When it comes to crime, homicide detective Jake Carrington plays for high stakes . . .

Assigned a missing persons case, Lieutenant Jake Carrington investigates a local Mob boss. The trail goes cold, but the Mafioso isn't taking any chances, and soon the heat turns up from another quarter. Turns out there's more than one dangerous suspect . . .

Kyra Russell is drop-dead gorgeous and Jake is only human. But despite their mutual attraction, Jake's suspicion deepens when he learns about her gambling problem—an addiction that cost her both husband and son. Even more disturbing is Kyra's day job. She runs a crematorium—and it's tied to the Mob. Now Jake will have to navigate a firestorm of treachery to get to the truth . . .

Previously published as *Burn in Hell*

Visit us at www.kensingtonbooks.com

Books by Marian Lanouette

Jake Carrington Thrillers
All the Deadly Lies
All the Hidden Sins

Published by Kensington Publishing Corporation

All the Hidden Sins

A Jake Carrington Thriller

Marian Lanouette

LYRICAL PRESS
Kensington Publishing Corp.
www.kensingtonbooks.com

Lyrical Press books are published by
Kensington Publishing Corp. 119 West 40th Street New York, NY 10018

All Kensington titles, imprints, and distributed lines are available at special quantity discounts for bulk purchases for sales promotion, premiums, fund-raising, and educational or institutional use.

To the extent that the image or images on the cover of this book depict a person or persons, such person or persons are merely models, and are not intended to portray any character or characters featured in the book.

Special book excerpts or customized printings can also be created to fit specific needs. For details, write or phone the office of the Kensington Special Sales Manager:
Kensington Publishing Corp.
119 West 40th Street
New York, NY 10018
Attn. Special Sales Department. Phone: 1-800-221-2647.

Kensington and the K logo Reg. U.S. Pat. & TM Off.
LYRICAL PRESS Reg. U.S. Pat. & TM Off.
Lyrical Press and the L logo are trademarks of Kensington Publishing Corp.

First Electronic Edition: July 2018
eISBN-13: 978-1-5161-0477-2
eISBN-10: 1-5161-0477-3

First Print Edition: July 2018
ISBN-13: 978-1-5161-0478-9
ISBN-10: 1-5161-0478-1

Printed in the United States of America

This book is dedicated to my amazing sisters, Cathy, Theresa, Brenda, and in loving memory of Florence, for believing and encouraging me to follow my dreams.

Love you all!

Chapter 1

"What's bothering you about the file, Jake?" Sergeant Louie Romanelli, Jake's partner, asked.

"There's nothing in it." Jake held out one piece of paper with only the initial information jotted down in chicken scrawl. "I can't find the CSI's report or lab reports, or for that matter, any interview reports. Stack's a seasoned detective. After two weeks of investigating a case there should be more in the file."

"So he screwed up," Louie said.

Jake studied his partner. He had an inch or two on him. Louie's olive complexion, dark eyes and hair was the complete opposite of his brownish-red hair and green eyes. They'd been best friends since childhood and partners for the last twelve years. He didn't trust another soul as he trusted and respected Louie.

"No, it's more than that. Something's off. I'm going to run with this one and shadow Stack and his movements." He shouldn't be discussing personnel issues with Louie.

"What, he's purposely not trying to close the case?"

Instead of responding, Jake stared Louie down.

"Son of gun! Are we going to find ourselves in another dirty cop case?" Louie asked.

"We might. You can stay clear of this one in case it is. That way when the shit hits the fan it won't land on you." As if Mondays weren't hectic enough, now he'd have to deal with Detective Stack.

The invisible "Wall of Blue" shunned the good cops by treating them as traitors for turning in a bad one. It didn't make sense. But he wasn't going to worry about it. He hated dirty cops. They gave the whole force a bad name.

"No, I'm your partner. We investigate together. Why the hell did they give you the Missing Persons' Department to begin with?"

"It's a temporary assignment I was told, while the brass interviews for a new lieutenant for the department."

Jake had his hands full. His recent promotion to lieutenant of the Homicide Department was enough to keep him working thirty-six hours a day. Now handling Missing Persons, he'd need to invent a forty-eight-hour day.

"Do you want to update me now or later?"

"Later. I need to get a handle on it. Why don't you run with the other case for now. And when you stop by with LJ tonight, I'll fill you in."

Jake wasn't going to speak about it here. He hoped Louie understood. Lately, the walls seemed to have ears. After Louie left his office, Jake spent the rest of his day looking through Missing Persons' personnel records. He wanted to familiarize himself with all the detectives from the department. But mostly, he wanted to see what opinion Carl Stack's retired lieutenant had about the detective. As acting lieutenant to the Missing Persons' Department he had to understand who was reliable and who wasn't in a pinch.

Next on his list, he had to review the cases of his own men in Homicide. Brown and Lanoue had closed their recent vehicular homicide case, but were still working the school shooting. He'd given his approval last week for them to bring in and start interviewing all of the students of interest in the hopes of shaking something out of the tight-lipped kids. From the team's reports on the incident, the victim had been a saint—straight-A student, class president, honor society pledge, and he held a job to boot. In his experience, all you had to do was dig deeper to get the shine to fall off. Only this time it hadn't. Thurston Crandall's secrets were rooted so deep down that a backhoe hadn't unearthed them.

Jake hit the intercom. "Brown, I don't see Crandall's parents' interview in the file."

"It should be there. I'll be right in, LT."

Kirk Brown walked into his office. At five-feet-eleven, Brown wore his brown hair in a military cut. He looked on the young side of his thirty-one years until you looked into his brown eyes. Jake handed him the Crandall file. While Kirk shuffled through it, Jake picked up Burke's file on the suspicious death of an elderly woman. Al's conclusion was the same as the one he'd come to: the woman hadn't died of old age. Someone had helped her along. Best bet was the sole heir who was knee deep in debt.

"LT, it should—"

His cell phone rang. Jake plucked it off his desk and hit the talk key. He held up a hand to quiet Kirk.

"Dina, how are you?" He hadn't heard from her in a while. A friend, one he had dated once or twice, until she got too serious. A nice woman who collected husbands like boys collected trading cards.

"I'm having a small gathering tomorrow night and I'd like for you to join me."

"I'm not sure. What time?"

"Around eight."

"If I can, I'll stop in."

He hung up and turned his attention back to Kirk.

"I don't see it in the file. I'll check my desk," Kirk said.

Jake emailed Al Burke, agreeing with his take on the suspicious death. He spun his chair around and looked out his window at the downtown area. Across the street from the station the staff of the Town Hall Café had started setting tables for the lunch crowd out on the terrace. The restaurant offered American cuisine with an Italian flair and stiff drinks. The owners, when they had remodeled, kept all the old wood crown moldings. Refinished, it gave the place a days-gone-by charm, while offering a classy atmosphere. It was one of his favorite places to dine.

He pondered the personnel files he'd recently reviewed. A couple of detectives from Missing Persons were a problem for him. Their service records were dismal at best and their politics left him cold. He wondered which one he'd have to deal with first.

Jake left the station at four and headed home. The dog he'd recently adopted needed tending. It hit as he walked in the door. *It's like having a kid.*

"What am I going to do with you, Brigh?"

Jake Carrington stared down the brown-eyed beauty, then bent to wipe the floor with the cleaner and paper towels. The dog had a nervous bladder, which let loose every time the doorbell rang. Adopting a dog now wasn't one of his brightest decisions. He didn't regret it.

Oh, he knew what he was doing. *We each understand cruelty.* They made quite the pair. Brigh learning to trust again, and him, trying to keep his mind occupied while dealing with the possible release of George Spaulding, the man convicted of killing his sister. Add to that, the loss of Mia, the woman he had fallen for. It had taken one look into Brigh's big, chocolate eyes for the dog to own him lock, stock, and barrel.

The bell rang again. Jake pointed to Brigh before he started toward the door. "Go lie down." Trembling, she inched her way to her bed. With one last look at the dog, Jake turned and opened the door.

"Why didn't you answer the door?" Louie Romanelli asked.

"Me and Brigh were having a much-needed conversation. You're early."

Louie scratched his chin, staring first at Jake then at Brigh. "Sophia's on the warpath with the kids. Before she turned it on me, I left."

The two constants in Jake's life were Louie and Sophia. He learned years ago not to get in the middle of their arguments.

This is all Louie's fault anyway. He pushed Brigh on me. Jake studied his friend and partner as he walked in the house. Brigh turned her big doe eyes up at him as if she knew what was running around inside his head. Not for one minute did he regret his decision to adopt her, but...it was going to take some big-time adjustments for both of them before they got used to each other. At least the dog kept him occupied and pushed Mia out of his head. And what was he going to do about her? Jake bent and gave Brigh a rub between the ears.

The two men went into Jake's comfortably furnished living room.

"Brigh and I need to get to know each other," Louie said. "LJ will be over after dinner to play with her. He figured with you here, the dog'd be more relaxed. He wants to avoid any trouble when he comes over to walk her."

Louie's teenage son had jumped at the chance to make money. Jake had hired him to walk the dog after school to keep Brigh from getting lonely. It was also insurance he'd have no surprises waiting for him when he got home from work.

"I'm glad he's agreed to walk her every day after school. Brigh's one skittish dog. She hates to be alone."

"Anything more you want to share on the Missing Persons' case?"

"Gee, Louie, it's only been a couple of hours since I last saw you. What, I'm now a miracle worker?"

After dealing with the last two cases, Jake had hoped for some downtime. Instead, he got another department and several murders to deal with. And what looked like a deliberate attempt to botch an investigation.

"You got something in your head," Louie said.

"I do. Who benefits if the missing guy never turned up?"

"Yeah, anything interesting there?"

"I believe he'll be one of our murder victims if he's ever found."

Jake sat on the couch. Brigh inched over, laid her head upon his lap. He stroked a hand over her coat.

As Louie approached, Brigh backed up, squatted and turned toward Jake. Pointing at her, Jake said, "Don't. It's all right. Louie, sit for a few minutes here but don't touch her."

"Have you heard from Mia?" Louie asked, changing subjects.

"No, and I told you the subject's off limits."

Louie shrugged.

"Now start to pet Brigh while I'm holding her. Once she gets used to you, I'm going to head to the pet store."

"You want me to babysit your dog?" Louie tossed him a pained look.

"Yes, until LJ shows up."

"Jake, it's a dog. She'll be fine on her own. Besides, I have to get home to dinner before I'm on Sophia's list along with the kids."

"Then I'll take her with me."

Louie cocked his head to the side, studied him and the dog, then left without another word. Alone, Jake and Brigh gauged each other.

"I'm not going to baby you." Brigh licked his face. *Crap, the dog already has me wrapped around her paws.*

On the ride to the store, Brigh stuck her nose out the window. Before heading in, Jake opened the window wider, then poured some water into the dish he'd brought along for her. It'd been a hot June and he didn't want Brigh getting dehydrated. Inside the pet store he picked up a few chew toys and more dog food. If he didn't get control, he'd buy out the whole damn store for the pooch. He decided he had enough stuff and got in line to check out.

A riot of red curls greeted him. He wasn't usually one for redheads but...he wanted to see the face all that hair belonged to. A small boy darted between him and the woman.

"Mom, can I get this for Zelly?"

He got his first look of the woman's face when she turned to speak to the child. Deep green eyes stared down at the boy. Her bowed mouth firmed as she spoke. "Trevor, we have enough stuff for the cat. Put it back. And apologize to the man for pushing by him."

"He's fine," Jake said.

"Sorry, mister."

The kid pushed past him. Jake smiled at the woman before she turned toward the clerk to continue checking out.

He paid the kid at the counter then headed to his car and put his purchases in the trunk, except for the chew toy, which he unwrapped and placed in front of Brigh. Once he was sure Brigh was okay, he walked across the lot to the grocery store. He had to eat too.

* * * *

Kyra enjoyed the last two days with her son. Yesterday, when the school nurse called her, she rushed over to pick Trevor up. Tom was unavailable and should've never sent the kid to class. The poor child was running a fever. But after two unscheduled days with Trevor, Tom had insisted she bring him home.

She stood on the top step of the place where she used to live, and at the insistence of the law, she handed her son over to a conniving bully. Tom's house, not hers. Each time she dropped Trevor off the fissure in her heart widened.

"You're welcome to come in," Tom Russell said.

"Trevor, give Mommy a kiss. And I'll see you tomorrow if you're up to it." She wrapped her arms around her son, ignoring her soon-to-be ex.

"If you'd get help, we'd be a family again."

She swallowed the barb that jumped to her lips. Instead, she said, "It's a dead issue, Tommy. Leave it be." She hugged Trevor one last time before she turned away and headed to her car. With each step, a knife jabbed at her aching heart.

She didn't remember when she'd given her soul to the devil. But she had. Leaving Trevor behind proved it. Her life, her son, her marriage, had been destroyed by no one but her. She pulled the car from the curb. Heading home to her cold, empty condo dragged her mood further into despair. Without her son, the place always reminded her of the morgue. Noise and people were what she needed. Turning the car around, she headed to the casino.

As she stepped off the garage elevator into the lobby, the cheap glitz, the noise, the thick smoke seeped into her bones and relaxed her. Ah, she was home, and better yet, her favorite machine stood empty. Slot machine therapy was better than any shrink.

* * * *

"Son of a bitch," Kyra whispered, two hours later.

Since she'd been here she'd dumped over three thousand dollars into the freakin' machine. *I can't believe this bitch sits down right next to me and hits the jackpot on the first spin. I'll never get Trevor back this way.*

Kyra Russell pushed her long, curly hair back over her shoulder. Why did the jackpot escape her? Ten grand would pay for the lawyer to fight Tom for custody. She stuffed another hundred-dollar bill into the machine and banged the maximum-credit button. Her stomach jumped with excitement as the wheels spun. Each time, her mind cheered *This is it!*

As the wheels rolled into place, a cold chill raced through her veins. One by one, they landed. By the time the second symbol stilled, Kyra realized she'd lost again. Her heart banged in her ears like a jackhammer on concrete, spiking her anger. *It's the next one,* she told herself, banging the maximum-credit button again. She needed to take a pee break, but didn't dare leave her machine for fear someone else might hit the jackpot after she'd primed the machine.

Kyra counted along with the attendant as he paid the woman next to her, seventy-five big ones. The attendant turned to leave. Kyra waved him down.

"Excuse me," she called.

"Yes, ma'am?"

"I need to use the restroom. Can you watch my machine or lock it down?"

"I have to call a supervisor over. It'll be a few minutes."

He pressed the button in his earpiece and whispered into it. After ten minutes, the supervisor came over and locked down the machine for her, and told her she'd need to be back within the hour or they'd release it.

"Thank you."

"Not a problem, Kyra," the supervisor said.

He had read her name off her reward card, addressing her like he knew her. *Well, screw him.*

She pushed off her seat and rushed to the ladies' room. Kyra didn't want to stay away too long, giving them a chance to reprogram the machine against her or reset it. She hated the new system with the tickets. Since they'd installed it, she hadn't won like she used to. Kyra was convinced the new system worked against her. She believed it was the reason she lost all the time.

Winning had been the norm when she first started playing. One night she'd won eight thousand dollars, and the next night twenty-five thousand dollars on one spin. The zing was indescribable when those wheels had rolled into place and the bells went off and the crowd surrounded her. On the night of her big win she'd gone home with twenty thousand dollars—she'd blown five grand trying to win more. Greed always took over. Winning excited her but not as much as the rush, the euphoria, she got while waiting for the wheels to fall onto the pay line.

The casino had treated her like royalty, had even given her a host. He'd gotten her into the popular shows or restaurants anytime she wanted. Nothing was too good for Kyra, as long as she showed up and put her money into the machine. She became a regular at the players' lounge—eat and drink for free. *Yeah, free, her ass. The cost was extreme.* Somewhere along the line, she'd lost her self-respect—along with her marriage, her son, and her savings.

As time went by, she'd put more money into the machines, hoping for bigger payouts. How it had gotten out of control she didn't know, but soon everything she loved would disappear. *The bastard doesn't want custody of Trevor—he wants to bring me to my knees.*

She'd rather die than lose Trevor. He needed her. She needed him more. Money the root of all evil—solved problems—her problems—if she just had some of it. Tears rolled down her face as she sat on the toilet. Not caring who heard her cry, she whispered, "Please, God, give me one big win and I promise I'll never gamble again."

She listened, but He didn't answer. She washed up and hurried back to her machine. Three hundred dollars left, her Visa card maxed out. Worse, the payment on her loan was due this week. Tommy—the asshole—had drained their joint bank account rendering her debit card useless.

She tried to stay away, honestly she did. But after a day, she'd get antsy. Her fingers itched. More than anything, she needed to get to the casino. Hell, it was hard to explain even to herself. She'd be pressed to explain it to anyone. No wonder the nuns at school had always preached against the evils of gambling.

Head down, her stomach in turmoil, she sat at her machine as she waited for the supervisor to come back—to unlock the machine. She itched to play. She needed the win. A hand landed on her right shoulder, startling her. Jerking away, Kyra turned. Muddy-brown eyes stared into hers. Joe Dillon's dark eyes matched his greased-back black hair. Small in stature, he nevertheless lorded over his people. *Crap, not the supervisor. Joe Dillon is not the person I want to see right now.*

"Kyra."

"Joe."

"How's it going?" Her host sat down next to her.

"Not good," she whined.

"I'm sorry to hear it. Your payment is due soon?"

Double crapola. "Yes."

"Why don't you leave the machine for a while? Come have something to eat with me?"

"Why?" *What does he want, besides money?*

"Let's discuss your loan payment over dinner, explore your options."

What options? There weren't any. All week she'd racked her brain trying to find a solution. Though a quiet guy, Joe scared her. He wasn't a person she'd want to cross. He worked for both the casino and the loan company. When she had gotten in trouble and owed the casino mucho bucks, he'd gotten her the loan. Her own bank had turned her down. Deep inside, she understood he'd destroy her.

He just might be the final nail in her coffin.

Chapter 2

"Kyra, no one's going to touch your machine. A break might change your luck."

"What the hell," Kyra said. Something had to change. "I can eat."

"How about a steak?"

"Fine."

They got up at the same time and bumped into each other. Joe sat back down. Kyra stood. Joe followed her as she started to head to the Trenton Steak House. Joe grabbed her arm and pointed to the private elevator. The ones that led to the Whale Room. She looked at him. He shrugged and grinned at her as he pressed the call button.

"What's up?"

"You need a real break, let's head upstairs."

Curiosity got the better of her, but she figured she'd find out what he was up to in good time. A second later, her legs went lax, her hands got clammy as fear smothered her. Dizzy, her breath hitched in her lungs. Damn, she shouldn't leave the floor with him. She owed seventy-five thousand dollars on the loan she had taken out from the private finance company Joe had hooked her up with. She paid off the casino. *Stupid—what a fool I am. I should've made a partial payment with the three grand instead of gambling tonight. They won't beat me up, will they?* A whirlpool of bile swirled its way up her throat. Tears welled in her eyes as she tried to blink them away before they fell.

"Are you all right?" Joe asked.

"I don't want to leave the public floor." Her voice cracked. There had to be a way out of this.

"I have a deal for you, but I can't discuss it in an open area. We'll discuss it upstairs, over dinner." He flashed a toothy smile.

His smile was meant to calm her, but it did the opposite. "What kind of deal?"

"We'll discuss it upstairs," he repeated.

"You're not going to break my legs or anything, are you?" she joked halfheartedly.

"No such thing, Kyra. Relax."

Now's the time to worry.

* * * *

The worst thing about a promotion—the paperwork. Call him crazy, or sick, but he'd rather work a juicy murder then process paper. Too bad Louie had taken lead on last night's case, and Burke had the old lady. Now he was sitting in the chief's office, with Shamus throwing numbers around for his departmental budget and his head was spinning. A necessary evil, but wasn't that what accountants were for?

His cell phone rang as he reviewed a column of numbers. It was Louie. God, he'd have kissed him if he'd been in the room.

"Excuse me," he said to Shamus. He pressed the talk button. "What's up?"

"We caught one," Louie said.

"I'll be there in a few." Jake ended the call as he turned toward his captain. "Commissioner, Captain, there's a new one."

"Somehow, I knew you'd find a way to get out of this," Shamus said. "Why don't you let Louie run it?"

"He's running the one we picked up last night."

"Louie's quite capable of handling both, Jake." Shamus leaned over to him, whispered in his ear, "I'm stuck, you're stuck." McGuire grinned as he leaned back in his chair.

Trapped.

He hit redial. "Take one of the junior detectives with you."

Jake grunted as Louie's laughter poured over the line. He cut him off mid-choke.

"Jake, evaluate both your department and Missing Persons. The mayor wants to cut our budget again. We're going to fight it, but I need proof and stats as to why cutting the force is a bad idea. I understand there's some deadwood in Missing Persons. You might want to start there. Don't give the mayor cause to zero in on your department."

He'd heed the warning. Velky had put a bullseye on his back when Jake had gotten the mayor's man, Captain Miller, kicked off the force for corruption. Politics—it didn't belong on the force.

He scribbled on his note pad. Two detectives from Missing Persons stood out. He'd be a happy camper if they transferred out or got laid off. The ones he had in mind had belligerently voiced their displeasure over the Miller incident. Did he, without cause, want to put them on the block? Their mediocre evaluations told Jake their former lieutenant hadn't held them in high regard either. It was his decision.

"You have something to add?" Commissioner Blake asked.

"No, sir."

He wasn't going to voice his opinion. This temporary assignment to combine both departments might be a permanent thing. He wouldn't put it past the mayor to meld them together for a laugh to overwhelm him. He'd have to wait and see. Budget cuts, his ass. This was the mayor's game to show who pulled the strings.

And Mayor John Velky was an expert at the game.

* * * *

Kyra needed to remember that the hosts were sharks. Their job was simple—they had to get you to put your money into the machines. They didn't care where it came from, or if it destroyed your life, as long as you put it into the machines. They got paid by their successes. Kyra guessed she was one of Joe's successes because her life was in shambles.

"Okay." *It can't be all bad.* Kyra gave Joe a sideward glance as he pressed the button for the thirty-sixth floor.

The elevator stopped. The doors glided open. She'd heard the rumors about this floor. Had always been curious to see it. The other gamblers in the private rooms had talked about it, but you only got to go up here if you were invited. A Whale. To the casino a Whale was defined as a person who spent big bucks. Not thousands, but hundreds of thousands, even millions—the casinos catered to them. What they asked for, they got: wine, song, and women. The Whales mingled with the casino owners and the big-name entertainers. The owners were their hosts.

Kyra stepped off the elevator and took in her surroundings with a keen eye. The Monet on the wall, the oriental carpets, and the fine bone china and lead-crystal wine goblets that graced the tables. Big money. All she needed was a tiny bit of it, she'd be able to survive—straighten out her life.

"Right this way."

Joe held out her chair. She sat and released the breath she had been holding since she encountered Joe.

"What do you want to drink? Dom Pérignon?"

Do they wine and dine you before they kill you? At least I'll have good champagne before I die. "Yes please." He smiled as he put his hand on hers. *He's good. I bet with his other hand, he'll shoot me.* "Why the special treatment?"

"As I said, Kyra, I want to discuss your payment options." He stopped talking as the waitress stepped up to their table.

From her peripheral vision, Kyra was aware that the waitress had placed cocktail napkins in front of each of them before putting down the champagne bottle, though she never broke eye contact with Joe.

"Can I take your order?" the server asked.

He ordered for both of them. She sipped her champagne and savored the cool bubbly sensation as it rolled over her tongue.

"How do you like your steak?" Joe asked.

"Medium."

"Two filet mignon, garlic mashed potatoes, and asparagus. Sound good, Kyra?"

"Yes."

"Irene, have the chef put on a chocolate soufflé for dessert."

"Yes, Mr. Dillon."

Kyra watched the waitress walk away to process their order.

I'm in deep shit. Nobody pampers you for nothing.

Rubbing her sweaty palms on her napkin, she wished for a towel to wipe the well of water away that had accumulated between her breasts. Kyra turned her attention back to Joe and waited for the bomb to explode.

"Kyra, you understand I not only work here at the casino, I'm employed by the people who hold the paper."

"The paper?" She understood him, but wanted him to make it crystal clear.

"Your loan, along with other people's loans."

"What kind of paper do they hold?"

"All kinds of paper. Whatever a person needs at the moment. My boss is a generous man. At times he offers an individual a deal to make the paper go away. That lucky person also walks away with some cash in his—or her—pockets."

Kyra stared, her champagne forgotten. Joe didn't look uncomfortable. In fact, he looked as if this was business as usual. Her mind raced. What kind of deal? Was it legal? Was this the answer to her prayers? The dread in the pit of her stomach surged. *Run, run for your life. A bit dramatic? Uh-uh!* At a loss for words, she nodded for him to continue.

"Do you want to make the seventy-five thousand dollars go away, and get some cash to fight your divorce and custody battles?"

Lord, he knows way too much about me. This can't be good. Whatever they wanted from her had to be illegal. But what?

"Do you want me to continue?"

"Yes." Desperation drenched her voice. She hated the sound of it.

"What we speak about today can't be discussed with anyone else, or there'll be serious consequences. Understood?"

She never broke eye contact with him—his look sent a cold, thorny pain into her spine. *I've been stabbed with an icicle. God, his eyes are creepy. Why didn't I ever notice that before? Once in, there's no getting out.* What were her choices? She had no money and her parents refused to bail her out. They had the money too. What kind of parents didn't care if she lost her son? What kind of grandparents were they?

Nobody but me will help me. Decision made. With some cash, she'd take Trevor and start a new life elsewhere.

"I understand. What do I have that your bosses want?"

"Ah, here's dinner. Let's eat first."

She didn't want the freaking food. "What exactly are you talking about here?"

"After dinner, Kyra." He cut into his steak and placed a piece in his mouth.

She ate, though she never tasted the food. When the waitress brought out the chocolate soufflé, she stared at it. A favorite of hers, but she had no appetite.

"Can we get this over with?"

"No, we haven't had dessert," he said, eyebrows raised.

She wanted to wipe the smug look right off his face but reined in her temper. Bit back her comment.

"Are you in a hurry to sign your life away? Eat the soufflé first," he said in a low voice. She had to lean in to hear him.

She picked up her spoon, only to slam it down. "Sign my life away?" Dinner purged its way up her throat.

"It's an expression." He shrugged.

A tear ran down her face. He reached over and thumbed it way. The gesture skeeved her out.

"After dinner we're going to take a ride. I'll explain everything. This offer comes from my boss at the loan company, not me—"

"I have to talk to them?" she yelled.

"Quiet. No, I'll be doing the talking. I wanted you to understand the terms. This offer comes from them, not the casino. Understood?"

Washing his hands of the act, clever him. "Yes." She resigned herself to her fate. There wasn't any way she'd be able to pay off the seventy-five thousand dollars.

"I want you right now, with discretion, to look at the guy in the corner. Take in every detail you see and retain it."

"Why?"

"No questions, do what I ask."

She turned, looked over her left shoulder toward the bar. Her gaze lingered on the man Joe wanted her to study. The guy filled the whole corner—he had to weigh three hundred fifty pounds if he weighed an ounce—gross. Greasy hair held in place by his comb-over. Revolting table manners. She kept her gaze moving until it landed on the bar. She signaled the waitress. *I'm stalling—how can I get out of this? The guy must be a Whale. Joe better not be offering me to him. I'll throw up on the spot or, worse, kill myself. Which will solve everything.*

"Can I get you something, miss?" the waitress asked.

"Yes, a glass of water, please."

The server walked away from the table. "Did you see the man I was speaking about?"

"Yes, and he's gross." Kyra didn't bother to lower her voice.

"I'm not going to tell you again to keep your voice down." She didn't like the hard edge his voice held. "We'll talk about him on our ride. You done?"

Joe got up without waiting for her answer, or her water. Running after him, she noticed each step he took slammed to the floor as he marched away.

Well screw him.

Chapter 3

Kyra caught up to him and tugged on his arm. "Why are you angry? I'm the one being put on the spot here."

"I'm angry because you show no discretion. You're rude." He turned back to the elevator.

"Rude?" She lowered her voice to a whisper. "You're the one who asked me to check out that gross excuse for a human being and for what? I'm not stupid and I'm not doing him." Her face burned. Her throat went dry. At her side, her fists curled. She held her temper on a tether.

"I didn't ask you to, did I?" He stepped into the elevator, adjusted his tie.

She stomped in after him. "What was the purpose of the look-and-see?"

"I already told you we'd talk in the car. Please don't cause a scene, Kyra. Like you, I need my job."

They rode down in silence. *Dear God, what have I gotten myself into?* Focus failed her. The trek to the car struck her as the final walk of a condemned woman. *Dead Kyra walking.* They reached his car. No surprise he drove a Mercedes-Benz SLK 55 convertible, silver. It was a beautiful, sleek car. *My dream car, in the exact model and color. Why him?* "Does it have a V8?"

"You like cars?"

"This is my dream car."

"Yeah, it's a V8, and it handles like a dream."

"I bet. What year is it?" He helped her into the car.

"It's last year's model."

Zooming out of the garage, he turned right, onto a back road instead of the highway. It was a smooth ride. The trees whizzing by the only acknowledgment of motion. Leaning her head against the seat, she noted its comfort. He started talking and drew her into the conversation and reality.

"I want to lay out the whole deal for you before you interrupt. Afterward I'll answer any questions you have."

"Okay." Tapping her finger on her leg was her only outward sign of nerves. She hoped.

"The group chose you for two reasons. First: you're pretty, with a great shape. Second: you hold a unique position."

Oh, shit! It's worse than I imagine.

"They set this up to give you a choice. You guessed the first choice. Mr. Garcia is a Whale and he likes redheads. You fit the bill. He spends millions at the casino each year. My boss likes to give him what he wants. He likes oral sex."

Her stomach shot up to her throat. She swallowed hard, forcing the contents back down.

Joe never looked at her. His face a blank.

"Your second choice involves your job."

"My job?"

"Remember, no interruptions until I'm done," he reprimanded. "You work at the cemetery, correct?"

He looked over at her, but she didn't respond. She nodded.

"Don't you do all the cremations there?"

"Yes," she whispered. This had to be a nightmare. Kyra pinched herself. *Nope, it's not.*

"Okay, this is difficult for me…" He paused, but didn't fool her. "They need you to dispose of a body for them."

* * * *

He'd stalled long enough. With his reports processed for the day and his review of his staff's cases completed, Jake headed home alone. Another long night with no one but Brigh to talk to. Mia's absence echoed through his halls. But tonight he had a choice. Go to Dina's party or stay home.

Did he want to socialize with other cops? Dina was nice enough. If Miller and his cronies showed up he'd leave. He didn't need a confrontation, especially with a dirty cop. It was something to break up the boredom. He knew most of the women she hung out with. And none interested him. He'd have to attend to see if she'd surprise him. Lord knew his life had been empty this last month.

Decision made. He drove into the garage. Brigh jumped up on him as he opened the inner door to the house.

"That's a good girl. Did you miss me?"

Jake rubbed his hands over Brigh's coat, than scratched her behind her ears as she licked his face. He let Brigh out the back door and waited for her to complete her business. After filling Brigh's food and water dishes he jumped into the shower to get ready for the party.

* * * *

Kyra woke with her head between her knees. Joe was holding it down. He'd parked the car on the side of the road. *Please tell me it's a nightmare. Did he say he wanted her to dispose of a body for him?*

"Are you all right?"

"No, I'm not. Are you for real?" Her curls curtained her face as she turned toward Joe to gauge his answer.

"I'm afraid I am."

His stare bored into her skull. What was she going to do? If she said no, would they kill her? They'd have to. Her other choice was to be on her knees with the dirty, disgusting man in the corner. It hit her hard. They'd picked him on purpose. They wanted her to get rid of their body, not do the man.

Her mind whirled around as she tried to come up with an alternative solution. Joe got back in the car and pulled out in traffic. *He better be taking me back.*

"There's no choice number three?" she asked, with no hope.

"I'm afraid not."

"You set it up this way on purpose. And that fat slob—not in this lifetime. You gave me only one real choice."

"You have two choices."

"Yeah. If I pick the man how many times do I have to do him?"

"Until he gets tired of you."

He can't be serious. Once would be too many times. Not that she'd even consider it.

"You're saying this wipes out my debt one hundred percent? That I walk away with cash. How much cash?"

She had to try to reason through the craziness. More than anything, she wished for a miracle. One to end the calamity her life had become. With more money she'd be able to provide Trevor with some stability in his life.

"You get a clean slate and one hundred thousand dollars."

A hundred grand? For that kind of money, who did she have to burn? The governor? "When do I have to give you my answer?"

"I want your answer now, but I'll give you until Thursday night. We'll meet at the casino for dinner in the Whale Room again. Afterward, we'll take another ride to discuss all aspects of the deal." *He mentioned dinner, like that alone will sway me. Joe's a freakin' idiot.*

She inhaled a couple of times to calm herself. He'd given her time. All she had to do was come up with a counter offer. Joe pulled into the casino parking garage and she realized she had a few minutes more to ask questions.

"Why me? I'm sure there are other people who owe you more money."

"You don't owe me anything. You owe my bosses. Why you? It's obvious—you have a unique job. My bosses find that and your beauty an asset. Remember, you're the one who put yourself in this position.

"You're small potatoes to these guys, a pawn, but right at the moment, a necessary pawn. Either take care of their Whale or take care of their body. It's your choice." As he parked, she watched his hand as he reached into his jacket. He pulled out an envelope and handed it to her.

"What's this?"

"I took up some of your time tonight. My bosses want to show their generosity." Joe dropped a thick envelope with cash sticking out of it onto her lap.

Without a word, he disparaged my character. The bastard's treating me like a hooker. It doesn't matter if I performed or not. Well, now I understand how Joe and his employer regard me. And all because I gamble? With force, she jerked the envelope off her lap and threw it in his face. Her body quivered with anger as she got out of his car. With her head held high, she walked away without another word. She checked her emotions and forced back the tears until she reached the safety of her vehicle. Once inside the car, her eyes erupted and the river of tears flowed. How in God's name did she save herself from this predicament?

You did this to yourself, Kyra. Joe's cold, unforgiving words echoed in her head.

She sat there, parked in the garage for a long time, unable to stop tears and find her mad. She pounded her hands on the steering wheel as she cried some more. She started to hiccup as the tears ran dry. She put the key in the ignition, took a deep breath before she drove away. On the dark stretch of road, her mind played back Joe's conversation. She knew her third choice was death. Right now it was her cleanest choice. One her son might be able to live with—and not know how low she'd sunk in life.

"I'm such a loser!" she screamed.

How'd I get this low? No pride, choice or self-esteem left. Forced now to give up total control over her life if she agreed to do what they asked. *I only need one big win. One win, dear God.*

The dashboard clock read eight o'clock. Too early to go home. The silence gave her time to mull over Joe's words and the deal. More than anything she wanted a drink. Where did she go on a Tuesday night? Then it hit her. Dina's party. She'd go, Lord knew she needed to get her mind off her problems for a while.

* * * *

Kyra knocked on the door. Dina swung it open. A big smile spread over her face as she hugged her before pulling her into the apartment. Dina was a work friend. They weren't close, but she needed human contact tonight. Kyra looked around the room and smiled. The ratio of men to women were in the women's favor. More men meant more choices.

"I'm glad you came," Dina said in her sing-song voice.

"Me too. I needed a night out. Thanks for inviting me."

"I'll get you a drink and introduce you to some people." She leaned in and whispered, "People as in men." Dina winked. Her infectious giggle brightened Kyra's mood.

Kyra rolled her eyes for effect. Dina had been trying to set her up since she heard about the divorce. She studied Dina. Long black hair, beautiful black eyes, high cheekbones to die for, full lips, and a nose a little too big for her face. Otherwise, she'd have been flawless. Gracefully, Dina glided back to the bar to get her drink. Kyra watched her every movement. Dina was graceful, while Kyra was clumsy.

"I'm good, Dina. I don't need a man in my life right now. It's too messed up." Why didn't Dina understand? She'd been divorced twice. Dina always had a boyfriend.

We each have our vices. Dina's is men—mine's the casino. She held a genuine affection for Dina. She didn't have a mean bone in her body, plus she was a great admin.

Dina was one of those women who always needed a man around and wished it for her friends too. Kyra didn't. In fact, since she'd found gambling, she'd lost interest in sex.

"Divorce is confusing. What do you want to drink?" Dina jumped from one subject to the next.

"I'll have a rum and Coke with lemon."

Dina mixed the drink while Kyra scanned the room to see if she recognized anyone.

"Here it is."

Turning back to Dina, Kyra accepted the drink. "Thanks. I'm glad I came." Kyra smiled.

"Me too. Ohhh...he's yummy." Dina crooned, looking across the room.

Kyra followed her gaze to the front door and had to agree. She'd seen him somewhere before but where? A looker, in a rugged kind of way, he stood about six feet tall with brownish-red hair, more red than brown. His comfortable, broken-in jeans shaped a firm ass. He wore a light jacket with a tight black tee under it, displaying a well-defined chest and abs. "Who's he?" Kyra tried for casual.

"Jake Carrington. Lieutenant Jake Carrington. The perpetually single male. Attentive, hot and a great date, but don't get serious—commitment phobia," Dina warned.

"Sounds lovely."

"Oh no you don't. He'll break your heart. You don't want a relationship until you date him. Then wham—once he's got a hold on your heart, he walks away. Oh, but what a ride." Dina grinned like the devil.

Kyra laughed. It was something she needed after the day she'd had. "I wouldn't mind the ride." Laughing, they both turned back to the bar.

* * * *

The redhead caught his eye the minute that Keller from Illegals opened the door. She seemed familiar. Instead of greeting a bunch of his fellow cops, he walked up to the women.

"Want to share?" Jake asked, amused when both women jumped.

"I didn't see you there, Jake." Dina leaned over and kissed him on the cheek.

"Hi, Dina. What's new?"

"Nothing, you?"

"Same old thing." He stood there, looking between Dina and her friend. Years of reading people and situations told him they were up to mischief.

"Um, Jake, this is my boss, Kyra."

"Hi, Kyra." He held out his hand. She took it. *Nice, firm handshake.* "Hello."

Redheads weren't his thing, too close to his own coloring, but this one... He realized he'd held her hand a little too long and dropped it.

"You're Dina's boss. You work at the cemetery, right?"

"I do."

"What do you do there, Kyra?" Her name rolled off his tongue. He liked the sound of it.

"This is a conversation stopper. I cremate people for a living."

"Where's the joke?" He stared into her eyes, waiting for the punch line.

"No joke." The corner of her mouth tugged up.

"Interesting." He reached behind the bar, grabbed the bourbon, poured four fingers. For the life of him he drew a blank, words escaping him.

"What do you do, Jake?"

"I'm a homicide cop."

"Interesting."

He liked a woman with spunk and this one oozed it. "I asked for that one."

"You did."

"You look a little nervous. Don't like cops?"

"I have no problem with them. Never talked to one before."

"Ouch." Jake frowned.

He had a live one here, but she was hiding something. Something about him made her nervous. It must be his job. Even in social situations he read people. It was what made him a good cop and what had annoyed Mia. She was trying to camouflage her nerves. It might be fun to discover her secrets.

"I'm told I can be a bit abrasive."

"Yeah? Who told you that?"

"My soon-to-be-ex-husband."

Another conversation stopper. The three of them stood there in an awkward silence.

"Who wanted the divorce?" Jake asked. Both women looked at him like he'd grown a third eye. *Oops, wrong question.*

"He did, but it's mutual," she said, annoyance clear in her tone.

She offered no more. He should move on, say hi to the guys. But Kyra held his attention, and few had since Mia.

"Kyra—Gaelic isn't it?"

"Yes. My name warns you, in case you missed the red hair and freckles."

Laughing, he said, "Me too."

"You don't say."

"You don't take any guff, do you?"

"I always imagined if I was interrogated, there'd be a bright light," she halfheartedly joked.

"Interrogated? I can accommodate you." He winked. "Handcuffs and all."

Kyra choked on her drink. "Thanks, I'll pass on both."

She was fire and playing with her might not be smart. He'd find out soon enough.

"We've met before."

"Have we? Where?" Kyra studied his face.

"At the pet shop. You had an active kid with you."

"My son Trevor. I remember now."

Neither noticed Dina move on to another group. Jake looked down into Kyra's sad, vivid green eyes. For some reason, they tugged at his heart. *Great, Jake, how stupid—just what I need, more baggage.* He hadn't gotten over Mia. They still hadn't talked since the night she walked out. But still, he had no business flirting with another woman. It meant nothing, but how long should he wait for Mia to make up her mind?

"I lost you there for a moment. Where'd you go?" Kyra said, snapping her fingers.

"Oh, nowhere important." He shrugged.

"Fine." She looked embarrassed, turned away from him. Jake laid his hand on top of her arm to get her attention.

"I'm sorry. I didn't mean to be rude. I've no right to be talking to you. You're in the process of a divorce. I recently broke up with someone."

"It's okay, a little conversation never hurt anyone. Do you want to grab a drink somewhere?"

"Yeah, I'd like that," Jake said, as a smile tugged at the corners of his mouth. An entanglement wasn't what he need right now, but he enjoyed the banter with Kyra.

"Okay, where?"

"Is the Holiday Seasons good?"

"Yes."

Chapter 4

"I'll see you in the morning, Dina. Thanks again for the invite."

"Take care. I'll want details tomorrow," Dina whispered into Kyra's ear.

"Good night, Dina." Jake kissed her cheek.

"Be good." Dina smiled.

"Why? That's no fun."

Jake walked Kyra to her car. "I'll meet you there," Kyra said.

"You don't want to take one car?"

"No, it's wise to take both." *In case I want to do something foolish and go home with you.* He tapped her roof. "Lock your door."

"Thanks, copper."

Climbing into her car, she watched him in the rearview mirror as he walked away laughing. She pulled out of Dina's condo parking lot.

What the hell are you doing, Kyra? He's a cop...a freaking cop, for God's sake. How did I come from talking to... What do I call you, Joe—a hood, a criminal, the mob—to talking to a cop? Not talking, but going out for a drink with him. What kind of stupid has come over me?

Laughter bubbled out as tears poured down her face. She pulled into the bar's parking lot. Tilting the rearview mirror down, she wiped away her tears and checked her makeup. *I don't look good.* She reapplied her lipstick. *If I was smart I'd go home. This is going to cause trouble in the long run. But...how much can one drink hurt?*

A yelp escaped her lips as she jumped toward the center of the car at a knock on her window. She took a deep breath in and released it when she realized it was Jake.

"I didn't mean to scare you. Didn't you see me pull in?" Jake offered her his hand to help her out of the car.

"No."

"Were you crying?" he asked.

"I told you—nerves. We should do this some other time?" Cripes, what was she doing here? What was she, nuts? *He's a freakin cop.*

"You'll find I'm a good listener, if you need an ear."

Wish I'd met him last week. "I'm fine. Sometimes the pressures of the job, the divorce, life, gets to me. See? Whack-job. Run for your life." She laughed without mirth.

"Not running. Do you still want a drink?"

"I guess I do." Pretending everything was fine, she laced her arm through his as they walked into the bar.

* * * *

He didn't understand what provoked her tears, but she wasn't fine. Kyra had piqued his curiosity. Call it his cop intuition but something was off with her. He enjoyed a good puzzle. Kyra seemed stretched. No, more than that. She seemed afraid. Of him? No, not him.

"What do you want to drink?" He pulled out a barstool for her.

"A Cosmopolitan sounds good."

"Hey, Jake, how's it shaking?" the bartender asked. Walking down the bar to them, he stuck out his hand to Jake.

"Good, Pat. How's the family?"

"Everyone's good. Do I get an introduction?"

"Kyra, Pat Brennan, retired WPD."

"Kyra, an Irish name. And your surname?"

"Russell."

"Ah, nice, lass. Well, your first drink is on the house in this Italian bar." He winked.

"Thank you." Kyra smiled.

* * * *

After Pat served them, he moved down the bar, out of earshot. She should've stuck with the rum and coke, instead of mixing alcohols. Kyra sipped her drink, not wanting to let it go to her head. She was too close to the edge tonight. The booze might loosen her tongue. What would be her answer on Thursday? She hadn't come up with a counteroffer to get her out of the situation. Were they going to kill her? She knew in her heart she'd never be able to pick either one of the choices presented to her. Joe had to be crazy to ask. Kyra looked around the bar as if seeing it for the first time. Thursday night was a long way off. She'd put the decision away for later.

Tuesday nights were quiet here. At the other end of the bar, talking to Pat, sat a man downing shot after shot like this was a speakeasy and prohibition was in effect again. *I wonder what troubles he wants to drown? Who cares? His problems can't be bigger than mine.*

"Hey, where'd you go?" His hand on her arm brought her back to the conversation.

"I must have zoned out. What did you say?"

"It wasn't important."

"I'm sorry." *A big guy like him sulking. Who needs this crap?* "I had a shitty day."

"I asked how you got into your line of work."

"Oh, I was the secretary at the cemetery for six years. We built the crematory. I took the course, along with my boss at the time, to be a backup to him. A year later, he fell down on the job, died on the spot of a massive heart attack. I got the job by default."

"Ah, a rags-to-riches story," Jake joked.

"Yes, ask my creditors, they'll agree," she said, rolling her eyes.

"You're one tough cookie, Kyra." He stared into her eyes.

"Yeah, that's me. Good or bad?" She looked up at him. The intensity of his gaze unnerved her as he leaned an elbow on the bar, his body facing her.

"I don't know. I'll need to do some homework, study the subject." The boyish grin he flashed melted her heart. Who knew a simple smile had that much power.

"Well, there'll be an open-book test after," she joked back.

"There's nothing open about you." *Geez, the guy turns from joking to serious on a dime. Give me a freakin' break.*

"Instinct or guessing?"

"A little of both."

"Well, shit."

He laughed. "Yeah, it'll be fun getting to know you."

She watched him down his drink as she continued to sip hers. "Time will tell."

She liked him though he seemed as wound up as she was. *Job or personal problems...which one, Jake?*

"Would you like another drink?"

"No, I'm still working on this one."

"Why?"

"Funny, 'cause I'm a cheap drunk and I'd like to keep my wits about me tonight."

"That's no fun."

"Trying to take advantage of me?"

"No, hoping you'll take advantage of me." *Looks like he knows the power of that grin he flashes all the time.*

"It might still happen, the evening's young." She tossed him a flirtatious smile. It was time to test her wiles. She raised her glass and saluted him.

"Ah, a tease."

"Oh yes."

She discovered they had a lot in common, but he sent vibes he was still hung up, involved with someone else. She worked up the nerve to ask.

"Do you plan on getting back with the woman you broke up with?"

"I did in the beginning...now...?" He shrugged as he looked into his empty glass instead of at her.

Well, that shut down her line of questions and him.

"Can I ask why?" In his eyes the pain was evident.

"You can ask. I definitely have. I still don't understand why we're not together."

She lifted her drink, sipped and wished her own problems were relationship-related.

"I don't mean to unload on you, but I'm still in love with Mia. Before we move forward you should be aware of that."

"Thanks. I'm not looking for a relationship. My life's too complicated right now. I will tell you this—if you love her, go after her. Fix it. Love doesn't come around often."

"She doesn't want to be involved with me. I'm overprotective. Her words, not mine."

He looked miserable. She searched around for the right answer. "Did you overreact to something to make her accuse you of it?" *Oh shit, that wasn't it.*

"I can't talk about it, Kyra. You want another drink?"

"No, it's time to head home. I have an early day tomorrow." She stood, took her purse from the back of the barstool. "Thanks for the drink, Jake."

"I'd like to see you again. Do you want to go out to dinner Friday night?"

She reached into her purse, pulled out her business card. "The number on the bottom right's my cell number. Dinner sounds good. Call with the time."

"Good night," Jake said.

"Good night, Jake. Thanks for the drink and the company." She liked that he didn't try to kiss her. She waved to Pat, started to leave the bar. "Where are you going?"

"I'm not letting you walk to your car alone."

"Yeah, you might be a little overprotective," she said, smirking.

"All part of the service."

Together they stopped in front of her car, and she hit the remote. "This is me."

He reached around her. *He's going to kiss me after all.* She was disappointed when he opened the door to let her in. *Make up your mind, woman, do you want the kiss or not?*

"Thanks."

"You're welcome. I'll talk to you tomorrow."

"See ya." She closed the door, hit the lock button and drove out of the parking lot.

* * * *

Jake watched Kyra drive off. After spending an hour with her his opinion of her had changed from jumpy to cagey. She had issues bubbling under the surface. Oh hell, who was he to judge? He had issues too. *We both need a friend—that's all this is.* Plus her snarky sense of humor entertained him. It was good she wasn't looking for a long-term relationship. What happened with Mia might not be able to be fixed, but he had no desire to put his emotions through the wringer again. Though in his heart—Mia was the one. He shouldn't call Kyra. *Why start something I'm not ready to finish? And, I'm not going to talk about Mia to her or anyone else.* He started walking back to the bar, stopped at the door, then decided to go home. Before he got to the car his cell phone rang.

"Carrington here."

"Lieutenant, it's dispatch. We have a body at East Main Street and Meriden Road."

"I'm not on call tonight. Where's the officer in charge?"

"He's tied up on another call, Lieutenant. It's been a busy night."

"Okay, what's the address?"

"That's the address the caller gave us."

"Contact Sergeant Romanelli, and have the first officers on scene stand by. My ETA is about ten minutes."

* * * *

A block from the bar she pulled to the curb. "Idiot!" Slumped over her steering wheel, she hugged it tight to her chest. This wasn't the part of town a person wanted their car to break down in, never mind pulling over to cry. Right this minute, she didn't care.

She clutched at her chest as a piercing pain cut off her next breath. Panic tightened her muscles, making the shooting spasms worse.

Oh my God! I'm having a freaking heart attack.

Kyra merged into traffic, but had to pull over immediately when what looked like Jake's car flew by with sirens blasting. In less than five minutes she turned her car into the hospital emergency-room parking area. She sat there as she inhaled. Disappointment filled her when her breathing went back to normal as the pain dissipated. Not heart, but a panic attack. "No such luck, Kyra. You're not getting off that easy."

The hospital guard started walking over to her car. She slammed it back in gear, pulled out to head home. *I don't want to talk to anyone now.*

At the condo she climbed right into bed. Fifteen minutes later she got up and paced around her living room. Rocked with fear, she curled up on the couch with a blanket and turned on the television to clear her mind of Joe's horrific proposal. Surfing through the channels, she stopped on the one that played old soap operas. Nothing held her interest for more than a minute. She threw the remote, missing the television by inches, and went to the kitchen to retrieve her laptop.

She settled back onto the sofa with the computer and flipped it open. She had intended to catch up with the paperwork on today's cremations, but found she had no ambition. Instead she opened a new spreadsheet and listed all her bills and her loan balance in the left column. In the right column she listed her salary, her sole income. If she got a second job, it might help—but doing what? She had no skills expect for administrative ones. What kind of money did a part-time job pay? Minimum wage? She'd cashed in her savings bonds, her savings account, and part of her 401k. Tommy's compassion and forgiveness had gone away with the last withdrawal from the 401k. He forgave her for the withdrawal from Trevor's college fund. They had time to build it up again Tom said, but blowing their retirement ended their marriage. Tom was looking out for his own ass.

No matter how she arranged the numbers, the debt won over the income. Even with raises calculated into the equation, it would take her fifty years to pay everything off, including the interest. Her throat went dry. Her gut tightened, and her head pounded as she pushed her computer aside. There was no way out for her except to accept Joe's offer. It was hopeless. She did again what she'd done all night—she cried.

* * * *

Jake pulled to the curb and noted Louie hadn't arrived yet. As he climbed out of the car, he spotted the uniform. Kudos to Russo. He'd cordoned off the scene and had the bystanders pushed back. Frank Russo, a twenty-year veteran, understood his job. At five-eight, the guy packed a solid punch. Jake knew. A few times he and Frankie had sparred in the gym.

"How many people trampled my scene, Frankie?" Jake asked, surveying the body and surrounding area.

"No one, I got here before the EMTs, Lieutenant. When I arrived I found the body, not the caller. Nothing's been touched. It was obvious he was dead awhile. I didn't let the EMTs near him." Jake nodded for Russo to continue. "At first, with all his track marks, it looked like an overdose, but the head wound—"

"Give me a minute," Jake said, cutting off Russo before he gave his opinion of the scene. He wanted to form his own impressions before the uniform gave his. He walked over to the body, leaned down and studied it. Russo was right. The wound on the head wasn't created by his fall. Someone had whacked the poor kid hard on the noggin.

Louie sidled up to him with a coffee in his hand.

Damn, that coffee smells good. "You got one for me?" Jake asked.

"No, but I'll share. What have we got?" Louie asked as he took a sip.

The medical examiner pulled up behind Louie's car.

"How'd we get the top dog on an O.D. victim?" Jake asked.

A tall, lanky man of Chinese and American descent, Chen Lang always looked in need of a meal. The Doc carried his one hundred and eighty pounds on a six-foot-four frame. His skin gave off a translucent glow, the same color as the corpses he worked with. Short on staff, Lang spent many hours attending the dead and didn't seem to care if he saw daylight or not.

"Been a wild night, Jake, the team's spread all over the state," Lang said.

Jake stepped away from the body. Louie stood by his side. "After Doc Lang finishes up, I'll look for cash, needles, or his stash. But I'm betting it's gone," Louie said.

"I hope they left his I.D."

"What the hell have you been drinking? You stink of booze. Where are you coming from?" Louie asked.

"I was out. Is it that bad?" Jake blew his breath into his hand. He hadn't been on call tonight and it was nobody's business if he'd wanted a drink.

Dispatch had called him in when the lieutenant on duty was tied up on another homicide.

"Yeah, I better take the lead on this one. We don't want any questions when the case goes to court," Louie said.

Jake nodded.

The department was a political landmine at the moment. He stepped away from the scene. At his car, Jake wrote down his impressions. Diagrammed the angle of the body, and proceeded to make notes about the wound and the location of the needle marks. He'd compare them to Louie's and the crime scene team's tomorrow.

Chapter 5

At home after turning the scene over to Louie, Jake switched on the coffee pot, then turned on his computer. In a perfect world he'd explore a woman in real time, but something about Kyra had his gut screaming. With his coffee in hand he sat at his computer and started the run on her. He'd run her financials another time. It required a warrant. But Google should get him started before he brought in the heavy guns. At a later date he'd run her through the police data base.

Married seven years, to of all people, that ass Tom Russell. A man who threw his family's political connections around to intimidate people. The nouveau Russell family dynasty, created with smoke and money, thanks to an inheritance from his mother's uncle a few years ago. They had nothing but money. Russell Senior bought and sold people when it was prudent for him. Tom's parents considered themselves Wilkesbury royalty. Power-hungry people who tried to control other people's lives. Kyra and Russell didn't seem a good fit. Had he judged her wrong? Something always happened to deracinate love and put a divorce in motion. He'd have to check out the court docket next in hopes of finding the reason for it.

An hour later after reading the public documents, Jake sat back in his chair and contemplated Kyra's situation. The records listed her as an inveterate gambler. The petition requested that her husband be granted custody of her son. Why? Gambling wasn't a thing the court used to take away a mother's rights. It had to be the Russells' money at work again. Jake's curiosity was fully engaged. He'd investigate, but how did he bring up the subject without setting off alarms. No, he'd wait until she did. And what a coincidence that he was now investigating a case of a missing gambler. He didn't trust them, but no one, including himself, knew he had attended Dina's party tonight. Even so, what would Kyra have to do with the missing man? Friday night he'd throw the guy's name out at her, see if he got a reaction.

* * * *

Pulled from a restless sleep by the phone ringing, Kyra grabbed for it. The jarring tones echoed in her head. "Hello," she squeaked out. Damn, she'd spent the night on the couch.

"Kyra, it's Dina. Where are you?"

"Dina?" Disoriented, she reached for her watch. "What time is it?"

"Lord, Kyra, it's nine fifteen. The family's due here in twenty minutes."

"I'll be there. Please serve them some coffee. Thanks for calling."

Kyra slammed down the phone, ran into her bedroom and grabbed her clothes along the way. Once in the bathroom, she threw water on her face. Not bothering with makeup or a shower. Twelve minutes later she ran out the door.

I've got to get my act together. Where did the night go? Oh shit, I forgot my briefcase.

She made a U-turn, headed back to her condo. Running up the stairs, her business cell phone rang. Jingling her keys in the door, she put the phone on speaker and snapped, "What?"

"It's me again," Dina said.

"I'm almost there. I forgot my briefcase and had to turn back," Kyra said, frustrated.

"Mr. Marren called. You've got a breather. He and his wife are running fifteen minutes late."

"You're the best, Dina, thanks."

Kyra clicked off and sat on her couch to catch her breath. Restless, she popped up to make a cup of coffee. Good thing she'd turned back, she'd left her personal cell phone on the kitchen counter. She grabbed her coffee, phone, and briefcase, and headed out to work.

Damn it. I didn't call Trevor before school today. I'll have to call after school. Once she got to the office the pace didn't slow down. The Marrens arrived ten minutes later. After they signed all the releases, Kyra handed over their father's ashes. Later she met with the Collette family to explain the cremation process. By noontime, she was itching to go to the casino. She'd never been a clock-watcher, though today the red digital numbers burned a hole in her irises. She played online slots to soothe the craving and proceeded to lose two hundred dollars in six minutes. The money was gone.

She looked up when she heard a knock on her door. She minimized the window on her computer and called out, "Come in."

"I'm going to order lunch from the deli. Do you want anything?"

"Yes, get me a corned beef on rye, with mustard, nothing else, please."

Kyra fished around in her purse for the money and panicked. She knew she'd left the casino with three hundred dollars last night. She'd kept track of what she put in the machines. She opened every envelope, her change purse, and her wallet. All she found was a twenty. What had happened to the rest of the money?

She handed the twenty to Dina. After Dina left her office Kyra wrote down what she remembered about last night. As she counted up the numbers, her head began to swoon. A twenty—crap, pay day wasn't until Friday. Less than that now, and today was Wednesday. She'd spent more than she'd planned last night. How was she going to take Trevor to his favorite restaurant tonight? She hated to do it, but she had to break her promise to him.

Yanking her keyboard in front of her, she scrambled online and checked the balances in her new checking and savings accounts. Her stomach flipped—between the two accounts she had two hundred dollars to her name. Laying her head on the desk, she willed away the nausea. *Freak, the rent on the condo's due this week.* With care she checked every deposit and withdrawal. Each one coincided with a night at the casino. Oh God, she did need help.

If she got help, would it save her from having to pick one of the options Joe had presented to her yesterday? Dina returned with her lunch. Realizing her predicament, Kyra pushed her lunch aside, her appetite gone.

"Are you okay?"

"Ignore me. You know...divorce," Kyra said, hoping that covered everything.

"I know. How'd it go last night?"

"Like crap."

"You didn't like Jake?" She almost laughed at Dina's expression.

Walked into that one. She shifted gears. "No, sorry, my mind's somewhere else. He's fine, but he's on the rebound and is still hung up on the woman."

"Yeah, I heard, but I didn't believe."

"Well, he even used the 'L' word."

"No kidding? Well, it's about time Jakey Boy's on the receiving end. Are you going to see him again?"

"We set up a dinner date for Friday. I'm not sure I'm going to keep it." Kyra frowned. After Thursday night with Joe her life as she knew it ceased to exist.

"What's the matter?"

"I'm not comfortable dating. I'm not divorced yet." The truth of the statement surprised her.

"Tommy's not going to change his mind, is he?"

"No," Kyra whispered.

"Oh, I'm sorry, honey, let's change the subject."

They finished their lunch in silence.

* * * *

Wednesday morning at the station, Jake wrote up his reports on various cases while he waited for Louie to get back. Louie was out following up on some leads pertaining to the Wolinski case. An hour later, Louie walked into his office. Jake pointed to the chair in front of his desk. Instead Louie walked to the coffee machine and helped himself.

"How'd it go after I left the scene?"

"As you'd expect. Lang agrees the blow to the back of the head was the cause of death and it didn't happen when he fell. What party were you attending on a Tuesday night?"

Leave it to Louie to mix business and gossip. "I was at Dina's. Then I wasn't." He didn't want to tell Louie about Kyra yet. "I want to compare our notes. Did you get an ID on the kid?"

"Yeah, his name's Donald Kolinski, age twenty-seven. I notified his parents last night. They almost seemed relieved."

"Kolinski looked about forty, twenty-seven, huh?"

"Yep, heroin will do that to you. Also, Lang said he'd call with the preliminary this morning. Who was on last night?"

"Lieutenant Holmes overseeing the calls. Also Kraus and Burke were on covering Homicide. There seems to have been a rash of deaths last night, a lot from tainted heroin. Then they got the usual—violence, domestics and one or two natural deaths. The night shift was hopping." Jake handed Louie his notes and sketches from the scene.

"Better them than us. Okay, back to Kolinski. He's a small-time dealer who uses Danny Wallace as his supplier. And Danny was last seen with him. Wallace has a record as long as my arm for dealing, theft, and mischief, no charges or history of violence, but word on the street is he's now working with either Spike or the local mob."

"He's stepping down in the world. Let's start with him."

"No one knows his whereabouts. I put word out on the street that I'm looking for him. I'll do follow-ups when I locate him," Louie said, turning to leave his office. "Hopefully, he'll lead us to Spike, and close that case."

Spike was still wanted for the killing of nineteen-year-old, Xavier Orlando. The poor kid was shot through his door when Spike went looking for someone who had stiffed him on a drug deal.

"We ever find out his real identity?"

"No. Spike turned up one day and took over the trade with force. Vice hasn't been able to get his fingerprints. No one knows where he came from."

"Did Spike kill the kid for stepping on his territory?" Jake asked.

"It's one of the things I'll be looking in to," Louie said as he left.

* * * *

Around three o'clock, Kyra forced herself to give her mother a call. She wanted to speak with her son. Not up to the grilling, Kyra hesitated before she pressed in the numbers for her mother. *Suck it up, Kyra, you're going to have to listen to it now or later. Better to get it over with.* She banged in their number.

Sean and Margo Hannigan, otherwise known as her parents, had cut her off when they found out about the gambling. Each one had pulled her aside and told her they'd give her the money for the lawyer if she'd get help and promise not to set foot into the casino again, but she was unable to comply. Didn't want to comply, she corrected.

Her mother picked up the phone on the third ring, out of breath. "Hello?"

"Hi, Mom, what's wrong?"

"Nothing, I was outside when the phone rang. I forgot to take the portable with me."

"Mom, Dad tells you all the time to take it with you. What if something happened or you needed to call for help?" Kyra lectured.

"I'm fine."

"I'm running behind at work. Can you put Trevor on?"

"The bus hasn't come yet."

Kyra didn't respond.

"Are you there, dear?"

"Yes, Mom, have Trevor call me at work when the bus drops him off."

"I will. Kyra, how are you doing?"

She heard the concern in her mother's voice. *Ignore it. If she cared she'd help you out.* "I'm fine."

"You haven't been over since our conversation. We miss you."

"I don't want to do this now. I'm at work."

"We still love you. It's for your own good."

"Yeah, right. I have to go, make sure he calls me." She disconnected the call before her mother replied.

* * * *

Wednesday got away from Jake. A visit to Saul Church's elderly mother took longer than he had planned on. One that Detective Stack should've done at the beginning of the investigation. Saul Church no matter what, always called his mother. Since she hadn't heard from him in a couple of weeks she was convinced her son was dead. He owed the wrong people money since she had cut him off without a dime.

"Mrs. Church, do you know who these people are?" Jake handed over some pictures of mob associates, including Phil Lucci's twenty-year-old one.

After a careful study, she laid the pictures on her lap. "No, Saul never said, but the last three weeks before he disappeared, he was jittery and short tempered."

"Where did he gamble?"

"Wherever he found a poker game. He's a good son, Lieutenant, but the gambling took over his life. He lost all sense of decency. He stole from me, from his aunts, he even stole from his kids. His ex-wife blames me for pampering him."

"Are you sure he didn't take off to avoid the people he owes?" Jake asked.

"I'm sure. His landlord gave him two weeks to come up with the money or he'd be evicted. Saul asked me if minded if he stayed here until he got back on his feet." Mrs. Church wiped at her eyes with a pristine white handkerchief. "It will be my fault if they killed him."

"No it won't, Mrs. Church. Saul was a grown man who put himself in this situation, not you."

"I understand what you're saying, Lieutenant, but it doesn't help. I love him. And if you find him alive, I'll bail him out again."

Of that, Jake had no doubt. He stood. "I'll let myself out."

He left Saul's mother to her guilt.

Jake struck out with Saul Church's friends. They refused to meet or talk to him. He checked his watch. *Damn, time moved at the speed of lightning.*

* * * *

After work, Kyra went home, fixed dinner, but still had no appetite. Looking down at the food, she picked it up and dumped it in the garbage. Minutes later, food forgotten she surfed the channels on the television. The casino called to her like a scorned lover. Damn, the need to be there clawed at her. She got antsy if she didn't go. Spikes jabbed her brain as she paced her condo. She still hadn't decided what answer she'd give Joe tomorrow. The choices he'd given her made her want to throw up. She wasn't a hooker, for God's sake. Doing the disgusting, sloppy, fat guy was out of the question.

Burn a dead body? Trevor became her reason to accept the offer. Money equaled custody of Trevor. *And for God's sake, that's what I do for a living anyhow.*

Trevor didn't call after school. That was her mother's way of getting back at her for hanging up on her. Boy, that burned her ass. Kyra needed to talk to Trevor. He was the one good, pure person in her life—she couldn't lose him. After dialing Tommy's number, she got his voicemail. She left a message for Trevor to call her back.

What was the crime if she burned a dead body? Seriously, she'd have to look up the penalty for doing that. A hundred thousand dollars and no debt. She'd make sure she and Trev had a great life far away from all of them.

Decision made. Problem solved.

Kyra went to the liquor cabinet, took out the bottle of vodka, and poured some into a glass to reinforce her decision. She took shot after shot until she passed out.

The buzzer on her alarm went off eight hours later. Stumbling out of bed, she made it to the bathroom, dropped to her knees and threw up. Ten minutes after nothing but the dry heaves, she stood with the help of the counter for support. The taste of the mouthwash upset her stomach more.

The woman looking back at her in the mirror frightened her. Not recognizing herself, she examined the dark circles under her eyes that had appeared there this week—not a flattering addition. Her skin, paler than usual, almost translucent, emphasized a bleakness in her eyes she didn't recognize, which completed the transformation. Desperate and sick, she needed to pull it together to get through today. The pounding in her head didn't help—it grew louder with each movement. Her cell phone flashed missed call as she walked back into the room. She plucked the phone off the nightstand and listened to the voice message.

"What the hell is wrong with you, Kyra? Trevor waited all night for you to show up." Tom shouted into her ear. Oh God, she'd forgotten all about taking Trevor to the restaurant. What kind of mother was she?

All she wanted to do was crawl back into bed, and die. She'd make it up to him this weekend. And damn, she had to attend the board meeting scheduled for ten this morning. She'd lose her job if she didn't. Kyra willed her limbs to move to the bathroom.

After turning the faucets to the hottest point she jumped into the shower and exhaled. Oh, how she wished she didn't have any place to go tonight.

It took her almost an hour to get dressed, to look presentable. She put on her red suit, which showcased a little cleavage—the rounded tops of her breasts. She hoped the distraction kept the boys busy during the meeting. With her antacids in hand, she left her condo at nine thirty.

* * * *

Louie didn't like what he was hearing. The deeper he dug into Donald Kolinski's life the more depressed he got. Kolinski was a stock broker who hit it big on a few IPOs. To celebrate, he'd started partying with the other brokers. Wine, drugs and women. The more he made for himself and the company the more he partied.

"My son, Sergeant, got caught up in it all. We're not rich people. When he hit on that first IPO he found himself a millionaire overnight. Everyone wanted a piece of him. His boss gave him a twenty-five percent bonus and expected him to do again. I saw the pressure building. He'd become nervous and agitated. When he hit on the second IPO, the company celebrated him as the new golden boy. The owner even brought him an expensive sports car." Mrs. Kolinski stopped and stared down at the picture on the end table of her son standing in the trade room at the NY Stock Exchange with his thumb up. "The partying got worse. He'd miss work. And the money started to disappear. At first it looked like he was spending it on the women he was dating, but I found out it was drugs."

"What did you do about it?" Louie asked.

"When he made his first million, he put me on his accounts. After learning of his drug use, I checked the balances in his checking and savings accounts. I was astounded. He'd gone through two million dollars. Two million dollars, Sergeant, up his nose to escape his success. I immediately withdrew three million and put it into a CD that doesn't mature for eight years. I hoped that would bring him to his senses." Mrs. Kolinski's voice hitched. "It didn't. He accused me of stealing from him. Said I was no better than his boss. Three weeks later he was fired. With no money, he put his condo in the city up for sale and came home. It's been a downward spiral since." Mrs. Kolinski seemed wiped out.

"Do you have other children?" Louie asked.

"No, Don was our only one. I blame myself…"

"Karin, stop that. Don did this to himself."

Mrs. Kolinski took her husband's hand.

"If the two of you think of anything else that might help us, please give me a call," Louie said as he stood. "I'm sorry for your loss."

"We lost him a long time ago, Sergeant," Mrs. Kolinski said, as she wiped her eyes with the tissue she had crumpled in her hand.

* * * *

Thursday, Jake's intention to call Kyra lay by the wayside. Tonight was out of the question but he should still call and confirm tomorrow night's dinner date. Everything he'd read about her on Tuesday night intrigued him. Were the nerves he'd gleaned from her the result of the battle she had with her ex for custody?

He pulled her number out of his pocket and pressed it into his phone.

"What?" she barked.

"Is this a bad time, Kyra?"

"Sorry, bad day."

"You have a lot of them."

The woman was a Dr. Jekyll and Mr. Hyde. Call him crazy but the type intrigued him.

"No, it's your bad luck you happen to be there on the bad ones." She didn't elaborate.

"You're cutting out. Are you driving?"

"Yes, I need to pull over. Hold on."

Jake waited. He heard the engine quiet as it idled.

"You still there?" she said.

"Yes. I can call back when you get home."

"I'm out for the evening with friends."

He wondered if she was on her way to the casino. Gamblers were liars. Was she one? "I'm calling to see if we're still on for dinner tomorrow night?"

"Yes, that sounds good."

"You like steak or fish?"

"Steak is good."

"I'll pick you up at seven? Why don't you give me your address?" He knew it from his research, but decided not to let her know he'd looked her up.

"It's Unit 5, at the Laredo condos off of Meriden Road. I'll be ready."

"You sure everything's okay?" She sounded distracted. Was she with her ex?

"I have a headache."

"Big night?"

"Yeah, I had a pity party last night, got drunk by myself, and paid for it all day today."

"Been there, done that," he said. "I'll see you tomorrow night."

He hung up. Why was he pursuing her? Kyra wasn't encouraging his attentions and she wasn't divorced yet. The woman seemed to have more problems than he did. Why tangle himself up like that? *God only knows.* But something about her pulled at him. People made mistakes, good people. Jake considered himself an excellent judge of character. It was his nature to poke at something until he got to the source of a problem.

Chapter 6

Joe Dillon stood by the entrance connecting the casino to the garage as he waited for Kyra. Thirty-five minutes late. He wondered if she'd show. He took his handkerchief from his pocket, wiped his brow. Nervous as a bride on her wedding night, Joe hoped Kyra had made the right decision. They didn't care about the Whale or his needs. They needed her to dispose of Church's body. The bastard had turned state's evidence on his boss instead of paying off his debt—not a smart thing to do if a person wanted to live. Now he was frozen in someone's garage while they figured out what to do with him. It also meant a huge bonus for Joe if he pulled this off.

Phil had summoned him to his office on another matter when he'd overheard Phil speaking on the phone with his lieutenant about the mess Church had caused. It was then he got his nerve to speak up and put Kyra in the mix. He'd never tell her it was he who had thrown her to the wolves. If she picked the fat slob, he'd lose all respect for her. Kyra had it right the other day when she questioned him about picking Garcia. They'd given her a choice, though, she understood it was for show. A semblance that she was in control. She had better select the one they wanted her to. It didn't matter, either way she'd take care of their body. If she chose right she'd walk away with some money, if not...well, he'd leave the what-if up to Lucci.

Since the day he became her host he'd been intrigued by her job. Who accepted a position where they burned bodies for a living? He'd never understood undertakers either.

Joe had big plans for himself in the organization. This little deed moved him up faster in the organization without him dirtying his own hands. A win-win situation. He'd let Kyra believe his boss was associated with the casino, but it wasn't true. Yes, indeed, Kyra was going to be an asset to his career. About to turn and head back into the casino, he saw the elevator doors open. Joe watched as she rushed toward him.

"Sorry I'm late, Joe," she said.

"I was ready to give up on you."

Kyra held up a hand to catch her breath. "Heavy traffic slowed me down."

"Not a problem. Are you hungry?"

"I want to get this over with. We can eat later."

"I'd rather eat first. Afterward, we're going to meet my boss."

"Oh—I didn't know—you never said I had to meet him." She bit her lip.

"What's your decision?"

"I can't—no, I won't do your Whale, though you already knew that."

* * * *

Jake continued to wade through all the information he'd dug up on Kyra and Tom while Louie was out picking up Wallace for questioning. Until their petition for divorce, news on the couple was nonexistent except for a dismissed case of sexual harassment against Tom. Everything he read pertained to the parents and what candidates they supported. Or who they socialized with. The second thing he found on Tom Russell was an article about his promotion last year. Promotion, ha. He worked for his father's firm. Did it count when your father promoted you? Jake wondered.

Brigh sat on the couch with him as he tried to dig out information on the dismissed case. Jake spread the printouts of old newspapers across his coffee table, scanning them for any tidbits that might help Kyra. He found what he was looking for in the *Wilkesbury Daily News* three weeks later. The article stated the case had been settled out of court and all charges had been dropped. Hmmm. A place to start. Why wasn't Kyra using that case against Tom in the divorce?

He'd find a way to bring it up tomorrow. Make it look like he ran across the article in the papers. The last thing he wanted to do was shut Kyra down. It might be interesting to take her to the casino and watch how she played. For the little insight he'd gain into her personality was it fair to dangle her addiction in front of her? *No, it's cruel.*

* * * *

Joe's nerves relaxed as he exhaled. She looked nervous, but not out of control, which surprised him. In the last couple of days she'd aged. Her decision wore on her. But what was it? She walked with a slouch, also something new. Joe's six-year-old popped into his head, and his heart started to open to her, to her child. He slammed the door shut. He'd gone too far to go back now. *Remember your rule, Joe, don't get involved. She did it to herself.*

"It's seven thirty now. We're not expected before nine. Let's head upstairs." Joe took her by the arm and led her to the special elevator for the Whales.

"I'm not hungry. I've been sick all day."

"What's wrong?" He looked her over.

"I fortified my decision with vodka last night. Do I have to meet him tonight?"

"You're also a drinker?" he asked.

"I'm not," she snipped.

"Even stupider. Food and a Bloody Mary will make your head better." He hoped—needed her presentable when he introduced her to Phil.

During dinner he kept his eyes on her. Somewhere around dessert her color came back. He didn't want anything to ruin this night. It didn't bother him that this brought him deeper into the organization. He hated his casino job, though he understood it was a stepping stone to his real vision. Joe planned on retiring early. After watching all these gamblers take and take, then demand more—it was his time to take now.

Kyra had been quiet as they ate. It wasn't because of the hangover either. Her demeanor shouted defeat. Joe didn't want any surprises when they went to Phil's. He'd told Phil he'd explain everything she needed to know to her. This way he'd be protected. But Phil insisted on meeting her, thus sealing her fate. Joe understood deep down it wasn't going to be a one-time deal. He'd locked Kyra to Phil for the rest of her life. Once again, he shoved down his conscience, and looked toward his future. He watched her push away her plate. He signaled for the check as he checked his watch.

* * * *

Jake stayed behind the glass as Louie questioned Danny Wallace. Danny admitted being with Kolinski, but had nothing to do with his death. Jake listened in as Louie continued his questioning for another half hour.

"I hear you're working for the mob now," Louie said.

"Me, no way, man," Wallace said. His eyes roamed the room.

"Did your competitor kill him?"

"Who's that?" Wallace tapped his fingers on the table.

"Spike."

"Never heard the name before." Jake saw the lie.

"Nervous, Danny?" Louie asked. "You should be—right now Spike might be hunting for you."

"I'm not on his radar." Wallace clamped his mouth shut when he realized he'd said too much.

"Didn't you just say you hadn't heard the name before?"

Wallace scrubbed both hands over his face, "I did. Man, you're trying to connect me to the mob. I'm small potatoes here. I make a little money and stay clean."

"Yeah, real clean, hooking young kids on the junk. You're a real humanitarian, Danny boy," Louie said, disgust in every word. "If it was Spike or the mob who did the hit, you might be next, Danny. I'd mull that over. And when you do, you'll understand I'm your only friend."

"Yeah, like I'd trust a cop." Wallace stood. "Are we done here?"

"For now, but I got you in my sights. If I was you, I'd keep looking over your shoulder," Louie said as he packed up his notes. Wallace left.

"Nothing. He hadn't a clue who Kolinski was meeting after him," Louie said to Jake as he came into the room.

"Yeah, I heard. What's next?"

"Lucky me, I get to find all his junkie friends and question them."

Jake smiled. "Well, you can do my paperwork and I'll track down the people."

"No way. Have fun," Louie said as he walked away whistling.

Jake worked until well after eight reviewing his detectives' progress on their cases. It still bewildered him, the pile of paper the job produced. With a clear desk, he'd be able to give his attention to his own case load first thing tomorrow. Louie had left around six. Something to do with an event going on at school with one of the kids. Jake often attended, but he'd begged off this time. He loved Louie's kids like his own but this time he didn't want to go.

Louie and his family slammed into him reminding Jake he no longer had one of his own. His sister Eva's murder destroyed his family seventeen years ago. His mother was wasting away in the nursing home, his father dead. Last month with Mia he had something special. Something permanent. But she'd dashed his hopes. Could he ever forgive her for the cruel way she'd delivered that message?

He hadn't intended to go anywhere after leaving the station but Jake drove straight to Kyra's condo. On his way he called and got voicemail. Jake sat in his car, read the case file on the missing man while he waited. After a half hour, he realized his stupidity. Desperate wasn't endearing. Should he head home or to the bar? No, not tonight. Jake pulled the car out of the lot and headed home.

* * * *

Joe drove up in front of a lavish mansion. He pushed a button on the post connected to the security gate. A guard approached and checked out the car, including the trunk and undercarriage. The lawn—was something this big even called a lawn, with its gentle hills—rolled and butted against the house. The place had to have ten thousand square feet of living space. A limo waited in front with a uniformed driver standing at attention beside it. The overhead lights glinted off his gun. Many more guards spread out over the grounds and she assumed they were armed too. *Lord, please tell me I'm getting out of this alive.*

Joe stood beside her, waves of nerves rolling off him. Kyra had never seen him this way. For all his posturing, it seemed Joe was a peon here too. The guard nodded to both of them, then stepped back as he invited them into the foyer.

"Stay here. I'll announce you," he commanded.

"What have you gotten me into?"

"Nothing yet," he whispered.

"Don't bullshit me, Joe. You're the one who threw me under the bus. I'll do the Whale." She smirked as her words and their implications landed.

"You can't change your mind now. I already gave him your answer." He spit the words at her.

"No you didn't. You're as afraid of him as I am. Good." When the guard came back, she turned her back on Joe.

"Right this way."

The man led them down a long, tiled hallway covered in oriental rugs and original artwork. He opened a set of pocket doors and ushered them into a well-appointed office. A large, masculine, dark cherry desk stood as the focal point of the room. A floor-to-ceiling window behind the desk looked out onto the lake. It showcased the owner's power. It said, *I'm king and I'm dangerous. Don't waste my time.* A six-foot marble statue stood in the corner—a toga-draped Roman woman pouring water from a pitcher.

The couches and chairs were covered in soft, supple, beige leather. The walls were a dark tan, and the red rugs pulled the whole room together. Nouveau Riche. The owner made sure all who entered knew it. Even with the glitz, it was the man behind the desk who captured her attention. He had jet-black hair, beady black eyes, and a prominent hawk-like nose in a narrow face. The face wasn't handsome as it was interesting. He looked ferocious.

"Ms. Russell, it's a pleasure to meet you." As he stood to take her hand, she hoped she hid the surprise. He was the same height as her—small for a man, five feet four inches.

"I'm sorry we haven't been introduced." Her eyes never left his face.

"I'm Phil."

She tried to remove her hand from his, but he tightened his hold. Icicles flowed through her blood.

"What a surprise you are. Leave us, all of you," he commanded.

"Mr.—" Joe tried to speak.

"I said leave, including you, Angelo. We'll be fine here, won't we, Ms. Russell?"

"I…guess," Kyra said, watching everyone else scurry from the room. *I'm the sacrificial virgin being offered up to the gods.*

"Ms. Russell. May I call you Kyra?"

"Yes."

"A surprise you are, Kyra, both in beauty and intelligence."

They watched each other, assessing. "Why intelligence?"

Laughing, he answered. "Because you hold your tongue and observe. Not many women—no, that's not true—not many *people* are smart enough to keep quiet and listen. Do you understand why you're here?" He stared into her eyes.

"Yes," she whispered, turning from his piercing gaze.

He let go of her hand, offered her a seat. "Please sit. Help yourself, Maria outdid herself."

"No, thank you, I'm not hungry." She took the single chair by the couch. His laughter poked at her nerves. *What the hell is amusing him?*

"I like polite. Are you afraid I'll sit too close to you?"

Small talk and flirting, not what she'd been expecting. "No."

"Honesty. I like that too."

He sat in the chair opposite her. His eyes searched her face. Kyra adjusted her position and waited, back straight, hands folded in her lap, eyes lowered.

The silence filled the room. She understood he'd talk when he was ready. A smart man. He waited too. Intimidation seemed to be his game and he played it well. *Hell, it worked.* He wasn't going to lay his cards on the table until he made a decision about her. Hoping he got to it sooner, rather than later, Kyra reined in her temper. It took all her control to do it.

"Your color's brightened. Are you hot?"

"No."

"Are you annoyed?"

"No."

"You're sure?

"Yes."

"Did I do something to make you mad?"

"No, I'm nervous. I understand what you want from me. I don't have a choice. I'd like to get to the how and when," Kyra answered.

* * * *

Carl Stack packed up his briefcase to leave for the night when his desk phone rang. He grabbed it up. "Detective Stack here?"

"It's Eddie Johnson from dispatch, Carl. I have a Mrs. Church on the phone. She asked for Lieutenant Carrington. Isn't it your file?"

"It is. Send her over to me." Carl steamed at the nerve of Jake butting into his cases. He picked up the receiver once Eddie transferred the call over. "Detective Stack here?"

"Oh, Detective, I wanted to speak with Lieutenant Carrington."

"He's not available at the moment, Mrs. Church. How can I help you?"

The woman hemmed and hawed before she spoke again. "I need to tell the lieutenant something."

"When did you last speak with him?" Carl wiped the sweat from his brow.

"Yesterday, why?"

"No reason. What do you need to tell him?"

The bastard's gone over my head and is interviewing people on my case. What's got his panties in a twist? Carl took three antacids from the roll on his desk and popped them into his mouth. He had a good thing going here and he'd be damned if Carrington was going to ruin it.

"I was embarrassed to tell the lieutenant that my son told me if I didn't give him the money, the mob would kill him. God forgive me. I believed he was playing me again."

Freak, it's worse than I imagined. "I'll pass that on to the lieutenant, Mrs. Church. We'll do everything in our power to find your son." Lucci had already paid him to turn a blind eye on this one. That 'gung-ho asshole Carrington' wasn't what he needed right now. One more year and he'd be able to retire to a nice tropical island with his cash and live like a king. If he kept his head down and stayed out of Carrington's way he'd make it to his goal.

* * * *

"I can see you're nervous, but you and I haven't spoken about anything. How do you know what I want? Are you a mind reader?" He watched her stare at the floor.

"No."

"Look at me, Kyra." He waited until she raised her eyes to his. "Nobody, Kyra, knows what or why I do anything, it's how I've succeeded in life. Do you understand?"

"Yes."

"It's difficult to have a conversation with you if you're only going to give one-syllable answers."

Her eyes had drawn his attention from the moment she entered the room. Damn, they were mesmerizing. How had she wound up here?

"I'm sorry. This is a first for me." She shrugged.

He pressed a button on his desk. Moments later a maid walked in. "Yes, sir?"

"Bring a pot of coffee with some Danish."

"Right away, sir."

They sat in silence until the maid came back with the coffee. Phil moved around the room, trying to decide if he'd use her. In the thick of things, he couldn't care less about a tool. And make no mistake, she was a tool, but there was something about this one he wanted to get to know. *But business is business.* He cleared his mind, studied her some more. No matter how hard she tried to hide her nerves, they showed, along with her unhappiness. Her movements were jerky while her gaze scanned the room like a cornered animal. He poured a cup of coffee and handed it to her.

"Thank you."

"Why don't you tell me why you're here?"

* * * *

While he wasn't directly involved in Louie's investigation, he kept a close watch on it. Something about it niggled at him. Still trying to pull the thread from his mind, he got slammed back in time as it betrayed him. Jake's last case with its similarities to his sister Eva's was never far from his consciousness. The horror of it never left him. Shanna Wagner, a young girl, had been killed, thrown away like garbage because a man's ego refused to handle her rejection.

A cruel reminder he hadn't heard back on the results of the DNA test George Spaulding had taken a few weeks ago. Not that he needed one. Every chance he got, Jake studied Eva's file. He wanted to be prepared for the parole board when the time came. Inside his head, he understood murder. Though never far from his mind he wished in his heart...no use going there. In his sanctuary, his home, he philosophized, though it got him nowhere. From the beginning of time, man had killed man for his needs, wants and greed. Who was he to question the grand plan?

The Missing Persons' case files sat on the coffee table. Jake grabbed the top one, the Church file. He'd need to speak with Stack soon. *And won't that be fun.* He started reading it then closed it. He snatched up his phone and hit redial. Again it went to voicemail. What was Kyra up to tonight? Gambling? Dating? Reconciling with her ex? Like he had the right to ask these questions or even wonder. How stupid was he to get involved with an almost-divorced woman? Jake closed his phone. The Missing Persons file needed his attention, not his libido.

* * * *

Carl checked to make sure Carrington was in homicide and not headed down to Missing Persons. He grabbed several Missing Person forms off his desk and started to fill them in with bogus names and interviews. He'd fix Jake and make him out to be a fool. If Carrington couldn't find the people, he'd tell him he caught them at a floating crap game. He wanted evidence, he'd give it to him. His last lieutenant had never reviewed their files. It's a pity Caulfield had chosen to retire. Why of all the damn lieutenants in the department had they picked Carrington to run MP?

I better fill the rest of the forms out at home in case that bastard decides to stick his nose in my business again. And what should he tell Phil? God, he'd kill him for sure if he was the one who had set Carrington on him. *The time isn't right, but when it is, I'll inform him of the problem.*

* * * *

Where to begin, Kyra mused. She sipped her coffee and ignored the burning sensation in her gut. Her head spun with a dozen answers. "Joe Dillon's my host at the casino—I'm in debt way over my head—he made me an offer to pay off my debt. It's a chance for a fresh start," she said, as she looked deep into Phil's shadowy eyes. Phil was impossible to read and that bothered her.

She inhaled, and finished her story. Bile choked her.

"Is this out of the norm for you?"

Of course it is. "Yes. He gave me two options. Neither appealed to me, both were out of the question, but I don't have a choice." She dropped her head in defeat.

"Then why are you here?"

Her head jerked up. "Excuse me?"

"I asked, why are you here? It's a simple question." His voice hardened.

"I told you I have no choice."

"Who said?"

"I understood I had no choice when Joe presented it to me."

"We all have choices, Kyra. You can choose one of the options Joe presented to you or walk away and never look back."

"Without any trouble?"

"I don't cause trouble for anyone."

A lie I'm sure. "Okay."

"I understand you have a son. It must be hard to work full-time and be a parent." He smiled. Though he tried for benevolent, it missed its mark.

"I don't want to speak about my son."

Now she was scared from her head to her toes. It was evident Phil liked fear. Was that how he controlled people?

"Most times I can't shut a mother up about her children."

"Trevor doesn't come into this, understand?"

"Are you threatening me, Kyra?" He smiled without mirth.

"No," she whispered.

"Good. If I decide to use you, you'll have no say in anything. *Anything.* You got that?"

"Yes."

"Good. I don't hurt children. I'm insulted that after spending less than half an hour with me you believe I do." Anger peppered his words.

"Trevor's everything to me. I needed…I had to make sure." Her voice quavered.

"I understand. But *you* understand, if we move forward, I own you. *Own you,* Kyra."

She lowered her head, sat in silence. Her hands trembled. She paused to gather strength before she replied. "What you mean by 'own me?'"

"Exactly that. Do you need a dictionary?" He raised his left brow, the corner of his mouth twisted.

"No. I'm under the impression I'm here for a certain function. What other things do you have in mind?" She raised her head, making eye contact again.

"You're here for a certain thing which might have to occur on *more than one occasion*. Do you understand what I'm saying?"

"Yes."

"What are your reasons for accepting Joe's deal?"

She contemplated before answering. "I want my son back, Phil. I'll do anything to get him back."

"How did you lose him?"

"Gambling." The flash of anger burned up her neck as her emotions, as always, showed on her face. It was times like this she wished she was a brunette.

"I'm sure it was a tough lesson. How did it get out of control?"

"I—" She stopped. *I don't know isn't acceptable here.*

"Well?"

"I let it take control of me. At the time I cared about nothing else." She'd never said it aloud. For the first time, she realized the simple truth in her statement. Her heart—awash in shame—had to deal with the fact she hadn't put Trevor first.

"You didn't care about your son?" A cruel man. He pushed her buttons.

"From the moment I became pregnant, I loved and cared for my son. I can't explain it to myself. How can I explain it to you?"

"The answer should be simple. You control your actions. I control mine."

Cruel, yes. "I'm aware I made the wrong decisions, harmful decisions, decisions I have to live with, Phil, not you."

"You're annoyed. Good."

"Good?"

"Yes, good. Your answers are honest. Your anger is pointed at you, not at anyone else. I like that, because that's where it belongs."

His words crushed her. Kyra waited for him to continue his attack against her character. It baffled her when Phil got up and walked to his desk. He pulled out his chair then sat. Next, he opened a drawer. "Join me over here, Kyra."

The man's devious. He must be through testing me. She pushed off her chair, went to his desk. For some reason it hit her—that was the longest yard of her life.

"Why are you smiling?"

Startled. "Nothing."

He tilted his head at her. His scary eyes stared her down.

She exhaled. "I didn't realize I was smiling, because I don't want to." Studying him, she continued. "I have a habit of playing jokes in my head when I'm under stress. It relaxes me. The walk from the chair to the desk hit me as the longest yard." She shrugged.

"Do you understand why you're here tonight?"

"Yes. You're assessing me, trying to figure out two things. One." She held up her right hand, extended her index finger, tapping it on her left hand. "If I'm up for the task. And two, if I'm intelligent enough to understand what I'm committing to."

"Correct." He continued to stare.

"What's your decision?"

He laughed, taking her off guard.

"Why are you laughing?" Hating herself for asking.

"You."

Pain shot up her arm as she dug her nails into her palm. Fighting for control, she bit back the sarcastic quip on the tip of her tongue. Kyra lifted her head and stared at him. *Enough of playing the frail and helpless female—I hate being played.* She needed his answer now.

"Your decision?"

"Kyra, let's make it clear up front. I'm in charge. I'm always in charge. I don't put up with insolence. Understood?"

"Yes."

"I give people my answer when I'm ready to give my answer. Understood?"

"Yes."

He tapped his pen on the desk. Kyra waited, watching it bounce up and down. *The man's a control freak. It's obvious from the way he's conducted this interview.* She wondered if he realized how much of himself he gave away with his motions. He reminded her of her trustees at the cemetery on one level, the only difference, Phil was a dangerous man.

"I've come to a decision. I can't use you."

"May I ask why?"

"No."

She squared her shoulders, stood, held out her hand. He took it. Held it.

"Thank you for your time, Phil."

"Aren't you the polite one? I like polite employees."

Her head snapped up. "Excuse me?" He still held her hand.

"I am going to use you, Kyra, because it gives us both what we need. I needed to see how you'd react when things didn't go your way."

"I'm not sure they did."

He laughed. "Yep, honest."

Getting down to business, he outlined how the undertaker would show up with a legitimate cremation, and inside that coffin there'd be two bodies, not one. The legal cremation's paperwork covered both their asses if someone asked any questions. She wasn't allowed to take notes. She'd memorize the information until she got home. Once there she'd open a file on her computer and passcode for her eyes only. It took Phil an hour to detail everything. She'd be paid the one hundred thousand in large bills. The first burn had to happen within days or the deal was off. *Oh my God, I agreed to dispose of a body for the freaking mob. I'm going to hell for sure.*

He seemed surprised that she hadn't blink when he mentioned that the same fee applied for each body.

"Kyra, you understand this isn't a one-time deal?"

"I figured it out over dinner with Joe. Once in, there's no getting out," she stated.

"This concludes our business for tonight." He stood.

"Thanks, Phil." She extended her hand again.

He took it, then seemed to make a personal decision. "Kyra, are you free tomorrow night? I'd like to take you to dinner. It has nothing to do with the deal."

"I have a dinner date tomorrow night, but I can cancel it. It's a first date."

"No, don't cancel. We'll make it some other time."

"I don't have plans for Saturday night if you want to go then instead of Friday?"

"Yes, Saturday's fine. I'll call with the time. I prefer eating around nine. It's not too late for you, is it?"

"No."

"I'll send a car."

"Where are we going?"

The corner of his lip twitched up at her question. "There are some great restaurants around here."

"I live in Wilkesbury. Why don't I drive up here? That way you don't have to worry about getting me home."

His eyes twinkled. "Don't plan on staying the night?"

"No."

Laughing, he said, "Fair enough."

Chapter 7

Jake studied the Church file again. According to Detective Stack's personnel records he was a thorough cop. The Saul Church case didn't prove that to Jake. After his interview with Mrs. Church, he decided it was time to have it out with Stack.

He scribbled notes in the margin as he read the single-page report, then penciled a note on his calendar to speak to Stack about it. At this point he didn't want to outright criticize any of the new detectives assigned to him until it was necessary. Missing Persons and Homicide had to work through the bumps and personalities before the two departments melded together and became a unit. It was temporary, or he hoped it was. But who knew, with Mayor Velky in charge.

The file bothered him. Instead of moving forward, he read it for a second time. Even a rookie knew how to gather more information than this. He'd find a motive for why Stack hadn't handled it properly.

With that out of the way, he grabbed the next personnel file. Harold Walsh, a crony of the Miller brothers, now there was one who spelled trouble for him. A friend of the Millers was an enemy of his and an informant for the mayor. Why did turning in a bad cop—Captain Miller—have to play havoc with a good cop's—Jake's—career?

After reading about Harry's lackluster job performance, Jake moved on to Homicide's case load. All the files seemed in order and, if not brilliant, they did show a logical order of investigation. But there was no logic to the Church file. Was Stack burned out or crooked?

* * * *

Christ, now why did I go and make a date with him? Kyra replayed the entire interview in her head. She hated to admit she found Phil attractive, in a dangerous kind of way. What was wrong with her? Never before had she pursued the bad-boy type. And in two days, she'd accepted dates with two. Oh yes. Make no mistake. Jake Carrington was a bad boy, even if he was working on the side of good. Versus Phil, who was on the side of evil. The picture in her mind had Jake on her right shoulder, angelic. Her left shoulder showed Phil as Beelzebub. The absurd imagery sent her into a fit of laughter. She steered the car onto the shoulder of the highway to get back in control. Wrestling with right and wrong even at this age —boy, Sister Mary Catherine would be proud of her.

* * * *

Friday flew by. With one burial and one cremation, it gave her time to catch up on her paperwork. Phil called, setting the time for dinner on Saturday. He informed her the first body would arrive by the end of the day.

The undertaker along with one of Phil's henchmen would stay with the body throughout the entire process. Phil wanted to make sure she didn't call the police. Understanding his motive, she wasn't insulted. Their expected arrival time was three, three thirty. Around two thirty she walked out of her office and perched herself on Dina's desk.

"Do you have big plans for the weekend?" Kyra asked.

"Oh yes. You remember the guy with the blond hair from the party?" Dina smiled.

"There were a lot of guys with blond hair at the party. Which one?"

"The tall one."

"They're all tall to me." Kyra laughed.

"Oh, right, Shorty." Dina laughed. "Well, never mind. Ray's six feet and built. I'm hoping to see how built tonight." Dina wiggled her brow.

Shaking her head, Kyra kept her mouth shut.

"Tonight's your date with Jake, right?"

"Yep."

"We'll have to compare notes on Monday."

"Sounds good. Why don't you take off for the weekend? Everything's all set here for today."

Not out of the ordinary for her to let Dina go early on Fridays if they weren't busy. This gave her some quiet time to prepare for Phil's body.

"You sure?"

"Yes, enjoy."

"Well, you don't have to tell me twice. Thanks. Enjoy your weekend."

Kyra watched Dina grab her purse and head out before she changed her mind. After Dina left, she walked into the back room where the cremations were performed. The room housed two chambers—ovens—but the public didn't like that term. Inside this room there were three smaller rooms off to the right side. A processing room, because at twenty-five hundred degrees the larger parts of the bones, such as the femur and humerus, didn't burn to ash in two and a half hours. They had to be pulverized. What the family received was the pulverized bones with minimum ash. Windows in the chamber doors allowed the attendant to view the process while the burn took place. She never looked. *Ghoulish.*

The outside of the building didn't advertise that it was a crematory. The chambers were designed to do a double burn. It incinerated the body and all gases and odors as well. Outside the building, clean, white, odorless smoke filled the sky.

The other two rooms were for storage—one refrigerated, in case the cremation didn't take place until the next day, and one for supplies. Kyra checked her watch: 2:55. Another check of the chamber area satisfied her she was ready for their arrival. She headed out front to wait.

Kyra had to give it to Phil—his people were on time. They arrived at three o'clock on the dot. The funeral director stopped in the office. She directed him to the side of the building where she'd receive the body. Meeting the funeral director made her nervous. The more people who knew what she did for Phil, the greater chance she had of getting caught. The hearse pulled into the garage area at the side of the building. She walked out to open the first bay, instructing the driver to back in. Both doors of the hearse opened. The undertaker stepped out of the driver's side. After a few moments, the guard from Phil's house stepped out of the front passenger side. He nodded, but didn't say a word to her.

She pushed the church table with the hydraulic lift to the hearse and locked the wheels in place. The funeral director, along with Phil's man, loaded the coffin onto the lift. She assumed a family had sprung for the expensive coffin and not Phil. What a waste of money. A few thousand dollars down the drain, or in this case, up in smoke. The cremation caskets were made of a heavy-duty cardboard, cost a few hundred bucks, though it might not support two bodies. *Better not go there, Kyra.* She unlocked the wheels and started to push the casket along the corridor to the chamber room.

"Do you have your paperwork?"

"Yes." The funeral director looked petrified.

"Great. Are you staying through the entire process?" She looked at both for their answers.

"Yes," they said in unison.

"Okay. There's coffee in the little kitchen by the front door and a vending machine in the workers' locker room if you want anything."

"Why don't you get yourself a cup of coffee, Tony?" The guard spoke for the first time.

The funeral director looked from one to the other, then scurried from the room.

"Kyra, right?"

"Yes."

"I'm not leaving this room until the process is completed."

"Phil explained."

"Do you need to view the body?"

"No."

"Why not?"

"It's not my job to verify the body or the identity of the deceased. The undertaker is responsible for the paperwork and identification. It's the funeral director's job not to make a mistake."

"Convenient."

"Yes."

Her pat answer should she be questioned. She didn't look in the coffins. As long as the person was dead and the undertaker had the proper paperwork she didn't care.

Chapter 8

Phil's henchman made Kyra nervous. He didn't flex a single muscle as he stood watch at the oven door. He observed each of her movements from his post. It took all her strength to push the coffin into the chamber. Two bodies weighed much more than one. To protect her ass, she'd claim she had assumed it was a severely obese man. She wondered who they were. The two and a half hours while she waited for the cremation to finish dragged on. Pacing between the offices, she tried to settle down and process paperwork, though her mind refused to focus. She wanted to call Trevor, but not in front of Phil's guy. She'd wait until she got home.

At last, it's done.

"The burning part of the cremation is now over, Mr.—" He didn't introduce himself either at Phil's house or here.

"What's next?"

"What's your name?"

"It's not important. If Phil wanted you to know he'd have told you."

Kyra tried not to roll her eyes. "We have to let the ovens cool down for a good half hour."

"Then what?"

"Then I rake the remains—pull the ashes out of the chamber, and load them into the processor."

"What does the processor do?"

"Your larger bones in your arms and legs don't burn to ash at twenty-five hundred degrees for two and a half hours. They'd take five or six hours. We process those bones—grind them down to an ash-like substance. That's what the families receive in their urns."

Kyra watched for a reaction. Interesting. Unlike most people he showed no emotion at all.

"After you process everything, what do you do?"

"I place the remains in a plastic bag which goes into a plastic urn. This is what I return to the funeral director or family unless the funeral director supplies an urn. If he does I then place the remains in the one he brought."

"Once you can get into the oven, we're out of here."

"No, as I said, I have to process the remains, and pack them in the urn, then you're done. Got a date?" she joked. Stone face.

"Why can't you open the oven now?"

"It's called a chamber. There's a safety on it. It remains locked until it's safe to open. We don't want anyone burned."

"So, you can't open it?"

"Not unless you want to get burned to a crisp. It needs to cool down." Kyra stared at him. She'd be damned if she'd endanger herself.

"I'll take a cup of coffee now." He nodded to her.

Boy, if he's waiting on me to serve him, he'll be disappointed. "I'll show you where it is."

To the right of the front door stood the small kitchen for the staff. Kyra walked in with Phil's man. The smell of burned coffee filled the air. She dumped it into the sink and started a fresh pot. Together they stood in compatible silence as they waited for it to finish brewing. The funeral director had chosen to stay in his car for the duration of the burn.

Kyra's head snapped up when he said, "How did you get into this line of work?"

"Natural progression, a promotion of sorts. I was the trained backup and when my boss died on the job it became mine."

"Interesting."

Still not a muscle moved in the man's face. It reminded her of chiseled marble. "How did you come to work for Phil?"

He looked at her, turned, poured two cups of coffee, handed her one, and took the other. *Okay, he wasn't going to answer.* She decided to wait out the burn in the processing room. His hand latched onto her arm. Her stomach pitched upward. Fear tightened her gut, but she challenged him, looking down at his fingers before raising her eyes to look into his. Dead, onyx pools of liquid stared back at her. She almost jumped back. *He'd snap my neck if Phil ordered it.* She wondered if he'd killed the man she cremated today. *Best not go there, Kyra.*

"It's for your protection that you don't know—don't ask questions." He released her arm.

"Let's check on our guy." She exhaled.

When they reached the back room, her cell phone started ringing. She checked her watch. Not much time to change into a different outfit for her date. *Damn, I wanted to sex up my outfit.* She looked at the number. Was fate making the decision for her? Did Jake want to cancel? It served her right if he did after what she'd done.

"Jake?"

Her eyes followed Phil's man around the room as he poked his head into each room, lifting papers off counters. *Nosy bastard.*

"Are we still on for tonight?" She heard apprehension in her own voice.

"Yes, but I'm running late. I wanted to give you a heads-up. It's not a problem, is it?"

Problem? This is awesome. The gods must be working in my favor. "No problem. What time?" Kyra's energy level took a boost. Jake was what she needed. "Eight?"

"Yes."

"Are you still going to pick me up?"

"Yes, I'll see you later." She hung up.

"Who was that?" the guard asked.

"My date for tonight." She offered no more.

After waiting the allotted time, Kyra pressed the button on the side of the chamber. The door glided open. Intense heat filled the room. The remains were a hot, glowing red. Grabbing her tools, she started to empty the chamber, pulling the rake back she hit the guard in the stomach with the handle. He groaned, but she wasn't going to apologize. Aware he hovered behind her, she wasn't going to let him interfere in her job.

"If you wish to watch, it'd be better if you stood off to the side. It takes about fifteen minutes to get all the remains out of the chamber."

"What's the metal thing there?"

"If the deceased wore any rings or other gold jewelry, it will be the base metal the jeweler used to form the jewelry design before he dipped it in the gold. The metal will warp during the burn. The dental gold in the deceased's mouth will have melted. If the person had a plate in his head or leg there'll be a piece of unrecognizable metal at the end of the process. It will be removed and separated from the bone ashes. Sometimes, I even find remnants of the nails from the coffin."

"You mean my rings aren't pure gold?"

"No. Gold is soft. The higher the gold content, the softer the jewelry. A wedding band starts with a piece of metal formed into a circle. Next, the jeweler builds and bonds the gold around it. The metal doesn't melt but it breaks down—though gold melts at those temperatures. Before we process or grind the remains, we have to remove the metal."

"What do you do with it?"

"We discard it."

"You mean you throw it away?"

Kyra turned her back to him as she rolled her eyes to the ceiling. "Yes."

"I want the metal."

"Okay."

She didn't question him. Who wore the ring was none of her business. The less she knew the better off she'd be—she wanted to live. After removing everything from the chamber, Kyra carried the remains to the processing room and scanned them for metal. After she removed the items, she put them in a separate box for the guard. She pulverized the remains in the grinder and dumped them in a plastic bag before loading them into the plastic cremation urn. Handing him the ashes, she escorted him to the hearse. He opened the back, took out a box and handed it to her.

"What's this?"

"An urn."

"Okay, come back here." *Why the freak did he wait until after I was done, for Pete's sake? I want to get the hell out of here.*

He followed her back into the processing room. She transferred the ashes from the temporary urn to the ornate one, handing it back to him when the transfer was complete. He reached into his pocket and handed her a thick envelope. She didn't look inside. His smile surprised her—it brightened his whole face, revealing handsome features she had missed before. He should smile more often, he'd be less scary. She closed the garage after they pulled out, grabbed her keys and purse, set the alarm and locked up for the night.

Kyra rushed across town. She'd burned a body for the mob. For God's sake, the freakin mob. Though wrong, she'd now be able to afford a lawyer to fight Tom. But still, she'd burned her first body for the mob.

When she got home, she locked the door and pulled down the shades. Then she counted the money. Phil was true to his word. In the envelope was one hundred thousand dollars. If she didn't have a date she'd be on her way to the casino. Tonight after the date, she'd head there and try her luck. Now that she didn't need the money, she'd probably win and go back to how it had been in the beginning. A lawyer would make all the difference in the world for her custody battle. Confused, elated, she now had money, but frightened with what happened next. She'd have to push today's events from her mind before she went crazy.

She walked into her bedroom. This was a cold room, not like the one she'd shared with Tommy. She hadn't had time or money to decorate. A queen-size bed, with a white comforter thrown over it, and a dresser were all she brought for the room. She wasn't planning on staying there once she got custody back and the house. The windows had shades and sheers covering them. She moved her bed, pried up a floorboard with a flat-head screwdriver as she hammered the end of it for leverage. When it popped off, she put ninety-five thousand dollars between the joists before she banged the board back in place. She slid the bed to its original position. Tomorrow she'd have to buy a safe. She wasn't going to put this money in her bank account or safe deposit box.

She shoved three thousand dollars into her purse. The other two thousand went into her suitcase in the closet. Kyra started to get ready for her date. Later, she'd have to figure out why her conscience wasn't bothering her much. Who knew if any of her regular funeral directors had ever put an extra body in their coffins? Kyra never checked the contents, though she supposed the weight of the box was a dead giveaway. As long as who she burned was dead, her job was done. She'd have to research the law to determine if the disposal of a dead body fell in the category of a misdemeanor or a felony in the legal code. She had to be aware of the penalty if she got caught. Something she probably should've done before she agreed to it in the first place.

Chapter 9

Jake knocked harder than he'd intended. He hated when he ran late but he'd been searching for Guy Pollo for over a month for the overdose death of a teenager and today they had nabbed him. Louie had some family issues he needed to attend to. Jake had to stay to process the drug dealer.

Kyra opened the door as he knocked. *Stunning!* She wore a form-fitting shirt in black with white stripes. It draped her bosom and gave him an enticing view of her cleavage. The black pencil skirt with the slit up her thigh sent his imagination into overdrive. Sexy, yet classic. He liked that she finished off her outfit with a simple string of pearls instead of clunky jewelry. And all that curly red hair she left loose fell over her shoulders.

"I'm sorry about the delay."

"Not a problem. I'm a little overdressed. Have a seat while I go change." She closed the door.

"Don't change, you look great." He liked legs and the slit gave him a nice view of a great pair.

"Thanks. Where are we going?"

"Maxine's in Hartford. Have you ever been there?"

"Yes, it's one of my favorites."

Jake took the jacket Kyra handed him and held it up for her to put on. Cool for late spring, though tonight promised warmth. After Kyra grabbed her purse from the chair, Jake opened the door and waited while she set her alarm and locked up. For the date he'd switched out the department issue for his silver convertible. After he helped her into the car he pulled into traffic.

"Rough day?"

"Yes and no." He laughed.

"I understand that."

"We caught this guy today I've been looking for all month. He's the reason I ran late."

"As I said, it wasn't a problem."

"How was your day?"

"Busy, and more of the usual," she said as she shrugged.

"Bored?"

"I'm in a rut, I guess."

"Summer's almost here; that should brighten things up."

"It should." Kyra seemed…uncomfortable?

Good first-date conversation, Jake. Change the subject. "Are you sure you're all right?"

"I need to be honest, Jake."

"Okay." He glanced at her sideward. *Here goes.*

"This is my first first date in nine years and I'm petrified."

"Is that all? Didn't we go for drinks the other night? So, in reality this is our second date." He flipped her a quick smile before turning back to face the road.

"That helps."

* * * *

Once he'd put her at ease, Jake enjoyed Kyra's company. She turned out to be someone who listened. He spoke about his job, the recent promotion, but steered away from anything personal. Kyra tried to dig deeper but Jake was a master of avoidance. Before he knew it, they were at the end of the evening, sitting in front of her condo. *The awkward moment has arrived.* He didn't want to put any pressure on her. He relaxed back into his seat and let Kyra control what happened next. It'd make his life easier. While he waited her out he studied her face. Strong bones, wide almond-shaped eyes, and a bowed mouth had him hoping she'd invite him in for coffee.

"Earth to Kyra." Jake laughed as he nudged her shoulder.

"I'm sorry, trapped in my head."

"I get it." He leaned over, kissed her, brushing his lips over hers before he got out of the car. He walked around to her side, extended a hand, and helped her out.

"Thanks for a great evening," she said.

"I enjoyed it. How about we do it again next week?"

"Yes, that sounds nice."

At the door, he held out his hand for her keys. She dropped them into it. He unlocked her door, handed her back her keys but didn't open it.

"Do you want to come in for a cup of coffee or a drink?" Her voice cracked, endearing her to him.

"No, it's best I go home. Thanks for a wonderful evening. I'll call you at the beginning of the week to set up a time for dinner."

"Sounds good."

He leaned in and kissed her once more, gently. But it didn't take long for him to deepen the kiss when she offered encouragement. The urgency in it forced him to put space between them. He didn't take advantage of vulnerable women.

He ran his thumb over her cheek, and smiled down at her. "Now you can relax," he joked.

"I was relaxed," she shot back.

He laughed. "Liar."

"You're right. Good night."

"Bye. Lock your door."

"The protector?" Kyra joked.

"I love a smart-mouth."

"Well, you came to the right place."

"Not yet," Jake said.

"Bye."

He waited for her to close the door. When he heard the lock click into place, he walked down the stairs. Kyra was an intelligent woman who didn't flaunt her looks. Every time the subject turned to relationships, she somehow turned it back on him. Was he losing his touch? She never discussed her gambling problem. His cop senses zoned into how masterfully she dodged the subject whenever they came close to it. At the same time her eyes shouted "help." *Lord, I should be running— not wondering how I can help her.* He doubted she'd ask him for assistance even if she need it. The more they talked, the more he recognized she was hiding something. He'd need all his investigative skills to unravel her secrets.

Chapter 10

Kyra fell into a deep sleep the minute she hit the sack. It only lasted for a few hours before she awoke around four a.m. She shot to a ramrod position, her heart pounding wildly in her chest. It slammed into her head—she'd burned a body for the mob.

And Jake. What was she doing with him? She'd need a miracle to juggle the guilt, the cop, and the mob boss. By throwing herself in with Phil, she'd made matters worse. Now instead of being a gambler, a woman who lost her child, she was a criminal. She fell back against her pillow. How in the hell would she be able to manage it all? Why did everything come with a price?

The next morning around ten she woke for the second time, stretched, then climbed out of bed. She called Trevor before even making coffee. This morning she needed his light.

"Hi Tommy, is Trevor there?"

"Trevor waited for your call last night. What's with you lately? It's the third time you missed calling him. Is the damn casino more important?"

"You better keep your mouth shut. If I hear you told this to Trevor, you'll pay."

"Why? It's the truth."

"It's not." It took everything she had in her to find her calm before she answered him. "I love Trevor. He's everything to me and don't you fill his head with lies. I didn't go to the casino last night. I worked late. A last-minute rush cremation which made me late for my date," she said, to anger him.

"A date?" He didn't respond to anything else. A smile tugged at her lips. *Gotcha.*

"Yes, a date. I had a great time." *Rubbing it in, you bet. Childish, yes. It's about time I had a weapon to use against him.*

"Oh...I still love you, Kyra. We'd still be together if it weren't for your gambling."

What a load of crap. He's still a dick. "That ship has sailed. We both need to move on. What we have is Trevor. There, we did our best work." On the verge of tears, she hoped her voice didn't show it. She had come to hate him.

"Please put Trevor on."

"Before I do, can you come to dinner sometime this week?"

"Why?"

"Why? Because it'd be good for Trev...I miss you."

"What game are you playing?" *Boy, the bullshit's getting deep.*

"Playing? I don't understand. I miss you. I understand we won't be together again, but I'd like to be friends. It'd be good for Trev to have both of us at dinner."

He was up to something, but she didn't know what. He'd been angry at her when he found out about the 401k fund. The fight—a real knock-down, drag-out—was the most vicious they'd ever had. They'd both said things they couldn't take back. He told her there was no place in his life for her—to him, she was dead.

"Please put him on."

"I'll call you Monday." She heard him yell to Trevor. Then yell again, before she heard Trevor respond.

"Hi, Mommy." He sounded excited.

Her heart wrenched at his voice. Trevor represented everything good in her life. Guilt tugged at her heart strings. Praying he'd never find out how she'd crossed the line. How she'd broken the law. How she'd continue to break the law, whenever Phil told her to, for the rest of her life.

"Hi, baby."

"Mom, I'm not a baby. You promised not to call me one anymore." She heard the frustration in his voice. Oh, how she missed him. He'd always be her baby.

"I know, Trev, but remember, I promised not to do it in front of other people, but I'm going to continue to do it when we're alone, okay?"

"All right. I missed you last night."

The crater in her heart spread. What kind of mother was she? The date and work weren't more important than Trevor. Nothing was more important than him. Yet, she'd still forgotten to call three times in the last two weeks. Stress was no excuse. Tears filled her eyes.

"I missed you too, Trev. I worked late last night. I'm sorry." *Now, I'm lying to him. What have I become?*

"It's okay, Mommy. When am I going to see you?" He was still enough of a child that he switched between Mom and Mommy. She loved when he called her Mommy.

"I'm taking you to dinner this week and your father might join us."

"Cool."

She smiled at the excitement in his voice. She hadn't been that excited in a long time. Her nerves started to fray with the upcoming visit with Tommy. *What's he up to?*

"It is. How was school this week?"

"Fine."

She smiled at his usual answer. "What did you learn?"

"I don't remember," Trevor said.

"You don't remember? How come?"

"I don't remember," Trevor's voice squeaked.

"Did you learn new words?" Kyra persisted.

"Yes."

She laughed. Their conversations always went like this. She loved the routine of it, when she called. They spoke for another fifteen minutes. Her heart was empty without him, tears burned her eyes as she hung up.

Last night she had gone to dinner with a cop. Tonight she was going to dinner with a mobster. Later this week, she'd have dinner with her soon-to-be ex and her son. To even out the score she should find a priest and have dinner with him to round out this insane soap opera she called her life.

Kyra dressed in a hurry and drove to a bank she'd never used before. She purchased a bank money order for one thousand dollars and had the teller make it out to Tommy as trustee for Trevor. Her repayment into Trevor's college fund. It filled her with joy. The payments had to be timed as not to raise questions about where she got the money. Afterward, she'd gone to another bank and got another money order for one thousand dollars for the divorce attorney she wanted to hire. After tucking the checks into her purse she headed home to clean her condo. With the house clean, she filled the bathtub with hot, steaming, fragrant water. Kyra turned off her cell phone before slipping into the tub. As the hot water eased her physical aches, she let out a soft sigh hoping it relaxed her a bit as the perils of the evening lay ahead of her.

* * * *

At nine on the dot she pulled into Phil's driveway. She turned off the car radio as she waited at the gate to be announced. The guard acknowledged her, searched the car before he passed her through. Phil's man, the one who'd attended the cremation, opened the front door.

"We meet again." She gave him a forced smile, hoping he didn't read the fear behind it.

"I'll show you in. Phil's waiting for you." No smile, no conversation. He turned, leading the way.

Walking down the familiar hallway, they came to Phil's office. The man opened the door, and Phil invited her in with a hand gesture. *What the hell? Phil's still demonstrating who's the boss. A freaking power play, for Christ's sake. This so-called date was a mistake.* One she'd suggested out of fear of retribution for turning him down.

"Kyra, right on time. You look lovely tonight." He took her hand.

"Thank you." She stood at attention.

"Have a seat. I want to talk business before we start the pleasure part of our evening."

So this is the way it's going to be. "Okay."

"Not curious?" He stared at her.

"You'll get to it when you're ready." Kyra never wavered nor broke eye contact with him.

Laughing, he said, "You're quite different from any other woman I've had the pleasure of knowing."

"How so?"

"You're direct. Though afraid, you don't let the fear control you."

"What do you need from me?"

"I wanted to take a minute to say thank you. Angelo said everything went well yesterday. You were courteous to him." *The bastard is trying to find out how I'm dealing with it.*

"Phil, I'm good at my job. I agreed to do one for you. Like all my customers, you got my best."

"I like dealing with people who do their jobs well. Are you hungry?"

The change of subject caught her off guard. "Yes, I am. Where are we going?"

"We're heading to the shore for dinner, but first we'll have hors d'oeuvres here. We'll take the limo. You can pick up your car later. Is that all right with you?"

"Yes."

"Did you enjoy your date last night?"

She'd turned away then jerked back, eyeing him. "I'm not comfortable discussing my date with you. I'm sure you'd want me to extend the same courtesy to you."

A mean-spirited sound, something not quite a laugh came out of him. "Yes, I'd like the same courtesy. You fascinate me. While you work for me I need to understand your wants and needs."

"Fair enough."

"Let's move to the living room for hors d'oeuvres."

He led her down the hall toward the front door and turned right into his living room. Spectacular. A floor-to-ceiling marble-and-granite fireplace caught her attention as she walked in. High ceilings, and a room with soothing beige-and-blue color scheme. Understated furniture of the best quality filled the room. It easily held fifty people or more. It all spelled money and comfort.

"Beautiful," Kyra said, spinning around to take it all in. The last time she was here she'd seen nothing, blinded by nerves. *Get in, get out,* had been her goal at the time.

"I find it comfortable. I love reading in here. Ah, here's Maria now."

The maid put down the appetizers as Kyra settled on the couch. After Maria left, Phil walked to the bar and pulled out two glasses. Kyra never took her eyes off him, following his every movement.

"What can I get you to drink?"

"Rum and coke."

He mixed the drinks, brought them over and handed her one, then settled on the couch next to her. He held out the tray of hors d'oeuvres to her.

"Thanks." She picked up a stuffed mushroom and popped it into her mouth, closing her eyes as she savored the taste. The best she'd ever had, though she'd expected nothing less from him.

"I take it you like it." He grinned.

"Yes," she said, studying the platter. She chose another mushroom, stuffed the whole thing into her mouth to halt further conversation.

* * * *

Phil enjoyed watching her eat. Not shy, Kyra exhibited a healthy appetite and didn't push the food away like other women did. Phil followed her movements as she reached for the caviar and put some on a blini and placed it in her mouth. It was almost as good as eating it himself. Her eyes lit up with her pleasure. He reached for the caviar, sampled it, then smiled.

"Are you enjoying the food?"

"Yes. I'm not crazy about the caviar, it's the first time I've had it. I do like the stuffed mushrooms."

Yes, he was enjoying her. "I'm glad. How do I differ from the gentleman you dated last evening?" Damn, he hadn't meant to ask but his curiosity had gotten the better of him.

"That's a loaded question. Are you sure you want the answer?"

"You continue to surprise me, Kyra. Yes, I want the answer." More than he wanted her to know.

* * * *

Jake wondered what Kyra was up to tonight as he washed his dinner dishes. "It's you and me, Brigh. I wasn't smart enough to ask her out on a date."

The dog walked over, pushed her muzzle under his hand as her sad eyes looked up at him.

After he'd gotten home last night he'd written down everything Kyra had told him about herself. He filed it with the stuff he'd dug up on her online. He draped the dish towel over his shoulder as he sat at the table. He'd created a basic form years ago to organize the information he had gathered on a case. He found it helped him to plug the holes. Kyra's chart looked like Swiss cheese.

Was he looking at this wrong? If he divided it into threes, one column for motherhood, one for wife, and one for gambler, what did it tell him? He played around with the info on a second sheet but it didn't reveal a lot. Carl Stack's Missing Persons' case on the gambler was also on his mind. Did Stack's missing guy connect to Kyra, and if so, how? Did she owe the same people money?

He was positive she wasn't going to be happy when she learned he'd researched her.

* * * *

"You're both gentlemen. I like that in a man. Second, you're each on opposite ends of the spectrum..." *Crap, said too much. It has to be nerves.*

"Opposite spectrums of what?" Phil sat up straighter.

"Personalities." She tried to cover.

"You're lying. You went out with a cop last night. I'm not stupid. I don't hire someone without checking them out."

She fidgeted with her hands, as total unadulterated fear consumed her. What about Trevor? Was he safe?

"Kyra?"

In for a penny. As this man had said, he now owned her. "I met him this week at a party and made plans for dinner Friday night. Turns out he's a cop in Wilkesbury."

Kyra watched her words land. Phil's facial expressions were a study for a clown or actor—first it went from a deep-lined frown to a wide toothy grin. Crap, she'd put Jake in Phil's path. The bastard knew all along who she'd gone out with last night. Did he have her followed?

"Yes, I can see how we're different."

"Not different. You both seem dedicated to your professions."

He nodded for her to go on.

"It's why I'm not comfortable talking about it, besides the normal reasons. It's awkward talking to one man about another."

As he studied her she tried to guess the workings of his mind. Was he wondering if he'd be able to use her cop? Jake Carrington didn't strike her as corrupt.

"What kind of cop is he?"

"Homicide." Her eyes roamed the room, not focusing on any one item, as little points of ice raced up her neck. She didn't dare make eye contact with Phil.

"Relax, I'm not going to turn you in. What's his name?" *Did he already know?* Kyra wondered.

"I can't tell you," she said, as she turned back to him. "He has nothing to do with you. And most likely it will be our first and last date."

"Why not, is he married?"

If she wasn't mistaken, Phil was jealous.

"No. My life isn't mine anymore. Why drag someone else into it."

"So you like him?"

"He's nice enough."

"It's not like you to be evasive, Kyra," he said, staring her down. She dropped her eyes to the table.

"I'm not being evasive. I didn't talk about you because you never crossed my mind last night." *Shit, I shouldn't've said that.* "I didn't even tell him I had a date tonight. I understand the rules, Phil. Continuing to date him is a problem. I decided last night it was my first and last date with him."

"But you liked him?" he insisted.

She didn't understand where his jealousy came from. She owed him nothing, for Christ's sake.

"Yes, I do." He watched her struggle before she continued. "He asked me out again."

"What did you say?"

"He's going to call me next week."

"Did he spend the night?" She almost jumped out of her skin at the anger in his voice.

"It's none of your business, but the answer's no."

"Why?"

This whole line of questioning's ridiculous.

He must've realized he'd scared her and backed off. "I'm sorry. You're right. It's none of my business. Are you ready for dinner?"

"Yes, if I eat any more of the appetizers, I'll be stuffed."

* * * *

What just happened here? Anger pumped off of Phil and wrapped around her like a boa constrictor. He'd no right to ask those questions, but in them she found her answer to whether she should date Jake again. The relationship needed to end before it started. *I'll use a reconciliation with Tom to put him off.* It saddened her, but what choice did she have? Cops don't love criminals.

God, she'd lost her appetite but didn't dare beg off now. Stuck with Phil for the next couple of hours, she decided when dinner was done, she'd go to the casino to let off some steam.

On the drive to the restaurant she ignored Phil's pissy mood. Why the hell had she suggested tonight? She had the perfect out yesterday. Boy, did she screw up. Her relationship with Phil needed to stay a business arrangement, nothing more.

It took thirty minutes to reach the five-star restaurant. A swanky place overlooking the ocean in Rhode Island. It was obvious he was trying to impress her. The new black dress she bought this morning fit in well with the atmosphere and the clientele at the place he had chosen. She'd put her hair up for the evening, though it was impossible to contain all her curls. She'd hoped the 'do appeared businesslike instead of messy. A strand of pearls at her throat and pearl earrings were the only jewelry she'd worn.

Phil seemed to be a regular. Everyone greeted him with deference, from the maître d' to the waitstaff. They were escorted to a table with a beautiful view of the water. The maître d' started to pull her chair out but Phil brushed him away and did it himself, but not before he slipped the maître d' some cash. With some ceremony, the waiter presented their menus. Next he draped their napkins over their laps. Amused, she turned her attention to the sea. The three-quarter moon reflected off the water, a magical light beckoning her. The ocean resembled a smooth, dark plate of glass. She realized she wanted to share this scene with Jake not Phil. Phil's question pulled her back to the here and now.

"Is the restaurant to your liking?" he asked.

What's with this guy? "It's great."

"I'm glad you like it. The fish here's excellent."

"I'm not crazy about fish."

"Steak then?"

"Yes." She smiled at him.

"Steak it is. I ordered wine instead of cocktails. Do you prefer a cocktail?"

"No, wine's good for me." Killer first dates. How stupid of her to make two in one weekend.

"Are you nervous, Kyra?"

Déjà vu. Didn't Jake ask me the same exact question last night? "No, I'm not. This is my second date in nine years."

"The first being last night?" He cocked his head and pinned her with a stare.

"Yes. I forgot how stressful they can be." *Yep, déjà vu.*

"Relax, I don't bite." He grinned. "Unless, of course, I want to."

"Funny. What are you having?" She steered the subject to another topic.

"What do you want?"

"We're not talking about dinner, are we?"

"No. I'm interested in what makes you tick."

Shit, what makes me tick? It's none of your damn business, Phil. Deep down she understood he'd use whatever she told him against her at a later date. A point she had to hold in the forefront of her mind. She wanted and needed to guard her private life from the likes of him.

"I'm a boring person." Kyra tore her eyes from the ocean to meet his questioning gaze.

"I doubt that. Look at the job you have. Not many people do what you do."

"It's a simple and necessary job. Why don't you tell me about you? You're a blank slate to me."

"I keep my life private on purpose, Kyra. If this comes to anything, I'll share."

"Why don't you tell me what's not private then." *Will he kill me if he doesn't like what I say or do? This is excruciating. How many more hours are left of this date?* The clang of her machine called to her.

"It seems like work, doesn't it?" *A mind reader or is he bored too?*

"It does. Why's that?"

"Do you always answer a question with a question?"

"No more than you do."

"Clever girl." He laughed.

The waiter took their orders. As they worked through dinner and another bottle of wine, the conversation became easier. She had to be careful the wine didn't loosen her tongue too much. *Phil's the boss*, she reminded herself more than once and held back. When he relaxed, Phil proved to be a good date—attentive, funny, and knowledgeable in many areas, though he never revealed anything personal about himself. They left the restaurant at one thirty in the morning. The ride back to his house became awkward. Around two they pulled into his driveway. Phil knocked on the glass between them and the driver. The chauffeur lowered the window.

"Angelo, we'll be fine, give us a minute here."

"Okay, boss." Watching him exit the car, she wondered what Phil wanted.

"I enjoyed myself. I hope you did too."

"I did."

He took her hand and made circles on her palm with his finger. *Is this guy for real?* She didn't laugh or pull away. She wasn't sure what she should do.

"You're a patient woman. Would you like to come in for a nightcap?"

"It's late, Phil, and I have a long drive ahead of me. Some other time."

"You should've let me send the limo for you. If you're tired you're welcome to stay here."

Her shock must have shown. He added, "No strings attached."

"Thank you. A gracious offer, but I'm not divorced yet. I don't want to put myself in a compromising position."

"Smart. Will I see you again?"

"It's not wise to mix business and pleasure. You're my boss." She turned the light on over her head. Searched deep into his raven eyes.

"I don't see it going anywhere. Of course, you can't gauge where something's going based on one date. I'd like to see you again."

Kyra didn't respond right away.

"I'll tell you what, no pressure. I'll call you during the week. If you'd like to have a second date, we'll make plans."

"Thanks, I'll look forward to your call."

Leaning over, he turned off the light she had turned on, then took her in his arms and kissed her. Nothing, not even a spark. No current running through her like she'd experienced with Jake. More amused than mad when Phil slipped his hand up her front and cupped her breast, she placed her hand over his, and removed it before breaking the embrace.

"Good night, Phil."

A smile washed over his face. "Good night, Kyra. Drive with care. There are a lot of drunks out this time of night."

"I will. Thanks again."

The walk to her car had her debating whether she should go home or to the casino—willpower mixed with common sense won out. The last person she wanted to see tonight was Joe Dillon.

When she got home, a car parked in the spot next to her assigned one had its windows all steamed up. Kyra didn't recognize it. The hair on the back of her neck stood up. Should she get out of her car? *Call the police.* Phone in hand, she was about to open the door when the driver's door of the other car opened.

Chapter 11

A thousand questions ran through her mind as he tried her locked passenger door. Kyra stared at him. Why was he here? What did he want? Was that a new car? There was only one way to find out. *First, he invites me to dinner and now he shows up on my doorstep. What's his game?* Kyra unlocked her doors.

"What, were you at the casino?" Tommy accused.

"No. I had a date," she said.

"Another date? Who's the guy?"

"It wasn't the same guy, Tommy. Why are you here? Where's Trevor?"

"He slept over at my parents' house tonight. I had a date too, but she canceled."

She knew that "poor me" tone he used when he wanted something.

"Why are you here?" she asked again.

"I miss you, baby. When you said you had a date, it pissed me off…"

She pushed him back when he reached for her. "Tommy, let me remind you of your exact words. 'You're dead to me.' Do you remember them?"

He sat up straighter, a typical move he made when he'd been drinking. "I remember," he whispered.

"Good. Now get out of my car. There's nothing here for you."

"I'm sorry, Kyra, I still love you. I haven't dated anyone else. Did you have sex with him?"

Gripping the steering wheel, she fought for control. "It's none of your business, Tommy, though you should know me better by now."

Silence. She turned in her seat to face him. Not for one second did she believe the tears that rolled over his cheeks.

"I thought I did—then you betrayed us."

She blinked away her tears. "I didn't betray you. Do you understand addictions? Would it have been better if I had a drug or alcohol addiction?"

"Are you getting help?" He reached for her, she pulled back.

"We've been through all this before. Go home."

"I need you." In an instant he had her in his arms, his lips pressed to hers. She pressed her lips closed as she fought to get away.

"What are you, drunk or crazy?"

"Neither, I want to try to fix us."

"Fix us? That ship has long sailed. We can't take back all the things we said to each other or, more important, how you took my son away from me. No, we're through. Go home."

Tears ran down her face. Her heart ached. She'd almost given in to him. Then he grabbed her arm and squeezed it hard.

"Let go or I'll call the police," she yelled.

He'd never raised a hand to her during their marriage, though he came close the night he discovered she'd raided the pensions and the 401k.

"Please listen to me. We need to be a family again. I miss you, but Trevor misses you more. Please consider a reconciliation."

She wanted to go in and sleep for a year. Confused, angry, and frightened. *Tell him what he wants to hear*, a voice in her head shouted. *End this night now.*

"I will. I'll see you at dinner this week. We'll talk more then." She saw hope in his face though she knew she'd never take him back.

"Are you serious?"

"Yes."

"Why don't you lock your car? I'll walk you to your door." Tom was always a gentleman, but at the moment she didn't trust him.

"You don't need to walk me to my door. I've been on my own for months now." The pleasure she received rubbing it in his face was small. *Oh well, you take your fun where you can.*

"I deserved that." He leaned in to kiss her. She pulled back.

"Good night." She waited for him to get out of her car and climb into his. She wanted to stay put until he drove away but he didn't move. She realized he wasn't going to leave until she was inside. She rushed to her door, unlocked it, pushed it open, and waved to him as she stepped inside and slammed it closed. She threw the deadbolt into place before setting the alarm, her movements jerky as she slid to the floor in tears. She hadn't realized until that moment how frightened Tommy had made her. He seemed different tonight.

Her cell phone started to ring. "Phil?" *What the hell does he want at this hour?*

"I wanted to make sure you got home all right."

"I got in a few minutes ago."

"Did you run into any trouble?"

"No."

"You sound upset. What's wrong?"

"Nothing." She knew he'd never let it go. "My ex-husband was waiting for me when I got home. He wanted to talk."

"He didn't hurt you, did he?"

"Phil—no—I'm confused." *I want to go to bed.*

"Okay, as long as you're all right. I wanted to tell you again how much I enjoyed the evening."

"Thanks again, good night." She hung up first, stripped off her dress, and kicked her shoes across the room before she fell into bed in her underwear. She was asleep before her head hit the pillow.

* * * *

Out his back door, Jake studied the charcoal sky. Black fading to gray as the night shifted into day. Lightning lit the sky with a promise of a passing storm. If it had to rain on his day off, at least it promised to be brief. The clock on the microwave read four, too early to call Kyra and see if she wanted to join him for a picnic once the weather cleared up.

He'd had a restless night and picked apart the reasons. Stack's file continued to rattle around his head. Gambler goes missing, who's responsible? The answer's always the same. He owed someone a lot of money and took off. Or someone he owed took their due in a pound of flesh. In Church's case, which one was it? He'd look into who ran the gambling in Connecticut. That would be his starting point. According to Louie's voicemail, he was close to closing the Kolinski case. One down and several outstanding. Someday he hoped there'd be no names on the murder board. *And pink elephants will fly.*

Though a bit early, he showered and dressed. He'd go to the station to kill a few hours and put in some serious time on his cases instead of putzing around the house all morning. Before heading out, he'd walk Brigh to give her some exercise. The pooch was becoming lazy.

"Brigh, want to go out?" Jake rubbed the dog's head, grabbed her leash. "Hey, it's Sunday, do you want to come to work with me?"

Brigh licked his hand as if she understood and jumped up onto his leg. Chuckling, he took her outside. Brigh stood perfectly still. In the dark Brigh glued herself to his leg. He didn't fear the dog running away. A scaredy cat, but Brigh was living up to her Gaelic name. It meant *survivor, power, force, and strength*. The poor thing was all of that and sweet. How she'd remained gentle after all the abuse she'd taken in her first four months was beyond him.

After their walk, Brigh climbed into the back seat, while Jake sat at the wheel. It didn't surprise him to see Louie at his desk when he and Brigh walked into the bullpen.

"Why are you here this early? Sophia kick you out?"

"I have unfinished paperwork. I've also been catching up on your Missing Persons' files. Something's not right there. Oh, look who's here." Louie bent and rubbed Brigh behind the ears.

"It's the reason I'm here too. How'd the guys make out over the weekend? Any new cases?"

"One new homicide and a teenager gone missing, but she was found an hour later at her boyfriend's. I'm also working the Wade case. Looks like an accidental death."

"Looks like, why isn't it?"

"I need to check out a few things before I say," Louie said as he scratched his head.

* * * *

Kyra woke at nine—disoriented, twisted, and tangled in her sheets. She looked around for Tommy. Realizing it was a dream, she got out of bed and headed into the bathroom. Her head throbbed. *I didn't drink a lot last night. It has to be nerves.* Turning on the hot water for the shower, she climbed in.

The steaming water washed over her, easing the tension in her body. Her cell phone started ringing. Her eyes popped open at the ring tone. *Shit,* she got shampoo in her eyes.

"Screw it, I'm not answering it. It's probably Tommy anyway or worse Phil," she said aloud.

Thirty minutes later, with a sense of being half-human she climbed out of the shower. As Kyra toweled off she looked in the mirror. *Lord, I've aged this week*. If she wrote a book on all of last week's chance meetings and offers alone who'd believe it? They'd label it pure fiction. *I wish*.

On the way into the bedroom, she picked up her cell phone off the counter. Three missed calls. Scrolling down the list, she made a mental note of the callers. The first number she recognized as Tommy's, the next two came up unknown. Each had left her a voicemail. Hitting the voicemail button, Tommy's voice filled the air.

"Hey, Kyra...I wanted to say I'm sorry for scaring you last night. We're still married, and you with another guy...drove me crazy. It's my problem, sorry." He hung up. She pressed the save button. It might come in handy one day.

The next message was from Jake. "Hi, Kyra, it's Sunday, I was wondering if you had plans for today. If not, would you like to do something? Give me a call. Oh, it's Jake." Laughing, she wrote down his number and stored it for future use.

The last message didn't surprise her. Phil. What did he want? "Hello Kyra, it's Phil. I hope you got some rest last night. I wanted to make sure you were okay—if you'd like to do something today, let me know." At the end of his message she hit the delete key.

Jake's offer was the only one that sounded tempting. What was she going to do about him? Tommy's message confused her. Not for a minute did she trust his professed jealousy. It had to do with the divorce. She needed to behave in order to get Trevor back. It struck her, she hadn't gambled since Tuesday night. Didn't that prove she didn't need help? Ironic—here she had all this money and now she didn't want to gamble. All she wanted to do was spend time with Jake.

* * * *

Jake's cell phone vibrated in his pocket. Pulling it out, he looked at the number and smiled. He hated to admit it but he'd been anticipating her call. Brigh stood then rested her head on his lap.

"Hi."

"It's Kyra."

"I'm glad you called back. Do you have plans today?" He ran his hand over Brigh's back as he planned out what he'd do with Kyra today. He'd need to take Brigh home.

"I'm free."

"How about a picnic?"

"That sounds wonderful."

"I'll pick you up in an hour if that's good for you?"

"I'll be ready. I just got out of the shower. Lazy day."

"I'll help you dry off," his husky voice offered a promise of more, he hoped.

"Maybe someday in the future," she teased.

"Shot down again? Oh well."

"Wounded, but not killed."

"Then there's hope. See you in an hour." Her humor lifted his spirits. "Bye."

* * * *

Now for the hard call. Talk about playing with fire. Worse than fire— knives that cut deep. He picked up on half a ring.

"I'm delighted you called back."

"Hi, Phil."

"How are you today?"

"I'm good, thanks for your concern."

"Did he leave you alone?"

"Yes. I guess he got jealous when he heard I had a date. He's okay now."

"Want me to talk to him?"

A chill ran down her spine as his meaning hit home.

"Please, don't. I'm fine. Nine years is a long time to be together. Separating takes some getting used to." Why the hell had she gone on the date with Phil? He was nothing but trouble. Not that she'd had a choice.

"I understand. Do you want to do something today?"

"I'm sorry, Phil, I have other plans." She didn't elaborate.

"I'll call you during the week to set up dinner. Take care."

"I'll look forward to it." He didn't sound happy, but at least he didn't ask what her plans were. She didn't bother to call Tommy back. Perhaps tonight she might…

Kyra dressed with care. Her body tingled all over in anticipation of seeing Jake again. She put on her new jeans with embroidered red roses and a short-sleeve mauve top. She took the light green sweater out of the closet. It set off her eyes. The weather in June in New England changed by the minute. One hour it could be seventy degrees, the next fifty. Even with the sweater, she decided she'd take along her spring jacket. *I should have some money with me in case.* For reassurance she checked what she had left from the original three thousand she'd put in her purse on Friday. Six hundred fifty dollars was enough for today.

Kyra walked into her living room, draped her jacket and purse over the chair. She rechecked her makeup in the mirror by the door to make sure she hid the unflattering, deep dark circles under her eyes. Though she tried to calm her nerves, she paced the room while she waited for Jake. *A harmless picnic, or was it? Mob, cop, burned bodies? Playing with fire is becoming my trademark.*

* * * *

Phil didn't like being blown off. And that's what Kyra had done to him. She pulled back last night though he couldn't figure out why or what he'd done that turned her off. What kind of plans did she have today? Who was the lucky man—her ex-husband or the cop? Neither choice made him happy.

"What's up, boss?"

"Nothing, Angelo. Leave me be." Phil waved him away.

"You sure?"

"Yes." He reached for his desk phone. After picking up the receiver he slammed it back down and noticed Angelo still standing in the doorway.

"Don't you understand English?" he snapped.

"Sorry, boss. You want anything?"

"No."

Angelo left the room. Phil picked the phone up again to call Joe Dillon. When the call went to voicemail his blood boiled. *He better answer this time.* He redialed.

"Hello."

"Joe, it's Phil. Has Kyra been to the casino this week?" He didn't want small talk, he wanted answers.

"I haven't seen her, Phil, but I'll check to make sure. It surprised me she hasn't shown up here yet with her new found weal—" Phil cut him off.

"Don't say anything stupid, Joe," he warned.

"Sorry."

Phil slammed down his phone. He picked up his pencil, started tapping the desk, a nervous tic that emerged when he was aggravated. What was up with Kyra? Did she get smart and stop gambling? Who was she out with today?

It wasn't like him to moon over a woman. If he wanted one, he called one. They were a dime a dozen, but this Kyra was a different sort. Before working for him, she seemed to have been a woman with middle-class values. Gambling had taken her down. What was he going to do with her?

Was she telling the truth when she said she wasn't going to see the cop again? Frustrated, he snapped the pencil in half.

"Angelo!" The door swung open. Angelo's six foot frame filled the doorway.

"Yeah, boss?"

"Bring the limo around. I want to go for a ride."

"Right away."

Ten minutes later, pulling out of the driveway, Angelo asked, "Where to, boss?"

"Take Route 2 toward Hartford."

They drove in silence for a while. "What's the matter, Phil?" Phil looked up, met Angelo's gaze in the mirror. On rare occasions Angelo called him Phil. They went way back. Phil trusted Angelo more than any other person in this world.

"I'm off today."

"It's the redhead, isn't it?" Angelo pressed.

"Yes, Ang, it is. She got under my skin."

"Be careful there, women aren't your strong point."

He didn't need to be reminded. Women didn't like him and he didn't understand why.

"She's different."

"She is. I like her, but she's still a woman. They operate with a different code."

"She does have a code."

"Yeah, I noticed it when she did the cremation. One that might break her for not respecting it. Why are we going to Hartford? Are we going there to talk to David?"

"No."

"Then what?"

"I haven't figured it out yet, keep driving."

"She messed with your head last night?"

"No. I did."

"How?"

"I want more than she's willing to give. For some reason she's scared of me."

"Smart woman." Angelo grinned.

Phil left the conversation there. As they drove, he analyzed every word she'd spoken last night. Did she back off because he had put his hand on her breast? The kiss shocked him—he expected passionate, but it was as if he kissed a corpse. Didn't he turn her on? She seemed inexperienced even though she'd been married. Was she a one-man woman? Lucky guy if that was the case. Phil didn't like her ex waiting for her outside her door last night. If it continued, he'd personally speak with him.

He loved nothing more than a strong woman because it was an incredible surge of triumph when he broke her. Kyra might be too strong for her own good. If he couldn't break her, he'd kill her. No one refused him.

It had surprised him she hadn't gone straight to the casino once she got the payoff. Did the gambling lose its appeal to her? Or did she learn her lesson? He made a decision, tapped on the glass separating him from Angelo.

"Yeah, boss."

"Turn around, head to the shore instead." He'd let the natural cycle of things play out and try not to spy on her.

Chapter 12

Kyra's call had him putting the gambler's file on the back burner for today. After agonizing over Mia for the last few weeks, he looked forward to a relaxing day with Kyra. No pressure, no fear of screwing up, no anxiety. If nothing else but a friendship developed with her, he was okay with that. Jake called the deli on Highland Avenue and ordered lunch: two different kinds of sandwiches, fruit, drinks, and chips. The storm passed by once the sun had come up. The bright sunshine brought the warmer weather with it. He decided to take her to the beach, and not Kent Falls where he had taken Mia for their picnic. A day vegging out on the blanket getting to know her was what they both needed. He needed balance back in his life. His equilibrium had been off since the breakup.

With the top down on the convertible he headed to the deli, then to Kyra's. After knocking, he scanned the neighborhood. Low-to-middle-income earners owned or rented condos here. The department got a lot of calls to respond to this section of town for a variety of things. Why'd Kyra choose to live here? He'd have to ask.

"Hey." Jake leaned in, kissed her when the door opened. Again she set something off inside him. Something he liked.

"Come in. I need to grab my jacket and purse. Do you want anything?" she asked.

"No. I'm all set."

"Where are we going?"

"To Rhode Island to walk the beach, and have dinner on the shore. Sound good?"

"Yes."

A few hours later, after their walk on the beach, he led her to the car. He pulled out the blanket and the picnic basket. The weather cooperated. It was in the mid-seventies and the sun shone down on them with a mild breeze—its warmth holding the promise of summer.

"I like a man who comes prepared."

"Yep, I was a Boy Scout." He flashed her a mischievous grin and wiggled his brows.

"This is terrific, I'm starved."

"I hope you like what I brought."

"I like most everything. Did you fix this yourself?"

He laughed. "I could lie, but no. There's this little deli off Highland, they make great grinders. I popped in after you called me back and picked them up."

She reached in the basket and brought out the wine. Digging deeper, she found the sandwiches. He watched her check out each one before she decided.

"Mmm, which one's mine?"

"You pick, I'll eat anything."

"I'll take the—"

Jake turned to see what had left her speechless. "Something wrong?" Jake eyed the men approaching them. He went on alert.

"No—I'm—"

"Kyra?"

"Phil, how are you?" Jake noticed the tension stretched across her voice.

"Good. It seems we both had the same idea today. The weather's great, isn't it?"

"Yes, it is."

Awkward. Jake picked up a twitch at the corner of Kyra's eye. Nerves? He knew the man's face. Jake racked his brain for a name. The man she'd called Phil reached down, forcing Jake to take his hand. Jake pushed himself off the blanket, straightened to his full height as he took the man's measure. He towered over the guy.

"I'm Phil, Kyra's friend."

"I'm Jake."

He didn't like the guy on contact. Jake knew a hood when he met one. Tonight he'd spend time searching his data base. The guy seemed familiar. Too bad Kyra didn't give his last name. They didn't seem like a good fit. Did she date him? Was he her ex? No, wrong name for the ex. An awkward silence ensued as the men studied each other. Of all the beaches in Rhode Island, why did they wind up together on this one?

"Well, I'll let you get back to your picnic."

"Nice meeting you, Phil."

"Same here, Jake." Turning to Kyra, Phil said, "See you soon, Kyra."

"Bye, Phil."

The man seemed pissed. Neither of them took their eyes off Phil as he walked down the beach to meet up with the other man waiting by the shore line.

"Who's that?" Jake asked, sitting back down on the blanket.

"Last night's date. In fact, he called me this morning to ask if I'd spend the day with him. I turned him down."

"Why?"

"We're not a good fit, Jake. Besides, I had a better offer."

"There's something off about him."

"Like what?"

"I don't know. I'm going with instinct. Watch yourself with him."

"Lord, Jake, you are the protector of all things," she said, teasing him, throwing Mia's reason for ending their relationship back at him.

"I'm serious." Something in her tone...the edginess of it...

"You were about to pour the wine while I decided which sandwich I wanted."

* * * *

There was something off about Phil, but she couldn't tell Jake. To smooth things over she'd have to call Phil later. Kyra was sure Phil had figured out that Jake was her cop. *My life gets messier and messier with each passing day.* She choked on her saliva as the idea of Phil having her followed settled in. Damn, her head hurt. She'd address that issue later. It'd been ages since she had experienced the thrill of being with a man. The first bite of lust zinged around inside her as they ate their lunches in silence. With a full belly, a laziness had set in. She snuggled close to Jake for warmth as they lay on the blanket. The breeze grew cold when it shifted, with the winds coming off the ocean instead of the bay. After a while she fell into a deep sleep.

She stretched, yawned and sat up.

"You should have woken me sooner, Jake."

"You looked like you needed the sleep."

"I slept the afternoon away. Sorry," Kyra said. What an exciting date she made. God, she hoped she hadn't snored.

"Are you hungry?"

"You bet."

"Alleluia! I've found someone who can keep up with my eating habits."

* * * *

The place he picked to eat dinner was noisy and it smelled of fried fish. Damn, this was his favorite spot. Selfish of him, she hated fish. She had told him on their first date. He searched the menu for meat and was relieved to find she'd have a few choices. They ordered dinner and made small talk until the meals came.

"You must be an excellent interrogator."

"Why?" He popped a piece of lobster into his mouth.

"You have a way of pulling a person out of her shell."

Reaching over, he offered her a piece of his lobster, then laughed when she pressed her lips together. It would take the jaws of life to open them.

"Am I being too intrusive?"

"No, I...like your style."

"Good, because I like yours." He grinned.

Stuffed, they walked the beach again to let their dinner settle before they headed back. Jake put his arms around her to keep her warm. She triggered affection from him but she also kicked in his protective nature. He wanted to question her until she gave him the full scoop on her friend Phil. He hoped by the time they got home she'd have dropped his last name. Jake noticed she had spaced out on him.

"Where did you go?" Jake asked.

"The ocean makes my mind float, in a good way."

He stopped, turned her into his arms and kissed her. There was no doubt she did it for him. He wanted her right here, right now. With her encouragement he took the kiss deeper, forgetting where they were as his hands roamed over her.

"We'd better stop," she shouted over the sound of crashing waves.

"Why?"

"I...because I need to slow things down."

"I told you we'd go at your pace. But...I'm there already."

"I figured that out, Jake." A joke. She did that a lot when she was cornered. *Interesting.*

"Do you always use humor to get out of a situation?"

"Am I in a situation?" She stared.

"A question?"

"I'm not divorced yet," she said for the second time in two days. "Dating's confusing. I'm not a modern girl. I waited until I got married to have sex. I don't understand what's acceptable anymore. I want to go at my own pace. Sex isn't casual with me."

"Okay, but I'm available if you do decide you want casual sex." He flashed her a grin as he said it, trying to make her comfortable.

"Funny."

He drew her closer when she shivered. "Let's get back. You're cold, aren't you?"

"Yes."

At the car, he unlocked her door and held it open for her. Before she climbed in, he took her in his arms and kissed her again. *Damn, same reaction.*

"I'm warm now," she blurted out, face turning red. He loved how she blushed.

"I can make you warmer."

"I'm sure, but I'm hot enough right now, thanks." She offered him a shy smile and climbed into the car.

Shot down again. Oh, well.

* * * *

Pissed wasn't the word he'd have used. *I haven't been this angry in years. I bet that's the cop.* Phil had watched them for a while before he'd approached them. Kyra seemed relaxed, even animated, with that man. Last night with him she'd acted stiff and on edge. It was only after he had plied her with a lot of wine that she had relaxed. Phil reminded himself she'd made no promises. It didn't curb his anger. Who was Jake? The cop or the ex-husband? He'd have to do some research. He always liked to understand his competition and make no mistake—this guy was his competition.

Kyra blowing him off for this Jake fellow got him angry. She'd said she wasn't going to see the cop again but his gut told him Jake was Kyra's cop. *The bastard stood up to intimidate me.* Height didn't bother Phil. He'd dealt with being small his whole life—and he'd taken down much larger men than Jake. Toying with ideas on ways to torture Jake calmed him.

A little competition didn't faze him as long as he won.

The next morning when he woke, his shitty mood had worsened. He hadn't slept well. Kyra with Jake pissed him off. When she'd called last night, he ignored it. Let it go to voicemail. When his resolve gave way he listened to her message. It sounded businesslike, not personal, and that annoyed him more. She was certainly getting personal with Jake on the beach. He placed a phone call to Wilkesbury. His contact at the police department picked up on the first ring.

"Wilkesbury Police Department, Detective Stack speaking."

"Hi, Carl. Are you clear to talk?"

"I'm in the middle of something. Can I call you back?"

"Yes."

Carl had informed him another cop was close by, listening in on his conversation. When he'd set up this system, he appreciated Carl's caution. Phil'd await Carl's call back on a secured line outside the police department. He'd be patient. Ten minutes later his phone rang.

"Sorry to keep you waiting."

"No problem. I have some questions."

"Shoot."

"Do you have a cop on the force by the name of Jake? I don't have his last name. He's about six feet tall with reddish brown hair."

"The lieutenant," Carl said.

"Is he Homicide?"

"Yes. He's straight."

"What's his last name?"

"Carrington. You're not going to approach him, are you?"

"No. I met him over the weekend. I like to know who's who, you understand. I can smell a cop twenty feet away." *I'm talking too much.*

"I understand."

"Is he your boss?"

"He's my temporary boss. The brass got him running Missing Persons until they replace my retired lieutenant."

"One more thing, is he involved with anyone?"

"No, he's a player, but he did get serious with this woman last month but I heard through the grapevine that she dumped him. It messed him up."

Phil slammed his phone on the desk. Carl's word played over and over in head. *Hmmm! Jake was a player.* Was he playing Kyra? If he desired, he'd make Carrington's life unbearable. The idea warmed his heart. Yeah, if Jake became a problem he'd ruin his career. Even more, he liked the idea of Jake Carrington meeting an untimely death.

Wouldn't it be rich if I had Kyra cremate him?

Chapter 13

For a change, she woke with energy. What a wonderful weekend it had been and Jake had been the one who made it fantastic. The money helped too. But she needed to be careful around Jake. Damn, he was turning out to be more than a distraction. After two dates, she understood what Dina had meant when she said he grabbed hold of your heart and didn't let go. But if he found out what she'd done, he'd take her down and kill any chance she had in gaining custody of Trevor.

Why was she chancing it?

Like the gambling, she came alive around Jake. Was she substituting him for gambling? *Hmmm! Interesting.*

What am I going to do about Phil? Phil, Phil, Phil. He wasn't a man you brushed off. She needed to tread with extreme care when dealing with him if she was going to come out of this alive.

Phil hadn't returned her call last night. A control freak and her boss—Kyra had to keep that in mind at all times to make this arrangement work in her favor. Not good to mix business with pleasure. She'd correct her mistake today.

Her business cell phone rang as she walked into her bathroom. Not recognizing the number, she answered. "Hello."

"Ms. Russell?"

"Yes."

"I'm Stan Slawlaski from Bridgeport. From the Slawlaski Funeral Home?"

"What can I do for you?"

"Mr. Lucci told me to call you." Alarms started clanging in her head.

"Who is Mr. Lucci?" she asked. But she was sure it was Phil.

Silence.

"I must have the wrong number, sorry." The undertaker hung up.

A few minutes later, her personal cell rang. Phil's number.

"Phil?"

"Good morning. How are you today?"

"I'm fine and you?" *My, aren't we being formal today.*

"Good. A Stan Slawlaski called me a few seconds ago. I'm confused." *Oh shit, not another one this soon. This can't be good. And who else did he tell?*

"He called and asked for me, then he mentioned a Mr. Lucci. I didn't have a clue. Is that your last name?"

"Yes."

"What did Mr. Stan Slawlaski want?"

"He wants to arrange a cremation."

"Phil...this is between you and me, right?" Her stomach roiled. Who else knew what she'd done for Phil?

"Mr. Slawlaski works for me."

"How many people did you share what I'm doing for you with, Phil?"

"Kyra, remember, I don't answer to you, you answer to me. All Mr. Slawlaski knows is his next cremation will be done at your place instead of at the Bridgeport crematory."

Kyra looked at her watch. If she didn't get going soon, she'd be late for work. She needed to do her makeup and hair before getting dressed, but she knew the incident yesterday at the beach needed to be addressed.

"I'd like to come visit you tonight if you're free?"

"Why?"

"I want to talk about yesterday."

"What's to talk about?"

Oh yeah, he's pissed. Shit. "You seemed upset."

"Why, because you went out with Jake Carrington after you said you were cutting him loose?"

It didn't take him long to find out Jake's full name. "I did. When he called I changed my mind. The beach sounded wonderful." *Shut up, Kyra, you're talking too much.*

"I can't see you until ten o'clock. I have other plans."

Ballbuster. She swallowed hard. "I'll see you at ten."

Phil hung up without another word.

Shit.

* * * *

It was childish of him to put her off, but Phil wasn't amicable at the moment. It was easy to read her and the reason she'd blew him off. No sparks. Why not? Why the damn cop over him? Well, he'd remind her who owned her tonight.

"What?" he barked at a knock on his door.

"Boss—"

"I'm fine, Angelo." He waved him away.

Phil watched Angelo pull up a chair and sit across from him as he ignored the dismissal. He cocked his head to study Angelo.

"Don't understand what go away means, Ang?"

"We need to talk."

"About what?"

"The redhead."

"Her name is Kyra," Phil emphasized.

"She's trouble. I like Kyra. She can provide a great service for us, Phil, but she's not interested in a personal relationship."

"Be careful where you tread, Ang."

"It's not anything against you or her. It's not a good match."

"Why?"

"She sees you as her boss, nothing more."

"Why?"

"She was put out Saturday night when you brought her in here first to discuss business. You did it to remind her you were the boss."

Angelo's overstepping his authority, but I'll let him continue. They'd been together for many years. Phil respected him and his opinions. Angelo was his silent partner. A fact he didn't share with the world.

"It's only your opinion."

"No, it's you. I watched her the other day. She's a professional who takes pride in her work. You pushed her away before you even asked her out. You did the whole 'I own you' thing, didn't you?"

Phil chuckled. "I did."

"Well, that's not the way to win a woman, especially a woman like Kyra. Has she been back to the casino yet?"

"No, I'm surprised. It's obvious she has a problem, but no, she hasn't gone since last Tuesday. What do you make of that?"

"She's trying to get her son back."

"There's something missing in a mother who gives up her son." He subconsciously threw his own mother's desertion in his face. How she'd left him to fend for himself at the age of nine against a mean, drunken father.

"She didn't give him up, Phil. I did the research. Her husband greased a lot of palms to get custody. He was taken from her."

"Because of her problem," Phil stressed.

"Yes, because of the gambling, but most people don't lose their kids for that. Her husband's family is connected in Wilkesbury."

"What have you learned about him?"

Phil knew Angelo's research skills were the best. People would be surprised to find out how deftly he handled a computer.

"He works hard, but he hasn't made any big splash in life. He married young, had a kid, and works for his father. I understand the divorce is ripping him to pieces."

"He sat in wait for her Saturday night."

"He's the one who wanted the divorce. He blamed it on her gambling. She okay?"

"Yeah, it upset her. We should pay him a visit."

"Phil, don't. She seems to be able to handle herself. Let's keep her as a business tool."

"She doesn't want me to talk to him, but she wants to talk to me tonight about yesterday."

"Is she coming here?"

"Yes, I told her I'm not available until ten o'clock."

Angelo raised his right brow and laughed. "Pissy, aren't you?"

"I guess I am. I like this one, she's different. On another note, how are we going to use Joe Dillon?"

"He's ambitious. At the moment he serves a purpose. Why?" Angelo frowned.

"It seems... I haven't decided if we'll incorporate him into our organization yet. When I do we'll discuss it."

Phil tapped his pencil on the desk.

"Discuss what?"

"There's something about him I don't like. He had no qualms about setting up a woman with a small child."

"That's funny, since when does that bother you?"

"It's not funny."

"Yeah, it is."

It wasn't. And Angelo better shut up if he knew what was good.

Chapter 14

Kyra worked through her day in a fog. One minute she'd be smiling, the next, her stomach flipped upside down as Phil's sneer filled her mind. She had to keep herself alive and her son safe. She had to keep Phil as a business arrangement and nothing more.

Saturday night's dinner was nothing to write home about. On top of that, Phil was scary. She guessed if you ordered someone's death, you weren't a normal person to begin with. Did burning a body for him put her in Phil's class? Kyra hoped not. Though she burned bodies every day, this one…haunted her. Did he—or was it a she? —have a family? Before it destroyed her, she pushed it from her mind.

She was doing this to get Trevor back. That was all she had to remember. It was her job to dispose of bodies. As she scooped the remains of today's cremation from the chamber, she rehearsed what she'd tell Phil. The intercom speaker boomed to life and startled her.

"Kyra?"

She walked over to the intercom then depressed the button. "Yes, Dina?"

"Jake's on the phone for you."

"Thanks, I'll take it in here."

Kyra walked into the processing room and picked up the wall phone. "Hey."

"I wanted to give you a quick call. Tell you I had a great time yesterday."

"Me too."

"What night would you like to go out this week?"

"I can't tonight or Wednesday, any other night's fine." It tickled her when she realized she'd been waiting all day for his call. Her body turned into a furnace, the fire raging below whenever she talked to him or remembered the day she had spent with him. *When I'm with him I'm alive. But he could*

*get me killed. Somehow, that made it all the more thrilling, even better
than the rush I got from gambling.*

"How about tomorrow night?" She guessed the quiet, Catholic, good
girl was gone, replaced by this thrill seeker.

"Sounds wonderful, what time?"

"Seven?"

"Yes. How about I cook for us?" *Damn. That's asking for trouble.*

"No, I'll take you out."

"You sure? I don't mind cooking."

"Yep, this way we can visit without distractions."

"Distractions?" she said.

"Yes."

"Seven it is. See you then."

A huge smile spread across her face as she hung up. If she survived
tonight with Phil...best not go there.

* * * *

He'd blown the perfect opportunity with Kyra. He should've accepted
the dinner invitation at her condo. The attraction was growing though the
timing wasn't right. He'd wait for whenever she was ready. Jake liked that
she didn't do casual sex. How stupid was he? It made him want her more.

"Who's Kyra?" Louie asked.

Jake frowned at his partner. He hadn't heard Louie sneak into his office.

"A friend."

"A friend, as in female friend? Since when are you dating again?"

"Louie, it's none of your business."

"You used to be fun, before you screwed things up with Mia." The
disgusted look on Louie's face annoyed him. *My personal life is exactly
that, personal.*

Louie, his childhood friend and now partner, took a lot of liberties with
him. Louie's olive complexion made him look tan all year round. Black
hair and brown eyes on a six-two, muscular frame housed a nosy, fastidious
man he'd give his life for. Louie wore his suits like a second skin.

"I'm still fun, but it might help if you wore a skirt," Jake joked.

"Oh, you're a riot." Louie turned to leave the room but not before Jake
caught the frustration on his face.

"Sit down."

"Why?"

"I'll fill you in, and let me add a caveat. No gossiping."

"You're no fun," Louie repeated, shaking his head. He took a seat in front of Jake's desk.

"I met her last week at a party. We've been out twice. There's nothing more to tell."

"You mean you're not sharing anything else."

"Correct."

"No details?"

"There are no details to tell."

"She's holding out on you, huh?"

"You've got a one-track mind."

"What about Mia?"

Jake frowned. "I haven't seen or talked to Mia since she walked out on me."

"So you're going to move on, instead of talking to her?"

"It seems like it." He shrugged.

"Well, you're stupid."

Jake coughed into his hand to hide the laugh. "A fact that breaks my heart every hour of every day, Louie."

"Oh shut the hell up. I'm serious."

Louie and his wife had fixed him up with Mia. Jake experienced their joy when he fell hard for her. Louie loved his family and Sophia was the best wife a man could ask for. Together, Louie and Sophia were raising three well-behaved kids. Bestowing the honor of godfather on Jake at their daughter's birth showed how much they cared for and respected him. *My family.* Louie's wife, Sophia, though sweet and well-meaning, had caused the fight that had broken up him and Mia. Over the last few weeks, Sophia had been trying to apologize with numerous calls and voice messages, though he hadn't returned one call. Louie was caught in the middle as he tried to hang in the background which was out of character for him. It had put a strain on both their working and personal relationship. Jake figured Sophia had ordered Louie to stay out of it.

"What do you want me to say?"

"Why does everything with you have to be permanent?"

"Let's discuss the case, because this conversation's over," Jake said, reining in his temper.

"Just like that?"

"Yep."

"Someday you're going to be a lonely old man and it'll serve you right."

He understood Louie always had to have the last word and let him. He turned his attention to the case and pulled the file from his drawer.

"Did you get the lab reports?"

"Dwight Wade's blood alcohol level was one-point-six. I'd say he had a good time before he died."

"That's twice the legal limit. Did the autopsy report come in?"

"No, the M.E.'s office hopes to get it to us by tomorrow."

"I'm curious about the bruising on the body. How about the ballistics report?"

"Not yet." Louie scratched his head.

"Which hand showed the residue. His wife said he was right-handed, but the wound showed a left-handed entry. It'd be awkward to use your goofy side to shoot yourself, especially drunk."

"What the hell's a goofy side?"

"Snowboarding term. It means not your natural side." Jake watched Louie process the information.

"You're calling it a homicide based on what, your gut?"

"No. I'm waiting on the reports, but this guy was blind drunk. The entry's on the wrong side, especially for someone incapacitated. It's a bit suspicious. Mr. Wade had help getting to the great beyond. I'm sure of it," Jake said.

"Okay, I'll dig deeper into his life." Louie stood. "It's good you're dating again, but you owe it to yourself to be happy. You were happy with Mia. Settle it one way or another by talking it out with her. Otherwise it will fester."

"I'll consider it, Louie. Bring in the reports when you get them."

* * * *

Jake turned his chair to the window. His gaze traveled toward the new buildings that housed a branch of UConn. The city fathers fought for the campus to be here to bring more business to the downtown area—so far it hadn't. Only the pizza parlors did a booming trade, but the other businesses still seemed at a stalemate. The Palace Theater was the draw for an evening out when it had an act booked. A few bars and restaurants benefited on show nights. His eyes scanned the rest of downtown. It depressed him to see many closed businesses. Even though the tanked economy had hit Connecticut hard, it hit Wilkesbury harder. Jake still loved this city. An old factory town—in its heyday it held the prestige title of The Brass Capital of the World, though most of the jobs and manufacturing had gone overseas decades ago. At the turn of the century and well into the thirties it was labeled Sin City and folks from as far as Pennsylvania and Vermont came for a visit to experience the debauchery and to blow off some steam. Good old Wilkesbury had fought for respectability for a long time. The town was also known for its politics. In 1960 a hopeful John F. Kennedy campaigned here to a record crowd at three in the morning. Many had been there all day waiting to get a glimpse of the candidate. On his return trip to Wilkesbury two years later as president, Kennedy remarked that Wilkesbury might have been the easiest town to get a crowd in or out of in the United States or it was a town with a large democratic base. President Kennedy made a promise he'd never be able to keep. He promised to meet the enthusiastic crowd again at the end of his campaign in 1964.

Yes, his town was steeped in history, some good, some bad, but Jake loved this city. In the old buildings, he saw the amazing architectural designs of the various eras. Though most buildings were in need of repair, their beauty still shone through. It was the classic design of the twenties and thirties. Some enterprising people were renovating them and making unique businesses out of them.

A boy kissed a girl as they sat on a low wall on the college's property. Jake's mind turned back to his conversation with Louie. He'd never tell him, but Louie was right.

Without speaking with Mia he'd never be able to move forward. Ending a relationship mirrored a death. You needed to grieve before you moved on. He was fond of Kyra, but she wasn't Mia. Jake knew there'd be nobody else for him. He didn't want to hurt Kyra. He should end this thing before it went any further—before it became more difficult for him to cut her loose.

Cripes, his life had never been easy. A little reprieve once in a while, he shrugged the thought away and turned from the window as someone shuffled their feet in his doorway.

Chapter 15

After lunch, Kyra returned Tommy's call. She hoped to control the tone and content of the conversation. She hadn't bothered calling back yesterday. It was small of her, but she wanted him to suffer the way he had made her suffer. She sipped her coffee while the phone rang. No answer after three rings. She debated whether to leave a message or not when he answered.

"Kyra?"

Shit. "Yes."

"Why didn't you return my calls?"

Demanding? Sorry, Tommy, you don't have the right. "I had plans."

"Plans? Now, you're too busy for me? What if it was about Trevor?"

Don't play me. "Well, Tommy—" Wasn't it about time she started addressing him as if he was a man and not a kid? "If it was about Trevor, I'd hope you'd be smart enough to leave a message."

"Where were you?"

The jackass doesn't get it. "Out."

"Out where?" he yelled. Kyra pulled the phone from her ear.

"None of your business, Tom, you're not entitled to that information."

"Now I'm Tom?"

"Yes, it's time we both grew up and moved on."

Steam pushed through the phone—she was surprised her hand didn't burn. *That'll teach him to sit outside my house.*

"You want to play hardball, Kyra? You haven't a clue who you're dealing with."

"I'm not playing anything, you are. You're the one who sat outside my house in the middle of the night. It's called stalking. You're the one who kept calling yesterday. That's called harassment. And let me remind you,

you're the one who filed for divorce and took my son away from me. Now, why were you outside my house Saturday night?" Her temper rose. Her hands trembled as her face burned with hate. She inhaled to try to calm down. *Nope, didn't work.*

"I'm sorry. I miss you. It got me crazy you being with another man," he whispered.

Changing tactics, oh, such a Tommy move. "I can't help you. It's over, Tom, remember it was your choice." Her voice hardened.

"No forgiveness, Kyra?"

She didn't respond right away. Kyra tried to control her emotions. She prayed her voice didn't crack. "I'm giving you the same amount of forgiveness you gave me."

An echo vibrated through her ear when he slammed down the receiver on his end. Tears streamed from her eyes, blinding her as the realization smacked her square in the brain. This conversation ended any hope of reconciliation. Her stomach clenched as she doubled over, her muscles cramping. The door squeaked open. Kyra didn't bother to look up.

"I'm sorry. I overheard everything. Are you okay?"

Dina walked over and hugged her. rubbing her back as unstoppable tears flowed along with the sharp pain that was jabbing her in the heart. She leaned her head against Dina's stomach. Nine years of love turned to bitter hate. How did people survive? Dina wiped the tears from Kyra's eyes as she held her.

"I'm sor...sorry, Dina." She hiccupped.

"Oh, Kyra, let it out, honey. I locked the front door. We won't be disturbed." Dina continued to rub her back. "I don't understand why I'm crying."

"This happens when you accept it's over."

Her head jerked up and off of Dina as someone pounded on the front door. "Can you get it? I'll be in the bathroom."

Her legs wobbled like rubber bands when she tried standing. Forced to sit back down, she watched Dina shut her door as she headed into the main office. After a few minutes, she got up and headed to the bathroom.

In the mirror, puffy eyes greeted her. She wiped the tears falling down her face and repaired her makeup before she went back out. Work wasn't the place for this to happen. She rinsed her face with cold water then took a couple of deep, calming breaths.

She paced the small bathroom. *I should cancel Phil for this evening and reschedule.* "Yeah, right, like he's a man you can reschedule. Wise up. Phil can make your life a living hell." She realized she was speaking out loud. Everything echoed in this place. She made a decision. After work, she'd go to the casino, then to Phil's. Hopefully, it'd calm her down before she had to deal with him.

* * * *

Restless all day, Phil decided he wanted to see Kyra for dinner. He reached for the phone. Started to dial her number. Stopped. He had set the time to inconvenience her, but it backfired on him. He was the one who needed to see her. He finished dialing her number.

The minute she answered, he started right in, not giving her a chance to speak. "It's Phil."

"What can I do for you?"

Ah, businesslike, but her voice is off. "Are you crying?"

"No."

Why had she lied? It was something he'd pursue tonight. "Let's meet for dinner instead. My plans have changed."

"What time did you have in mind?"

Agreeable, good. "Why don't we do six thirty here? That way we can talk without being interrupted."

"I'll see you then."

Interesting. Kyra's mood had changed since the last time he'd spoken to her. Why? Did she have a fight with her cop?

* * * *

"Jake, it's Kyra."

"What's wrong?"

"My ex is following me. My God, I can't pry my fingers off the steering wheel. He's upset with me. I can't figure out why he's doing this."

"You sure it's him?"

"Yes, we had it out today. I'm heading into the Hartford area. Every time I change lanes he does too. It's as if he's glued to my bumper. Hold on."

"Kyra, don't put down the phone," Jake yelled to no avail. Kyra didn't answer him back.

He strained, listening for any unusual noise. Tires squealed. Kyra swore. *Helpless.* His pulse raced. "Kyra!"

"It's my ex. Wait, I have to switch lanes. I hope I don't get killed. Traffic's heavy. I'm going to put the phone down again but I'll keep it on speaker. If anything happens to me I want you to arrest Tommy for chasing me."

When Kyra let out a string of words a truck driver would've been proud of, he reached for his keys on his desk. He'd use the sirens to get to her if she'd tell him where the hell she was.

"Listen, shout out your location. I'm on my way."

"I'm doing eighty-five and he's still on my tail. Wait, I can squeeze between him and an eighteen-wheeler and make it off this exit. He won't be able to follow."

"Tell me where you are. I'll call the state police," Jake said.

Edgy, his nerves pinged in the silence.

"Take that, you bastard," Kyra shouted through the phone.

The tension stretched in her voice, Jake relaxed when she came back on. "I'm okay, I outfoxed him."

"Why don't I come over with dinner and you can tell me what happened."

"Thanks, but I'm on my way to meet a friend for dinner."

"I'm working late tonight. I'll swing by when I'm through. If you're home I'll stop in for coffee if that's all right with you."

"I might be late."

"Not a problem. Now tell me what happened. I want to document the incident on the record."

"I don't want it on the record this time. It's out of character for him. If it happens again—I will."

"Kyra, you need to document this incident. As you said, it's out of character. That's the part that scares me. It's for your safety."

"Yes...traffic's heavy. I weaved. If I went three lanes over, that car did too. I recognized Tom when he made the mistake of pulling up too close to me. He matched me move for move. No matter how fast or how slow I went he stuck with me. When I saw an opening for one car between two trucks I slipped between them when a car cut him off. As he passed I drove off the exit. He's never acted this way before."

"Acted what way?"

"He was waiting for me Saturday night when I got home. And he went ballistic on me after I told him I'm dating. He's the one who asked for the divorce."

"It doesn't matter who requested it. This kind of behavior doesn't lead to anything good, Kyra. Call me if there's another incident."

"Thanks, I will."

* * * *

Her phone call with Jake smoothed her nerves. Bizarre, how she went from talking to a cop to visiting with a mob boss. She'd be amazed if she got out of this alive.

Kyra pulled into Phil's driveway at six thirty. The guard at the gate waved her through. After a quick scan she pinpointed the guards on the hill. Phil loved his security. The front door opened before her fist made contact with the door.

"Hey, Kyra, follow me," Angelo greeted her.

Always business. No problem that's the way she liked it. "Okay."

Angelo led the way. At Phil's office, Kyra turned toward the door. *What's he grinning about?*

"This way." He pointed farther down the hall. "You'll be eating in the dining room."

Kyra turned to follow him to a part of the house she hadn't seen before. A formal, spacious room done in burgundy and beige, nevertheless inviting. *Whoever picked the art knew what they were doing.* She appreciated the artist's vision. but it was the chandelier that captivated her. Exquisite Swarovski crystal, if she wasn't mistaken. Her gaze continued to move around the room. The huge dining table sat fifty. At the head of it sat Phil. A king surveying his kingdom. He stood as she approached.

"Good to see you." He extended both his hands to her. Awkwardly, she raised her hands to his.

"Phil, this is a lovely room."

"I'm glad you like it."

So formal. "How have you been?" *Lame.*

"Good. You?"

"Fine." At a loss for words, Kyra disengaged her hands to stroll around the room, looking at the artwork.

"You seem nervous, Kyra. Why?"

"I guess I am." Desperate to get this part of the evening over, she continued, "It's awkward."

"Why?"

Not giving her an inch, she pressed on. "You seemed upset at the beach yesterday."

"I am. Or I was," he corrected.

"Sounds like you still are." She held up her hand to stop his reply. "I didn't have plans to see Jake again, as I told you Saturday night, but I like him. When he called on Sunday, I was happy to hear from him. While I was in the shower getting ready, you called." *A little lie.*

"Ah, I missed out by minutes," he snarled.

"No." She needed to be honest. "I enjoyed your company Saturday night, but you're my boss. I don't mix business and pleasure." She stopped pacing the room to look at him.

"So ours is a business relationship, nothing more?"

His blank face was unreadable. Not one iota of emotion showing. She cringed inside. "I'd like to believe we have a friendship developing."

"A friendship. How insulting, Kyra."

Oh boy, I'm screwed now. "Phil, it's not my intention to insult you. I like you, but I work for you. You made that clear on Saturday night when I arrived for our date."

"I did."

She studied him, paced some more.

"Please sit down. We can't have a conversation with you moving around the room. It's distracting."

"Sorry." She walked to the table, sat in the first chair on his right.

"Now, as I explained on Saturday, it was a date, nothing more. I knew you weren't attracted to me from the lack of passion in your kiss."

"Oh." She dropped her head.

"But it bothers me you're dating a cop."

"It has nothing to do with us or our business deal." She lifted her head, stared into his eyes and fought all the nerves trying to flinch under his gaze.

"You can't be that naïve. I'm not comfortable with you dating him. And, as I explained last week, I own you. And I'm forbidding you from seeing him again."

Kyra didn't break eye contact with Phil as she gave great care to her answer before she replied. She got up and started pacing the room again.

"You're quite restless, Kyra."

"I'm thinking," she shot over her shoulder.

Phil started to laugh. She jerked away, before marching to her chair. Kyra threw herself into it. "I'm glad I amuse you. It'd be unwise for me to dump Jake too fast. He'd question me on the why. It'd be best to let this burn out on its own."

"Explain."

"Jake and I hit it off right away, but he's still in love with the last woman he dated. I don't see this getting serious."

"Then why continue to date him?"

"He's good company. We have a lot in common."

"I can see that—you're a criminal and he's a cop."

The sarcasm wasn't lost on her. She refrained from shooting her own nasty quip back at him. Phil's jealousy floored her. Kyra didn't have to be told how stupid it was to date Jake, but for the first time in her life she was alive with excitement. Was it worth the risk, the thrill?

A tray filled with fruit and cheese sat in front of her. She grabbed a piece of apple with a slice of cheese, stuffed them both into her mouth.

"Stalling, Kyra?"

"No, I didn't see where that required a reply." She chose another piece of cheese.

Phil stood. It was his turn to pace. At the window he stopped with his back to her. After a long silence, he spoke.

"I like you. I can't explain what it is about you that makes you different from the other women I date, but you're special. I'm sorry we didn't connect and I accept your decision. Who knows, sometime in the future…"

She released the breath she had been holding. "Thank you."

"I want to make this clearer than I did before, no matter what, if you tell the lieutenant, or sic him on me, you're dead. Do you understand?"

Kyra started choking on the slice of cheese she'd swallowed. She grabbed her glass of water and drank.

"Yes, I've understood that since the beginning. I can't see any reason for discussing our business with Jake."

"Good. Let's eat. I want to discuss this funeral director out of Bridgeport."

"Okay. How many more bodies should I expect this month?" God, she hoped he spaced them out. If Phil kept up this pace, it'd bite them both in the ass.

Chapter 16

Jake noted the time and place of the incident then typed up the complaint form. If he saw Kyra tonight he'd have her sign it. If not, he'd bring it around to her at the cemetery tomorrow. It was imperative that she formalize Russell's stalking. Too many of Jake's murder cases over the years had started out as a domestic call. He tapped a finger on his knee. There was nothing simple about a domestic. Love did crazy things to a person. People who claimed to have loved their victims tore them apart, or hacked them up. Most murders involved money or love. But love was the most vicious.

A knock on his office door pulled him from his macabre thoughts.

"LT, we got one. Armand's at dinner. I didn't want to disturb him as long as you were here."

"No problem, Kirk. I welcome the distraction." Cop humor. Over the years it had worked its way into his head. "What've you got?"

"Officer on scene reports a possible suicide."

"Let's head out."

Ten minutes later, Jake pulled to the curb. Kirk Brown pulled in behind him. As he waited for Brown to get out of his car, Jake studied the house. Small, white, with black shutters. All the window treatments were closed. Officer Fisher walked up to him. Jake admired Stella Fisher, a good cop in his eyes.

"LT, woman in her forties, wrists sliced, we found her in the tub. The house is as neat as a pin. Nothing has been disturbed. It's owned by a Victoria Wiggins. The dead woman matches her description. The thing is, she buried her son a month ago," Officer Stella Fisher said.

"Quick work, Stella, thanks." Jake appreciated an officer who didn't trample a crime scene. "EMTs here?"

"Yes, but I didn't let them in. It was obvious she's been dead for about two hours or more."

Nodding, he walked inside with Brown. Fisher trailed behind. "Is there a note?"

"There's one sticking out of her purse."

Jake studied the body, the position, the angle of the cuts. "Where's the weapon that cut her?"

"It might be in the tub, Lieutenant. I didn't drain it yet."

Jake knelt beside the tub. The position of the body was wrong. The head was by the faucet, not the feet.

"Collect your water samples before you pull the plug. And be careful, the weapon might still be in there," he said over his shoulder.

Armand Lanoue arrived on scene as Jake and Brown were finishing up. Jake turned over his notes and observations to him before leaving. He'd wait until McKay finished his autopsy but it looked like an open-and-shut case of suicide even with the body at the wrong end of the tub.

The note was found in her purse. It stated she didn't want to live without her son who had died the month before. Death again became the answer for lost love. The wrong one, but an answer all the same.

* * * *

Phil tapped his fork on the table and measured Kyra. She didn't seem to mind what she did for him. He'd bide his time, because he wanted her. And he always got what he wanted, one way or another.

"I'm not sure. After the Bridgeport one there might be one more."

"In case I get another call, who are the funeral directors I'll be dealing with?"

"You won't be dealing with them out of the blue again. I'll call you first before one shows up. I've already spoken with Mr. Slawlaski. He won't call you again."

A cold shiver ran down her spine. She hoped Mr. Slawlaski wasn't going to be one of her burns.

"If it's possible, can I get a little notice? It worked out well last week, because I let my secretary go home early. That way, no one but me sees Angelo."

"We'll see." He liked the way her mind worked. She protected herself as well as the people she was dealing with. It showed character.

He pressed a button. The maid walked in minutes later with a tray of food and started serving. Tonight's dinner consisted of manicotti and sausage. He marveled at how she ate. Wondered how she maintained her figure, though she hadn't touched the sausage.

"How's dinner?"

"Great. You were right, Maria's a wonderful cook."

"You don't like sausage?"

"No."

"I'll keep it in mind. Let's talk business."

* * * *

Jake left the scene of the suicide around a quarter after ten. It was too late to head back to the station. He'd type up his notes when he got home. As he drove, he made a U-turn when he remembered he'd promised Kyra he'd stop in. And he had the incident report with him for her to sign. Who was she having dinner with? He'd never asked, but in his gut he knew. Yesterday, her reaction to that guy Phil had bothered him. Kyra wasn't forthcoming either. Was he jealous or protecting her? His answer shocked him—both.

When he'd done a statewide search of known criminals with mob associations a Phil Lucci came up. No recent arrests, no recent picture, but the picture of Lucci at nineteen looked close enough to the guy on the beach on Sunday. He'd bet his badge on it. The question was how did he approach Kyra on the subject? Was she familiar with Lucci's background?

A little after ten thirty Jake watched Kyra approach her assigned parking spot, then drive past him before turning back. He climbed out of the car when she opened her door and walked around and helped her out.

"Sorry, I didn't mean to scare you. Smart move, by the way, driving past until you knew who was in the car."

"Yeah, I'm getting smart. I noticed the city plates and figured it was you."

"I...I was out on a call and figured I'd stop by on my way home. I should've phoned."

"No, it's okay. I'm surprised. Were you here long?"

Distracted. He knew when he wasn't wanted. "No, I got here about five minutes ago and decided to do some paperwork. I was finishing up when you pulled in. I have tonight's incident report for you to sign."

"Oh...do you want to come in for a cup of coffee?"

"You don't look like you want company. Is everything all right?"

"No, come in. That incident with Tommy played on my mind all night."

"How was dinner?"

"Awkward."

"Why?" He didn't have a right to question her, but that didn't stop him.

"Jake, I had dinner with Phil."

They'd reached the door. Turning, she looked into his face. Was she looking for a reaction from him? If so, which one did she want? Jake gave her his best cop stare.

"How'd it go?"

"As expected." She shrugged, unlocked the door.

Jake scanned the place when they walked in. Kyra stopped to hang up her jacket in the closet by the door. She dropped her purse on the wrought iron table standing beside it.

"Do you want regular or decaf?"

"Real coffee has caffeine, accept no imitations," he said.

"So, the cliché is true—cops, coffee, and donuts?"

He hit his stomach. "Does this look like I eat a lot of donuts?"

"Sorry, I lost my head but I do have coffee cake, if you're interested."

"Ah, you set me up. Well played." He grinned. "I'd love a piece."

"We're talking about the cake, right?" she joked.

"Well…"

She punched his arm. It was good to see her relax. She took the cake from the cabinet, cut two pieces, and brought them to the table with the coffee. He watched her over the rim of his cup as she ate the cake and waited her out.

Changing the subject, she shifted gears. "Yes, I'm tired. I'm whipped from my full weekend and busy Monday."

"There wasn't a problem with Phil tonight, was there?"

"No, there wasn't a problem. He wasn't happy, but what could he do about it? I don't want to date him."

"I should leave. I stopped by to make sure you were okay after the incident with Tom and to get you to sign the report."

"As you can see, I'm fine, but tired."

"Kyra, there's something about him. I can't explain, but my instincts are never wrong. Be careful dealing with him."

"Who, Tom?"

"No, I was talking about Phil but I'd watch out for Tom Russell too. I'm on call tonight if you need anything…anything, Kyra." He pulled his notebook out of his jacket, started writing in it.

"I'll be fine."

"Here's my beeper number, you have my cell." He put the notebook away and stood.

She took the paper with his numbers on it and placed it under the salt shaker.

Kyra stood with him and walked him to the door. "I appreciate your concern, Jake."

He leaned in, took her chin in his hand, lifted her face, and kissed her. A slow, tender kiss that pushed heat through his body. At her response, Jake deepened the kiss as she pressed into him and wrapped her arms around his waist.

"You keep it up...I won't want to leave," Jake said.

"Isn't that my line?" Kyra asked.

"Cute."

"You don't have to rush off."

"It's almost eleven. It's for the best. Tonight's not the night, but it will be soon," he promised, kissing her again. "Get some sleep."

"Will I see you for dinner tomorrow night?"

Jake tightened his hold on her as he rubbed her back and whispered in her ear. "Yes." He gave her another kiss, nothing gentle this time.

Her voice cracked. "You sure you want to leave?"

"I don't but as I said, it's for the best."

He waited until he heard the lock click into place before he walked down the front steps to his waiting car.

Chapter 17

Seconds after she'd locked up for the night, her phone started to ring. *What does he want?*

Should she answer it or not? Her finger hovered over the reject button. *We said everything there was to be said today.*

Void of emotion, Kyra wondered where all her love for Tommy had gone. Checking her watch, she decided to answer it. It might have something to do with Trevor.

"Is Trevor okay?"

"What? Yes, he's fine. I'm…sorry to call you this late, but I didn't want to leave…I'm sorry, Kyra. I get crazy when you're with someone else. You're mine."

"No, Tom, I'm not. And stop following me. I'm not rehashing today's conversation. Remember who started the proceedings." She rubbed her temple where a sharp pain shot down into her left eye. Tonight she'd run the gamut from crazy killer to cop to an even crazier ex-husband. What had she done to deserve all this drama?

"You're not going to take any blame here?" Tom asked.

"I do take blame, every single hour of every single day when I walk in the door and Trevor's not here. I don't need to be reminded."

"Only Trevor, you don't miss me?"

What to say? Since he'd filed, she'd lost both her faith in him and her love. He'd been nasty. Had she ever understood who the real Thomas Russell was?

"I did in the beginning, than you started all your shit—it shut me down."

"What if I said I was sorry?"

"It's a little too late for 'I'm sorry,' Tom." Kyra held her hand up in mock quotation marks. Too bad he couldn't see them.

"I hate when you call me Tom."

"Get used to it. Oh, and I filed a complaint tonight about you for following me. You could've gotten us both killed." It was time to play hardball.

"You've become a bitch, Kyra."

"I'm protecting myself."

"Protecting from what?"

"You."

"Does this mean you're canceling dinner on Wednesday?"

The question threw her for a loop. What's he up to?

"No, I'm not, but we'll meet at Trevor's favorite restaurant instead of the house."

"Why?"

"You scared me tonight and Saturday. I don't want to be alone with you." She waited for his reply. The silence continued. "Are you still there?" Silence. "Tom?"

"Yes." She barely heard him.

"Give me a call with the time to meet you at the restaurant. It's late. I need to get to bed."

"Alone, Kyra?"

"This is the last time I'll give you an answer to that question. Yes, and remember you have no right to ask."

"Bitch."

"Yes, I am. I became one when my husband kicked me out of my home and took my son away from me. You left me with nothing."

She slammed down the phone, not able to control the tears pouring down her face. Her heart ached where Tom slashed, his words sharper than any knife. She'd never show Tom how each plunge with his sharp tongue ripped her heart apart.

It'd been a little over a week since she'd been to the casino. Though she itched to go, something had changed. She didn't need it anymore. Now the only thing she looked forward to was spending time with Jake. She wondered why? If only it had happened before she had destroyed their lives. *Oh Trevor, I'm sorry.* She cried herself to sleep.

* * * *

His plans with Kyra for dinner kept Jake going all day. He hoped she'd confide in him tonight. He rang the bell, delighted when Kyra opened the door wearing her apron, with a dish towel dangling in her hand—call him crazy—she looked sexy in that getup.

"Weren't we supposed to go out?"

Shit, her face dropped. Open mouth insert foot, Jake.

"I wanted a quiet evening at home. If you want, we can still go out," she stammered.

"No, you went to all this trouble."

"You did say you wanted to go out, but…"

He'd embarrassed her. Kyra turned to go into the kitchen. Jake gently took hold of her arm and turned her back to face him. He wrapped one arm around her waist, lifted her chin with his free hand, and searched her eyes.

"Let's start over. I didn't mean to sound ungrateful."

"You didn't." He hoisted her to her toes as he brushed his lips over hers. *Such a tiny thing.*

"Better?"

"Yes. Come into the kitchen while I put the steaks on."

"We don't have to eat right away." He wiggled his brow.

"We should."

Dinner—foreplay—the lines blurred. Anticipation with each mouthful whipped his mind and body into a frenzy. Kyra was charming, at times shy, and most of all she was a tease. He'd better help out with the dishes before he said another stupid thing. He grabbed for the plates at the same time she did. His glass of water tumbled all over the bottom of his shirt and onto his lap.

"I'm sorry." He jumped up to get a towel but she beat him to it and started blotting the water from his lap. He tried to snatch it from her as his voice cracked.

"Give me the towel, Kyra."

If it wasn't so embarrassing he'd have enjoyed the way her face burned red as she handed him the cloth. "I'll be right back."

Gone for a few seconds, she returned with a large beach towel. "Here, why don't you go into the bathroom and take off your shirt and pants. I'll throw them in the dryer. Good thing it was only water and not the wine. It won't stain."

"Ah, I love your plan. I wondered how you'd practice your wiles on me and get me to disrobe."

"I'm a creative woman, but it seems like you're stealing my line."

"Times have changed."

"Not that much."

Jake took the towel from her and headed to the bathroom. His ears tuned in to the clanging of dishes as Kyra finished clearing the table. It was hard to keep his mind off her hands when she had tried to pat up the water from his lap. The doorbell sounded. Had she invited anyone else? Christ, and him without his pants.

"Tom, what do you want?"

Jake listened in as a drunken Russell talked, slurring his words. "I want my wife."

Kyra's scream pierced Jake's heart.

Cursing, Jake wrapped the towel around his waist as he burst into the living room. His vision blurred red as he spotted Russell mauling Kyra.

"I'm not your wife. Get your hands off of me!"

"You're still my wife. The divorce isn't final," he slurred as he pushed her hard up against the door, grabbing her left breast with no finesse.

His anger spiking, Jake ran across the room, the towel wrapped around his waist dropping as he came up behind Tom. He pulled Tom off Kyra and spun him forward. Russell threw a blind punch that glanced off his shoulder. Jake's right hit its target hard as he landed a punch in Tom's stomach. Russell doubled over. Jake finished him off with a left cross to the jaw. Tom stumbled back. Jake encased his right leg around Tom's, tumbling the drunken Russell to the floor.

Jake captured Tom's hand and jerked his thumb backward. Russell screamed and ceased struggling.

"Kyra, grab my handcuffs off my belt."

Kyra ran to the bathroom, located the handcuffs, then ran into the living room with them. Jake took the bracelets from her, pulled Russell's hands behind him and restrained him. He tightened them to pinch into Tom's wrists. He whispered into Tom's ear as Tom started to struggle again.

Still on his stomach, Russell swiveled his head to stare down Kyra as he struggled with his bound hands. "You slut, you're my wife." Tom turned to look over his shoulder toward Jake. "Don't you care that you're dipping into another man's goods?" he screamed at Jake.

Jake was proud of Kyra. She knelt down on the floor by Tom's head. "Listen, and listen good, Tom, because I'm only going to say this one more time. I'm not your goods and never have been. I was your wife, but not anymore. Don't ever come back here."

"How long have you been doing him?"

Jesus, the man didn't get it. The guy's an ass.

"Kyra, you should press charges. He's not going to stop."

"I don't want to give him a record."

"He's been stalking you. This is the third incident within as many days. And he tried to rape you. You need to press charges."

Jake watched the battle play over her face as he'd seen it play over other victims' faces.

"Walk away for a few minutes before you decide. It's the smart thing to do," Jake said.

He hadn't gotten off of Russell yet. Russell tried to move, Jake put pressure on Tom's back with his knee as Kyra walked away from them. Jake watched her pace the kitchen. *I hope she asks herself the right question. Will this get me custody of Trevor?* She had to press charges for ammunition to gain custody. If she didn't come up with it, he'd ask it.

Jake grabbed the cuffs and yanked Russell to his feet. "I want you to put your back to the wall. Good, now slide down it."

"Why can't you put me on the couch?" Russell whined.

"Because the floor is where the animals sleep," Jake said, heading for the kitchen. "Kyra, I have him handcuffed. You need to make a decision. I'm going to tell you from experience this will escalate if you don't do something now to protect yourself. You need to have him arrested. Tomorrow you also need to apply for a restraining order."

His heart broke for her as the tears fell from her eyes. "I will," she whispered.

Jake walked over to her, still in his boxers. He put his arms around her, holding her close. He thumbed away a tear. "It's for the best and for your safety. It should also help with the custody battle."

"I understand that but..." she said again as she placed a hand on his arms. "What do you want to do?"

"Arrest him," she said, anxiety filling her voice.

While he radioed for a patrol car, he kept his eyes on both of them.

"I'm having you arrested for attempted rape, Tom," Kyra said.

"You're mine."

Wondering if he'd feel the same way tomorrow when he sobered up, Jake cocked his head toward the guy. The arrogant bastard didn't get it. He read Tom his rights.

"Uh, Jake?" Kyra said.

"Yes?"

"You better put on your pants and shirt before the patrol car gets here."

"Good idea."

He left the room, headed to the bathroom to fetch his clothes. Behind him Tom cursed at Kyra.

The patrol car arrived within fifteen minutes. Jake talked to the officers. When they took Tom away, he was still cursing. Then, like all pathetic men who had no control, he threatened her again.

"You'll pay for this, Kyra," Tom yelled as the officers dragged him from her condo.

* * * *

Jake closed the front door as Kyra sank onto her couch and had a good cry. He walked over and gathered her into his arms, cradling her to his chest. He didn't say a word while she cried. He let her get it all out. The silence filled the room as she ran out of tears. Rubbing her back in comfort, he kissed the top of her head then rested his head on hers. He wanted to kill Tom at that moment. The anger coursing through him wasn't important right now. He didn't want to upset Kyra any more than she was.

"I'm sorry. It seems lately all I do is apologize."

"Shush, rest."

Pushing away from him, she looked up. "I told you I had baggage."

"This isn't your fault." If nothing else, he wanted her to understand that. It always amazed him the way the victims took responsibility for the actions of others.

"I'm glad you were here. I'd never have been able to stop him on my own." She shivered against him.

He hugged her tighter. "Me too. Don't let him in if he comes back. Call 911 right away, then call me. Understand?"

"Yes." She pressed closer into him as his adrenaline evened out. Domestics were the worst calls. Kyra didn't understand how dangerous Tom Russell had become.

Chapter 18

Kyra pushed off Jake's chest and straddled his lap. She placed kisses on his cheek, nose, and lips. At his response, she parted her lips, slipping her tongue into his mouth, teasing, biting and sucking. He hardened against her upper thighs as she ground her hips into his. There was a violence in her kiss as she searched for what she needed—love, acceptance, distance, and forgiveness. Desperation shoved her forward as she explored his mouth, hoping to ease the passion welled up inside her. Did she dare ask for more?

"Sit next to me," he said, his voice hoarse as he pulled back to look at her.

Why was he lifting her off his lap? Jake placed her beside him on the couch. What had she done wrong? Tonight she needed him. Was he going to turn away from her, leave her in turmoil?

"Your emotions are all over the place tonight. I won't take advantage of you when you're this wrung out."

"You're not. I want you, Jake. I'd hoped tonight we'd see how far the night took us."

"I had the same idea, but Tom changed that. Why don't you get some sleep? Don't follow through on dinner tomorrow night. Right now you shouldn't be alone with him."

"We're meeting at a restaurant, not his house. But I don't want to ever see him again, though I promised Trevor I'd be there. I hope you keep him in jail. This way I'll take Trevor out by myself."

Boy, he went from sexy man to cop in under sixty seconds.

"Make sure you're never alone with Tom. Trevor's a child. Explain to him that from now on it's either you or Tom, not both. If you insist on dinner and you don't want me there, make sure you take someone else with you."

"I will. Can you find out where Trevor is? I hope he's not with a babysitter again. If he is, I need to pick him up."

"I'll call the station and have the arresting officer ask Tom."

"Thanks, I'll relax once I speak with Trevor."

Kyra got up from the sofa and started to pace back and forth between the kitchen and the living room while she watched Jake place the call to the station. She walked back into the living room as he ended the call and sat on the couch next to him.

"Trevor's spending the night at Tom's parents."

"At least he's safe, though he's been spending a lot of nights there. I don't like Tom's parents," she rambled on, still embarrassed by Jake's rejection.

"Nothing terrible about it, some people are hard to be around. It takes a lot of patience to be in a room with the Russells."

"You've had dealings with them?" He always surprised her.

"No, but they're pompous people. They throw their money around and expect everyone to jump through hoops for them. I don't trust politicians. I should go and let you get some rest."

"Please stay awhile, I don't want to be alone." She stared at her cuticles as she picked at them. Jake took her hands in his.

"I'll stay for as long as you like."

It dawned on her he was still in his wet clothes. "Let's try this again. Why don't you give me your shirt and pants. I'll dry them for you."

"I'll keep them on, thank you."

"Afraid I'll attack you?"

"I'm trying to do the right thing here, by keeping my hands to myself. You're making it quite difficult," Jake said, his voice strained.

"Good."

"Good?"

"Yes, good. I told you I want to make love to you. I've never been more sure of anything in my life. Don't make me beg. I don't care about Tom. I want to put him out of my mind."

"I want to make love to you too, but we should talk first."

"About what?" Kyra asked.

"You."

"I'm boring."

"No, I find you enticing and obviously so many others do too."

She wanted to wipe that stupid grin right off his face. *Lord, what does a girl have to do to get laid around here?*

"What do you want to know?"

"Everything."

"I hate talking about me."

"Then talk about your son."

"Trevor's the light of my life. He's full of energy, smart, and funny. The divorce is killing him. Six is a tough age. He's too young to understand what's going on."

* * * *

He watched her face light up. At the same time pain filled her eyes as she spoke of her son. Jake wondered if she'd tell him why she was losing custody of the kid. She didn't seem the type to abuse a child, but then again, you never knew. The job had taught him that everyone was capable of violence.

"Kyra." He took her hand, looked into her eyes. "Why don't you have custody of Trevor?"

"I have a gambling problem." Kyra tugged her hand free of Jake's. He grabbed it back.

"Gambling, like betting on sports?"

"No, casino-type gambling." She dropped her eyes.

"You shouldn't have lost custody over a gambling problem."

"You do if you're married to a Russell in this town."

Jake watched her checks flush, then he took her chin in his hands and raised her head. "Look at me. You made a mistake, but losing your son's a high price to pay. Can't you fight him?"

"I don't have enough money to fight back but I'm saving, though I doubt I'll have enough in time." She dropped her eyes, breaking contact with his. *Something's off here. What is it?*

"How much do you need?"

"What?"

"I asked how much do you need, and what about your parents?"

Her forehead creased and her lips pursed into a thin line before she answered him. The question wasn't difficult, why was she stalling?

"Kyra?"

"They won't help."

"Why?"

"Jake, this isn't any of your business. This is all too intimate to discuss with you."

"You're willing to sleep with me, but not talk to me." He hid the hurt. Damn if she wasn't hiding something. How much did she owe on her gambling debt? Was she so broke she had no money left over to fight for her son?

"It's…oh, Jake. I can't…I don't know."

"Talk it out. It might help."

"Yeah, and push you out the door."

"I'm not going anywhere."

"Right."

Russell had done a number on her. "Please, Kyra, talk to me."

"Okay, here goes. Tom wanted to go to the casino, because he found our life boring. We never anticipated how it might grab hold of me and not let go. I started playing the slots. A little here. A little there. Next thing I knew, it became an obsession. I lost control. At first, I was winning big. Then I started losing. The more I lost, the more I tried to win."

Jake listened without interrupting. She was embarrassed, the white skin of her neck changing colors until it matched her hair. He knew it was hard for her to open up, but he had a knack of drawing people out. But he wanted the whole story before he formed an opinion.

"There's no reason for you to be embarrassed, Kyra. People make mistakes."

"You don't understand. It was a major mistake. I used Trevor's college fund."

"You can pay it back."

"I've been working on it."

"So, after nine years, Tom kicked you out over that?"

"No."

"Then why?"

"I used my pension fund and my 401k and his. I processed a withdrawal with his signature."

"I can see why he was angry. But together you should've sought help for the addiction. If his retirement fund is what pushed him over the edge and not Trevor's college fund…"

"He threatened to press charges against me for forgery."

"But he didn't. Instead he filed for divorce?"

"Yes." Tears washed down her face.

She stood and started pacing the room. Jake went to her and took her in his arms. He knew there was more here she wasn't telling him. Patience was something he'd developed over the years. "You didn't answer my question. Why won't your parents help you?"

"If I went to Gamblers Anonymous and promised to never set foot in the casino again they'd help."

"And you're not willing to agree to those terms, even to gain custody of your son?"

"It's not the terms, Jake. It's my parents trying to control me. Tom also tried to control me throughout our marriage. I'm sick of it!" she yelled. "You're right, the price is too high. I didn't know Tom was going to pull the custody thing or I'd have agreed. By then, it was too late, the judge had ruled. Tom's parents had already greased the right palms."

Jake tightened his grip on her as she tried to push away. "Kyra, look at me. There're ways to fight these people. Are you still gambling?"

"I was. I haven't been back since last Tuesday."

"Why?"

"I lost again. I realized the stupidity of my actions as I tried to win the money to fight Tom. You'll never understand how much I hate myself for what I did to Trevor's life. How I screwed it up. A child needs both his parents at his age."

"Kyra, it can be fixed. I understand how you can blame yourself. I blamed myself for years for my sister's death." *And still do,* but he wasn't going to share that.

"What happened?"

"A classmate of mine raped her, beat her and murdered her. Eva asked me for a ride that day, but I refused because I had a date. It was only five minutes out of my way. Five freaking minutes out of my way. If I'd said yes she'd be alive today." The guilt, the pain, the horror of it, slammed into his life at unexpected moments. It woke him from sleep, invaded his work. He sat up and wondered how much longer he'd be able to handle it and the job? He shoved the gruesome reflection from his mind.

"Then it would've happened on another day. You can't fight fate or blame yourself for someone else's actions." She rubbed his back.

"I can and do," he whispered.

"Did they catch the guy?"

"Yes, he's in jail, but he's up for parole again."

"How can the parole board consider letting him lose on society?"

"The prisons are overcrowded."

"That's no excuse."

"I attend his parole hearings. I give testimony against him each time. This ensures they'll keep him behind bars. I also bring pictures of what he did to her along with all the physical evidence, including the DNA reports, to show how Spaulding's violent act can't be forgiven and that he's not fit to rejoin society. And I don't care how old he was at the time of the crime.

It kept him locked up. Now, after all these years, he wants his DNA tested again to prove it wasn't him. He did it. Of that I have no doubts."

"It must still be raw."

"It is."

She let him lead her back to the couch. They sat down. "Do you want anything?"

"Yes, to get back to talking about you."

Great. "There's nothing else to say."

"There's a lot to say. You never said if you had a problem."

"I do."

"That's a big step, acknowledging it."

"I understand that."

"What's your plan to gain custody?"

"Well, Tom helped tonight with his actions. I've also saved up money for the lawyer and to repay Trevor's college fund."

"That's why you live here, bare to the bone?"

"Yes. What I need more than anything is to have Trevor back with me. My heart has a hole in it without him here."

"I can imagine. Do you have enough money now?" Her shoulders jerked at his question. Interesting. He wondered why.

"I'm almost there. Each week, when I get paid, I add to it."

Every time he brought up money, she dodged him. Why? "If you need my help, I'll be a character witness." Was there another reason the court ruled against her? His instincts buzzed.

"Thanks."

"It's hard for you to accept help, isn't it?"

"Yes. I like being independent. But I appreciate the offer. Oh, I have a big favor to ask. I need a date for my friend's wedding next weekend. Do you want to go?" Kyra fiddled with her hands.

Jake took hold of them. "Yes, just let me know the time and place."

* * * *

With nothing more to be said on the subject, they sat on the couch in silence, not an uncomfortable silence, but a soothing one. Kyra snuggled closer to Jake, needing the warmth his body supplied. He hadn't judged her or walked out, a mark in the "pro" column for him. Was he disgusted with her or did he consider her a fool?

Kyra turned and kissed him. The kiss turned from a thank-you to passionate in under a second. Again, she probed his mouth—the heat shot through her, settling between her thighs. She wanted this man, wanted his hands, tongue, and mouth on her. His mind excited her. Never with Tom had she experienced these sensations Jake invoked. His gentle caress was a far cry from Tom's bruising one. The fire, the pleasure, shot in and around her as he tweaked her nipple between his thumb and finger. Incredible—she was ready for him, and the man hadn't even taken off her shirt. She inched her hand over his jeans and rubbed as he hardened with each stroke. She swallowed his moan as he crushed his hips into her hand.

Jake broke off the kiss, stared into her eyes, questioning as he unbuttoned her blouse. In a swift movement, he stood, extended his hand to her, and tugged her up off the couch.

"Kyra…are you sure?"

"Yes, I'm sure. I don't want to be alone tonight."

"I'll spend the night on the couch."

"What is your problem with getting laid, Jake?"

"Kyra!"

All the way into the bedroom they kissed while groping each other. He slid her blouse off her shoulder while trailing kisses down her neck to the swell of her breasts. He reached behind her to unhook her bra and came up empty.

"What kind of bra is this?" He looked into her eyes.

"Front loader."

"Christ, there should be instructions with these."

He moved his hands to the front, fussed with the closure. Kyra gripped them and guided them until he released the hook. Once freed, his mouth explored her as he teased along the way. The rhythm of it drove her wild. The anticipation built as he slid his right hand under the waistband of her skirt. A moan caught in her throat as his hand penetrated her defenses.

But apparently not ready to end the exploration he tugged her skirt off. Whispery kisses sent her off the edge as she grabbed hold of his head.

"Easy." He laughed, continuing to tease her.

"I can't. In me now," she screamed as she writhed.

"Patience, darling."

"I can't."

He tugged off her thong and continued his exploration. She exploded. Breathless, she whispered, "I want more."

Laughing, he rubbed his hands up and down her legs. "Hmmm!"

He started to remove his boxers when she pushed him onto his back. Straddling him, she worked them off for him. Empowered by the orgasm, she wanted to give him the joy he'd given her.

Shamelessly, she bent over. Kissing him, she slipped her tongue between his lips. Kyra pulled back and smiled. She skimmed his throat as she echoed his every move. He fisted his hands in her hair. Her scalp burned as he tugged. She slid her hand down the length of him, cupping him as she massaged. Kisses replaced her hand as her mouth caressed and tugged until he started to pulse. Not wanting him to come yet, she released him and sat up. A sly smile played upon her lips.

"You're killing me, Kyra, take it all," he begged.

She moved up his body and lowered herself onto him as she kept the same tempo, the same motion as her mouth. Slow and steady. His eyes never left hers as he held her hips. When she slowed the pace to tease, he pumped her hips faster. She saw his green eyes become determined right before he flipped her over and with fast, long strokes he thrust into her until she screamed out as she smoldered with her second orgasm. Her body and mind were floating. *This is what they write songs about.* Tom had never brought her to this level of release. She wanted to do it again and again. Should she ask?

Jake collapsed on top of Kyra. "You're incredible."

He seemed to realize he was crushing her because he pushed up and off, letting her draw in air.

"Yes, it was exceptional."

He stretched out beside her, comfortable in his nakedness, he draped an arm over her. Kyra reached for the covers. "Don't, I want to look at you. You're gorgeous and don't even realize it." Ridiculous to be embarrassed, but she was. How should she respond to that? *He's high on sex right now.* She lay there in a contemplative mood, content in their silence.

"Are you okay?"

"Yes, this was amazing."

"It was."

"You know..." How did you explain mind-blowing? Kyra turned on her side to face him. "I never experience sex this way. It was intense, satisfying, incredible, and awesome. Should I go on?"

Laughing, Jake said, "No. I get it."

"Good, because I'd like to get it again," she said.

"My pleasure."

"Oh no, my pleasure," she said, as she rolled on top of him.

They made love well into the morning hours. Each time Jake made love to her, he brought her to orgasm—the experience euphoric. In the beginning, Tommy would take his time, initiating foreplay, but after the first year, he'd climb on top of her, satisfy himself and climb off. After sex with Tom she'd been an empty husk, an instrument for him to satisfy himself and the hell with her. Not once with Tom did she ever achieve an orgasm and was led to believe it was her fault. As the sun came up, so did Jake. Kyra smiled as she responded to his touch.

"Where did you go?"

"I'm right here."

"Do you want to talk?"

He's cute. "Talk is overrated. I like action."

"A woman after my own heart."

* * * *

Two hours later he puttered around the kitchen and made coffee while he waited for her to wake.

"I've died and gone to heaven," she said, coming into the room.

"Good morning, sleepyhead. Do you always sleep in?"

"Sleep in? It's six thirty. What are you, one of those morning people?"

"I love the morning. Coffee?" He held up the pot to entice her.

"Is there a God?"

He stared at her.

"Yes, coffee please. You're tough. No sense of humor?"

"I have a sense of humor though not over coffee. I even made breakfast."

"Do you want a key?" she said, sipping the coffee. "You can cook and offer great sex at the same time."

"Hate to eat and run, but I have to get going. Remember, don't meet him alone tonight. If you don't want me there, make sure someone else is. Stay safe."

"Thanks for breakfast, especially the coffee."

He walked over to her, bent, kissed her, then straightened. She stood, grabbed his shirt, and kissed him back. No peck—a kiss filled with promises of more. He liked that.

"I'll call you later. And, Kyra, I had a great time last night."

"Me too, I'd love a repeat performance."

"How about right after work?"

"You're on."

Chapter 19

Wednesday, Angelo, along with the same funeral director from the previous cremation, showed up at three thirty as Phil had promised. She directed them to the garage in back to unload the body. At three forty-five her cemetery laborers started coming in to clock out for the day and stow the equipment they'd used.

The foreman, Dunn, walked into the cremation room. He eyeballed Angelo and the funeral director.

"You need a hand, Kyra?"

"No thanks, Joel, I'm all set."

"If you're sure, I'll see you tomorrow."

Kyra noticed Joel hadn't budged. She walked into her office, sat at her desk, and started processing the paperwork for the legitimate cremation. She'd yet to put the body in the chamber. The air stirred as Joel entered and closed the door behind him.

"What can I do for you?"

"You sure you're okay here by yourself?"

"Yes, they've been here before."

"You have my cell number?" Bless his soul. Joel had a crush on her.

Kyra waved goodbye to him. She wondered what Angelo was up to. As she turned, she watched him walk into the hall. Was he eavesdropping? He came back with a cup of coffee. She got up from her desk and headed into the chamber room. The oven's thermometer showed it had reached the right temperature to load the casket.

Angelo walked in. "Do you need an extra hand?"

"Sure, help me guide it in."

It was heavier than even the first body she'd processed for Phil. *Even without knowing I'd know there were two bodies in here.* What had this one done to earn Phil's wrath? God, she hoped someday it wasn't her in the box. Once they had the body in the chamber, Kyra hit the close-door button and ignited the flames. She walked out of the chamber room to the break room to grab a cup of coffee. The pot's contents reminded her of sludge. Angelo followed her into the room with the cup he'd poured minutes ago. The air smelled of burned coffee. She wished for something stronger to calm her nerves, but coffee had to do. Two and a half hours locked up with Angelo while the cremation took place unnerved her.

To keep busy she made another pot. He dumped the contents of his cup into the sink and rinsed it out. Someone had taught him well. She approved. The smell of the brewing coffee filled the air. Angelo didn't seem in a talkative mood today.

"Is everything okay?" she asked. "I spoke with Phil earlier today. He was quite short with me. No social 'how are you.' Is he pissed at me?"

"Yes. He doesn't like to be shot down. Are you still seeing the cop?"

"Yes." She swallowed her smile. *Yes I am, all of him.*

"That bothers Phil, and, if truth be told, me too."

"Why? One doesn't have anything to do with the other."

"You can't be that naïve. The world is interconnected." Second person in a week who had mentioned her naiveté.

"I can keep my business life separate from my personal life. Phil shouldn't worry about it," she said, annoyed.

"He's been burned before. He needs to be cautious. Excuse the pun."

"I won't betray him. I made a deal I plan to honor."

"In our line of work, it's good to be careful. It keeps you alive."

She accepted the veiled threat.

They lapsed into silence. Angelo stood at attention in front of the chamber, same as the last time. The funeral director sat in his car. Kyra processed paperwork on the legitimate burials and cremations she had performed this week. A car pulling up outside had her racing to the window.

Angelo left his post. He walked over to join her. They reached it at the same time. Angelo bumped her out of the way, forcing her to move to the next one to peer out at her unannounced visitor. *Crap.* Jake stood outside, studying the building. *What does he want?*

"It's the guy I'm dating. We have plans for tonight. I'll get rid of him," she said, nerves dancing through her stomach. Angelo placed a firm hand on her upper arm and squeezed.

"I'm going to send Stan back here while I wait in the car. Don't take long to get rid of him. I don't want any trouble. Understood?"

Oh boy, did she. "Yes."

Knees shaking, Kyra went to the door, unlocked it and held it open a few inches.

"I'm glad to see you lock yourself in." Jake leaned over and kissed her on the lips.

"Precaution, it's part of the job. To what do I owe this surprise?" She didn't invite him in.

"I was in the neighborhood and I decided to stop by instead of calling to see if you're still going tonight ."

"I'm glad you did." She folded her hands together to keep them from shaking.

"Are you okay?"

"Yes. I mean no. I didn't plan on going to dinner with Tom, but it's the only way he'll let me see Trevor today. I must see for myself that Trevor's okay." *Excellent recovery, Kyra.*

"I'll be there, but I'll be late. Make sure you don't leave with him."

"I won't."

"Where are you meeting them?"

"The Burger Joint, Trevor's favorite."

"No bar."

"Nope. You'll have to have a milkshake." She laughed.

"Poison, I never touch the stuff."

"Try it, you'll enjoy it. Hey, I'll see you tonight. I've got one cooking. The funeral director is in the back waiting for me. I'll see you later."

He whispered in her ear, "I can't wait for a repeat performance."

Blushing, she said, "Me either."

* * * *

She walked back into the chamber room, startled when she slammed into Angelo's chest.

"Touching," Angelo said.

"You were eavesdropping?"

"Yes, I wanted to check out your cop."

"He's not my cop. I've had two dates with him. I don't own him."

"How far have you two gone?"

She hated her cream coloring. The heated flush spread from her head to her shoulders. Sure her skin matched the flaming red of her hair, she replied, "It's none of your business."

Laughing, he said, "Relax, I didn't mean anything by it, but now I know."

He reached out, gently touched her cheek. She pulled back. "Why are you taking chances, dating a cop?"

"He's the first man I've dated since being separated. The woman who introduced us didn't tell me he was a cop."

Talking too much. Angelo was synonymous with danger. More so than Phil.

"I don't want any trouble. I'm doing the job I promised and I'd like my private life to remain private."

"As long as it doesn't interfere with us, it will."

"Great." She needed a shot for her frayed nerves. First Tommy and his insane actions last night. Now Angelo. What was next? If it wasn't for Trevor, she'd run away and start over. Unless she was fired, Kyra knew she'd be doing Phil's dirty work for the rest of her life. Did the people she burned have families? Were they looking for them?

Were they the same kind of people as Phil or were they ordinary people like her, trapped in a mistake?

Kyra blinked those people from her head. If she didn't she'd go crazy.

And why wasn't she willing to throw Jake away—was he her new addiction? He was special, someone she wanted a long-term relationship with. One of a kind. She understood he slid from gentle to hard in a matter of seconds when a situation called for it. If she continued to work for Phil, why continue to date Jake? She stepped into her office to get away from Angelo, saying she had to finish up the paperwork on today's burials.

The timer went off at six o'clock, signaling it was time to process the remains. Kyra headed back into the chamber room and started emptying the oven.

"Do you have an urn with you, Angelo, or do you want me to put the remains in one of the plastic ones?"

"I have one with me. I'll get it. How much longer before you're finished here?"

"Another half hour. I still have to remove any metal before I run them through the processor."

"You mean the grinder." He smiled.

"No, the processor." She forced a smile.

"Right. I'll get the urn."

* * * *

Jake sat in The Burger Joint parking lot waiting on Kyra. At the crematorium, she hadn't invited him in. In fact, she kept the door at an angle to block his view. Who was she hiding? Though he liked her, more things had started to bother him. Another piece of the puzzle didn't fit. After they finished with dinner with her ex, he'd ask her straight out who was at the crematorium today.

A car pulled into the parking lot too fast. Jake started to climb out of his car to give the driver a warning when he realized it was Kyra. He took a few moments to study her. *Harried*, both this afternoon and now and she'd lost weight this week. No matter how he dissected it, he kept coming back to her affiliation with Phil Lucci. How had she wound up on a date with him in the first place? And who had introduced them? He was going to get answers tonight, one way or another.

He knocked on her window and smiled when she jumped.

"Thanks for meeting here," she said.

"No problem."

"I need to get inside. I'm late."

* * * *

"Not a word, Tom. I'm here to see Trevor." She gave her son a kiss.

"I want to apologize..."

"Not here, not now. I promised Trevor dinner. That's why I'm here."

"That's it?"

"Yes. To ensure that nothing happens, Tom, my friend Jake is with me."

"For Pete's sake, I was drunk."

"No excuse. If you start in I'll leave. But we will have this discussion at a later date." She turned to Trevor. "Wow, look at you. You're almost finished."

"I was hungry. Can I play in the ball pit?"

"Yes."

Trevor stayed in place and stared at both his parents. Russell stared, tried to intimidate Jake. Jake stared him down until Tom looked away first. He took a seat at a nearby table.

"We'll talk later," Tom demanded.

What an idiot Tom was using that tone on Kyra. But Jake noted time and place of the threat to add to the file.

"I have plans later. We'll talk when it's convenient for both of us."

Russell grabbed Kyra by the wrist, Jake stood but sat again as Kyra waved him down.

"Your little stunt last night isn't going to gain you custody."

Kyra dropped her voice to a whisper, but Jake heard every word. "You mean your stunt, don't you? Remove your hand, and the charges stand. You will not ruin our son's life with your petty grievances. Act like a man for once in your life. Take responsibility for your actions. You can't rely on your parents forever."

Russell's face flamed cerise. It looked as if he'd explode on the spot. Jake relaxed as Tom let go of her wrist. Kyra put her burger down to rub her wrist.

"Are you ready, Trev?" Russell stood and grabbed Trevor by the arm.

"Ouch, you're hurting me, Daddy." Trev tried to pull his arm away from Tom's grip. This time Jake walked over and sat beside Kyra.

"Tom, let him go." Kyra's tone brooked no room for argument. People were looking their way.

"Sorry, buddy. I didn't realize how strong I am."

"I'll take Trevor home when he finishes his dinner. He needs to play awhile longer. It's why he likes it here," Kyra said.

Tom looked down at her then at Jake. "I don't want him near my son."

"Shut up," Kyra said. "Trev, why don't you go play in the ball thingy while Mommy talks to her friend for a minute? You can finish eating when you come back."

Children aren't stupid and Trevor's no exception. Trevor looked from his mother to his father then at Jake before he left them to their fight.

"Well, aren't we good parents?" she said.

"If you'd control that snide tongue of yours we'd be in a better place."

Jake watched daggers shoot from Kyra's eyes. "You're a fool, and an arrogant bastard. You started this the minute I walked in. It's neither the time or the place...but we'll have this out when it's convenient for me."

"Oh, you bet. Have him home in an hour or I call the police." He stormed out.

An hour later they took Trevor home. Jake drove with Kyra in her car but didn't get out when she went to the door. He listened through the open car window as Kyra and Tom spoke. Russell seemed subdued.

"Can we please talk, Kyra?"

"I won't be alone with you, not after last night. You've changed."

Good girl. Jake was glad Kyra stood at the door and didn't go in.

"You make me crazy, you always have."

"Oh come on. Stop the bullshit and grow up. We're divorcing. Remember, going to the casino was another one of your bright ideas.

Accept responsibility for your actions. Isn't that what you said to me before you kicked me out and left me with nothing?"

"We can't get past it, can we?"

"No." She turned to leave.

"Kyra, I am sorry. I assumed you'd stop gambling and come to your senses. I screwed up."

"Yeah, you did." Shoulders slumped, she returned to the car. Jake pushed open her door. Kyra drove around the block then pulled to the curb and stopped the car. Jake took her in his arms while she cried it out.

"Why don't you drop me back at my car then I'll follow you home?"

She pulled into her condo parking lot a little before he did. Jake opened her car door, helped her out. "Come on, I'll fix you a drink."

"I warned you about baggage. Remember, it's your own fault for hanging around," she said, trying for humor, but missed her mark.

"Yes you did, but I told you last night I'm not going anywhere," he said.

"It seems like a lifetime away right now."

Arm in arm, they walked up the stairs to the condo. Once inside, Kyra started toward the kitchen but Jake stopped her.

"Sit down and relax. I'll get it. What do you want to drink?"

"You don't have to wait on me. I'm not injured."

"I want to wait on you. Say thank you and sit down."

"Thank you, I'll have—"

"I know—a rum and coke."

"Okeydokey… I'll sit right here."

It cut right through him when Kyra sat and propped her feet on the coffee table, as she dropped her head on the back of the sofa. Her eyes closed, her mouth drooped.

Jake walked to the doorway between the living room and kitchen with drinks in hand and a compress for her head, but stopped short. Helpless, he stood and observed her try to deal with it all. The agony on Kyra's face ripped at his heart. Never had he seen a more pathetic expression.

He'd heard every word she and Tom exchanged, but more, the hurt in Kyra's voice resounded in his head. Jake gave her credit for controlling her temper and emotions in the restaurant. In the same situation, he'd have been all over Russell, unable to hold back his temper. He walked farther into the room, talking as not to startle her.

"Here's your drink. No, don't get up." He sat on the edge of the couch and pressed the cold compress on her head.

"Thanks you make a good nurse." She smiled

"Don't insult me. I'm a doctor. Want to play?"

"Insult you... You just set back an entire profession, though playing doctor does sound good."

"Rest."

"Lord, Jake, you spend more time trying not to get laid." She smiled into his shocked face. "What?"

"I'd never have guessed you had such a gutter mouth. I like it."

"Good, I'm trying it out."

"Smart-ass."

"That's me." Kyra sat up, kissed him.

"How did I rate a kiss?"

"For being there and not judging me."

"Lie back down and rest for a bit. It's been a tough night. Do you want anything?"

"Only you," she said, as she circled her arms around his waist. Jake hugged back as he leaned his forehead on hers.

"Not going to rest, are you?"

"You rest your way. I'll rest mine." She snuggled into him, nestling her lips to his neck under his jaw.

"I won't be responsible for my actions. You're making me crazy."

"Promises, promises." She laughed.

He pushed off the couch, started to walk from the room.

"Hey, where are you going?"

He came back and looked down at her. "Hay? What am I, a horse?"

"Sorry. Where are you going, Jake?" She exaggerated every word.

He picked her up off the couch, and carried her into the bedroom. "I'm off to do battle. I pray I'll survive."

"We can only hope."

"Oh, you'll have to do your part to make sure I do. But you might be the death of me yet."

"Hmmm."

Unceremoniously, he dropped her on the bed and dove in after her.

Chapter 20

After a harrowing day, Jake rang the doorbell. He'd promised Kyra he'd stop by when his shift was over. When she opened the door she looked sexy as hell, all tossed from sleep.

"I woke you, didn't I?"

"That's okay. I must've dozed off."

He leaned over and gave her a kiss as he snugged her to his body.

"Do you want coffee?"

"Do you have a beer?"

"Yes, sit down."

He followed her into the kitchen. "You should have told me you were tired."

"I'm good, it was a busy week and…" She reached into the refrigerator, moved things around until she found the beer.

Jake took the bottle she offered. They walked back into the living room. He caught a glimpse of the paperwork as she turned the pile over. He'd spotted cremation forms, spreadsheets, and a bank statement. It wasn't the content that bothered him, it was the way she did it. And damn, it wasn't any of his business, but she had piqued his curiosity.

"I haven't told you that I've been assigned to the Missing Persons Department along with Homicide until they find another lieutenant. The brass isn't in a hurry to replace him either. Which sticks in my gut, but that's another story."

"You don't seem happy about it."

"It's more work, not more money or recognition."

She tucked her legs up under her and pulled the afghan off the back of the couch as she smoothed it down. He wished her hands were roaming over him like they did over the blanket.

Distracted, the drawn look around her eyes had him changing tactics. "I should leave and let you sleep. After our week I bet you're exhausted."

"No, I was looking forward to your company. Tell me about this new department."

"All right. It's what the name implies, Missing Persons. When an individual is reported missing, the detectives take the information but don't act on it until after forty-eight hours unless there's foul play suspected. You'd be surprised how many don't want to be found. It all depends on the evidence, it either stays a Missing Persons case or it's turned over to Homicide."

"Does it happen often?"

"Eight out of ten times the person shows up, but the one they turned over to me the other day I believe is dead."

"Why?"

"He's been missing for almost two weeks. His apartment was ransacked. I took his mother over there to check it out and she didn't find anything missing. Somebody was looking for something. A heavy gambler, according to his ex-wife. He'd bet thousands on the games each week. She said he'd even bet on how fast an elderly woman crossed the street before a light turned red." He should ask her now about her problem.

"Did he owe somebody a lot of money?"

"His type always does. And the stupid ones try to get away without paying."

"You always pay," Kyra whispered.

Drawing her into his arms, he held her close. He decided to go for it. "This guy was deep into the mob. That's an unhealthy thing, when you can't pay." He turned her chin up and looked into her eyes. "You're not into the mob, are you?"

Her body jerked at his question. He held on tight as she tried to pull out of his embrace. Her head bounced off his chin. Taking hold of her face again, he stared deep into her eyes for his answer.

"Where did that come from? I have enough trouble with Tom now you want to add more?"

"I had to ask."

"Why?"

"There are times when I look at you…your voice and expression scream desperation. It breaks my heart."

"I am desperate. I'm losing my son, and it makes me angry, and sick." She stood. Paced the living room. She almost knocked over the planter by the reading chair. He'd made her mad, too mad. *There it goes again. Damn gut.*

"I'm sure it does." He got up off the couch and walked over to her, but she turned away before he took hold of her. *If Kyra isn't lying, she's holding something back.* "I should leave."

"Yes, that's a good idea. I'm tired."

"I didn't mean to upset you—"

"I'm cranky. As I said, it was a hell of a week with Tom, and an exhausting one with you." She smiled up at him but it didn't reach her eyes.

"It was a great week with you. Are you kicking me out because you're tired or pissed?"

"A little of both."

He took her in his arms, started rubbing her back. "It wasn't my intention to make you mad, but after talking to this guy's family today I got a better picture of a gambler. I want to make sure you're safe."

"I'm safe. I haven't heard from Tom today. Hopefully he got the message."

"Let's hope. Do you want to go out to dinner tomorrow night?"

"Sure."

"I'll call you. It's your turn to pick a place."

"You don't have to leave. I don't know why I'm bitchy tonight."

"I'm leaving anyway, you need sleep." He kissed her good night once they reached the door.

"I'm sorry."

"Stop apologizing. It's okay to let off a little steam. I hear it's even healthy."

* * * *

She locked the door behind him, set the alarm and fell back against the door, sliding to the floor the exhaustion took over. *Please dear God, tell me I didn't cremate Jake's dead guy this week. What are the odds? Why did I assume that all the bodies from Phil came from the other side of the state? My God, does anything lead back to me? Will Jake have to arrest me?* Her stomach flipped. *What will happen to Trevor if I have to go to prison?*

Question after question rolled around in her mind. Her queasy stomach started to erupt. Jake and Phil were trains on the same track, heading toward a colossal head-on collision. *And I'm the engineer responsible for keeping them from colliding.* Kyra went to bed to sleep on it.

Restless, one question kept her awake. Jake's new case—did she cremate the guy? If so, her life had just taken a nose dive into the gutter.

* * * *

On the drive home, he chided himself. He'd been too heavy handed about the gambling and the mob. It shut her right down. If she was in deep, he'd try to help her. But if she didn't admit her collusion with Phil, how could he? Every time he approached the subject, the way she reacted was off. His research into the Church file and the head of organized gambling in the state led back to her friend Phil.

The next morning, when he arrived at his office, Jake found Louie sitting in his chair sipping coffee. The coffee machine had been a gift from Sophia and Louie when he'd been promoted to lieutenant. And Louie had treated Jake's office as his own personal haven since. Knocking Louie's feet off his desk, he grabbed a cup before he sat down.

"Comfortable, Louie?"

"As a matter of fact, I am."

"Get your ass out of my chair."

"Grumpy, aren't you? What, didn't get any last night?"

"Curb your vulgar humor."

"How's Mia?"

"You know, Louie, you cross a lot of lines. Because we go way back doesn't give you the right to interfere with my life." He sat, stared Louie down.

"Who's interfering? I was inquiring after Mia."

"We're done, Louie. Why can't you get that through your thick, Italian head?"

"My thick Italian head? What about your thicker Mick brain? What's got your panties in a twist?"

"Nothing, I have a lot on my mind," Jake said.

"Yeah? Like what?"

The curtains on his glass wall had been open since he claimed the office for his own. If he wanted privacy he'd need to shut them. He stared out into his bullpen. Noted some detectives talked on phones, others typed away on their computers, a couple stood around drinking coffee. Stalling, he searched for an answer to Louie's question. Did he want to involve Louie in this mess? Last night, after lying awake for many hours, Jake played all the rumors and suppositions around that Phil Lucci ran the gambling and prostitution in the state. Because Lucci hadn't been arrested since he was in his teens didn't mean he wasn't dirty. His cop's brain shouted out that Phil Lucci was involved in the disappearance of Church, which connected Kyra in a roundabout way. Spinning his chair toward his window he stared out at the hordes of college kids going to and from class. For now he'd keep his suspicions to himself until he had something solid to connect them. If Kyra was involved with the mob, then, and only then, he'd bring

Louie in on the investigation. He didn't want to prejudice Louie against Kyra. Louie loved Mia.

"Let me see. I'm running the Homicide Department, which includes overseeing everyone's cases. The paperwork on the administrative side of things is an endless pit of hell. Now I'm running the Missing Persons Department, which involves mountains more of paperwork, along with us working our active cases," Jake said over his shoulder.

"I guess I'll forgive you," Louie said. "But on the serious side of things, I did the follow-up on Mr. Wade's drinking buddy the night he died. You remember that pesky case about the man who died with high blood-alcohol levels."

Damn, he'd put that case out of his head. "Don't bust my ass. Did you get anything?"

"Kevin Long claims he left Dwight at the bar around ten o'clock. He starts his work day at six a.m."

"Did it check out?"

"I didn't check it out last night. I've got it on my to-do list today."

"Okay, keep me in the loop."

"You sure there's nothing else on your mind?"

"Sure, now get out of here. I have a boatload of reports to process. Louie, close the door on your way out."

After Louie left, Jake went over to what he'd privately deemed the fishbowl and pulled the curtains shut. Back at his desk he turned on the computer and typed in the name Philip Lucci. He had a hit on Phil Lucci, not Phillip Lucci.

Not a second after Louie closed the door someone knocked. "Come in," Jake called out.

"LT, the medical examiner called a suicide on the Wiggins woman," Detective Armand Lanoue said.

"Thanks, Armand."

Turning back to his computer, Jake studied the sparse record on Phil Lucci. He had a sealed record at the age of fifteen, a burglary charge at nineteen—he served two years of a fifteen-year sentence and then nothing. *For a man his age there should be more.*

"You got smart after that, Phil, didn't you?" Not for one minute did he believe Phil had kept his nose clean. "Where did you do your time?" Jake kept peeling layer after layer off Phil's file until he was satisfied there was nothing else to be learned. He'd wait on running his financials—he needed a warrant for that.

Leaning back in his chair, he let the information settle into his mind. Phil had done hard time at Radgowski, now called Corrigan Correctional Institution, in Uncasville. The place housed some tough characters. Lucci must've gotten quite an education as a resident.

Jake would have to check to see if any of the prison guards were still around. If so, would they remember Phil?

More important, why had Kyra dated him? Even once? It bothered him, her association with Phil. Since Kyra wasn't going to tell him, he'd find out who put her in front of Lucci if it killed him.

Various questions popped into his head. Angered him. How much money did she owe? She had stated her relationship with Phil was strictly business. What kind of business? Was he pimping her out? No, it wasn't her style, though he'd seen stranger things on the job. Also, the other night she'd seemed inexperienced. According to her, her husband was her first and only lover until him. Truth or lie? And what difference did that make? Was Phil was threatening her son?

And the most disturbing question. *Is Kyra using me?*

The ringing phone startled him. "Yes?"

"It's Kyra. I wanted to apologize again for last night. I shouldn't have taken my mood out on you."

"It's okay, really." *What are you into?*

"You're positive? Because you sound a little off."

"I'm distracted with some research I'm working on. Where do you want to go to dinner tonight?"

"Do you want to try the new restaurant in Southington?"

"It's a steak house, isn't it?"

"Yes."

"You eat too much red meat."

"What are you, the beef police?"

"How about we head to the shore for a fish dinner?"

"I hate fish, but it sounds good, as long as it's not too late. I have Trevor tomorrow."

"We'll stay around here then. Is eight good?"

"Perfect."

After he hung up, Jake stared at the phone for a long time. She seemed normal enough today. Was he reading more than there was into her friendship with Phil? Why date him, a cop, if she had something going on with Phil? Kyra wasn't stupid—dating him put her in harm's way. It had to be her gambling. It rattled him that she might owe the mob. He didn't want to come to any conclusions without all the facts, but he needed to go where his gut led him.

* * * *

It was a warm night. He decided the convertible with the top down was called for. Settling Kyra into the car, he climbed in and put on his seat belt.

"Do you want the top up or down?"

"Down, it's a beautiful night for it."

"Don't care about your hair?"

Smirking, she said, "You can't mess it up, it's always wild and curly."

"I love that." He reached over and ran his hand through it, pulling her to him for a kiss before putting the car into gear and driving to the restaurant. He'd forgotten to make reservations. They made their way into the bar to wait to be called. It was standing room only. The only open spot available put them in front of the restrooms. And still they were pressed up against other bodies.

"Terrific atmosphere, Jake."

"I picked it for you." He grinned.

"Well, at least you get to check out all the pretty girls."

"There's only one I'm interested in, and that's you."

He loved how her face flushed red. "Thanks."

He leaned in to whisper in her ear but stopped mid-word. His mind froze. The room faded away.

"Jake."

"Mia!"

Unconsciously, his body shot into attack stance. For a month, he had the words planned on the off chance he ran into her. Now, confronted by Mia, his tongue ceased to function. The room, the bar noise, eased back into his consciousness. He wanted to let loose all the bottled up anger but didn't with Kyra beside him. Mia's absence these last few weeks had filled him with agony. Seeing her now brought back the pain.

"I'm Kyra." She reached her hand out to shake Mia's.

"Sorry, Kyra. Mia, this is Mia...Kyra Russell. Kyra, Mia Andrews."

"Hi, I won't hold you up. It was nice meeting you, Kyra. Always good seeing you, Jake."

What was wrong with him? *Talk to her*, his mind screamed. He sipped his beer while his future slipped away. Now wasn't the time to clear his mind, especially in front of Kyra. He turned back to her. Deep green eyes bored into his.

"Why don't you go talk to her? It's obvious you want to. I can take your car home."

"We're on a date, Kyra. I'll talk to her another time." He rubbed his thumb over her cheek. "Are you trying to dump me?"

"No, but I'll never have your whole heart, will I?"

"Do you want honesty?"

"Always."

If only you'd give it to me. "I've never lied to you. The answer's yes."

"Carrington, party of two," the hostess announced.

Jake raised his hand and said, "That's us."

He had to walk by Mia to get to their table. Jake noted she was with her girlfriends, not a date. It made him feel better. Their eyes locked as he passed. If he wasn't mistaken, he saw jealousy in hers.

Their waitress came over as he was helping Kyra into her seat. She took their drink orders. Jake was ready for another but noticed Kyra hadn't touched hers.

He hoped he was wrong about her connection to Phil Lucci. During dinner he tried to hide his moodiness while he kept Mia in his line of sight. He faltered a few times in the conversation but was able to recover.

"Are you all right?" Kyra asked.

"I'm sorry, I'm not great company tonight. Seeing Mia threw me for a loop."

"Stop apologizing, it's not necessary. Why don't we call it a night and head home?"

"I'll be right back then we'll leave."

Jake bumped into her as Mia walked out of the women's room.

"I see no grass grew under your feet, did it?" Mia said.

"Don't start. You want to talk, call me."

"Goodbye, Jake." Before Mia turned away Jake saw her anger, but more, he saw the hurt in her eyes.

Jake gently took hold of her arm, forced her to look at him before dropping them back at his side. "What do you want from me? Because I'm lost here."

"I miss you," she whispered.

He almost reached for her but instead steeled his arms at his side. "I miss you too, but remember it was your choice—"

"No, it was yours. You asked for more than I wanted to give at the time."

"It's been over a month."

"I know."

"No, you don't. You haven't a clue. And now, because I'm with another woman, you want to do this. I can't—" Jake turned away from her and walked into the men's room.

He heard someone coming in behind him, turned from the urinal. "For God's sake, Mia," He said as he zipped up.

"No, Jake, you listen. It's been hell for me too. How do we fix this?"

"I'm on a—" A man walked in, looked at the both of them then marched out without doing his business.

Jake never took his eyes off her. "I'm on a date. Call me tomorrow to set something up. I'm not doing this now."

* * * *

Sitting with her back against the wall, Kyra followed Jake's path. It wasn't right but she admired his ass as he walked to the men's room. Then watched as Mia cornered him.

What the hell? Disbelief hit her as Mia pushed her way into the men's room after Jake. *What balls that woman has.* How should she handle him when he came back? Confront him or comfort him?

Never taking her eyes off the men's room door, she held her breath. When Mia exited Kyra locked eyes with her—Mia broke contact first, but not before she noticed her tears. It'd be interesting to see Jake's reaction came out. Jake left the men's room, his head forward as he walked straight to the table. Kyra noticed him signaling the waitress for the check before he sat. *He must be a great cop.* His face held no expression—blank, flat eyes had replaced his beautiful passionate green ones.

You're in there somewhere Jake, but where? Kyra's sympathy hadn't beat out her anger. Her mind in a jumble, she needed to know where she stood. She had no right to ask. He'd been honest with her from the beginning. But, she wanted much more.

The waitress brought the bill. Kyra's mind kept throwing questions at her while Jake settled up. "Are you ready?"

She nodded.

He came around the table and pulled out her chair. Thank goodness they didn't have to pass by Mia as they left the restaurant. Together they walked to the car in silence.

Jake opened her door. She started to climb in but he tugged her into his arms. As he held her he whispered into her ear, "I'm sorry I ruined your night."

Kyra put her arms around him, rubbed her hands up and down his back, offering comfort. "You didn't. It's no one's fault we ran into her tonight. I wish I could erase your pain."

"You being here's enough." She wondered if that was true.

At her door, she asked, "Do you want to come in?"

"Yes."

Once inside, Jake took her into his arms again. Kyra leaned up on her toes and pressed her lips to his. Jake pulled back, looking into her eyes.

"I care for you, Kyra. You understand that, don't you?"

"You don't need to reassure me."

"I'm not. It was a little awkward tonight—shit, a lot awkward." He broke the embrace, paced the room.

"Is this the first time you've seen her since the breakup?"

"Yes. Every emotion I had rushed back and whacked me upside the head."

"You're so poetic." Kyra forced a smile, hoping to relax him.

"Right, more like idiotic. Still want me to stay?"

"Yes."

"Why?" *Oh Jake, I'm not giving you up without a fight.*

"Because I enjoy your company. And tonight you need a friend—I'm your friend." He came back to her, gave her a hug.

"Thanks." *Christ, I was hoping for more.*

"You're welcome. Do you want a drink?"

"No, only you."

"Well, you're in luck. I'm available."

"That makes me the luckiest guy alive."

"You sweet-talking devil, come into the bedroom before you spew more lies."

"Not lying."

Chapter 21

Jake hunted up his phone and looked at the display. Kyra caught the frown before he blanked out his expression. Not cop blank...guy blank.

"A problem?" she asked.

"It's Mia," he said.

"Why don't you take it in the other room?"

Silence. She hated silence. The phone stopped ringing...more silence.

Awkward, awkward, awkward. What do you say to a guy when you're naked in bed with him and the love of his life calls? Another round, or I'll kill her for you? What is the proper etiquette?

"I'm not going to talk to her right now."

"Your choice." She shrugged then rolled away from him.

He caught her and turned her back to him. She settled in on top of him. Kyra was torn. Jake never lied to her, but how was she supposed to handle this—Mia intruding in her bedroom?

"Does she always call this early?"

"No."

"I see." Kyra's temper flashed. She tried rolling off him again, but he tightened his hold on her.

"You see what, Kyra?"

"Calling this early is a way to find out if you slept alone last night." *Jesus, I sound jealous. I should be rejoicing—this is my ticket out of danger. And a way to get Jake out of Phil's sight.*

"She only wants to talk."

"Right," Kyra said, more annoyed with Jake than with Mia. How stupid men were. "Doesn't it seem strange she wants to talk all of a sudden after seeing you out with another woman?"

Silence.

He stroked her back. Kyra waited.

"You're probably right."

Oh, good. Now what? Kyra tried to push off Jake and again he held her to him.

"I'm going to call her back later to see what she wants. One way or another I need to hash things out with her. Do you understand?"

Ball's in my court now. "Yes and no."

"I love a straight answer."

If she let go, she'd have a much simpler life. *But the heart wants what the heart wants.* Had she replaced her gambling with him? Not something she wanted to get into right now. "You need to speak with her. You belong with her, not me." The tears welled in her eyes.

"Are you're walking away?"

"I'm not. I like you and I haven't had this much fun in years." Kyra smiled into his chest even as a tear slipped down her cheek. Once again she was on the short end of the stick.

He rolled them over. Now on top, Jake pushed up on one elbow and thumbed away her tears. Her heart screamed *choose me.* Her brain screamed *run.*

"I care for you, but I'm confused about Mia. I don't have a better answer for you."

How sick was she? With the threat of losing him looming over her, she wanted him even more. It was like putting more money into a losing machine.

"Kyra," he choked out.

"What?"

"I don't want to hurt you."

"Jake, if you stop now, I swear I'll kill you."

"You shouldn't threaten a cop."

"I'd get away with it. Justifiable homicide."

"Kyra…"

"How did we go from playful teasing to…dread, pain, rejection?"

"I should go."

"If you leave now, don't bother to come back."

She shoved him away and surged off the bed. She paced naked around the room. Her body was a heat missile filled with rage. Or was it jealousy?

"Please come back here."

"Why? Mia accomplished her goal. Since you received that damn phone call, your mind's been on her and not me."

"It's been on the both of you." His honesty killed her. He got up and walked to her with his arms held open for her. She stepped into them. "I told you in the beginning there were issues."

"Issues are one thing, leaving me hanging in the middle of the act is another."

"I wasn't leaving. You acted like you wanted me to go."

"When someone says 'I should go,' I get the impression they're leaving." She stepped away from him, resumed her pacing.

"I was giving you the opportunity to kick me out, but you didn't take it." She didn't have words.

"Kyra?"

"You're right, I didn't."

How did she say what was on her mind without scaring him away?

"Jake, I've come to care for you a lot more than I planned on, but with that said, I need to know that when you're with me—you're with me."

"I've always been with you. Last night, running into her blindsided me." Jake reached for her, but Kyra wasn't ready to settle. She'd probably regret what she was about to do for the rest of her life. What choice did she have? The red haze of anger encompassed her, blocked any rational decision making process. The hurt fueled her temper clouding her judgement. Now wasn't the time for decisions. Past experiences taught her that.

"You should leave. Go talk to her and take a couple of days to mull things over. When you have your head on straight, give me a call." Kyra reached for her robe. She started to put it on. She got an arm through one sleeve before Jake backed her up against the wall. The robe slid off. He put his hands around her bare waist. She wanted him. She looked up into his eyes, amazed when she saw hurt, not anger, in them.

"Don't push me away, Kyra, not now."

"I'm angry and confused. You weren't supposed to steal my heart and now..."

"I never intended to hurt you. And now...where do we go from here?" Jake's phone rang. He checked the number. "I have to take this. It's Dispatch."

Kyra watched her lover become the cop. She listened as he repeated a name and an address as he wrote them on his note pad. She wondered who had gone missing or, worse, who was dead?

"I'll check it out." He hung up, turning to Kyra. "I need to get going, but I'll call this afternoon. We'll finish this conversation tonight?"

Why am I complicating my life? It's the perfect opportunity to let Jake go—but I can't.

He raised her chin until she was staring him in the eye. "Kyra?"

"Talk to her first, before you call."

"I will."

Why did life have to be cruel? After Jake dressed and left, Kyra climbed back into bed, pulled the covers over her head. Last night Mia had seemed as shocked and hurt as Jake. This wasn't her fault either. All along, she'd envisioned Mia with warts, but instead she was glamorous. *Pity for Mia. Where the hell did that come from?*

Alone for the first time since she got her first look at Mia, dread plowed through her. It had shocked her to learn the woman with the body of a lingerie model was Mia. Tall, leggy, with midnight colored hair styled in a blunt-cut and vivid blue eyes, was her competition. For some reason she'd pictured Mia as a short blonde with a curvy figure.

Well, at least Jake didn't go for a stereotype. It lightened her mood some when she realized last night she wasn't a replica or a replacement.

* * * *

Jake left Kyra's condo and headed over to pick up Louie on the way to an address on the east side of town Dispatch had given him. The woman purported to have information about Saul Church, the man who'd disappeared a few weeks ago.

"What does she know?" Louie asked.

"Dispatch didn't say."

Jake drove into the apartment complex where Saul Church lived. Chances of finding Church alive were getting slimmer as each day passed. His gut told him Church was dead, but he needed to follow the leads. Chugging the rest of his coffee, he tossed the cup in a garbage can on his way out of the car.

"Which unit?" Louie asked.

"8E."

"Not much for conversation this morning?"

"No."

"Alrighty then," Louie said, knocking on the door.

"Mrs. Standish?" Jake asked when it opened.

"Yes."

"I'm Lieutenant Carrington. This is my partner, Sergeant Romanelli."

"Can I see some ID please?"

After she inspected their badges, she opened the door wider. "Come in. Sorry for getting you up early, but I wanted to talk to you before everyone else in the complex got up. I don't want to be tagged as nosy."

"I understand," Jake said, and did. Mrs. Standish was the go-to person in the neighborhood for any gossip. "What do you have for us, Mrs. Standish?"

"You don't want coffee or anything?"

"No ma'am, but thank you for asking." Jake made a show of taking out his notebook and pen to move her along.

"Sorry, Lieutenant, but I need my coffee before we begin." She walked into what Jake assumed was the kitchen. Once she came back out, they took seats in her living room. She started right in on her story.

"I mind my own business, but that day something made me get up from my soaps to look outside. I can't say it was a noise or anything..."

Jake figured this was going to be a long story. "Mrs. Standish, what did you see?"

"I'll tell this my own way, Lieutenant. Anyway, I see these three guys banging on Mr. Church's door. When he didn't answer, they kept on banging. It was obvious Church didn't answer his door. I was about to go out there to tell them he wasn't home when the door opened. I didn't see who opened it, but I assumed it was Saul. The men walked into the apartment and I went back to my soaps." Jake stared at her.

"Is that all you saw? Can you describe the men?"

"I'm not blind, son. Of course I can describe them. It's why I called the station." Jake watched her get up, head back into her kitchen. He was about to go after her when she returned with a note pad.

"Here we are. I wrote down everything because it didn't sit right with me, especially after they left with Mr. Church between them. Let me tell you, he looked scared."

Frustrated and ready to beat her with a stick, he asked, "You saw Saul Church leave with them? Are you sure?"

"I heard another commotion. I got up and went to the window again. That's when I saw them. And yes, I'm sure." It took great effort for Jake to hold his temper.

"And you never saw Mr. Church again, after that day?"

"No. You know, Lieutenant, I did call to the station that day, but the officer who answered asked if I saw a weapon. I didn't. His tone was insulting. I'm sure he put me down as a crank."

"I'm sorry for that. Why did you call back?" Jake asked.

"I saw his name in the paper this morning..." Mrs. Standish shrugged.

"I'm glad you did. For your safety, I'm not going to put your name in my report."

"I'm in danger?"

"I can't say, but take precautions."

"What kind of people are they?"

"I don't know."

If he was right, and the mob was involved, and he told her, she'd repeat it to anyone who'd listen and then she'd be dead. No, he wasn't going to tell her. He looked over at Louie. Louie nodded.

"Mrs. Standish, please don't talk to anyone about what you saw."

"I'm not stupid, Lieutenant."

Jake and Louie questioned her some more. When he was satisfied she had nothing else to give them, they stood. She walked them to the door.

"Thanks for your time."

Jake stood outside his vehicle and scanned the neighborhood. Over the top of the car, he said, "Will she or won't she?"

"She's already told anyone who'd listen."

"You're right," Jake said.

"What else is bothering you? You almost lost your temper back there. That's not like you," Louie pressed.

He told Louie what had happened between him, Kyra, and Mia.

"What are you going to do about the both of them?"

"Damn if I know," Jake said, frustrated. They drove the rest of the way to the station in silence.

* * * *

Back at the station, Jake requested the dispatcher's call sheets from the day Mr. Church went missing. It matched today's call sheet. Which was unfortunate, but Mrs. Standish was right—the dispatcher had put her call down as unfounded, no action needed. Was the dispatcher an idiot, or working with Stack? If they had acted sooner... It's hard to play the what if game. Jake walked into his captain's office and shut the door behind him.

"Problem?"

"Yes. There's a Missing Persons' case I'm working. A woman called in when she saw the man being escorted from his home. The dispatcher put her down as a crank." Jake handed McGuire the dispatcher's sheet.

McGuire studied it, took off his glasses, and pinched his nose. "How do you want to handle this?"

"I want to question the dispatcher without identifying the caller. She's in her seventies. She doesn't need any trouble."

"Trouble from the dispatcher?"

"No, the mob." Jake watched McGuire's forehead wrinkle.

"A hit?"

"Yep."

"Why?"

Jake updated Shamus about Church's gambling debts.

"Do we need to offer protection to the witness?"

"It'd be wise, but I'm not sure she'll take it. She's a tough old bird."

"You're overseeing the department, but why are you working this one?"

Again Jake filled McGuire in on Stack's case. He gave Shamus a minute to process the information.

"Have you questioned Stack?" McGuire asked.

"No, not yet. I can't say why—it's..." Jake stopped, stared and waited for McGuire to catch up.

"He's dirty?"

"I've got no proof. But where there's smoke...I need time to investigate the crime. See where it leads me."

"Keep me informed. When you're ready to question Stack, let me know. How's your department getting along?"

"It's going. Burke and Kraus are still looking for Spike. Lanoue and Brown closed the hit-and-run. They're still working the school shooting. I have no conflicts running both departments."

"Things are going to heat up if you're right about Stack and the mob."

Jake didn't doubt it—every cop's nightmare was turning in one of their own. He didn't believe in the "Blue Wall" when it pertained to a dirty cop. He hoped he could withstand the heat, yet again.

Chapter 22

The tower of files now covering his desk gave him a headache. Jake grunted at the boatload of paperwork he'd acquired. He needed to get his case reports done and handed in. It bothered him some that he'd put Stack in McGuire's line of sight, but he trusted McGuire to withhold judgment until all evidence was presented. McGuire would throw Stack to Internal Affairs for a full investigation if he found documentation pointing to his corruption. Jake's gut told him Carl Stack was as dirty as they came. An experienced investigator doesn't ignore a case unless he wants to. Decision made, Jake pulled all of Stack's physical case files himself for the last six months, heading off any talk that would have resulted from requesting them through proper channels. Tonight, over a beer, he'd review them.

He didn't leave the office until eight o'clock. It hit him on the way home that he hadn't called Kyra as promised. He speed dialed her as he drove. The call went to voicemail right away. After leaving a message he dialed Mia's number.

"Hello?"

"I see you called this morning." Controlled—that's what his voice sounded like to him. He wondered if it sounded that way to her.

"I did."

"What do you need?" *Nice, Jake.*

"Can we set up a date to talk?"

"Ah…has anything changed?" With gut clenched, a rush of nerves overtook his entire body. White knuckles gripped the steering wheel while his other hand pressed the phone closer to his ear. A sharp inhale filled his ears. Jake waited her out while his stomach rolled like a sea in a hurricane.

"I miss you," she whispered.

"You didn't answer the question," he said.

"Can we meet and talk?"

"If nothing has changed, why bother?" It struck him that he was being a hard-ass. *Why?* He couldn't say, it baffled even him.

"I didn't say it hadn't."

It isn't like Mia to play games. What's she up to?

"Jake?"

"When?" Mia's tactics hardened his heart instead of softening it. Call him a bastard, but he wasn't giving an inch. For a whole freaking month he couldn't get her off his mind. Was it Kyra? The look on her face this morning had torn him apart. He'd never meant to hurt her. Hadn't he warned her he was screwed up? It was the reason he hadn't promised her more. Was it an excuse to keep his distance?

"Tonight or tomorrow?"

"It's been a long day. I walked in the door minutes ago. Why don't we do this Monday night?" He didn't remember if he'd made plans with Kyra for tomorrow and he wasn't going to cancel on her if he had.

"You have plans with Kyra tomorrow?"

"I'm not going there, Mia. Do you want to meet on Monday night or not?"

"Yes."

"Seven thirty. Do you want me to come to your place or do you want to come to mine?"

"I'll be in the area Monday, why don't I come to your place."

Jake hung up. Tried Kyra's number again. The phone echoed in his ear as it rang. Was she ignoring him or out? And if so, with whom?

* * * *

Kyra hadn't been to the casino in over three weeks. She'd used super-human control to ignore her urges to go, but tonight they had won out. The machine she loved was occupied. She scanned over several others until she picked a new one and stuffed her money in. For some reason, she didn't get the normal rush. Her mind was on Jake and that bitch Mia. Why couldn't she leave Jake alone?

She slammed her palm on the spin button. As wheels fell into place, she didn't get the old thrill as the three red sevens appeared across the screen. Bells clanged as the machine announced she'd won the jackpot. Wasn't it always the way? You won when you didn't need the money. No excitement. What was wrong with her? Her adrenaline spiked now when she was with Jake. The irony wasn't lost on her.

The phone vibrated in her pocket. Taking it out, she saw Jake's number and pressed the ignore button. She wasn't interested in what he had to say. He didn't want to continue their relationship, she was sure it was the reason he was calling. She played while she waited for her message light to come on. When it did, she hit play and listened. He apologized for not calling today and explained he'd only gotten home from work a short time ago. He asked if she wanted to do something tonight or tomorrow. Well, at least he didn't break up with her on the phone. Tomorrow wasn't good. She had Trevor all day. She'd planned to take him to the beach.

Tonight, if there wasn't any traffic, she'd be home in an hour and fifteen minutes. Had he talked to Mia yet? Kyra decided to call him in the morning. It wasn't good to be available every time he called. Easy, conflict resolved. She played for another half hour. Boredom set in before long. She cashed out, then headed home earlier than planned.

Her life had changed. Should she thank Jake or blame him? It wasn't long ago she'd break out in a sweat if she didn't go to the casino. Now it held no draw. Or was it Phil and his corpses that had turned her off to gambling? How many bodies before she got caught? She'd never be able to develop a long-term relationship with Jake while she continued to burn bodies for Phil. A lightning bolt slashed through her head as a headache formed.

* * * *

Weary, limbs heavy, mind zinging around like a tornado, Jake jumped into the shower, washing away the day's stress. He'd head over to Kyra's now that he had his second wind. How ironic was life—he, the player, being played. Never before had he wanted a long-term relationship, and now he wanted one with two women. Different in appearance but the same in their core where it counted. Good-hearted women. Kyra had snuck up on him. It'd been a mutual attraction. A distraction, she called it. He was looking for a friend and found much more in her. Warm, compassionate, funny, a wonderful lover with many secrets. He didn't detect a mean bone in her body. Kyra's lack of faith in him, along with her friendship with Phil—if that's what it was—held him back. If she lied, and she worked for Phil, his career was in the garbage. Even if she hadn't lied, his instincts told him she wasn't telling him the whole truth. And if she was such a big gambler why hadn't he witnessed it? Had she given it up? How deep was she into the mob? That was a conversation he still needed to have with her.

Then there was Mia. In an instant she'd stolen his heart, set it ablaze, then a second later she'd ripped it to shreds. Could he forgive her? What changed her mind? Her temper seemed to match his—was that good or bad?

He'd have to pick one, but who? When and if push came to shove? It was Mia. Murder was much easier to figure out than women.

He climbed out of the shower, dried off and picked up his phone to check for new messages. Damn, Kyra hadn't returned his calls. With his finger poised over the redial button, he debated his course of action then tossed the phone on the bed. An in-person visit was called for. He dressed. He had to try to convince Kyra he wasn't out to hurt her, he only needed time to sort through everything. The clock on the nightstand burned the time into his brain in big red numbers: 9:00. Not too late for a Saturday night visit. Hunger pangs reminded him he hadn't eaten lunch or dinner today. He made a quick sandwich, turned out the lights, and headed to his garage. The bell interrupted his steps as he walked through the connecting door. Did Kyra have the same idea he had? He walked to the front door and looked out the peephole.

What the hell?

* * * *

Seven o'clock on a Saturday night and Phil didn't have any plans. Kyra invaded every one of his waking moments. He hadn't talked to or seen her for over a week. Tempted, he stopped short of knocking someone off to see her. How bizarre was that? The girl wasn't interested in him—but he found her intriguing. He'd call her on Monday because he didn't want to seem pathetic. Why should he tell her he was alone on what people called 'date night'? Was she out with the cop? His cell phone rang. "Yes?"

"It's Carl Stack."

"Why are you calling me?"

"We have a problem. We need to meet now."

"What kind of problem?"

"I don't want to discuss it on the phone. I can be there in an hour."

"No, not here." Where? He racked his brain, then chose. "There's a pizza place on Route 2 before Foxrun. We'll have privacy there. One hour, Carl." Phil slammed down the phone. *Damn idiots, can't anyone do their jobs right? This had to be about Kyra's cop. Why did Carl sound scared? Well, there's one way to find out.* He reached for his intercom, hit Angelo's extension.

"What's up?" Angelo asked, walking into the library.

"Carl asked for a meet. The little shit sounded scared. We're going to meet him at Bruno's place in an hour."

"Is Carrington on his back?"

"He didn't say. Carl doesn't scare easy—something's up."

Cheered at the need to do away with Carrington, Phil leaned into the chair. The library was his favorite room. High-back chairs cushioned for comfort were upholstered in burgundy and blue. The reading lights sat on the tables by the chairs to illuminate the books he loved. And the blazing fireplace kept him warm on a cool night. In prison, he'd learned the benefit of reading. They'd helped him keep his sanity and taught him much. Angelo had no penchant for books. He preferred those stupid video games.

* * * *

Phil frowned when he walked into the restaurant. Carl Stack had beaten him there. He must have been on the road when he phoned. Stack stood with hand extended as Phil and Angelo approached his table. Phil took Stack's sweaty hand but didn't linger. After he let go of it, Phil wiped his hand on his trousers.

Phil didn't ask Angelo to sit. He continued to stare at Stack as he took a seat across from him. Angelo walked to the back of the restaurant. After checking out the place, Angelo returned and took up a position by the front door.

A typical pizza joint. Old-world with red-and-white checkered tablecloths, empty Chianti bottles sporting candles with wax dripping down their sides, and an old jukebox on each table where for a quarter your favorite songs filled the place—nothing recorded after nineteen seventy.

Not standing on ceremony, Phil asked, "Okay, Carl. I'm here. What's this all about?"

"Jake Carrington."

Phil's stomach dropped to his feet. If Kyra had betrayed him... "What about him?"

"He's been assigned as my acting lieutenant for Missing Persons."

"And?" Patience for this idiot was limited.

"And he's reviewed all our cases and decided to work Church's case because, and I quote, 'I seem too busy to be working it.' The bastard's got a tough reputation, Phil. He's a black-and-white guy, no gray. He gets results."

"What caught his attention?" Phil was trying to look at this from a logical standpoint. Sweat poured down Carl's face. "Carl?"

"That's the point, I wasn't working it. I was trying to let it cool off before going back to it and declaring the trail had gone cold."

Phil didn't respond as he stared Stack down. This Carrington fellow was smart, from everything Phil had heard about him. Carrington had probably figured out Carl's involvement. Would the trail lead back to him, thus endangering him and his operation? For Carl's safety, he hoped not.

"Were there any witnesses to the incident?"

"No. The missing person report was filed by his mother. When I put the file together who knew they'd give us a temporary lieutenant. Christ, he's running two departments now. Where he finds the time is beyond me."

"Is this the way you do everything, Carl? Half-assed?" Cops were either gung-ho or they were lazy shits who turned a blind eye for a dollar. He hated both kinds. "What's he going to find?"

Carl shrugged. "I don't know. Jake's a good investigator. His close rate is eighty-five percent or better. If anyone can find Church, Carrington can."

"I don't understand what you're talking about." Phil smiled.

"You asked me to—"

"Don't go there."

"But—"

"No buts. Start doing your job, and you shouldn't have any problems with him."

"I'll ask, though it's a longshot he'd give it back to me."

"Well, it's in your best interest to convince him to, if you understand my meaning. Make sure nothing comes back on me, or you and I will have a problem." Phil nodded to Angelo. Ang came over to the table as Phil stood.

Stack started to stand. Phil leaned over and pushed him into his seat, then whispered into his ear, "Remember, I don't know you or Church."

Angelo scanned the parking lot from the doorway. When he was satisfied, he nodded to Phil. Angelo had the door of the limo open by the time Phil reached it.

"Is he trying to set us up?"

"No. He's a screw-up. Now he's got to deal with someone who takes his job seriously. What a small world. Stack may be the one who puts Carrington onto us, not Kyra. If he does, we may need to arrange an accident for him."

"Is that wise, Phil?"

"Why, because Carl's a cop? He's dirty."

"It doesn't matter. If someone offs him, the cops will come after us with a vengeance."

"Cops like Stack flip faster than any criminal. They understand how the system works and they'd sell out their mothers to save their own hides. Our job is to make sure he doesn't flip, agreed?"

"Agreed. I won't let it get that far. You seem calm about this new development."

"I'm not, but it'll give me a chance to see how Carrington operates. Then I'll decide his fate too."

Chapter 23

Jake continued to curse as he looked out the peephole. What the hell was she doing here? There's one way to find out. He opened the door but didn't invite her in.

"I'm sorry, Mia, you caught me on my way out." Brigh inched over to Mia, sniffing her leg. "Give the dog a few minutes before you pet her. She's skittish."

"I was in the neighborhood…and that's a lie. I drove by, hoping to catch you. Do you have five minutes? How cute." Mia gestured to Brigh. "When did you get her?"

"A couple of weeks ago. Mia, I don't have time to talk now." He wasn't giving an inch. He wasn't prepared.

"Oh…" She bent and scratched Brigh behind the ears.

Christ, she'd started crying. The dog, with a quirk of her head, accused him of causing it. Jake hated when a woman cried and it wasn't like Mia to do it. He stepped back as he opened the door wider to let her in. She pushed past him, her eyes fixed on the open door to the garage.

"I'm alone."

"She seems nice. Are you seeing her again?"

Her tears had dried up. "Who I see is none of your business, but the answer's yes."

"She's pretty."

"She is." Jake wasn't offering any encouragement. He turned his wrist up and checked the time. It was close to nine thirty. "I have to get going, I'll see you Monday night."

"Jake—" She choked up again.

He waited.

"Can't you give me five minutes?"

"I'm late. I don't want to keep her waiting."

"Is this how you treat someone you supposedly love? I stopped by to talk—to tell you that I love you and want to try again."

"And I love you—but if I recall, it wasn't enough for you." Why was he being cruel? Did he want to push her away? Hell if he knew.

"I'd like to start over. To be honest, I'm miserable without you."

"More than a month has gone by, Mia, and now you decide to do this after you see me out with another woman? I'd have been more apt to believe you if this conversation had taken place before last night's encounter." Brigh hadn't left Mia's side. *So much for loyalty.*

"I've been trying to work up the courage to see you. This has nothing to do with what's her name—Kyra?"

He walked around her to sit in one of his living-room chairs. Mia took a seat on the couch. Brigh choose to comfort Mia and laid her head on her lap. "You don't have a type, do you?"

"A type? No, I go for the person."

"It's like dating yourself, with her coloring."

"Believe what you want, but this conversation is useless. And, I repeat, I'm late." He started to stand. Brigh lifted her head and looked from Jake to Mia.

"Jake, please, a little help here. It was hard to swallow my pride and show up tonight. How do you want to do this?"

"I'm not doing this until Monday night. And if you keep pushing, not even then." Did he or didn't he want her back in his life? Wasn't she the one he'd been pining over? It took everything he had in him not to back down. He was being a hard-ass but she'd forced the issue. No one was going to lead him around by the balls. Love was one thing, to be played, another.

"It's going to kill me knowing you're with her."

"Damn it, Mia. You're the one who walked out."

"You gave me an ultimatum."

"You walked—"

The doorbell rang. Brigh ran to her bed. Jake got up, walked over to the door and opened it without looking through the peephole. Standing there with a bottle of vodka was Kyra. Her smile dropped.

* * * *

Kyra saw Mia standing in the living room, noticing the tears run down her face. Kyra looked back at Jake. He reached for her, but she evaded him and turned away. She ran down his steps. When she reached her car, he was right there beside her.

"It's not what it looks like."

"Oh? What does it look like?" Jake put his hands on the roof of the car, enclosing Kyra as he stared into her eyes.

"Kyra, I made plans to talk to her on Monday. She showed up here unannounced when I was on my way over to your house."

"We didn't have plans." She couldn't look at him, and started to turn away.

Jake took hold of her shoulders and inched her around to face him. He cupped her chin in his hand to keep her from leaving. "You weren't answering your phone. I didn't like the way I left you this morning."

"I was out." *He looks guilty as sin, why? He never promised me anything.* Kyra was torn. She should be jumping for joy, that it was about to come to an end.

"I still wanted to see you. Before you rang the bell, I'd asked her to leave."

"I don't care." It was taking all her willpower to hold back any more tears.

"Kyra—"

"Figure out what you want, before you call me. I can't play this game right now. I have too much baggage of my own. Good night." It would've been more effective if he hadn't still had her pinned between him and her car.

"Kyra, I'm not trying to hurt you. Come in. I'll get rid of her. Please."

He'd captured her heart. She wanted him, but now was the perfect opportunity for her to leave and stop all the questions. To uncomplicate her life. If Jake dumped her she'd only have two left to deal with. She'd quit her job, get rid of Phil, and the divorce got rid of Tom, and—and what? Would Jake investigate her? Find her connection to Phil if she left town without a word?

She must have taken too long to answer.

"Kyra?" Jake leaned in, whispered into her ear. "Kyra, don't leave like this, please."

"I don't want to make a fool of myself." Her voice broke. "I'm fighting to keep it together." She'd heard the hurt in his voice, the plea. *Christ, what should I do?*

"I'll send Mia away and come to your house."

"Why not talk to her and get it over with?"

"I'm not ready. I need a friend to talk to."

"Only talk?" She tried to smile, but failed to hide the pain.

"Yes. You run the game."

"Game, huh? I haven't had possession yet."

"You don't realize it, but you've had it all along."

"I'll go home. I don't want to get into a clawing match."

"I'll see you in a little while." When she turned away from him, he spun her back and kissed her. "Kyra, I don't have the right at this moment, but I want you to understand that I care for you. Thank you for being there for me."

"Christ, this is screwed up. I'll see you at my house."

He helped her into her car. She watched Jake in her rearview mirror as she drove away. She noticed Mia in the doorway. Had she eavesdropped? How much had she heard?

* * * *

"I guess you didn't have plans with her after all?"

"Let's get back to our conversation. Are you coming over on Monday night?"

He watched her struggle with her answer. "I want to, but from what I saw, it doesn't look like there's room for me in your life."

"Don't make a decision until we talk."

Her eyes were filled with tears. What? Does she turn them on and off at will? How had he managed to reduce two women to tears in one night? All he wanted to do was the right thing. It was never his intention to hurt either one of them.

"I'll call you on Monday. I can't do this right now."

Jake and Brigh walked her to the door. Together they waited until she got in her car and drove away. He shut the door and leaned his head against it for a moment.

"Well, Brigh, that's Mia. What do you think?" The dog walked over to her bed and started to gnaw on her chew toy. He'd get no help from her. Jake headed into the garage. Why had Mia shown up unannounced? Did she want to reconcile or was she playing games with him? God knew he wasn't up to any.

* * * *

Jake knocked on Kyra's door fifteen minutes later. Her puffy eyes greeted him. He clutched her to his chest. It tore at his heart to see the pain he'd caused her.

"I'm sorry."

"This isn't anyone's fault."

He eased his way through the door, never letting go of her as he closed and locked it. "This has been a tough weekend. Why don't we do something tomorrow?"

"I have Trevor tomorrow, but I have to have him home by seven. We can get together after I drop him off."

"Do you want me to leave?"

"Why'd you come if you didn't plan to stay?"

"I pushed myself on you tonight." He shrugged.

"You didn't. I wanted to see you. Do you want to talk?"

"Nothing was resolved. I don't understand why she stopped in unannounced after we had made plans for Monday. We didn't discuss anything. I had asked her to leave right before you rang the bell. I didn't lie. I do want to talk about you though."

"Why don't we go out for a drink or two?"

"I'm not in the mood for a drink. I want to stay home."

He grabbed her, kissed her hard. He ran one hand up and down her back as the other hand held her head to his. He needed this woman tonight. Not for talk but that was what he was going to do. He needed answers. He stared into her eyes and led her to the couch.

"Kyra," he choked out.

"Did you only come over for sex tonight?"

He released her, stalked around the room. "No—yes—I don't know. I knew I wanted to be with you. I didn't plan any further than that."

"Come into the kitchen. I'll fix you a drink."

"I don't want a drink. I want you." He sat down on the couch, rested his head in his hands. He laughed a bitter laugh. "Christ, I've never been this twisted up in my entire life."

* * * *

She sat down beside him and drew him into her arms. She'd no intention of letting him leave. Kyra knew he needed her. She brushed her hand over his hair as she pressed her lips to his forehead and whispered in his ear.

"Come to bed."

"Kyra, I didn't mean...I don't want to use..."

"Shush, come."

With Kyra leading the way to her bedroom Jake followed. She made love to him the same way he'd made love to her on their first night, with a gentle tenderness. It didn't lack passion, but it was comforting. Accepting. Later she held him while he slept, not able to get her mind off Mia.

Why had she shown up tonight when he'd asked her not to? Jake had told Kyra that he cared for her. Was he trying to make Mia jealous? Had Mia even heard him say it? The moment had no clarity except for the pain crushing her heart. Damn. Against all that was smart, Kyra had gone and fallen in love with him. Sleep eluded her. Instead she watched while he did. Both times he had stayed with her, he tossed and turned, his dreams haunted. If she gave him to Mia she'd have smooth sailing ahead. Deep in her heart she understood she was the wrong woman for Jake though she didn't want to walk away.

It wasn't a matter of could she, it was a matter of safety. Both his and hers.

Chapter 24

Her mind active she never fell into sleep. Kyra watched Jake jerk awake before he relaxed into his surroundings.

"How is it possible you're awake before me?" he asked, one eye open.

"It's still early, go back to sleep."

His eyes twinkled down at her. "I don't want to sleep."

"Let me guess what it is you want to do." Kyra had come to a decision during the long night. And though it hurt, she knew she would do the right thing by Jake.

"Is that an offer?" He rolled over, taking her with him.

"Oh, you don't want breakfast?" she asked, her eyes flirting under her lashes as she tilted her head up.

He laughed. "Only if you're breakfast."

"Wow, you're in luck. I am."

An hour and a half later they sat at the kitchen table. Kyra enjoyed watching Jake cook. "I could get used to this. I hate cooking."

"I find it relaxing, besides, I like to eat." Jake dished out eggs and bacon onto her plate.

"This is good. I have to leave here by nine thirty to pick up Trevor."

"You have plenty of time. It's only eight o'clock. Are you kicking me out?"

"No. No. Eat, relax. I have plenty of time to shower and dress."

"What are you doing with him today?"

"We're heading to the beach. I promised him."

"You don't want me to go with you?"

Kyra played with her eggs. Moved them around her plate. How did she answer him? She picked up a slice of crispy bacon and crunched on it. All the while, his eyes penetrated hers. "No, I don't, Jake. Right now Trevor doesn't need any new people in his life."

"Relax, I understand. If you're up to it we can do something tonight."

He picked up their dishes and brought them to the sink and started washing them. Kyra walked up behind him, wrapped her arms around him and laid her head against his chest.

* * * *

Trevor's excitement over being at the beach had Kyra's head spinning. She tossed the blanket on top of the sand. She reached into her tote bag, took out his toys and spread them out on it as she watched him run to the water's edge. She pulled her book from her bag but was afraid to take her eyes off him. Every few minutes, Trevor would run back to the blanket to show her some creature or other treasure from the sea.

The routine got her dizzy. He sat down on the blanket after one such trip and started talking.

"Mom, why doesn't Grandma like you?"

"Sometimes grown-ups put their noses where they don't belong. Grandma puts her nose in the wrong place all the time. Why?"

"Well, she and Daddy got into a fight about you."

"Trevor, it's not polite to eavesdrop on someone's conversation." Boy, she wished she'd been a fly on the wall.

Trevor ignored her. "Grandma called Daddy stupid. She said she couldn't believe how he pushed himself on you, and in front of a cop." He took a deep breath.

"Trev, I'm sure your grandmother would be upset if she knew you were telling me this."

"I don't care. She's mean." *From the mouths of babes.* Kyra didn't correct him because he was right.

"Mom, what are charges?"

Oh boy. "Sometimes—when someone gets in trouble with the police—they charge them with whatever crime they committed. Why?"

"Because Daddy asked Grandpa to make the charges go away. Grandpa shouted at Daddy, 'Not this time.'" *If the bastard tries to get the charges dropped, I'll sue the whole freaking system. Calm down. Protecting Trev is all that counts.*

"Then Grandpa cursed." Trevor giggled. "Do you want me to tell which one?"

"No, Trevor, just because an adult curses, it doesn't make it right. You're still not allowed to say the word, understand?"

"Yes."

"Good, now go play."

"I'm not finished, Mom. Grandma yelled at Daddy for a long time too. She said something already hit the papers. Daddy said he was sorry, he was drunk. Grandpa told him it wasn't an excuse. Grandpa yelled at him the way Daddy yells at me sometimes."

It was wrong, but she didn't tell Trevor to stop this time.

"Grandpa and Grandma were both yelling at Daddy and forgot I was there."

"I'm sure. Sometimes grown-ups get angry and they fight, but they still love each other."

"Not always. You and Daddy don't love each other anymore, do you?"

"No, we don't, but we both love you. You understand, Trev?"

"Yes." He stood. "I still love you too." He surprised her with a kiss and a hug before he ran down to the water again.

Kyra played the conversation over in her mind. She wanted to ask Trevor more questions but he didn't deserve to be put in the middle any more than he already was. One thing was for sure—Tom had to be pissed at his parents. Well, it was about time they made him take responsibility for his actions.

On the ride home from the beach, Trevor asked, "What's cus...od...dee?"

"Do you mean custody?"

"Yeah, that's it. Grandpa said Daddy blew the custody thing. Grandpa was mad because of all the people he had taken care of to make it work for Daddy."

Interesting. "Daddy and I are divorcing, Trevor. Who you get to live with has custody of you. It means to take care of you. I want custody of you and your father also wants it."

"I want to live with you, Mommy." It warmed her heart when he called her Mommy.

"Me too, Trev. When we go to court, you can tell the judge what you want, okay?"

* * * *

At six fifty-nine she dropped Trevor off to an annoyed Tom. He tried to get her to come in, but Jake's voice sounded in her head.

"Hey, buddy. Did you have a good time?"

"Yes, we went to the beach today, Daddy."

"Great, Trev. Be a good boy and go to your room. I need to speak with your mother."

Trevor threw his arms around Kyra and kissed her goodbye before heading to his room. As soon as Trevor was gone, Tom started in on her.

"Why don't you come in for a few minutes?"

"I'm not coming in. I already told you I'm not going to be alone with you. What do you want to talk about?"

"Do you always have to be such a bitch, Kyra?"

"Safety first, Tom."

"All of a sudden you're afraid of me?" he spat out.

Incredible, the guy's an ass. "Let me spell it out for you. YOU. TRIED. TO. RAPE. ME. Don't play innocent."

"It was a mistake."

"Oh, you bet it was. Good night."

"We need to make decisions about Trevor. You know—school, shopping, vacations?"

"The court will decide that for us."

"You bitch. Nothing's changed."

"We'll see. Good night."

The door slammed behind her.

Chapter 25

There were benefits to starting your morning with great sex. Kyra started the day energized. She'd kicked Jake out around seven then hopped into the shower before heading in to work.

"Don't you look well rested," Dina said.

"I'm good. Busy weekend."

"So, you're still seeing Jake?"

"I am." The phone rang.

"It's your line, Kyra."

"Okay, I'll take it in my office." She walked in, closed her door, settled herself into her chair and grabbed the phone. "Hello."

"Good morning."

Crap! "Morning, Phil." *What does he want now?*

"I haven't heard from you in a while."

Icicles jabbed at her spine. "Hi." She knew he hadn't called to talk. Why didn't he cut the bull and get to it?

Phil laughed without mirth setting her nerve endings on edge. "Still talking in one-syllable words I see."

He's baiting you, pull it together. "I was taught to speak when I have something of value to say."

"It's always smart to hold your tongue. I heard Jake Carrington is now heading Missing Persons. Is that correct?"

If he asked the question, he already knew the answer. "Yes, he mentioned it in passing."

"What case is he working on?"

"Phil, I haven't a clue. He was annoyed and passed a comment how he now had the department, nothing else, no case names, nothing."

"Hard to believe a man wouldn't discuss his job. What do you talk about?"

"I'm not comfortable with this conversation."

"I want to make sure I'm not the topic of conversation."

What a conceited bastard. Like I'd give Jake a reason to scrutinize me.

"I don't discuss you at any time with anyone, Phil."

"Oh, curiosity got the better of me. Come to dinner this week."

She wasn't expecting this invitation. "I'm booked the rest of the week, but open tonight." That should send him scrambling, she hoped.

"Tonight's good. Shall we say seven?"

Damn it, there was no way out of this. She'd need a good excuse to continue to date Jake. Because the subject wasn't closed as far as Phil was concerned. She couldn't figure out if she was more scared for Jake or herself. "Okay."

"I see you were at the casino last Saturday. Did you enjoy yourself?"

A warning bell rang in her brain. "I didn't, Phil. I guess that phase of my life's over. Or at least the urge isn't as strong."

Joe Dillon, that bastard. Now that's one body I'd do for free.

* * * *

Jake stopped in at the cemetery unannounced to ask Kyra to lunch. Over the meal he hoped he'd be able to pull more information out of her about Lucci. He chatted a few minutes with Dina to catch up on the gossip. She always knew what was going at the station, even before he did. And for someone who didn't work there, her information was always on the money. How she got it baffled him.

"Go on back, she won't mind," Dina said.

"This is a nice surprise." Kyra stood near one of the ovens with the door open. The heat blasted into the room as the roaring sound of the fire echoed through his head. "You don't mind that I dropped by, do you?" He closed the door behind him.

"No, not at all, if you don't mind that I have to continue to work while you talk. It's a busy day."

Kyra walked over to a door, opened it, and rolled out a cardboard coffin on a church truck. He watched as she put two cardboard rollers spaced about three feet apart on the oven floor. Kyra wheeled the body to the opening, pushed it off the stand and onto the rollers into the chamber, then she closed the oven and readjusted the timer.

Jake flinched at the ease in which she did her job. He followed her into the processing room where she turned on the processor—the grinding noise pieced his ears. The idea of bones crushing away in the machine gave him pause. "I hoped you had time to join me for lunch." Not that he was hungry now.

"Can I give you a call? I'm processing this one now, and got another one in the other chamber. Besides, didn't we make a date for tomorrow?"

"I wanted to see you. Pick your brain about the case I'm working on."

"What case?"

"The Missing Persons' case, the gambler I spoke about?"

"I don't see how I can help you." She turned her head to look at him.

"I need to understand the habits of a gambler. I'm not asking to insult you," he added quickly. "I understand you're not gambling anymore. It'd help me to get into his mind—understand the victim, know the killer," Jake said.

"I don't have a problem with helping you. Where did he gamble?"

"He gambled on everything." Jake spoke over the irritating noise.

"Ah, there's a big difference between us then. I only gambled at the casino. I don't even buy lottery tickets. I guess it was the lure of the machines, the bells and whistles."

At last Kyra hit the stop button. The room fell into an eerie silence except for the roar of the ovens in the other room.

"Is Church's way of gambling any different, I mean—from the way you did it?"

"I can only speak about myself, Jake." He noticed how she squared her shoulders for a fight. It wasn't his plan to make her uncomfortable, but he'd hoped this line of questioning might lead him to Lucci.

He walked over to her, ran his hands up and down her arms, looked into her eyes. God, he wanted this woman and wasn't that sick, in this room of all places?

"Your gambling doesn't bother me, Kyra, unless it got you in with the wrong people." The phone in the processing room rang.

Her shift in mood landed like a punch in his gut as she turned away from him to answer it. After a few minutes she hung up.

"It's a crazy day, Jake. This one won't finish before eleven and the other one by noon. Now I have one that will arrive about eleven. I won't be able to break for lunch. I can't leave the ovens unattended. Why don't you ask your questions now?"

"I don't want to bother you while you're working."

"It's not a bother, and this way my morning will go faster. Shoot."

"If you owed someone money and didn't have it, what would you do?"

"I'm not proud of this. I used my son's college fund and my 401k. Did the guy have assets?"

"We didn't find any. No one's seen him in three weeks. He might've skipped to avoid his debt?"

"I can't answer those questions, for two reasons. First, what were his gambling habits? And second, who did he owe money to and how much?"

"I understand. Your friend Phil's a bookie. Well, actually not a bookie, per se, but he runs the gambling in the state." If he wasn't looking at her he would've missed the flinch. He'd hit a sore spot.

"I didn't know. He's never offered me his bookie services."

"What other services was he offering you?"

Kyra tightening her fists at her side didn't get by him. He'd stepped over a line. "That's damn insulting. You don't deserve an answer but I'll give you one anyway. As I've told you before, Phil and I are friends. I'm sorry you don't like him, but how did we go from your missing guy to this?"

"Your friendship with him doesn't add up. How did you meet him?"

"Not to get an attitude here but what business is it of yours?"

"I'm trying to look out for you."

"I don't need looking after. He doesn't run the casino. I took out a loan and paid off the casino. I've had no business dealings with Phil."

"Have you seen him lately?"

Kyra laughed at him. *I guess I deserve that.* "Are you jealous?"

"Yes, but that doesn't have anything to do with the question."

"It certainly does. What's going to happen tonight when you see Mia?"

Damn her. "You haven't answered my question," he said, annoyed.

"You haven't answered mine."

"Because I don't have an answer for you."

"You can't do any better than that?" Her attitude had him wanting to shake and kiss her at the same time. "At least be honest, Jake. It's Mia all the way. Without realizing it, you've been using me to make Mia jealous."

How had she turned the table on him? "Christ, no, where did that come from?"

"For the last three weeks all I've heard was how much you loved Mia. Now that she's back in the picture you're confused. What's up?"

"I'll say it again. You're a tough one. I enjoy being with you, Kyra. Are you going to tell me there's nothing more than friendship between us?"

"I can't tell you a lie. But don't mistake excellent sex for anything more than what it was."

"Don't be insulting." Why was she deliberately trying to piss him off?

"I'm not, I'm being honest. You're afraid to face Mia because you don't want to be hurt again."

He stared at her. Kyra had hit the a sore spot. A knock interrupted the argument.

"I hate to interrupt, but your eleven o'clock cremation's here. I sent the funeral director to the garage." Dina looked back and forth between the two of them before she eased out of the room.

"We'll talk tomorrow after your session with Mia."

Jake stared after Kyra as she walked out the connecting door to the garage. He left without another word.

* * * *

Kyra pulled up to Phil's gate at six fifty-five. Once again, the guard searched her car before clearing her to continue on her way to the house. She drove to within feet of the front door and parked. Before getting out, she checked her mirror to make sure her makeup was intact. Satisfied, she climbed out and rang the bell.

She followed Ang to the dining room where Phil was already seated at the head of the table.

Phil stood and waited for her to come to him. Surprised when he kissed her on the lips, a shudder of revulsion passed through her. "Have a seat. Maria will start serving."

Maria brought in the first course, a salad and Italian bread with olive oil and herbs to accompany it, instead of butter. Kyra grabbed a hunk of bread, swiped it through the oil, and placed a piece in her mouth, figuring she'd let Phil steer the conversation.

"Kyra, besides missing you, I need to discuss Jake Carrington."

Hoping she showed no reaction, she replied, "Why?"

"I find him interesting, don't you?"

"I do, but for different reasons."

He nearly spit his wine out as Kyra smiled at him. "Oh, how you amuse me." But he got serious fast. "I want everything you have on him, understand?"

She stared at him. *Why did I accept his dinner invitation? It was a bad idea.*

"What do you want to know?"

He'd poured her wine. Sipping it, she studied him over the rim of her glass and continued when he didn't answer. "He's a gentleman. I enjoy his company."

"Stop the bullshit." It surprised her when he spoke to her in such a harsh manner. "What cases is he working on and how far has he gotten with them."

"I was serious when I told you he doesn't talk to me about work. He mentioned, in passing, he's overseeing Missing Persons and is working on one of their cases but his main focus is still Homicide."

"What case in Missing Persons?"

"I don't know." Maria walked into the room and picked up their empty salad dishes. Phil waited until she left. They sat in silence. A few minutes later, Maria returned with their dinners. Steak for her. Fish for Phil.

She'd lost her appetite. Though she tried to keep her hands still, the tremors continued. Folding them together, she held them on her lap under the table to hide her fear. The way Phil looked at her made her skin crawl, as if a thousand tiny bugs slithered over her flesh, devouring her inch by inch. She resisted the urge to scratch. *Calm down, Kyra.*

"Eat. Did Carrington tell you who he was working with in Missing Persons?"

"Yes, he mentioned it. Why?"

"No reason. You're sure he never said the name of the case he's working?"

"I'm positive. Is it a name I should know?"

"No." He put a piece of fish in his mouth while he continued to study her.

"Who told you I was at the casino Saturday?"

"It's not important, but I'm sure you can figure it out."

"Why is my being there important?" She was pushing and knew she shouldn't.

"Everything about the people who work for me is important." She cut into her steak and took a bite—*Freak this, I'm in deep trouble here.*

"How seriously are you involved with Carrington?"

"It's not going to be an issue going forward." She frowned.

"Why?"

"He's meeting tonight with the woman he says he's in love with."

"I see." He tapped his fingers on the table. It drove her crazy. "And that's it? If he decides to start dating her again, you're going to back away?"

"Yes." She answered his questions when she could with one word, knowing it irritated him. Petty, yes, but who cared? Certainly not her.

"You continue to surprise me. It's obvious you like him. Why give up without a fight?"

She took another sip of wine while she formulated her answer. "He loves this woman, not me. Why fight to stay with a man who doesn't love me?" She heard the strain in her voice, but tilted her head and quirked her eyebrow.

"Yes, why indeed? Well, it's not important. You'll tell me what happens when you decide? Dessert?"

"No thanks, I'm full."

"It's not like you not to enjoy your food. Does it bother you, Jake's meeting this woman?"

"Yes and no."

"I see."

She was sure he did, and against her better judgment, she asked the next question as they got up from the table. "Why are you interested in him, Phil?"

Snakes crawled over her flesh as he wrapped his fingers around her neck and slammed her up against the wall, his hand squeezing the air from her lungs—his other gripped her upper left arm. His strength overpowered her. Two of him appeared in front of her as her vision blurred.

"Phil..." she struggled. "I can't...breathe."

"I told you when you agreed to work for me you were not to ever question me. What about that you didn't you understand?"

"I'm sorry, I was making conversation," she choked out, fighting for air.

"I don't like to be lied to, Kyra. There will be consequences if you lie to me."

"I haven't lied to you about anything." Her voice was hoarse. He still held on to her neck but loosened his grip as he searched her eyes, his onyx ones piercing hers.

"Why don't you admit you love the guy?"

"Because I'm not sure I do."

"Then you're lying to yourself."

He let go of her. She rubbed her neck as she gasped for air. Her mind was frozen. Angry, scared out of her wits, all she wanted to do was leave and never see Phil again. What was she going to do if he left a bruise? Jake would pick right up on it. Question her about it.

The maid walked into the room, inquired if they wanted coffee served. Kyra didn't want coffee—Christ, she wanted to get the hell out of there. She'd seen something in Phil's eyes—not to be dramatic, but it wasn't human. If she wasn't mistaken, her fear fed him. It excited him. How sick was he?

"We'll have it in the parlor. After you."

This man's nuts. He's acting like everything's normal. Didn't he just grab my neck in his hands and almost choke the life out of me? She took the chair by the couch, not wanting to sit next to him. An escape route was what she'd need if he reached for her again. Scoping out the room, there wasn't a chance she'd escape alive. Angelo was never far away, but she understood he'd never help her.

Her brain misfired, her vision blurred, her concentration fading as she forced herself to sit through coffee and bullshit. Phil eventually brought the conversation back to business.

"I'll have another body for you by the end of the week. What day is good?"

"I never get too much notice. It's best to call ahead. Tomorrow is a light day. I'd be able to do it around two or three."

"I'll call if that works out."

Dismissing me. Thank God. He stood—so did she. Phil walked her to the front door, leaned over, and whispered in her ear. "That was a small demonstration of my strength. Don't play me, Kyra, or you'll be dead along with your son." He stepped back and said, "Good night."

Racing to the car, she jumped in and drove a little too fast down the driveway. Escape was her single goal. Phil threatened her son. *Oh God, what have I gotten myself into?* She'd kill Phil if he touched Trevor.

* * * *

"Was that necessary?" Angelo asked.

"Yes, you heard the whole conversation?"

"I did. She wasn't lying to you."

"No, but I don't like the way things are going in Wilkesbury. I gave her a reminder of why she should be loyal to me."

"The problem in Wilkesbury is Stack, not Kyra—he should've been the one you gave a demonstration to." Angelo eyed Phil.

"Oh, don't worry, Ang, he'll get his demonstration soon. I trust him less than ever since Carrington became his boss. Stack's got no spine." Phil looked out into the distance. "Was she's telling the truth when she said she wasn't in love with him?"

"What difference does it make if she's not going to see him anymore? I do have to tell you my opinion of Carrington will fall if he drops her. She's one hot woman. I wonder what the other woman looks like."

"She was holding back tonight. I'll get what she knows, all of it, when I'm ready." He scratched his head.

"She wasn't, Phil. Why do you have a bug up your ass about her?"

"I don't trust her."

"You're still pissed she picked Carrington over you, aren't you?"

"Don't be ridiculous, this is business."

"Make sure you keep it business. We have too much at stake here."

"Don't threaten me, Angelo."

"I'm not threatening you. I'm warning you, and I emphasize—WE have a lot to lose. Your affection for this woman shouldn't play into this."

"You underestimate me. I'd never let a woman undermine me. But I will have her someday, mark my words."

Shaking his head, Angelo eyed Phil. "You scare me."

"Good. Now, no more talk about this. I did want to ask you about her gambling comment. Do you believe she's lost interest?"

"It seems that way. Perhaps gambling was a way to end the marriage."

"Well, it did the job. I didn't bring up the attempted rape, neither did she."

"Phil, it's between her ex-husband and her—don't get involved. It's obvious she can handle herself."

"Don't dictate to me. I'm not going to do anything now. I'll bring it up at our next dinner date." His lips pressed together in a thin, mean smile.

"What date did you schedule it for?"

"I didn't. It'll be at my whim, not hers."

Chapter 26

Yesterday, after he left Kyra's office her statement about him being afraid played over and over in his head. Was there any truth to it? And again, she'd avoided the subject of Phil Lucci. What was he to her? Even today he couldn't get it off his mind. Jake was grateful for Louie's call. "Go."

"Nice greeting."

"I'm not in a nice mood, Louie."

"The warrant for Church's apartment has come through. Do you want to swing by the station and pick me up or do I meet you there?"

"Meet me there. I'll be there in twenty minutes. I have one stop to make."

"Okay, boss." Louie called him boss when he wanted to bust his ass. *What I need, another clown.*

Alone time was what he wanted to sort through his cases. He drove as far as the entrance of City Park and threw the gearshift into park. Jake pulled out his notes. One thing continued to eat away at him. Was it incompetence on Stack's part in the way he handled the Church case? He kept coming back to a big fat no. Then there was his and Louie's case—the death of Dwight Wade. His gut screamed homicide, though Louie had no leads. He hoped Louie's morning had been more productive.

Jake tried to keep his mind on his cases. Not succeeding, he put the car into drive and headed toward Louie's location.

Outside the apartment complex Jake spotted Louie's car but no Louie. Jake hoped he hadn't entered Saul's place without him. A quick scan of the parking lot showed Louie chatting up Mrs. Standish. After five minutes, Louie gave him a wave. Jake headed over to the pair.

"Lieutenant, you remember Mrs. Standish?"

"I do." He gave her a curt smile.

"Lieutenant, Sergeant Romanelli was telling me you don't have anything new on Mr. Church."

"It's unfortunate but he's correct. Please remember what I said in our initial interview. For your own safety, do not talk to anyone about this." His mind on the search, Jake turned away from her.

"I haven't, but I did tell the sergeant there've been people snooping around again." Jake's attention snapped back to Mrs. Standish.

"I took her statement—we can review it while we execute the warrant," Louie said, with a crooked grin.

Jake nodded to him. "Mrs. Standish, you've been a great help. Thanks." He headed again toward Church's apartment. He heard Louie behind him.

"She called again?"

"No. She was outside when I drove up. I stopped and said hello."

"What did you get?"

"Descriptions of the guys who came the second time and a license plate number." Louie smiled when Jake pulled up short.

"That's great. As soon as we're done here, run it."

"I have Brown running it now. Who put the bug up your ass today?"

"I've got a lot on my mind."

"Such as?"

"The usual."

"Oh, that's clear. Glad I asked," Louie said.

"Let it be. We have a job to do here—can we get to it?"

"Sure. Want to grab a beer after work?"

"Can't. I'm seeing Mia tonight."

"Oh." Thank God Louie didn't pursue the conversation.

They got the search done and called in the crime unit in hopes of finding fingerprints to identify the men who had escorted Church out of his apartment. Jake had requested the warrant and done his own search because the file showed Stack had done neither. Sloppy, sloppy work. The more Jake played with it—the more he came to the same conclusion. Purposeful carelessness. Not for the first time, Jake wondered, who owned Carl Stack?

As if reading his mind, Louie asked, "Jake, are we going to get into it with IA?"

"It looks like it. I can assign you to handle only the Wade case. It will clear you. This way you don't have to put up with any of the bullshit when it hits the fan. It's going to blow wide open soon."

"No, I'm in this with you all the way. If he's dirty, he deserves everything he'll get." Jake had known what Louie's answer would be, but he had to give him a choice.

"We investigate this one by the book. I don't want it to come back and bite us in the ass."

* * * *

Exhausted, Jake walked through his front door at six thirty. He wanted a shower and something to eat before Mia showed up. A quick check of the clock had him swearing. Time was not a commodity he had a lot of lately. Forgoing food, he decided to jump into the shower even though he was starving. The search of Church's place used up their lunch hour. And damn, he and Louie had turned up nothing new. Not one solitary clue. Nothing on his computer to indicate Church hadn't left of his own accord. Where was he? At least today's search had kept his mind occupied and off his suspicions about Kyra and her relationship with Phil.

The hot water gushed over him, easing not only his body but his mind. Tonight he needed to concentrate on Mia. Was Kyra right? Was he afraid of being hurt again? Was that why he'd been cruel to Mia on Friday night? At the restaurant, their break-up had rushed back like a tidal wave, crushing him. How different the first post-breakup encounter with Mia had gone from the way he'd pictured it. It wasn't like him to push reality aside and wish for the impossible—did he want a lifetime with Mia?

The bell echoed down the hall as he dried off. Right on time. He wrapped the towel around his waist and answered the door.

"I'm sorry, I only got in a short while ago. Why don't you make yourself comfortable while I dress?"

"I'll make coffee," Mia said.

"No, I need something stronger tonight. Help yourself though. Why don't you get acquainted with Brigh."

He left Mia and Brigh to figure each other out and headed back to his bedroom. He tossed on a pair of jeans and a shirt but didn't bother with shoes. He walked toward his kitchen five minutes later buttoning up his shirt. At the entrance, he took a few seconds to study her while she played with the pooch. Two drinks sat on the counter. *A beer would have hit the spot tonight, but a mixed drink it is.* She wore a deep blue, sleeveless dress with spike heels. When she turned to hand him his drink, he noticed how the dress set off her eyes, tonight a deep sapphire. He accepted the drink. Sipped it. Stalled.

"I haven't eaten yet," he said. "Can I make you something?"

"No thanks, I'm not hungry, but you eat." Mia continued playing with the dog. "She's a beauty."

"She is," Jake said, as he slapped some meat on a slice of bread.

He scarfed down the sandwich as he followed Mia into the living room. His eyes swayed in rhythm with each movement of her hips but her back was rigid. *She's as tense as I am. Poised for a fight.* Mia sat on the couch. He placed his drink on the coffee table and took one of the chairs.

Christ, who's going to start? Mia didn't say a word. Neither broke eye contact with the other. Brigh had to know something was up, because she went to her bed and ignored them. He stared, she drank. Lord, he wasn't a coward, but he was sure acting like one. Stalling, he grabbed his drink off the table and took a sip to wash down the food that had stuck in his throat.

"Do you want to go first?" Jake asked.

"Where do we start?"

"I'm not sure."

"Conversation between us was never forced. Why are we having such a hard time now?"

"That's a good question."

"Is there a chance for us?" Mia asked.

Well, that got right to it. "I hope there is."

"You were pretty mean the other night." *Not a question, a statement.*

"I didn't expect to run into you after all this time. You blindsided me." He rubbed his chin. "I have mixed emotions—love, anger, sadness—"

"All are powerful and yet out of all of them you chose to go with anger. Why?"

"I'm not one of your damn patients."

"This is the only way I know how to do this. Do you have a better idea?"

"No." He couldn't read her. Tonight she portrayed the Ice Queen. No emotion showed through her armor. Unlike Friday night's raging episode.

"Why did you lead off with anger?"

"Because you walked away without a word. And you tried to force me into a confrontation in a public place," Jake said, as he rubbed his temples.

"I didn't walk away, Jake. You gave me an ultimatum and when I left, you didn't come after me. I wasn't worth the fight."

"Oh for Pete's sakes, Mia, you're wrong. I gave you the space you asked for. You're the one who said you were only able to do casual—I want... wanted more with you."

"You asked for too much too soon. I was scared. You said it had to be all or nothing."

What the hell did she want? "How can you believe that's all we were together? I love you. I always will. I waited more than a month for you to call, and nothing. We didn't even run into each other." Knowing it had to be brought up, he continued. "I met Kyra at a party. We clicked. Neither of us wanted a commitment. She's in the middle of a messy divorce."

"You seem close."

"We are."

"Are you saying time made you realize it wasn't true love with us?"

"Damn it, I didn't say that, Mia, and don't put words in my mouth. Kyra's been a good friend and a little more. She's backing away from me because, and I quote, 'You don't look at me the way you look at Mia,'" he said, frustrated.

Jake watched her process the statement. Understood she was analyzing it. He picked up her empty glass along with his and walked into the kitchen to make them another drink.

"Jake." He turned back.

"Yes?"

"It still doesn't explain your reaction to me the other night."

"I hear nothing from you in over a month and then bingo, we run into each other and you profess you missed me as you try to hash it out in a public place. I don't do shows. What did you expect? That I'd leave Kyra there and run off with you?" He walked back into the room with the empty glasses, banged them down on the table. He looked into her eyes, drinks forgotten.

"A girl could hope." She shrugged.

"Well, that was childish. I don't plan on hurting her. If I do, it will be as little as possible. She's going through a tough divorce. And I don't want to add to her stress."

"You sound as if you care more than you're willing to admit."

"No, I'm willing to admit it. I care for her, but not in the same way I care for you." He pushed to the edge of his chair, took her hands and rubbed his thumbs over them. "Has anything changed?"

"I love you, but I saw another side of you the other night I didn't care for."

He let go of her hands, got up, paced and threw her words back at her. "I saw a side of you that annoyed me. You tried to manipulate me. Was it that I didn't jump at your commands, is that what you didn't like, Mia? I won't be cornered. Or was it the part where I was defending myself from an attack? Tell me exactly what bothered you."

She stood, walked to him, backing him into the wall as she jabbed him with her pointer finger. "You were mean. God, you went for the jugular."

He gently took hold of her finger then moved his hand down to her wrist, his fingers rested on her pulse. "I guess I wanted to hurt you as much as you hurt me. But you, too, went for mine. If we hadn't run into each other, would you have called?" Jake locked his eyes onto hers as he tried to gauge her answer.

"I was working myself up to it."

"What a coy answer. And how long was it going to take?"

"I don't know."

They talked for hours, and before they knew it, it was twelve o'clock. Both agreed they were miserable without the other—but they had issues they needed to work out. The biggest issue for Mia at the moment was Kyra. For Jake, it was Mia's lack of commitment.

"Things moved too fast for us, Jake. If we can take it slow I'd like to start over and see where it takes us."

"My love for you hasn't changed, Mia. If you're not sure, then why bother."

"I love you, but we have some real issues we need to iron out before I make a lifetime commitment to you."

It hit him, nothing had changed. Mia still held some part of herself back. What was wrong with him? All the women he cared for sheltered secrets. None were sharing. "What does this mean for us?" he asked.

"It means we continue to date. And build a relationship on things we learn about each other"

"I'm not your father," he said, frustrated.

"I never said you were. You don't have a clue where I come from and who I am. You don't know my family, my dreams, or my fears."

"You're wrong. You're a writer with an illogical fear of commitment. And you blame all your problems on your father and you overanalyze everything. You're not your family, Mia. I do know you. You're warm, funny, smart and withdrawn. Our relationship isn't built on sex." Control was the key here, he understood, as he suppressed his anger, he needed Mia to understand it was her he wanted—not control over her—in return he expected her love and respect. Without both they were nothing.

"What are you going to do about Kyra?"

Jake refused to answer. He still didn't understand where he stood with Mia. "Jake?"

He took care to find the right words before he answered her. "What do you want me to do about her?"

"You're a piece of work, playing the shrink with me. That's Psych 101."

"I'm not playing. Are we a couple or not?" After five hours he still hadn't a clue, and it was killing him. She still wanted it all while giving nothing back. No one in this world made him as crazy as she did.

"We can still date other people if you like, but I won't sleep with you if you're dating someone else."

"The way to find out if we want to be together is to be monogamous."

"I agree."

"I have plans with Kyra this week that I need to keep, but tomorrow I'll let her know that at the end of the week we'll no longer be dating." Jake watched Mia's face twist into a scowl. Instead of joy, he read annoyance.

"Why the end of the week? You can honor your commitment to her, but why consider it a date?"

"It's a courtesy to her. Kyra was there when I needed her. I'm going to be there for her." *I'm not backing down on this damn point. How can she be unhappy with my decision? I owe Kyra. I should run while I have the chance.*

"I guess I don't have a choice, do I?" Mia asked.

"This choice is yours as all the other choices were. You've been in control since the beginning."

"You call this control?"

"Why are you picking a fight?" Jake asked.

"Let me make it clear. After this coming weekend, you have sex with Kyra and we're through."

Mia started to pack up her things and walk to the front door. "I understand and have no problem with that. What night will I see you?"

"Next week, after you're done with Kyra, that's when." She leaned into him, gave him a peck on the cheek. She still wanted total control.

When Mia pulled away he closed the door. Then he fixed another drink, replaying the entire conversation over in his head. Cops and shrinks— what did they have in common? They analyzed everything and weighed the outcome. When had his life become one big pissing match with Mia? Was he a fool to want her, that he was willing to let Kyra go?

Drink in hand, he headed to the bedroom. Sleep eluded him. How could he avoid hurting Kyra?

Chapter 27

Kyra pulled off the road for a while on the way home because she was trembling all over. Once she got home she downed two shots of vodka. Still it didn't quiet her fear. The pressure behind her eyeballs felt as if they'd pop out of the sockets. She inhaled deeply, but the sensation clung to her as if Phil's fingers continued to squeeze the air, the very life, from her lungs. God, he'd kill her for asking a simple question. The urgency, more than ever convinced her she had to tell Jake about Phil. But the idea of going to jail held her back. Besides, what if Phil went after Trevor? Prison, if it insured that Trevor was protected, was a small price to pay for her son's life she decided.

The realization hit her hard. Tom was right. She didn't deserve custody of her son. If she gave Jake Phil, then she'd have to tell him what she did for Phil and end their relationship. Did it matter? After tonight, she'd lose Jake's respect and he'd run back to Mia. Kyra clenched her stomach as tears ran down her face. How did her life get this far out of control? She'd thrown the man she loved into the arms of another woman. And this wasn't about Jake, it was about keeping Trevor safe.

It was for the best if she upped and disappeared with Trev. He'd adjust to the new location after a while. It would be the best thing for him. And her bastard in-laws, wouldn't they be smug about it? *I told you, Tom, she wasn't worth it, but did you listen?* Oh yeah, one more reason to disappear. With close to three hundred thousand dollars she'd be able to handle anything that came her way. She'd have her choice of places to relocate. She'd go into the Witness Protection Program after she testified against Phil and disappear.

She'd need to plan. On her next weekend visit, she and Trevor needed to disappear into the vast lands of the Midwest. Was it fair to Trevor to uproot him from all he knew? But wasn't it best for a child to be with his mother? Tom had become dangerous since she left him. She should leave the country to be safe. She'd get Trevor a passport. They'd both need fake ones anyway. Untraceable ones. Which one was better or safer for Trevor—Witness Protection Program or leaving on her own? She wished she could ask Jake.

Was he sleeping with Mia tonight? It burned a hole in her as she envisioned it. She had no claims on him, but he'd become her new obsession. Though fun, it was no better than her gambling.

Up early, she dressed in a sleeveless turtleneck and paired it with a light jacket. Phil had left slight bruising on her neck. She dragged herself into work. Kyra walked into the office, bypassing Dina without a word, and sat down in her chair. A few minutes later, Dina came in with a cup of coffee and placed it in front of her.

"Thanks. I didn't sleep last night. I'm going to lock myself in my office to get some rest."

"Jake's seeing the other woman?"

"Dina, I can't speak about it," Kyra said, on the verge of tears.

"I overheard everything yesterday. If you need to talk about it or want to get a drink after work, I'm here."

"Thanks for being a good friend."

Around three o'clock, Phil called. "Kyra, I'm sending the undertaker over now. He should be there in an hour."

Crap! Nothing like giving someone notice, but another one hundred grand will help me and Trevor disappear. "Phil, this means it won't be finished until after seven. If any of my trustees stop in, they'll question why I'm processing this late."

"It can't be helped. One hour." He hung up without waiting for her reply. Kyra wished someone would off Phil.

* * * *

Around five a.m. Jake decided sleep wasn't happening. He needed a shower to clear his head. With bagel and coffee in hand, he headed into the station. First thing he did was check his emails. Damn, no fingerprint results from yesterday's search. After leaving the lab a voice message he panned through the rest of the emails. One from Louie on the Wade case caught his eye. Jake switched gears from Missing Persons to Homicide. *Cripes, my head's crowded.*

Louie had stopped in unexpectedly yesterday on Mrs. Wade and caught her with Wade's best friend. The friend Wade was drinking with on the night he shot himself. The same friend who, according to his statement, left Wade at the bar drinking and alive. Louie's conclusion agreed with Jake's—it looked like both the wife and the friend had killed Wade. Jake made notes on the printed report for Louie to check out the life insurance policy, including the beneficiaries. Plus, he wanted Louie to investigate Mrs. Wade's alibi more thoroughly. Another interview with the wife and the friend, Kevin Long, after Louie dug up that information might be the key to unlocking this case. At least something was popping on one of his cases.

He put aside the Wade file and took out his file on Church. After reading both his notes and the lab reports, he read Louie's. He put his feet up on his desk and closed his eyes to let the information ruminate. The number one clue to the case was Stack's lack of action. He didn't like looking at another cop, but there were some who acted like they were above the law. His brothers in blue pissed him off sometimes. They'd make Jake the target of their anger if he locked up Stack. He didn't want to put Stack in front of IA until he was sure, but it rang ninety-nine-point-nine percent in his head that it was. Jake slid his feet off of his desk. He grabbed his phone and pressed in Shamus's extension. He was surprised when his captain picked up instead of his voicemail.

"What's up, Jake?" McGuire asked.

"I'd like to take you for coffee this morning, or lunch today."

It upset him to toss Stack in front of his captain, but there was no choice. A dirty cop made the job more difficult for the honest ones. Jake understood better than most, he'd taken a lot of shit over the Miller brothers' deeds.

"Is this about what we discussed yesterday?"

"Yes," Jake said, as he made notes.

"There's no mistake?"

"I'm ninety-nine percent positive, but I want to bounce it off of you. I'm not ready to make it official yet."

"We'll go after roll call," Shamus said.

After he hung up Jake turned toward his window, put his feet up on the casing, and closed his eyes again. He ticked off the steps required to prove or disprove Stack's innocence. It drained his energy. Stack threw open his door, jolting him back to the present. Jake turned from the window and studied the man. Stack was looking for a fight. His body language signaled his attitude long before he opened his mouth. Carl looked like he'd slept in his suit.

"Yes, Carl?"

"I'm going to close the door, Lieutenant."

Jake nodded. "What do you need?"

"I want a damn explanation of why you're interviewing people behind my back and working my case. What gives you the right?" Stack asked, a blood vessel pounding at his temple.

Oh yeah, here we go. "I spoke with the people you didn't bother to talk to."

"Like Mrs. Church? The poor woman has enough stress with her son missing and now you've added to it by barging in on her and giving her false hope."

"False hope. You think he's dead?" Jake asked.

"I don't know. I can't find a trace of him. No one I spoke to has seen or heard from him in three weeks."

"I don't see any interviews in your file?"

"Because they're in my briefcase. I planned on going back around to reinterview everyone, but I can't find them either."

"And that doesn't strike you as odd, Carl?" Jake hadn't broken eye contact with Stack.

"Why are you working my case?"

"It's standard procedure when a lieutenant takes over a department to review all cases, Carl, and give his attention to ones he finds that aren't being handled according to procedure. This one wasn't."

"How so?" Jake gave Stack credit for reining in his temper.

"The usual trail of an investigation isn't detailed here. An empty case folder except for a single call sheet. There are no lab reports, no evidence that a CSI team had been called in. There are no interview records in the folder either. That's why."

Stack took an unoffered chair as he folded his hands over his bulging belly before he spoke. "Lieutenant, this guy's been reported missing before. If you checked my notes, you'd see he gets involved in poker games around the state and doesn't know when to call it quits or contact his family. His mother's jumped the gun three times in the last three years." Stack smiled. It reminded Jake of a teacher talking to a slow student. *Well, Carl, you don't know me.* Though it might've been fun to play with Carl for a bit, Jake decided this situation needed a head-on-collision approach.

"I saw your notes, which were inadequate by the way. You didn't follow procedure."

"I'm frustrated—investigating Church takes time out from my other cases, from people who are really missing and require action. I did interview his gambling buddies. They believed he'd caught another game he'd been carrying on about. A high-stakes game."

He's good. He'd missed his calling. Stack was an excellent actor. "I understand frustration, but procedures are in place to not only protect the public, but to cover our asses. By not following regulations you lost valuable time in the recovery of this person. It looks like this time he's actually missing. And where was this game supposedly held?"

Jake studied Stack as he searched for an answer. "His fellow gamblers said Church never told them. I'd be glad to take the case back and check again all the usual spots where he plays to make sure he's not off on a winning streak."

"Good idea, but we'll work it together, and from different angles. You pursue your angle. I'll follow the evidence—it's pointing to a grab."

"What evidence?" A bead of sweat ran down Stack's cheek. Carl swiped at it with irritation. *Good, he's losing his cool.*

"Some kids in the neighborhood saw him escorted from his house by three men." Jake withheld Mrs. Standish's name.

"When did they come forward?"

"They didn't." Jake wasn't giving anything away. He wanted Stack to ask.

"They didn't? Then who told you they saw something?"

"Because I canvassed the neighborhood and found witnesses." *It's called doing your job.*

"Lieutenant, you sure they're not pulling your leg?"

"I didn't get where I am today by being gullible. I've more than paid my dues on the street, Carl. I'm absolutely sure? Yes, as sure as I sit here. This case was mishandled."

Carl jumped up, banged his hand on the desk and pointed a finger in Jake's face. "You put that in my file and I…I'm going to the union…to my rep. You can't take a case from me, you arrogant bastard. If you're looking for a fight, Lieutenant, you've got one." *Now we see the real Carl Stack.*

"I'm reserving action and judgment until we resolve the case. You're dismissed."

Stack stood there with his mouth gaping. He started to talk, stopped, then regrouped. After a few moments Stack started speaking in a quieter voice—Jake assumed he did it to cover his outburst. "I'm not looking for a fight, but I won't back down either."

"You've been dismissed, Detective. And, Carl, I don't take insubordination from my men, let that be your first and final warning."

Jake watched Stack storm out of his office. He'd tipped his hand on purpose to put things into motion. Stack's next move was crucial. Jake had to pay careful attention before he chose a course of action to proceed against Carl.

Moments later Louie walked into his office without knocking. "What was Stack doing here?"

"I'm not going to discuss personnel with you, Louie." Jake was aware his door was partially open.

Louie stared at Jake, shrugged, and changed the subject. "You get my report on the Wade case?"

"I did. I agree with your findings."

Jake handed Louie a copy of his printed report, with his notes and directions on it.

"Did you arrange a follow-up interview with both of them?"

"I'm interviewing them together today."

"Good, but read my notes before you do. I'm sure you've already got the insurance information. Make me a copy of it and nail down the wife's alibi—then we'll reinterview them. Let's see who breaks into a sweat first."

"I already started the process on the life insurance policy. I've booked the interview room for noon."

"Push it out to later in the afternoon. This gives you more time, plus it gives them each more time to sweat the details."

When Louie left his office, Jake typed up his notes on the meeting with Stack. He printed out a copy to hand to Shamus over coffee. The meeting told Jake two things. One, Stack wasn't stupid. He clued right in to why Jake had taken the case from him. And two, he knew how to cover his ass. Jake needed to find the other complaints and review dates and times of the reported disappearances. He opened the Church file, reread Stack's notes. What was he missing? Stack hadn't listed the dates of the other reported disappearances. *It's time to dig out the buried information on other cases Carl might've let fall by the wayside.* Time he didn't have. If he had to, he'd reinterview Mrs. Church.

* * * *

Stack knew Carrington was an ace investigator. It took all the control he had not to lose it at his desk. Sweat dripped down his back as he tried to figure out his next move. He had to be sure Carrington was able to put his hands on the old files. He took blank complaint sheets from his drawer and loaded them into his briefcase before he headed out on the pretense of following up on a case. Instead he headed home. At his kitchen table with the complaint sheets, a calendar, and a tall glass of gin and tonic in front of him, he got to work. He was more afraid of Phil Lucci than he was of Jake Carrington. The lesser of two evils—Jake might destroy his career, but Phil owned his life.

The more he drank the more courage he found. He'd find a way to disgrace Carrington. Bring him up on charges. *I'm sure the Miller boys would help me out.* His thoughts amused him. He needed to pull it off and raise his worth in Phil's eyes. Leverage was the key. The information he supplied Phil on each case or helped make disappear meant more cash for him.

How to do it and come out of this clean? He slapped his head as an idea entered it. He'd ask Phil to have one of his women file a complaint and make sure Carrington was the investigator. Then have the woman file a sexual harassment charge or claim rape against the lieutenant. That ought to tie him up for a while. Stack laughed as he fixed himself another drink. The idea of that arrogant bastard defending himself amused Stack through his third drink. Without thinking, he picked up his home phone and called Phil.

"Hello."

"Phil, it's Carl."

"What number are you calling me from?"

"I'm home, don't worry."

"You stupid bastard, are you drunk?" *Who is he to talk to me like that?*

"Nobody's going to trace my phone. I have an idea about how we can stop Jake Carrington from interfering in our business." Stack rubbed his ear. The bastard had slammed the phone in his ear. Anger spurted out of every pore. Who did he think he was?

An hour later, on his way to sober, Stack had to take a chair. His head spun, his stomach heaved—he'd called Phil—and on his home phone, no less. Jesus, he was losing it. Not only did he give Carrington ammunition, he'd made Phil Lucci mad. *The last thing a person wanted to do was make Phil Lucci mad and me being a cop didn't matter to Phil. How do I fix this? I'll leak the information I have, then if he whacks me it will lead right back to Phil. Calm down. I'm privy to Lucci's organization and where all the bodies were buried.* Somehow, that didn't settle his nerves.

Nothing ever went right in his life. His wife had left him. His kids didn't talk to him and his girlfriend had called him a pig and dumped him last week. Now he'd aggravated Lucci and his nice, easy job looked like it was going away. What should he do? Cash in his bonds and take off. Hell, why should he let Carrington scare him?

Stack's bravado didn't last long. He poured himself another drink for courage, this time more gin than tonic.

* * * *

"Angelo, get in here," Phil shouted.

"I heard. Stack's becoming a real problem. We need to take him out now."

"Agreed, how do you want to do it?"

"I have a few ideas, give me a half hour to set it up." Angelo said.

"I'm playing with several of my own, but nothing smart."

"I need to make a few phone calls. Let's discuss it after I do some research." Angelo left the room.

Phil sat at his desk, steaming over the new developments. Though he knew this screw-up had nothing to do with Kyra, it all seemed to lead back to her and her cop. It'd best if he got rid of Stack and Kyra together or did he need to stagger them? If he did this right, he'd be able to lay the blame for Kyra's death on her husband and Stack's on Carrington. Phil smiled. A different scenario for each played out in his head. He'd wait to see what Angelo came up with before he presented his ideas on the subject. Oh yes—he rubbed his hands together and smirked—those two disposals would bring him immense joy. What a shame to waste a woman like Kyra, though—he'd get a little taste of her first before he did the deed. Show her what she'd missed out on by choosing the cop.

Chapter 28

At his meet with Shamus, Jake outlined everything he'd discovered about the Church case. McGuire agreed Jake hadn't enough evidence at this time to present an official complaint to IA. Shamus gave Jake the go-ahead to continue his investigation. The captain laid out the guidelines. More to cover their asses instead of Stack's, in case the investigation blew up in Jake's face.

The meeting took about an hour. Jake got back to his office around ten thirty. He created a password-protected file on his computer and made sure to name it something unrelated to Stack. He was reaching for his cell phone to call Kyra when Louie walked into his office. *I need to remember to close my door.*

"Here are your copies of the life insurance policy. Mrs. Wade's the sole beneficiary. Last month, Dwight Wade increased his policy from fifty thousand to two hundred fifty thousand. It looks like that was his death warrant."

"Looks like it. How about her alibi?"

"It's hard to substantiate. She was at home with the children while her husband was out drinking."

"Call the bartender at that dive again and reverify the time Kevin Long left that night. Then call his employer to see what time he started work the next day. It's surprising the guy didn't die of alcohol poisoning with his level of intoxication. Also ask the bartender if it was normal if Dwight Wade got that trashed when he was there."

"I'll get back to you on this. I changed the appointment with Mrs. Wade and Mr. Long to four thirty this afternoon, at her house instead of here."

"Good."

When Louie left, Jake reached for his cell phone again as it started to ring. He had to call Kyra. Looking down at his phone, he narrowed his eyes. *Why is Mia calling?*

"Carrington."

"Jake, I wanted to touch base with you today."

"Aren't we supposed to connect on Monday?" He didn't have time for personal bullshit.

"I was curious. How did it go with Kyra?"

"I haven't talked to her yet. It's been a busy morning." Pissed off at the idea of Mia checking up on him, Jake took a deep breath before he said something stupid.

"Oh, I'll give you a call tonight?"

"No, let's leave it for Monday, like we planned. I don't mean to rush you, but I have to go. It's a zoo around here today."

After he hung up, Jake walked over to his door and closed it then punched in Kyra's number.

"Hey."

"Kyra, are you okay? You sound terrible."

"Nice way to greet someone, Jake. I had a bad night." Her voice sounded strained. Was he the cause?

"Me too. I'd like to see you tonight. Are you free?"

"No, but damn reasonable." Her attempt at humor failed.

"What time's good?"

"Eight."

"Do you want me to bring dinner?"

"That sounds good, I'll see you later," Kyra said.

Jake placed his phone on his desk. Stared at it as if it had burst into flames. She'd hung up on him, not waiting for a reply. Kyra continued to surprise him. Unlike Mia she didn't ask about last night. Thank God she didn't force his hand. His news was better dealt with in person. For dinner he decided on the Steak and Brew. A quick email to the place with his meal choices and time of pickup done, Jake turned his attention back to the Church case.

A ping announced a new email. *My fingerprint results. Way to go, Neville.* Jake raised his coffee cup in a salute to the nerdy lab tech. One set belonged to Church, one was an unknown, the other two sets belonged to known criminals with mob connections. Gus Spinela, age forty-two, did two years at Somers for assault. Two years. Jake's head throbbed at the injustice of it. Why did they bother to get these guys off the street when the system put them right back out there again? The second guy was Patrick

Doyle, age thirty-seven. He did five years for assault with a deadly and racketeering. Racketeering? Enforcer was more like it. Nowhere in either file did Phil Lucci's name come up—the name that came up in both files was an Angelo Rainford.

Jake's run on Angelo Rainford showed he'd done one stint for armed robbery twenty-five years ago—well, well, look here. Angelo did his time at Radgowski, at the same time that Phil Lucci did his time there. Angelo, two years younger than Phil, gave him a thread to follow. Jake didn't believe in coincidence. There had to be a connection. Following the trail, Jake grabbed a pad. He started with Stack, he drew a line, then added Church. Adding another line to continue the pattern forming. Jake added both Spinela and Doyle along with the unknown man. Next, he added Rainford and Lucci. Adding a last line, he drew one from Lucci back to Stack. He wasn't sure why, but Jake put Kyra's name in the center. What did she have to do with Stack and Church? Lucci was the only connection here to Kyra. Or was he? *There was an Angelo at the cemetery that day. Lucci should be in the middle, with Kyra on the fringe of things.* He made the corrections.

* * * *

It was going to be a hell of a night. First, he needed to explain about Mia to Kyra. Then deal with her emotions. After that his urgency to extract what Kyra knew about Phil Lucci had become paramount to saving her. If the dominos fell, Lucci would neutralize Kyra in an instant. Jake had ignored her connection to him in the beginning. Now, it bit him on the ass. Christ, what if she was involved in Church's disappearance?

Had Kyra worked him from the get-go? Love and hate fought with each other in his heart. They'd met at Dina's house. Stack wasn't there. The thing that flagged Kyra was her gambling and the fact she dated Lucci. Gut versus heart. Jealousy versus fear for her? Was this the excuse he was going to use to end the relationship? He'd chosen Mia, not Kyra. If Kyra was involved what capacity did she work for Phil Lucci? All those questions spun around in his mind. Some answers dropped hard from his subconscious to his conscious mind. Shaking his head, he repressed them, listing them as absurd.

He needed to focus. Caffeine should do the trick. He pushed up from his desk to grab a cup. With mug in hand, he emptied his mind as he stared out his window. This day had gotten away from him. Shifts reported in, shifts went home. Three o'clock, but his and Louie's day wasn't done. They still needed to interview Mrs. Wade and Kevin Long. Jake rubbed the fatigue from his eyes. No sleep last night didn't help matters.

A quick stretch worked out some kinks before he glued his ass to the chair and continued his research. The printout on Angelo Rainford bothered him. Like Phil, Angelo had kept out of the system after serving his time. All that meant to Jake was that Lucci and Rainford had learned how to stay under the radar. There was no speculation about Angelo's recent activities as there was in Phil's. He scratched his head. Either Angelo had learned crime didn't pay or he'd become a more cautious criminal. Jake opted for more judicious, which made Angelo more dangerous. He turned to his computer, searched for a photo of Angelo in his prison files but came up empty. He'd have to search old mug shots for any photo even if it was over twenty years old to identify Rainford. Jake typed up his request and sent it out to the state police. He figured he should have something back by the end of the week if he was lucky.

* * * *

Driving home to shower and dress before he picked up dinner, Jake reviewed his day. The Wade interview brought a smile to his lips. Louie had taken the lead, easing Mrs. Wade through her previous statements, questioning this, pointing out that, in his quiet, fatherly manner. Jake had observed over the years how effective this method was for Louie, nailing a suspect or a kid to the wall. For her part Mrs. Wade relaxed, her body sinking deep into her sofa, answering Louie's questions and embellishing her answers as her confidence grew. Jake stood behind Mr. Long and waited for Louie to finish off Mrs. Wade.

"I don't understand why you keep asking the same questions, Sergeant." *Here we go.*

"Mrs. Wade, Dwight didn't shoot himself."

"I know that, Sergeant. Dwight wouldn't do that to me or the kids. He loved us."

"Then how do you explain how he died?"

"I don't know, maybe he was playing a game. A stupid game," she emphasized, almost yelling as she stared down Long.

"A game?" Louie tilted his head right, then locked his eyes on hers.

She continued to stare at Kevin Long, her husband's best friend and drinking buddy, and avoided eye contact with Louie. Kevin Long sat at attention, aware Jake was still behind him. It didn't take long after that for Mrs. Wade to break down and tell the whole story.

It seemed Dwight Wade and Kevin Long had gotten fall-down drunk and decided to play Russian roulette with Dwight's gun, thinking it was unloaded. Dwight lost. Long was the one who'd come up with the plan. He convinced Mrs. Wade she wouldn't receive any insurance money if it looked like a suicide. Long staged a robbery gone wrong. He acted as if he was a concerned friend. He didn't want Mrs. Wade and her children to be in dire straits as they grieved. Long had played her and dug her further into his crime. Both faced charges, Long for murder and Mrs. Wade for abetting after the fact. Jake's sympathies were with the kids, not Mrs. Wade. In her grief, greed won over justice. She should've turned in Long immediately instead of concocting a scheme to get the insurance money. Kids were always the ones who paid the highest price. Now they didn't have a father or a mother.

* * * *

With the food in hand, Jake knocked. Kyra opened her door to let him in. She looked exhausted and skittish. She wore a deep blue T-shirt, with a blue-and-green scarf wrapped around her neck, paired with jean shorts. On such a warm night the kerchief looked out of place.

"Let me help you with that." Kyra reached for one of the bags Jake held.

"I'm good." He walked past her to the kitchen and put the food on the table.

She'd already set the table with china and wineglasses. He'd been hoping for something stronger.

"The table looks nice. You didn't have to go to all that trouble."

"You're supplying dinner, I'm supplying the atmosphere." Her stance reminded him of a victim waiting for the next blow.

His stomach muscle clenched knowing he'd be the one to deliver it. He wanted to put her at ease. Jake walked over to her, took her in his arms, and kissed her hello. He reached to loosen the scarf, but she stopped him and pulled back. *What the hell?*

"So…do we talk over dinner or eat first?" Her voice cracked. The sound killed him. He should do it like he did notifications, fast and brutal, then deal with the aftermath.

"Whatever you're more comfortable with."

"Truth be told, I'm not comfortable with either. I'm getting dumped here, aren't I?"

He took her chin in his hands, tilted her face up and stared deep into her eyes. "I never meant to hurt you, Kyra. I do care for you and cherish our friendship, but I love Mia."

"I knew that from the beginning but it's unfortunate my heart didn't listen." He wiped the single tear that ran down her face with his thumb.

"Let's sit and eat. I'll tell you about our meeting last night."

"Do I want to know?"

While they ate, Jake filled her in on his conversation with Mia. "I told her I needed the week with you."

"Why?"

"We have your friend's wedding Saturday. I promised to go with you… and I didn't want to cut us off from each other that abruptly."

"So, after next Monday that's it? No more contact, phone calls, or visits?"

"No, that's not what I meant, I …" Frustrated, he didn't understand how to finish his sentence.

Kyra put down her fork and looked at him. "Jake, Mia's not going to want me around, and who can blame her? I need this time with you too—you've come to be a big part of my life. You've helped me to overcome—so much."

He pushed his plate away at the same Kyra did. He didn't have much of an appetite either. Taking her hand in his, he brought it to his lips. They sat in silence for a while, letting time slip away before Jake got up to clear the table.

"Leave the dishes. I have less than a week with you and I want to use you good—so good you'll be too tired for her."

"I've never known you to be vindictive." Jake quirked an eyebrow.

"Who knew?" She grinned.

They walked into the living room, sat on the couch together. Jake liked Kyra's choice of music. She'd set the mood with a bluesy jazz CD playing in the background. Loud enough to enjoy, quiet enough to talk. Two scented candles burned in their holders on the coffee table. The candlelight cast everything in shadows. It seemed appropriate.

He draped an arm around her shoulder, drawing her closer to his body. He kissed the top of her head. After dropping his bomb, he understood it wasn't time to bring up Phil Lucci. *Coward.* Once again, he tabled the subject. Was that for Kyra's sake or his?

"What's wrong?" Kyra turned and stared into his eyes.

"I'm happy and sad. I know my decision hurts you…"

"It does, but I've been expecting it since the moment I decided to date you. You were always honest with me. I'm trying to be grown up here—so don't make me cry."

Pulling her closer, he whispered into her hair. "I won't." She turned, banging her head into his chin. "Now I'm going to cry," he said, rubbing his chin.

Laughing, she said, "Sorry. I wanted to look at you." She swung her legs over his lap as she wrapped her arms around his neck.

His voice hoarse, he said, "We shouldn't—"

"Shush," she answered, kissing him.

He returned the kiss, getting lost in her and her generosity. How was he going to be able to give her up? Had he made the right decision? Why was he questioning himself now?

"I want to be fair, Kyra."

"I have you until Monday. Mia be damned. The rest of the week belongs to me."

"I don't want to hurt…"

"Understand?"

"Yes."

* * * *

Kyra kissed him again as she unbuttoned his shirt. She trailed kisses down his throat as she spread her hands between the material and his skin. She loved how the muscles tightened under her touch. She'd miss him more than she wanted to admit. Hurt—but relieved—the guilt and lying now ceased. In the short duration he was still hers, she'd enjoy every inch of him before she took off with Trevor. If loneliness set in, she'd amuse herself at any one of the casinos across the country.

He switched positions, lifted her up as he cradled her in his arms, carrying her off to the bedroom. Their lovemaking was tender, consuming and distant. Or was all that in her mind? Had Jake already checked out or had she? She got the physical release, but emotionally, she was drained. Tears fought to escape. Was this her punishment for gambling—the loss of all that was good in her life? *Christ, how Catholic is that,* she turned her laughter inward. *Bless me, Father, for I have sinned…* Words from childhood that held no meaning for her now. Her soul was beyond redemption.

Jake's arms drew her in. Until that moment she hadn't realized she'd turned away from him.

"Are you okay?"

"Yes," she whispered.

"Do you want me to leave?"

"No, I need you here tonight."

He tightened his grip around her. For one more night, she'd clutch at the safety he offered.

* * * *

In the morning, she woke to the aroma of coffee and bacon. She'd eaten more bacon since dating Jake than she had in all her life. She'd miss being waited on. Before she went into the kitchen she splashed water on her face and brushed her teeth. *Toothpaste, what a way to ruin a good cup of coffee.*

"Hey," she said, walking into the kitchen.

"She lives." He laughed.

"Barely. Where's my IV?"

"Coming right up, ma'am." He handed her a cup of coffee, sipped his own.

"Thanks." Looking over the rim of the cup, she took a deep breath. *Get a backbone, Kyra, and ask the forbidden question.* "Are you coming back tonight?"

"I want to."

"Do you want to have dinner here?" They were treading lightly as though it were the morning after the first time.

"Yes."

"I'll make it. What do you want?"

"I'll bring it."

"Don't like my cooking?" She laughed.

"It's not that. Eat your breakfast and stop busting my chops."

Jake left for work an hour before Kyra. She was going to make the most of the week. She'd enjoy Jake— he wouldn't soon forget her. She wanted to cry but she'd do it when she was alone, because it was her own stupidity that had gotten her involved with a guy who admitted he was in love with another woman.

Chapter 29

Angelo walked into Phil's office. "Here's the plan I came up with to get rid of Stack."

Phil took the file Angelo handed him, studied it. After a few minutes, he looked up. "I like it. This way there'll be no body in Wilkesbury or here. I don't want anyone looking at us."

"That's the plan. Why don't you call him and get him down there? We won't have to worry about Carrington investigating it because it's not his jurisdiction."

"Even better, Ang, I'll tell him I want to discuss his phone call."

Angelo chuckled. "That'll put the fear of God in him."

"To entice him I'll tell him I also want to discuss some new business. I don't want to scare him away." Phil tapped his finger to the side of his head. "Find a place on Route 16. I don't want it anywhere near here. Let's cover all the bases."

"When are you going to call him?"

"Now's a good time." Phil punched in Stack's cell number.

After he hung up, anticipation built within him. Call him sick, but he liked dishing out punishment to people who deserved it. And Carl Stack deserved everything he had planned for him. Now that Stack was dealt with, Phil turned his mind to Kyra, to decide what she deserved. What most women deserved, in his opinion, was a good, swift punishment. It was the only way they understood who was in charge. Without warning, he was jolted back to the first encounter with his mother, years after she had deserted him.

She'd walked out the door when he was nine and never looked back. Left him to fend for himself against an angry drunken excuse for a father.

Phil recalled every beating, every nasty word his father had spoken to him. Phil Sr. was a disgrace to the human race—a lazy, foul-mouthed, fist-swinging drunk who expected people to wait on him hand and foot.

Phil didn't blame his mother for leaving. What he blamed her for was leaving him there and accusing him of being a carbon copy of his father. He cursed her for walking out. *Ah! Look at what you missed out on, Mother.* He looked around his spacious office with its Italian leather furniture, pricey art, and his view of the lake. She should've had more faith in him.

* * * *

Beautiful Louisa Lucci was a naïve woman who had wanted much out of life but had settled for Phil Sr. when he knocked her up. He promised her the moon. What she got was a life of hard work and abuse. The day she walked out of Phil Lucci's house all she had were the bruises from the last beating and a few dollars, but she was determined to survive—and survive she did, until her son caught up with her on that rainy Monday morning in June...

Sitting in the café, he studied the waitress. A beauty in a used-up kind of way. Tall and thin, she looked about sixty, though he knew she was fifty-five. With her head down, she walked over to his table, slipping the pencil from behind her ear as she grabbed her pad from her apron pocket.

"What can I get..."

Ah, recognition. At least she knows her own son.

"Phil?"

Of course she recognized him. He was cursed, his face and build a replica of his old man.

"Yes, Mother." He had relished the stunned, cornered look in her eyes.

"I-I... How are you?"

"Is that the best you can do, Mother? After all this time, that's all you have to say to me?"

The conversation never improved after that. He left the restaurant and parked a block away. And each day as she left work, she had to pass by his car. He'd sit there and stare. On the fifth day, he got out of the car and walked up behind her as she rushed by. He dragged her into a dark alley. She jumped when the rats scurried from under the discarded newspapers. His grip tightened on her arm as he pulled her deeper into the shadows. He wasn't even going to validate her by killing her in her apartment.

He left her with the garbage. It was exactly where she belonged.

"This is for leaving me with that bastard." He took his knife from its sheath, brought it up, digging it deep into her skin, he cut her still beautiful face.

"No man will want you now, but that doesn't matter," he cooed in her ear. "Because you're not leaving this alley alive. Do you understand that, Louisa?"

"Yes," she cried. "Please, Phil, what do you want? I have some money stashed away."

"Where?"

"In my closet in the red hatbox."

"Louisa, I'm going to take your money and your life. What I wanted was a mother." He kissed her cheek and watched her shudder at his touch. Then he spun her around to face the wall. With a slow deliberate motion he dragged his knife across her throat from left to right. He made sure that each tooth of the serrated blade hurt and that she was aware of the pain as she died. The blood shot out of her neck. It drenched the wall. After the life drained out of her body, he dropped her to the ground and walked away, exactly like she had walked away from him. It was his nineteenth birthday. It was one of the few times he had dirtied his own hands.

A tinny sound bubbled up from his throat.

"Hey, Phil, I lost you there." Angelo snapped his finger.

"I'm reminiscing."

"Uh-huh, anything good?"

"It depends on how you look at it." Phil curled his lips. "Now let's discuss Kyra," Phil said, rubbing his hands together.

"Why don't we wait and see how your meeting goes with Stack first?"

"Getting squeamish in your old age, Ang?"

"No. To be truthful, Phil, she's done nothing wrong and doesn't deserve this."

"Well, she did, and I make the decisions here."

Angelo squinted and said, "*We* make the decisions here, Phil. You're talking to me. Doing anything to her will bring down a lot of heat on us right now—heat we can't afford with what we have going on. Any attention will derail our projects."

"You don't think there'll be heat killing Stack?"

"There will be but we can handle that. Carrington is a guy who'll hunt down anyone who hurts what's his. Ask the guy sitting on death row who killed his sister."

"From what I understand, Ang, he's dumping Kyra this week for his old girlfriend. It won't be a problem."

"Even if he dumps her, he'd still come after whoever hurts her. It's not worth it—plus, she's kept her side of the bargain. She's a good contact to have."

"We've paid her too much. If she continues, we need to renegotiate her fee."

Phil wasn't giving in. He'd deal with Angelo some other time. Kyra needed to go, no matter what services she performed.

"That can be done, but not right now. We also need to find a backup for her in case she gets fired or quits before we're done with her."

Or dies.

Many ideas popped into his head to accomplish the task. He'd make sure he'd be the one who got to do Kyra up close and personal. She'd pay for her arrogance, her rejection, her betrayal. It got him hard, imagining ways to take her out.

* * * *

Jake liked order. Order in his job. Order in his life. Order in his paperwork. How had everything gotten this far out of hand? He'd broken his golden rule and had gotten involved—not with one woman, but two. 'Love'em and leave'em' was a motto he'd always lived by. His job came first, though at the moment he found it hard to concentrate. Two women, each different and intriguing in her own way.

The sound of the intercom interrupted his personal melee. "Yes, Katrina?"

"Detective Stack asked me to relay a message to you."

What the hell is his game? He has my cell phone number. "What is it?"

"He's following a lead on the Church case. He'll call you later with an update."

Stupid son of a bitch, taking off on his own.

"Did he leave his location?"

"No."

"Son of a monkey." Jake swore under his breath. It would be his fault if Stack got killed. He'd pushed him too hard—forced his hand.

"Excuse me?"

"Nothing, Katrina. Thanks."

Jake hung up, wondering what and where his lead had sent him. He'd welcome any lead at this point, because he'd hit a wall on the case. Church had pulled a Jimmy Hoffa, leaving not one damn clue as to his whereabouts. Or to who had done him.

Edgy, he got up from his desk, left his office, and landed by the community coffeepot in the bullpen. In mid pour, Louie snuck up behind him. It took all his control not to yelp.

"Something wrong with the machine Sophia and I gave you?"

"No."

"You look perplexed."

"I am."

Stack was a personnel issue. He shouldn't discus Carl with Louie, though he'd be an asset with his puzzle-solving mind. He decided to break the rules yet again. Procedures, like rules, stood as guidelines, not absolutes.

"Want to do lunch today?" He put the pot down, emptied the untouched contents of his cup into the sink attached to the counter.

"You still working that Missing Persons' case?" Louie asked.

"Yep, why?"

"I was wondering. Where do you want to eat?"

"Anywhere private's good."

"Come and get me when you're ready."

Jake's gaze tracked around the bullpen before landing on Louie's back as his partner walked to his desk. Ten desks, all clustered in the middle of the room. Around the perimeter of the room were four hard, wooden benches. Family members of prisoners, victims, attorneys, and the general public used them. Two of the benches were occupied. One with a crying, elderly lady—Jake figured she was here for a kid or a grandkid. The other held a pair of teenagers trying to look tough, but not succeeding. Out of the ten desks in the bullpen, there were detectives sitting at four of them, the others must have been out on calls. Two were on the phone and two sat with suspects or witnesses answering questions. Not to pat himself on the back, but his department ran well. Homicide investigations were logical. You followed hard evidence, most of the time.

He smacked himself on the head. A Missing Persons case should run the same way as a homicide—with one exception—the body was missing. He'd been out of sync on this case all along as he tried to follow someone else's investigation techniques. He ran to his office, grabbed the file, opened it, rearranged it. Either way he looked at it, Church's disappearance was an organized effort. He was sure of it. Gambling made for strange bedfellows.

* * * *

Stack drove through Middletown on his way to meet Phil. The streets were busy this time of day. Middletown more affluent than Wilkesbury, offering a mix of restaurants and shops to suit many tastes and budgets. Phil calling out of the blue had him worried. It had seemed like Phil had forgiven him for his indiscretion. Was it new business or a ploy to lure him into a trap? Something he should think about, but he needed the money. He drove over the Portland Bridge at a mere ten miles per hour. The damn construction was going to last another year. He checked the GPS to see how much longer before he'd be able to turn onto Route 16. The little bar Phil picked was halfway for both of them. *Good choice, Phil. Liquid courage, and I sure need it.*

Damn, if that bastard in front of him didn't hurry up, he'd be late. Another screwup and he'd be dead. He wanted a little extra time to check out the place before he met with Phil. Pulling into a mini-mart, he checked his weapons. The Glock in his ankle holster was loaded, the safety off for a quick grab and shoot. An old-fashioned kind of guy, he liked his .38 Special, which was in his shoulder holster, loaded and at the ready.

He didn't trust Phil. Stack had learned early on in his career to listen to his instincts. They'd kept him alive for many years. He drove out of the parking lot heading east, and found the bar five miles down the road.

Stack pulled up to the front of the plaza and parked close to the road. He surveyed the entrance and all the cars, trying to pick out Phil's ride. Nothing came close to his usual mode of transportation. After assessing the front lot, he drove around to the back. The back wall of the restaurant sported two small windows. One screened wooden door stood wide open leading into the kitchen. A silver four-door BMW 330SI sat close to the back entrance. It was one he'd seen Phil use before. Carl wrote down the license plate. He drove around to the front and parked as close to the building as possible.

Inside, blinded by the darkness he had to squint to see. *Not good. Why aren't the lights on full? Was he in Angelo's sights right this minute?* A shiver ran up his spine. Did his greed have him walking into a setup? When he called Katrina he should've left his location for Carrington. Hindsight was great, but leaving wasn't a choice. He reached into his pocket, touched the knife for comfort.

His vision cleared as his eyes became accustomed to the low light. He took in the whole room, noting exits. A bartender the size of Texas stood behind the bar, washing a glass. A mirrored wall with shelves housed the liquor. It also gave the bartender a view of the room with his back turned. A glossy wooden bar had ten stools lined up to it. On the right side were booths, and in the last one he spotted Phil. Stack's internal antenna went up—where was Angelo? Phil never traveled alone. In slow, careful steps he approached Phil, his eyes scanning the room but he made sure to keep Phil in his sights. He reached Phil's booth and took a seat opposite him. It bothered him that his back was to the front door.

"Where's Angelo?"

"I have him doing other things today, why?"

"I've never seen you without him."

Stack placed his folded hands on the table. Phil grabbed them and applied an incredible amount of pressure. Stack tried not to squirm. In a second, he'd lose.

"Who I travel with, Carl, is my business. Is that clear?"

"Extremely." *Arrogant little prick.*

Phil released his grip. Carl refrained from rubbing his hand. He'd be damned, he wasn't going to give Phil the satisfaction.

"Good, now let's get down to business." *The man's a psycho.*

Phil talked for what seemed like an hour, detailing what evidence he needed Stack to pull for him. It was standard stuff Phil normally requested over the phone. Stack wasn't a nervous kind of guy, but Phil set off his alarms today. When the meeting came to an end, he decided to forego a drink and head right back to Wilkesbury. He slid across the seat and started to stand. Phil signaled for the bartender. Carl's breath whooshed out. His hand automatically reached for his ankle holster.

"Tony, bring us a couple of beers," Phil said to the bartender, turning back to Stack with a smile. "Nervous, Carl? You're sweating."

"No, it's warm in here. I have to pass on the drink. I'm expected back at the station. I'm still on duty."

He straightened, releasing his hold on the gun.

"One beer won't hurt you."

What choice did he have? "I guess it won't hurt." *Screw Carrington.*

The bartender delivered the beers to Phil. He didn't like it when Phil twisted off the caps and handed him one. He hesitated before bringing it to his mouth.

"Something wrong, Carl?"

"No." He sniffed the drink. He wasn't taking any chances. No odor. He took a large gulp. The beer cooled his parched throat as it slid past his lips and tongue. *There's nothing like that first sip.* After a few seconds bitterness attacked his taste buds. He should've left last month for his tropical island.

"Something's wrong with this beer." He wiped his mouth on his sleeve and eyed the bottle.

"Why?"

"It's bitter as hell."

Phil sniffed his bottle. "Mine isn't," Phil replied, and took another sip. "You want to switch?"

"No."

With keen eyes, Stack studied the bottle, rolling it between his hands. He decided he'd had enough. Carl pushed the bottle toward the center of the table. Phil reached for his, knocking it over. It spilled all over him. Stack jumped up. *Stupid son of a bitch. I'm sure he did that on purpose.*

"I'm sorry." Phil motioned the bartender over.

Sorry my ass. Stack grabbed the cloth from the guy and wiped the excess drink off his pants. He threw the wet towel on to the table and turned toward Phil.

"I should get on the road." Using the spill as an excuse he left the bar.

Out in the car, he racked his brain. Why had Phil summoned him? Most times he received his orders from Phil on the phone. Why meet for this? *Christ, now I smell like a brewery. All I need to complete my day is for some hick cop to pull me over.* Once in his car, he started to drive back down Route 16.

Dozens of daggers jabbed at his stomach. The convulsions forced him to bend at the waist. His face along with his neck stiffened. Incredible sharp pain shot through his body. Next, spasms hit his arms and legs, pinning his foot to the accelerator as his body arched backward. He had no control of the car. His back arched farther back, his head digging into the headrest. The ceiling his only view, he prayed he didn't kill anyone. Sweat dripped off his forehead, burned his eyes. *That bastard poisoned me. The pain! What the hell did Phil give me? He made sure I'd suffer. Oh, God. May the bastard rot in hell. What did I do...to deserve this?* Praying for death. Fighting for life, he fought each spasm of pain as it racked his entire body. The car shot across the road, hit the guardrail before it crashed through it and bounced off trees and bushes before landing in the middle of the swamp. The excruciating pain didn't let up as fear magnified each of his five senses when the cold water seeped in and washed over his body. He tried to scream for help, but no sound came out of his paralyzed mouth. The water engulfed him.

Chapter 30

Grateful for Louie's silence, Jake never let up on the gas pedal as they sped through Middletown. After Stack left the message with Katrina, one question stuck out with Jake—who had Stack met today? *Whoever set up the meeting must think we're getting too close to the truth on the Church case.*

"Tell me again what the state trooper said?" Louie asked.

"Stack smelled of beer, but he knew for a fact that wasn't what killed him."

"How can he be sure?"

"He said, and I quote, 'The cause of death was written on his face.' He emphasized that we'd need to see it to understand."

"Oh good. I love a mystery."

"It's not funny, Louie," Jake snarled.

"I didn't say it was. Calm down. I don't understand why the state trooper didn't give you all the information. What's the big freaking secret?" Louie tilted his head and stared.

"We'll see."

The turn came up fast. When he spotted cop cars, fire trucks, emergency response vehicles and the meat wagon, Jake figured he was in the right place. He pulled to the side of the road behind a hook-and-ladder truck. He understood all the manpower. They'd responded to an officer in trouble. He climbed out of his car as did Louie and together they walked down the embankment. Jake went on alert as he sensed the mood of the responders. The conversation was respectful, quiet, the attitudes somber. None of the usual dark humor—cop humor—you heard at a scene that relieved tension. It might've been any one of them. They were here to help, and also to reaffirm that they were alive for another day.

A trooper with stripes on his arm greeted them. The man matched Jake in height and Louie in coloring.

"Sergeant?"

"Lieutenant Carrington?" He held out his hand at Jake's nod. "I'm Sergeant McDermott. You must have broken the speed barrier."

"We ran hot. This is Sergeant Romanelli." McDermott shook Louie's hand.

McDermott pointed farther down the embankment. "It's not pretty." He started to walk down toward the stretcher.

The body was covered by the standard white sheet. Jake walked behind McDermott, Louie behind him. His mind was firing questions all over the place, his footing careful. Jake wondered how the trooper wore that hat all day long. Weird what popped into your head before you viewed a body.

The last conversation he had with Stack cycled in his head. It hadn't been kind. Accusations—he'd accused Carl of throwing a case, suspected him of taking bribes to look the other way. He'd have to live with it though the facts hadn't changed because Stack died. Carl's death confirmed his suspicions. This was a stupid move on the part of the killer. It drew more attention to him. The killing of a cop brought down more heat than the devil supplied in hell for an entire year.

Louie cursed behind him. Jake turned around and contained his laughter at Louie's scowl. Louie had stepped in something, ruining Mr. Fastidious's shoes. Jake turned back without comment. His gaze traveled to Stack's car, which sat on the embankment. It had already been pulled from the lake in order to retrieve the body.

Over his shoulder, he asked Louie, "Are you ready?"

"Yeah."

Trooper Sergeant McDermott pulled the sheet back as Jake and Louie surrounded the stretcher. Jake sucked in a breath. Louie gagged. Even experienced as they both were, nothing prepared them for this. Stack looked like a corpse from a horror movie, with his twisted features and stiff body. Rigor mortis had already set in. That baffled Jake. He walked over to the coroner.

After introducing himself, Jake asked, "Isn't it too soon for rigor mortis?"

"Certain poisons will bring it on sooner. If my guess is right, someone liked to read," the coroner replied.

"Why is that?"

"The set features, the early rigor mortis tells me, and it's only a guess, you understand—they had to have used strychnine or something like it to poison him. That shit's only used in books...mostly. You want someone to suffer, strychnine would be your substance of choice."

"How fast does it react?" Jake asked, while the sergeant and Louie listened in.

"Ten to twenty minutes, depending on the contents of the stomach. If alcohol was involved—and I don't know for sure it was, but his breath smells of beer— I'll know more once he's on my table," Doctor Tim McCoy from the state's medical examiner's office said.

"So we look for a bar within ten to twenty minutes from here. Thanks, Doc." Jake turned to Louie and the trooper.

"Lieutenant, I understand if you go looking for answers and do your own investigation. I would if it was one of my men. But I want to caution you, this is our case and we don't want it tainted. You need to take one of my guys, or one of the locals, with you. You'll get your answers faster that way around here and it'll keep the chain of evidence intact."

"Thanks, Sergeant. I don't mean to step on anyone's toes. This case ties into one of my Missing Persons' cases."

"Name's Cal, Lieutenant. Aren't you Homicide?"

"I'm Jake, this is Louie." Jake nodded toward Louie. "I—we are, but for now I'm also running the Missing Persons' Department. Stack was attached to that unit. And off the record, Sergeant, I think both cases tie into the mob."

The sergeant let out a low whistle. "Whatever I can do to help, I will. I'll keep you in the loop. It doesn't make sense for us to duplicate our efforts."

A veiled warning, he'd need to heed.

He needed a quiet space to scribble down his first impressions and place this piece into the puzzle. He had to analyze and process the crime scene and the why of it. Stack's family would need to have a closed coffin. It'd take a miracle for the undertaker to rid the face of the last painful minutes of Carl's life. He didn't like him personally or professionally, but nevertheless, nobody deserved to suffer like that. Looking around, he observed the woods and water. The drop off the road was a good fifty feet, if not more. According to the sergeant, Stack had sailed through the guardrail before landing in the swampy lake. Jake made a note to ask about Stack's speed when he flew off the road. Louie walked over while he was writing.

"Christ, I'm going to see his face in my dreams for a long time."

Jake continued writing.

"And look at my shoes," Louie said in disgust.

"You can look at that body with all the pain and suffering that was inflicted on Carl and still comment on your shoes? You've become hardened, Louie." Jake quirked a brow at him.

"I guess, but I paid a hundred twenty-five bucks for these shoes. They were comfortable, now they're trash," he said, aggravated.

Not caring about Louie's shoes, Jake walked back to the body. "McDermott, how many bars are in this area?"

"From the direction he came from, I'd say two."

"Do you have the names?"

"I plan on visiting them after we finish up here. You're welcome to accompany me."

I've been put in my place. "That sounds good."

What choice did he have? If he didn't like the answers he received with the state trooper present, he'd come back at another time. It wasn't his case, but damn it, Stack was one of his men. No way was Jake going to let the trooper relegate him to the back of the investigation.

* * * *

After Stack left, Phil and Angelo enjoyed a leisurely lunch at the bar. "You ready to go, Phil?"

"Not yet, Ang, I want coffee and dessert. I expect when we head down Route 16 there'll be quite a scene where Stack landed." Phil's grin spread from ear to ear as he anticipated the scene.

"It's stupid to be seen in the area."

"Stop being such an old lady and enjoy your work."

"That's the difference between us, Phil. I don't enjoy it. I do what's necessary."

"You can lie to yourself, I won't. While we're driving, I want to discuss the next phase of the plan."

"We should wait and see how this investigation goes before we move forward. It might fan the flames and bring the whole department down on us."

"We'll see." Obsessed with Kyra, she'd become his Helen of Troy. She was distracting him when he needed to concentrate on business.

Ten minutes later, they found the site. Phil beamed. A lot of response for one guy. At the intersection to Route 66, Phil told Angelo to turn around and head back home. As they pulled into the commuter lot, Phil spotted Jake Carrington—lights flashing, sirens blasting.

"He got here fast."

"Who?"

"Carrington's in the green car with the lights. This is even better than I imagined. Wait a few minutes, Ang. I want to see Carrington's reaction when we drive by."

"Phil, the guy knows you. Look at his reaction on the news. I'm taking a different route home."

Angelo pulled out, headed straight on Route 66, bypassing Route 16. Pissed, Phil said nothing as he stared out the window like a petulant child. Angelo had made the right move not taking Route 16—Phil would be damned if he'd tell him. *Round One to me. Did Carl leave a trail back to me, and if so did the final battle come down to Carrington and me after all? How ironic.* Still steamed over Stack's lack of discretion after using his home phone to call him, a deep-seated anger at Carl had clouded his judgement. He hoped Stack had hidden his payments well over the years. *I'm sure I'll find out soon enough.* Angelo was correct. Killing a cop brought on the heat but Stack's sloppiness had become a liability. Phil hated slipshod work. He didn't mind the heat. He'd gauge Carrington and his methods before he offed him.

Enough of Carl Stack. I need to move on to the second part of my plan. Kyra. He smiled as he plotted to tie up all the loose ends. Though Phil continued to tell himself taking caring of Kyra was a smart business move, deep down he understood it was her rejection that fueled his decision to get rid of her. And he didn't care. Phil ignored Angelo's suggestion to let Kyra go for another time. He also didn't care that Angelo wasn't on board with it. Kyra was his to do with as he wished.

"Ang, are you all set to put the move on Tom Russell into play?" Phil held the police report detailing the arrest of Tom Russell on attempted rape charges.

"Yes, I'm going to use Pat Doyle again. Russell's been out drinking most nights, getting shitfaced. The ass claims he misses his wife. The guy's a joke. What's that in your hand?"

"It's Russell's police report from when he tried to rape Kyra in her condo. He didn't check to see if she was alone, the idiot. Guess who was there?"

"Carrington?"

"Yes." Phil tapped a finger to his chin.

"Anyone who'd throw away Kyra is a jerk. What the hell did she see in that guy?"

"She was young when she got married. This is a great opportunity for us. In one move, we take out Kyra and Carrington."

Angelo pulled over to the side of the road, turned toward Phil. "Phil, aren't you doing the same thing? She's a useful tool, and she can continue to be, if we use her right."

Phil didn't like the way Angelo stared him down. He knew they were partners but Angelo seemed to be pushing too hard lately. Phil didn't need anyone, not even Angelo. Smiling at him, Phil decided he needed to reconsider Angelo's usefulness.

"My mind's made up, Ang. She has to go. Now that we see how it works, we'll find another patsy to do the cremations, and at a much cheaper rate. An opportunity like this isn't going to present itself again. We need to use it. Get me home, I'm tired."

He waved his hand as an indication for Angelo to turn around and start driving. Anger sparked across Angelo's face, but who cared? This subject was not up for debate. Why was Angelo pressing the matter? Why? Did he like her too? Phil had never known Angelo to cheat on his wife—was Kyra the exception? Jealousy raged within him, burned his gut until bile scorched his throat. *Calm down, Ang wouldn't do that. Shake it off, Phil. You're losing it.* The car slowed down as they approached the house. Before Angelo had a chance to open the door for him, Phil stepped out of the back and started walking away from the house. Angelo raced after him.

"What are you doing?" Angelo asked.

"I need some quiet time to play with ideas for the next phase. I'm going for a walk." Phil turned. Angelo slipped alongside him. "No, Ang. I need time alone." *What's with this guy? Calm down, he's doing his job, but this is my home. I swear, if someone comes after me here I'll string them up by their balls.*

"If you don't want me to walk with you, I'm sending a couple of the guys to follow at a distance. This isn't the time to be careless."

He reached up, patted Angelo's check. "You worry too much."

"You'll do me this favor? Take the two guys with you."

Angelo snapped his fingers. Two guards took up position behind Phil. Phil ignored the concern in Angelo's voice and continued to walk away. "Not a problem, as long as they keep their distance."

* * * *

Kyra woke filled with anger. As the morning progressed she decided to take the afternoon off. She chose the casino to burn off her anger. Right from the beginning, she knew Jake wasn't hers, but damn if she

hadn't fallen a little in love with him anyway. Why did she always go
for the unattainable? Life was unfair. In all the time she'd been with him
she'd gone to the casino only once. Why did Mia get to keep Jake after
she threw him away? Wiping the tears that ran down her face, she pulled
into the casino's ramp garage. She headed to the level and the general
area where she always parked. The garage wasn't that busy this time of
day, most people worked. Well, she hoped to hit it big early, that way
she'd get home in enough time to see Jake tonight. Funny, getting to the
casino used to consume her. Lately, it was a distraction to keep her mind
off her messed-up life and losing Jake. She stepped into the elevator and
hit the button marked C for the casino floor. As she got off the elevator,
she walked right into Joe Dillon. *Shit!*

"Er, sorry...Kyra! What a surprise."

Startled, Kyra kept moving. Joe at her elbow. "Weren't you leaving, Joe?"

"Why don't we visit for a bit? I get the impression you're not
happy to see me."

"Do you even need to ask that question? I'm pressed for time here.
Leave me alone."

She increased her pace, walking away from him. Kyra didn't bother
to see if he followed. There was one thing she was certain of—as soon
as she walked away he'd be on the phone to Phil, reporting her arrival.
Kyra wished there was a way to give Joe what he deserved—an oven at
twenty-five hundred degrees.

She should give his name to Jake, or even Phil—*that's mean.* For the
first time today a smile flirted across her lips.

She walked over to the five-dollar section. Kyra threw a one-hundred-
dollar bill into her favorite machine. A shadow crossed over her. Looking
up, she stared into Joe Dillon's mean, muddy eyes.

"What?" she spit out.

"I don't deserve this kind of treatment." Joe looked dejected.

"You bastard, you set me up with a mob boss for brownie points. You
think I should thank you? Stay away from me. I won't tell you again. Got it?"

"Shut up, Kyra, use a little discretion."

"Did you when you threw me to the wolves? Disappear now, Joe, or I'll
scream for help," Kyra said, her anger digging its fingers into every nerve.

"You'll regret this," Joe said.

"I already regret having ever met you. Now run along and report back
to your boss, you little weasel."

She turned back to her machine, stuffed another hundred in. Joe was
trouble, but she found she didn't really care. Once again, her life was

crumbling. She looked over her shoulder and watched Joe walk up the stairs, his cell phone glued to his ear. The little snitch had to be talking to Phil. That meant she had to hightail it out of there. An encounter with Phil right now was not on her agenda. Joe had actually saved her a ton of money. She pressed the button to redeem her credits and took her ticket to the cashiers to cash out before heading to the garage. *I should've gone to the other casino. Phil's too involved in this one. What I do with my time and money is nobody's business but mine.*

As she raced to her car, her cell phone started ringing. Thinking it was Phil, she almost pressed the ignore button, but it was Jake's number flashing on the screen. She answered the call right before it went to voicemail.

"Jake," she said, winded.

"Is this a bad time?"

"No, I'm climbing into my car." Damn it. Joe was leaning on her car.

"Kyra, everything okay?" Jake asked.

Ignoring Jake, she emphasized Joe's name. "Joe Dillon, what are you doing hanging around my car?"

"Hang up now," Joe said.

"No."

She heard Jake shout her name. Never taking her eyes off Joe she put the phone back to her ear. "Jake."

"What's going on, Kyra? Are you safe?"

"I don't know. Joe Dillon's my casino host. We had words a while ago and now he's at my car."

"Kyra, don't go anywhere with him." Jake shouted into the phone.

"I won't—"

"And don't hang up," Jake said, cutting her off.

"Joe, Lieutenant Carrington wants to know why you're following me?"

"I'm not following you but now that you're here we should go for a ride to discuss why you won't talk to me," Joe shouted as he grabbed her wrist and pressed down hard.

"Ouch! You son of a bitch, let go of my wrist," Kyra said.

"Kyra, this isn't a game. I said get into the car, now," Joe demanded.

"No." Scared shitless, she wasn't going to back down. *Where are the security people?*

In her ear, she heard Jake tell her to scream. Then she saw the security car. "Jake, there's a security car coming at us."

Kyra said that not only for Jake's benefit—she hoped the mention of security calmed Joe down. He dropped her wrist. The look on his face, along with his tone of voice, had frightened her. The man was ready to snap. In that second, she recognized the face of murder. Orders from Phil? No, it's not his style. The asshole had to have lost it. Joe knew she had a cop on the phone but came after her anyway.

"Kyra, are you in the casino garage?"

"Yes."

"Walk back to the elevator and get a security guard if the one in the car doesn't stop, understand?"

"Yes."

"This isn't over, Kyra," Joe said as he strode away.

The security car stopped. "Is everything all right here, Miss?"

"It is now, please wait until I get into my car." The guard nodded. "Thank you."

She climbed into her car and hit the lock button. "Joe's leaving." Kyra said into the phone. "I'm in the car with the locks on, Jake." Kyra waved off the security guard.

"Okay. What's going on, Kyra?"

"I don't know."

"Why are you at the casino?"

What do you care? You're gone as of next week. "This week's been upsetting. I came here to escape. After a few minutes I ran into Joe. We had words, it's the reason I decided to leave. That's when you called. Great timing by the way," she said, rambling on.

"Words about what?"

"Nothing I want to share, Jake." Silence. What was he thinking? "Are you still there?"

"Yes." *Oh good, now I have someone else pissed at me.*

"I'm sorry, thanks for your help. Uh...why did you call?"

"I was going to suggest we go out tonight, but I'll bring dinner instead. We need to talk."

Damn him! "About what?"

"Is seven good?"

"Yes."

After she hung up, she put her car in drive and started to pull out of the garage. She drove past Joe Dillon as he stood by his car, his eyes throwing knives at her. Should she call Phil? If he did set this up, would he send someone more professional to deal with her when he learned she didn't go with Joe? Why have someone grab her, and in broad daylight? It didn't make sense. Halfway through dialing Phil, Kyra changed her mind. Over the phone, she'd never be able to tell if he was lying. Plus, she wanted to put distance between her and the casino—or, more to the point, Joe.

Shivers ran up her spine and settled in her neck. She didn't want to be in Phil's zip code, whether he ordered the abduction or not.

Chapter 31

Jake's gut told him Kyra was in deep trouble, yet she acted like it was nothing. Didn't she trust him by now? Once again, whenever she was in trouble it reverted back to the casino. Which reverted back to Phil Lucci. He'd been calling to cancel on her tonight until he heard Dillon threatening her. Kyra had to have picked up on the deep hatred in the man's voice, because Jake had and he didn't even know the guy. What was that about? And why was she there, at the casino, in the middle of the day? He had assumed she had given it up. All he had were questions with no answers.

Kyra had the answers. But she wasn't sharing. He'd get to the bottom of it before she became one of his murder victims. His desk phone rang. Jake grabbed on the second ring when he recognized the extension for the state lab in Farmington.

"Jake, it's Tom Jones from the state lab." The guy took serious ribbing over his name. The idiot got drunk at the last Christmas party and sang his heart out—tone deaf bastard.

"What's up?"

"I did the blood work on Stack. He had poison in his system. A poison you don't see often," said Jones.

"What was it?"

"Strychnine."

"McCoy at the M.E.'s office guessed it right at the scene."

"I'd guess the killer's a reader. Mystery writers of days gone by loved to use it. The thing is, Jake, someone wanted him to suffer, and suffer he did with the amount he had in his system. It was an over-the-top kill. Dead the minute he ingested it."

"Wait, you said it took ten to twenty minutes to kill?"

"It does. What I mean is once he ingested the high dosage he was the walking dead. It took his body time catch up."

"Thanks, Tom. Email me a hard copy. I owe you one."

The cause of death was extreme. Stack had pissed off someone. But who? Jake opened his email, printed out the lab results, and headed down to Missing Persons. He needed to interview each and every one of his detectives who'd worked with Stack. It wasn't going to be fun.

A group of detectives stopped talking when he entered the bullpen. Jake understood their resentment, but he didn't care. He had a job to do.

"Listen up. I got the tox report back on Carl. It's not good. He was poisoned." Jake looked around him as he took in the expression on each of their faces.

"The poison used was strychnine, which caused extreme pain in the vic—I mean Carl." Jake waited out the murmurs before he continued. "I'm going to interview each of you to see if you knew what Carl had been working on or if he had complained about any threats. Any one of you who wants in on this is welcome to participate, though you need to understand the state police consider this their case and their jurisdiction. Physically it is, but Carl was one of us, and we'll work this until we get him justice. Understood?"

"Lieutenant, I'm in, and I'm sure everyone else is too," Detective Joe Green said as he looked around the squad room. "Are the state police going to share?"

"The sergeant in charge said yes," Jake replied. "I'll set up in my temporary office down here. Detective Green, I'll start with you." Jake turned toward their old lieutenant's office. The detectives' groans and whispers behind his back irked him.

Green walked into the office and shut the door without being told. He looked as though he had something to say before they began. Jake waited him out.

"Lieutenant, we've all heard of your reputation. Some of us even know you, but Carl was ours. We heard you were investigating him and threw him to the rats in Internal Affairs. Is that true?" Green stood at attention, every muscle in his face taut.

"Take a seat, Green. Whether Stack was being investigated or not won't interfere with the investigation into his death. And to answer your question, no, I did not turn him in to Internal Affairs."

Jake stared him down while he spoke. Green still stood. Jake gestured to the chair, again he waited him out. Green sat, his back straight, at attention.

"I'm serious about wanting in on the investigation."

"I understand that, Joe. Can you be objective?"

Green studied Jake for a few minutes. "Objective how?"

"You might not like where the investigation leads."

Jake scanned the office—he hadn't done anything to it because it was a temporary assignment. And if the brass officially melded the two divisions, Missing Persons' didn't need as large of a staff as it had now. Damn, the last lieutenant had not filed a report in five years. The paper clutter on the desk gave him a headache. He directed his gaze back to Green.

"Well, Joe?"

"Carl was a loner. He never socialized with anyone in the department. He had his own agenda, but he was a solid detective. You're saying he was dirty?"

"No." Jake didn't elaborate.

"But you're not saying he's clean?"

"Same answer."

"What are you saying, Lieutenant?" Green made "Lieutenant" sound like a curse.

"I'm saying Detective Stack's death gets every consideration, as any other homicide does, and more, because he was one of us. If there's an investigation into his practices, that wouldn't play into the homicide investigation—unless his dealings with undesirables are the reason he's dead."

Green nodded. "I'm in."

They shook hands across the desk. Jake ran through each interview with precision. He found out a lot about Stack and his personality from Green and the other detectives, but nothing about his actions. Not everyone was forthcoming because of the rumors of the potential IA investigation. Green had contemplated his words and came around after a bit, but the rest treated him like a traitor and were noncommittal. One even refused to answer questions without his union rep being present. *Detective Carrusso deserves watching.*

The phone rang. He didn't even get a chance to greet the caller. "Jake, Sergeant McDermott here. We've found a witness who saw Stack leaving a bar on Route 16."

"Excellent. Didn't we conduct interviews at all the bars this afternoon?" Jake held up a hand as Detective Green walked into his office. *Shit, I should learn to close my door.* Jake listened to McDermott, took notes, then paused as he tapped his pencil on the desk.

"I'll be there in about fifty minutes depending on traffic." Jake hung up and turned to Green. "What's up?"

"New leads on Stack?"

"Yeah. Close the door." After reading Detective Green's jacket, Jake had decided to use him in the investigation.

"I don't want this to get around. Trooper Sergeant McDermott found a witness putting Stack at a bar around noon."

"You're not going to tell the other guys?"

"Nope. I'm sharing with you because I'm going to make you the lead detective with me on this. No one but you will be privy to this until I deem it necessary to share with the rest of the department. Understood?"

"Yes...I mean no. You don't believe someone in this department killed him, do you?"

Green's quick. "No, this is how we run a homicide investigation, Green. It's on a need-to-know basis. Also, the witness doesn't want to be identified. She's scared." He'd call Louie later to explain why he was using Green instead of him.

Green nodded.

"Grab your jacket. We're heading out."

Traffic was light. Forty-five minutes later they approached the strip mall where the witness worked. Green had said little while they drove. Jake glanced over at Joe. Green's face was a study in concentration. Had he made the right decision, using Green on this case, or was he too close to the victim? Jake hated when he second-guessed himself. As they pulled into the parking lot, Green spoke for the first time.

"You never answered my question before. Was Stack dirty?"

Jake looked over at Green, made direct eye contact, and decided to take a chance. "Yes."

"Jesus." Green wiped his brow.

"If you're not comfortable working the investigation let me know, because you'll take heat if he is, I mean was, and we expose it."

"I can take the heat. I hate dirty cops," Green spit out. "I will tell you, he was weird."

"How so?"

"He never wanted to work with a partner. Balked when ordered to on a case. On different occasions he'd get a phone call. He'd tell the caller he was busy and he'd hang up. After a few minutes he'd leave the squad room with his cell phone and step outside the building. It always made me curious." Green scratched his head.

A good cop with good instincts, glad I trusted him. "I might be wrong. His last case file isn't jelling for me."

"How so?" Joe Green asked. His brown eyes inquisitive as he unbuttoned his jacket.

Jake ran through the Church case with Green. Joe didn't respond. After a long period of silence, Jake asked, "Well?"

"He never followed procedure. That in and of itself doesn't mean much, but I can't fathom why he didn't interview any of the neighbors or process the scene. He was a solid investigator. My gut says he didn't want it solved. Right?" Green turned and faced Jake.

"That's my take."

Jake climbed out of the car, waited for Green to join him. Together they approached the *Treasured Things* shop. The bell overhead rang as they entered a shop cluttered with delicate items. A petite woman with jet-black hair stood behind the cash register. Jake put her at close to fifty. He looked around for McDermott. Not seeing him, he dialed McDermott's cell. Cal answered on the second ring.

"It's Jake Carrington, we're at the store. Do you want us to wait for you?"

"No, I already interviewed her and emailed you my notes. I thought you'd want a shot at her alone. Her name's Joyce Swisher."

Subtle. McDermott kept him in the loop, but delayed the information. Jake didn't begrudge him. He would've played it the same way.

"Thanks, Cal."

Jake interviewed the clerk, who turned out to be the owner of the store. She said Stack had parked toward the street at the end of the lot, although many spaces were available in front of the bar. After a few minutes, he pulled out of the parking lot. Minutes later, she walked out back to throw out some garbage and noticed his vehicle behind the building. He was casing the place—her words—and she planned to call the police. As she reached for her cell phone, he left. She went back inside. A customer distracted her when she re-entered her store. Stack was forgotten until she was interviewed by the state police and heard about the accident.

"Lieutenant, that's all I know. It's horrible he had to die, but he wasn't acting right. If I had just called he might be alive..."

"Did you see him enter the bar?" Jake asked.

"No, sir, I didn't. I never saw him again," Swisher said.

"Were there any other cars out back you didn't recognize?"

"No."

"Thanks for your time, Mrs. Swisher."

"It's Miss, Lieutenant." She gave him a full smile while she patted her hair.

The woman was flirting with him. It took all kinds. With a tight smile he walked out of the store with Green. "Not a word, Detective. Understood?"

Jake detected a smile on Green's face but let it go.

"Yes, sir," Green said.

"What did you learn?"

"That Stack was nervous about his meeting, and he didn't trust whoever that was."

Jake nodded at him. Green was smart. He climbed in the car, waited for Green to do the same. "Why here?"

"Excuse me, sir?"

"Call me Jake. I said why here? What significance does this place hold? Green, sorry, Joe. Do you prefer Green or Joe?"

"Either works, Lieu—Jake. You want me to run the place, see who owns it?"

"Yeah, I do."

Green pulled out his laptop and started the search. Jake drove out of the parking lot and headed back to Wilkesbury. He slowed down where Stack's skid marks showed him crossing the road and pointed it out to Joe.

By the time they reached Wilkesbury, Green had the data on his laptop that Jake had requested. Efficient.

"It's owned by a holding company, called Limited Holding, LLC," Joe said, as they sat in Jake's car in the police garage.

"Run it deeper. I want all the names of all the principals involved in the business," Jake said. "Also..." Tapping his fingers on the steering wheel, he added, "Run all businesses that are held by that company. Let's see how deep their pockets are."

* * * *

In the lobby of the station, they broke off. He headed to Homicide. Green headed over to Missing Persons. The low-grade headache he'd been fighting off all day intensified when he got a load of the pile of paperwork on the desk, waiting for his attention. The hours in the day didn't triple, though his work load had. It was well after five when he checked his watch. He cursed and called Kyra.

"Kyra, I need to push back our dinner to around eight thirty, is that good with you?"

"If you need to cancel, I'm fine with it." *Not getting out of it this time, Kyra.*

"No, I'm going to be late. We need to talk."

Chapter 32

She wished Jake had called to cancel their plans for tonight. He'd been trying to have this talk with her for a while now. *You don't have to talk to him, Kyra. Who died and left him boss? Oh, grow up.*

Imitating a television gangster in her head, she watched the whole scene play out. *I don't wanna talk—I don't talk, it's as simple as that. What's the worst scenario? I don't get my week's worth of sex from him before he drops me for another woman?*

Damn it, she needed the connection. And wasn't that pathetic? She wanted him even when he planned to dump her. The argument played out in her head—it was a no-win situation. The itch to be with Jake was much stronger than any itch she ever had for the casino.

Jake arrived with dinner around eight thirty. He put the Chinese food on the counter. Kyra scanned the selection.

"There's enough here for ten people," she said.

"I didn't know what you liked." He flashed her the smile that always warmed her heart. "I got a little of everything."

Good, with Jake eating he'd be too busy to talk. Jake looked tired and discouraged. Is this what Mia did to him? Or was it the case or today's incident? Kyra's stomach jolted as it raced into her throat. She didn't have a clue how she'd explain today's episode. If she talked to him, took him into her confidence, would he keep it? Or worse, lock her up.

She wanted to come clean and walk away. The one reason she hadn't done it before was Trevor. She needed to think about him. Tom was not a stable parent. Trevor needed his mother. *I'm not the best person in the world. But I'm a good mother. I love my son.* She spooned some pork fried rice onto her dish along with boneless spareribs and an egg roll smeared with hot Chinese mustard before sitting down at the kitchen table.

"That's it?" Jake asked, eyeing her plate.

"This is my idea of Chinese." She watched him shake his head then pile the food onto his plate.

She turned her attention back to her dinner. Tonight was supposed to be all about sex, not her life. She should cut him out and avoid the complication of his curiosity. Or was it more? Had he discovered something about the cremations? She paled not liking the turn her mind took.

"You okay?" he asked, concern laced through his voice.

"Yes—I'm—I'm fretting over the upcoming court date for custody."

He grabbed her hand. "I told you I'd testify as a character witness."

Tears streamed down her face as he repeated his offer. "Thank you," she whispered.

Jake continued to hold her hand as he rubbed his thumb over the top of her knuckles to calm her. The simple gesture ignited her passion. She leaned forward and gave him a kiss. He took the kiss deeper. *Excellent, he's distracted.* He broke the kiss. Placed her hand on the table.

"I'm not hungry," Kyra said.

"Sorry, I am," Jake said, wolfing down his food.

She picked up her fork and started playing with her food. Throughout her whole life, she'd been able to predict if something bad was about to happen. Her stomach's contents swirled as a warning. She got the same sensation every time she rode a rollercoaster as it hit the top of the track, that slow agonizing pull that built up the fear until it dropped you over the edge, defying gravity and logic. Since Jake's call today in the middle of the encounter with Joe, her stomach had been churning.

Jake continued to shovel food into his mouth as she stared at his lips. When had he last eaten? Plate clean, he put down his fork, wiped his mouth on the napkin. Kyra understood the time had come.

* * * *

Drunk, Tom Russell rolled out of O'Malley's bar on East Main Street. He searched the parking lot. Most of the lights were broken or burned out. Once the location clicked into his mind, he made his way to his car. He fumbled for the key fob in his pocket as a man materialized from the shadows. Tom ignored him. His concentration focused on the lock.

"Mister, you okay to drive?"

"What's it to you?" Tom cursed as he pushed on the key fob, missing the open button several times. Tom gripped the hood for balance when the man pounced on him. A fist landed hard in his kidneys.

"What the freak?" he screamed as he started to fall to the ground.

The man spun him around, yanked him up by his jacket, then started pounding his fist into Tom's face and stomach. Drunk, disoriented, he was no match for his assailant. He hadn't landed one punch. Tom tried to focus because the man was speaking to him, but pain exploded in his face and body, the words noise in his ears. Muddled, but Kyra's name floated through the fog. He better not have attacked her. The man blurred in his vision as the blood dripped down his forehead into his eyes.

"Take my money," Tom murmured, slumping against the car. If the man hadn't held him up with one hand as he beat him with the other, he would've been on the ground. *Doesn't anyone in the bar hear what's going on out here?*

"Can you hear me, Tom?" the man asked as he stopped pounding on him and continued to hold him by both of his lapels.

"Yes," Tom said, praying the fight was over.

"Good. Now listen and listen good. Kyra says to back off or there'll be more of this. Understand?"

"Kyra..." *Kyra wouldn't do this...was it her cop?*

"Yes, Kyra."

"Who are you?" Tom wiped off the blood that ran down his chin with the back of his hand.

"Understand that Jake won't put up with you messing with his woman. Got it? The next time the beating will be worse."

Tom hit the ground when the man let go of his jacket and walked away.

* * * *

"Let's sit on the couch and talk," Jake said.

She led, he followed. On the couch, he turned his body to face her. *She's wound tight as a drum,* he realized. Kyra put her feet up under her and sat on them. Jake stared at one of the candles and got lost in the flames as they danced with the movement of the air.

Blue to yellow and then back to blue. More than anything, he wanted her to speak first.

"About what, Jake?" She was playing dumb.

"What went on today at the casino?"

"I don't know. The man snapped."

He locked his eyes with hers. "Why did this guy, your casino host, right?" She nodded. "Try to force you into the car?"

"Before he did that he tried to talk to me inside the casino. I told him to blow off and that I didn't ever want to be associated with him again."

"Why were you there to begin with? Didn't you say you weren't gambling anymore?"

"I haven't been, but today I wanted an escape from my life. I took the afternoon off. I was headed to the beach when an urge to gamble came over me. I turned the car toward the casino. What business is it of yours, Jake?"

"You're annoyed that I'm questioning you?"

"As a matter of fact, I am. Why does it concern you? As of next Monday, I'm not in your life. Your choice, remember?"

He'd wondered if she'd go on the defensive. It confirmed his suspicions. "I remember, Kyra. I'm concerned for you. You might've been hurt today, or worse, killed."

"I appreciate your help and your concern. The guy just blew a gasket. I'm sure he won't try that again. Besides, I wasn't even there for an hour. I was bored and on my way out when he approached me. It's the reason I was in the garage in the first place."

Jake lined up his next set of questions. Delicate, but he had to ask. Kyra wrapped her arms around her waist as she waited him out. Jake shifted into a more comfortable position. He unwrapped her arms and took her hand in his.

"Kyra, I've been putting this off since I first met Phil Lucci. Are you aware that Phil is the head of the Connecticut mob?"

"I knew something was off with him. It's one of the reasons why I stopped seeing him after two dates."

No tics showed. Kyra was either a good liar or she was telling the truth. Truth, he decided, but she was holding something back. He needed to pull it from her without shutting her down. The headache from earlier intensified, drilling stakes through his eyes.

"Since I met you, not everything has jelled for me. Something's off. I can't put my finger on it."

"You're a piece of work. Now that you've decided not to date me anymore, you're going to start playing games?" *An excellent offensive player,* he speculated.

"This has nothing to do with anything. I've been asking to speak with you on this subject since the beginning."

"But you always got sidetracked with sex—isn't that correct?" Kyra tilted her head to the side. He wanted to wipe the skeptical look right out of her eyes.

"No."

"Yes, Jake, at the beach on that Sunday, you acted jealous when I introduced you to Phil. Ever since you've had him in your sights."

"That's ridiculous. I deal with human garbage every day. Let me tell you, Phil Lucci's at the top of the pile. His kind kills people because they look at him wrong or he got up on the wrong side of the bed. Women are a means to an end with men like him. He has no respect for them."

"Lower your voice, Jake, you're shouting."

The front door bell rang.

He stared at her back. How had she put him on the defensive? Kyra got up to answer the door without looking through the peephole. Two uniformed cops stood in the doorway. She turned to Jake.

"You have visitors," she said as she turned toward him.

"Mrs. Russell? Kyra Russell?" the tall officer asked, the other one stood at attention.

"Yes?"

"Mrs. Russell, a Tom Russell has sustained serious injury tonight when he was attacked after leaving a bar in downtown Wilkesbury."

"Is my son okay? Is Tom okay? What happened? Where is he?" The questions tumbled from her mouth. Jake pushed to his feet.

"Mrs. Russell, can we come in?" The tall officer continued to address her. The other one stood quiet.

"Yes."

She opened the door wider to let them in. Jake walked over to her and put his arms around her shoulder, drew her close to him. He nodded to the cops. Santos he knew, and respected. Anderson he didn't trust.

"What happened, Santos?" Jake asked.

Kyra disengaged herself from his arms as she pushed the door closed. "Officer, answer my question. Is my son okay?"

"Mr. Russell was alone at the time of the attack," Officer Anderson said.

"I don't understand. Why was he attacked?" The cop ignored her.

"Where were you tonight between eight thirty and nine thirty?" Anderson continued to question her.

"I was right here with Jake," Kyra said, bewildered.

"Lieutenant...this is kind of awkward...I need your whereabouts between the same time frame?" Officer Santos asked while Anderson studied Jake's face.

Kyra jumped in. "Why?"

He looked from one uniform to the other. "Because he believes you and I were behind the attack. Isn't that correct, Officer Anderson?" Jake stared hard at the cop.

"Mr. Russell said his attacker told him the beating was from Kyra Russell. The attacker also said, and I quote, 'Jake said the next time the beating would be worse.' Lieutenant, do you know Mr. Russell?"

"Yes I do, Officer. I had the displeasure of meeting him a few of weeks ago when he tried to attack Mrs. Russell. I had to pull him off of her. They're in the middle of an ugly divorce and custody battle. Russell is a devious man, he might've arranged the beating himself to gain the court's sympathy. In fact, Mr. Russell tried to rape her when I was at her condo visiting. It's on the record. Here's my statement for your report: outside of the incident where he tried to rape Mrs. Russell, I have never laid a hand on him nor have I ordered anyone else to lay a hand on him. He's being vindictive to Mrs. Russell by incriminating her, and me by association." *Christ, this was going to be all over the station house tomorrow.*

"Thank you, Lieutenant. Mrs. Russell, the attacker, according to Mr. Russell, stood about five-feet-eight inches tall, with wheat-colored hair. He guessed the attacker's age around thirty-five to forty, with a stocky build. Do you know anyone who looks like that?" Kyra stared at the officer.

"Mrs. Russell?" The officer prompted.

"My foreman at work looks like that, but Tom knows him. Officer, this doesn't have anything to do with me. I'd never hurt Tom, for crying out loud. I need to find out where my son is."

The description clicked something inside of Jake. "I have a case that might cross with this. One of my suspects matches that description."

"I'll look into it, Lieutenant." Officer Anderson turned from him toward Kyra.

"Who are you calling, Mrs. Russell?"

"I'm calling Tom—where is he?"

"He's outside in the cruiser."

As Kyra started to rush outside Anderson stepped in front of her and blocked her exit.

"I can't see him?"

She looked up at the officer. Jake stepped over to Santos, not Anderson, and started speaking in a low tone.

"Lieutenant, Miller is after your ass. Lieutenant Stein was on call tonight but he called Miller in to take this one when he heard your name mentioned. Watch out," Officer Santos whispered.

"Thanks, Jose, I will," Jake said.

"I need to see how he is and where my son is. If I can't go out there, bring him in here," Kyra said, as she walked up to Jake.

The officers were doing their duty, but the lack of leeway bothered Jake. Who had set up this situation? *Not Miller this time, but it had to go back to Kyra's gambling and her connection to Lucci.*

* * * *

When the cop blocked Kyra's path Jake had taken out his phone to call Shamus. The way this was going down, he was sure it tied back to Kyra's gambling, Lucci, or Stack's death. Or some combination of the three. First, he'd need to find the connection. The description fit one of the guys who'd abducted Church. One of Phil's men? He looked at Kyra while he waited for the captain to answer. When he did, Jake explained everything to him.

"Why are they questioning you?" Captain McGuire asked.

"Because the attacker used my first name."

"You're not the only Jake in the city."

"I'm the one dating Kyra Russell though," Jake said, holding back his temper at being played.

"Innocent or not—" Jake went to interrupt him, but the captain forged on. "I know you're innocent, but it's going to put you in front of Internal Affairs. I won't be able to stop that. Who'd go out of their way to throw you to them?"

"Several."

Crap, life's gotten a hell of a lot more complicated. His eyes bored holes through Kyra. Now, more than ever, they had to finish their conversation. Glassy eyes told him she was in shock. Or she deserved an Oscar for her performance. The first priority was to get hold of any and all information on Tom Russell. The captain's voice pulled him back to the here and now.

"Jake?"

Yes?"

"I said we'll meet the first thing tomorrow morning, around seven."

"I'll see you then." Jake hung up, walked back over to Kyra.

"I'm going outside to talk to Tom, you stay here," Jake said.

"Ah…Lieutenant…I can't let you talk to the victim yet." Officer Santos looked uncomfortable.

"Jose, have you ever known me to hurt a suspect or victim?" Jake asked.

"No, sir, but I have my orders," Santos said, as he adjusted his collar.

Of course he did. Jake and Jose's boss didn't get along, not since Jake had cost him a promotion and got his brother thrown off the force. As the investigating officer on a police brutality case five years ago, Jake hadn't invoked the "Wall of Blue." The officer had been found guilty of excessive force and, instead of being fired, he'd been demoted. It took young Miller a couple of years to re-earn his stripes. His brother, the captain at the time, who'd encouraged the excessive force, had been fired and lost his pension. Sergeant Ralph Miller had been gunning for Jake ever since.

Ten minutes later, the doorbell rang again. This time Officer Santos answered the door. Standing there were Captain Shamus McGuire and Sergeant Miller. Miller walked over to Anderson and Santos, the captain walked over to Jake.

"Cap, why are you here?"

"I looked up to see who was running the investigation and decided to take it over to cut through all the BS."

"Thanks," Jake replied. McGuire always had his back.

McGuire walked over to Anderson, Santos and Miller.

"Officer, if Mr. Russell's injuries are serious why isn't he at the hospital?" McGuire asked, addressing his remarks to Officer Santos.

"He requested a visit with Mrs. Russell, Captain," Officer Anderson answered for Santos.

"An injured victim belongs in the hospital, Anderson. This is quite unusual. You've put the department in a situation that might wind up in a lawsuit unnecessarily. I'll have your report on my desk first thing tomorrow on the reasons you overlooked the victim's health to grant his request. Depending on your report, this might put a black mark in your file," McGuire said, making his displeasure clear.

"Officer, if you allow Mrs. Russell to see Tom Russell, make sure she's not alone. She had him arrested for an attempt of rape two weeks ago. His actions tonight are probably retaliation for that. Understood?" Jake asked. "And remember she has rights too."

"Yes, sir," Santos said.

Jose Santos was a good cop. Jake liked him. Too bad he was caught in the middle of this. Sergeant Miller would throw him under the bus the minute this scenario played out wrong. The only thing this was going to do to Jake was inconvenience him for a while—having to deal with IA was a pain in the butt—but it never scared Jake like it did other officers. He knew he was clean and he'd prove it. The real questions were who had beat up Tom Russell and why?

He watched Miller approach them.

"I'm sorry to inform you that you have an appointment tomorrow morning at nine o'clock with Internal Affairs." *Sorry my ass.* Miller's feral grin spoke for itself.

"IA isn't a problem for me, Miller. But I see you still haven't developed proper investigative procedures." Captain McGuire put his hand on Jake's shoulder to stop him.

"This isn't the place for either of you to air your dirty laundry. Sergeant Miller, there should have been a more involved investigation into this matter before you notified Internal Affairs. Your treatment of a decorated officer is deplorable. Your personal likes and dislikes don't belong at a crime scene nor on the job and will be noted in your file." McGuire walked over to Officer Santos and whispered to him.

"Payback's a bitch," Miller whispered to Jake before he turned away and joined Santos and McGuire. It cost Jake to hold his tongue. After a few minutes, he checked up on Kyra who sat on the couch.

"Are you okay?"

"No, Jake, I'm not. No one's told me where my son is."

Jake walked Kyra over to the four cops. "Cap, Mrs. Russell has asked several times about the location of her son. She's yet to receive an answer. She has also inquired about Mr. Russell. Can I take her outside to talk to him?"

"No, she can't speak—" Miller said.

McGuire interrupted Miller's answer. "Mrs. Russell, I will take you outside. Why isn't your son with you tonight?"

"My husband...ex-husband...has temporary custody," Kyra stated. Jake saw her embarrassment.

McGuire escorted Kyra out of the condo to the cruiser, leaving Jake and Miller alone with the two officers who worked directly under Miller.

"This isn't over, Carrington." Miller stormed out the door without another word.

"I'd watch your back, Lieutenant. Miller's one mean son of a bitch," Santos whispered. Jake nodded to him. He stared at the door Miller had slammed shut.

Fifteen minutes later, alone with Kyra, Jake sat down next to her on the couch and wrapped his arms around her. Drained of emotion, Kyra's tears flowed as he held her.

"Trevor's okay?"

"Yes, he's with my in-laws again. Poor Trevor. He can't stand my mother-in-law. He said she's mean. Let me tell you, the kid's correct in his assessment."

Kyra blew her nose into the tissue he'd supplied during her crying jag. He got up, grabbed the box this time, and handed it to her.

"I'm sorry I have to ask this. But did you have anything to do with Tom getting beaten tonight?"

"Oh my God, Jake, no. I'd never do anything like that to anyone, especially Trevor's father."

He didn't doubt her. "Okay, asked and answered. Who are his enemies—personal or business?"

"No one."

"Was it Phil Lucci?"

Her eyes widened, then filled with anger. Her voice high. "What is your freaking fixation with Phil Lucci?"

"Calm down." He rubbed his hand up and down her arm. "I'm not fixated on Phil Lucci. But I don't believe in coincidences. Today someone tried to grab you from a garage, then later in the day someone attacked your husband." Jake stared into Kyra's eyes as he tried to gauge her reaction to his logic.

"Let's get something straight right here and now. Tom is no longer my husband. Joe didn't try to kidnap me. He was leaning on my car. And yes, he was insistent, even grabbed my arm...but he wasn't going to hurt me."

"This is why we have homicides. People read situations wrong all the time. That man had plans to get you into the car one way or another. The only thing that stopped him from forcing you to go with him was me on the phone. Why don't you get that?"

"For what reason? I have nothing he wants."

He turned his head away in disgust. He'd been in this situation many times with a victim. It staggered him, her inability to comprehend what had happened in the garage with Dillon this afternoon. Or the danger it presented.

"Kyra, someone has a hard-on for either you or Tom. I'm guessing it's you. I'm also guessing that whoever did this is sitting back laughing, knowing he also threw me into the mix. That points to one person, whether you like it or not. What does Phil Lucci have on you?"

Chapter 33

Speechless, Kyra stared at Jake. Words stuck in her throat. Did she dare trust him? Was she in danger? If he arrested her, how much time would she have to spend in jail? If Phil had beaten up Tom, was she an accessory after the fact? The questions swirled around in her head. It made her dizzy.

"What do you mean, 'have on me'? For Pete's sake, Jake, this isn't the movies. I don't work for Phil Lucci. I have nothing Phil Lucci wants. I'm tired of answering these questions. Is this how you're going to justify dumping me?"

"Kyra—"

With tears in her eyes, she turned away from him, pushed off the couch to stand, then pace. She started to turn back, not realizing he'd come up behind her. She slammed into a wall of muscle. Jake's arms encircled her as he held her to his body. She loved when he did that. Relaxing into the embrace, guilt overtook her. She tried to spin out of his arms but he snugged her to his body before he released her and ran his hands up and down her arms before he rested them on her wrists.

"Look at me."

She raised her head, looked into his beautiful green eyes, and lied. "He has nothing on me. What stupid person beats up Tom to get back at me? I don't give a rat's ass what happens to Tom as long as Trevor is safe. It's you that someone's trying to incriminate. Why mention you, if this was payback for me?"

"It's not me," he said, never breaking eye contact with her.

"After today's incident the one person who comes to mind is Joe Dillon." She grinned inward. *Excellent, Kyra, throw Joe under the bus.*

"I'll mention it to the investigating officer."

* * * *

Damn it, she lied to my face.

Her pulse had jumped when he held her wrists. He needed the truth and it looked like she wasn't going to give it to him. He made a decision.

Jake released her. Sat on the couch with his head in his hands as he reviewed everything. He raised his eyes and pinned her with a look.

"I'm going to get my answers, Kyra. Whether they come from you or someone else, I will get them." He pushed off the couch. He towered over her. "I'm leaving." He walked to the door, grabbed the knob, froze when she called out to him.

"I don't know what you want me to tell you. I have no answers."

He opened the door, stepped over the threshold, turned back one last time to give her another chance to speak.

"Jake, please listen..."

"Do you know a Detective Stack?" Changing tactics, he watched for a reaction, a knowledge of the subject. He got none.

"No, should I?"

"How about a Saul Church?"

"Same answer."

He believed she told the truth this time. That was something.

"Who beat up Tom tonight?" he asked again.

"I told you, I don't know," she screamed.

Disgusted, he left without another word.

* * * *

Why were Jake and the police accusing her? She didn't have anything to do with Tom getting beat up. And who were those other people he asked about? Did she burn them?

Had she seen the last of him? No, not in a million years. Her luck wasn't that good.

Collapsing back on the couch, she let the tears flow again. How was she going to get out of this mess? She tried to push up off the sofa, but her legs went to jelly beneath her.

She reached for the end table, grabbed her cell, and pressed in Tom's number. He answered on the third ring.

"What do you want?"

"I wanted to make sure you got treated. Are you alright?"

"What a stupid question. Of course I'm not okay. You didn't have anything to do with this, did you?"

"No. I told you that before."

"Are you serious with that cop?"

"No. We're through."

Tom didn't reply. "Tom?"

"He's a fool."

"Thanks. Do you need anything?"

"I want our family back together..."

"It can't be fixed, Tom. Do you need me to pick up Trevor from school tomorrow?"

"No...okay, yes, we can go out to dinner after you drop him off."

"Tom..." She didn't hide the annoyance in her voice.

"I meant with Trevor, Kyra, don't go freaking out on me."

She hung up and started pacing. An idea began cooking in her brain. Tomorrow, she'd pack up all the money she'd gotten from Phil, then get Trevor from school. Together they'd take off for parts unknown. She'd make it work. All she needed to do was a little research to find the place for Trevor to be happy. Give him back the stability he deserved. Tomorrow she'd buy a new car. *Trevor has clothes here.* She ran through the inventory at her house. She'd buy whatever else he wanted on the road. She'd pick somewhere warm.

She walked through the kitchen to the connecting door to the garage and opened it. She rarely used it because most of her stuff was stored in there. Kyra grabbed her GPS from the car then returned to the living room. She lifted the lid to her computer and signed on. The more she researched, the more excited she got. Men were a complication she didn't need or want. Goodbye Jake and Tom and good riddance Joe and Phil. From now on it was her and Trevor. Nothing else mattered. There'd be no stress in her life. With her destination chosen, Kyra poured herself a drink, put her feet up on the coffee table, and closed her eyes.

The one person or thing she'd miss was Jake. Her parents also, if she was being honest. Though they'd been a pain in her ass lately, they were still her parents. They loved Trevor. Once she settled in after a year she'd contact them, but first she had to make sure she disappeared without a trace. The Midwest might have been better, but she didn't like their winters. *No, don't second guess your choice, Kyra. Arizona it is.*

* * * *

A little too fast, he pulled into his garage. *She lied.* Determined to find out what was going on with Kyra, he headed into his home office. After booting up his computer, he ran searches on Kyra's, Tom's, and Phil's finances. While that was running, he made phone calls to a couple of snitches, then a friend at the FBI. He wanted to know if they ever looked at Stack with an eye to the underworld. He also wanted everything they'd collected over the course of their surveillance on Phil Lucci. With those fires stoked, he went into his kitchen. He mixed a drink, then sipped it on his way into the living room to try to unwind.

He contemplated the outcome of his searches when Dina popped into his head. Wasn't she the one who'd introduced him to Kyra in the first place? Without looking at the time, he reached for his cell phone and punched in her number.

"Dina, it's Jake Carrington," he said, as she started to speak.

"Is something wrong?"

"No—why?"

"Well, it's after midnight."

"I'm sorry, I didn't look at the time, but it's important."

"Go ahead," she said, her voice heavy with sleep.

"Dina, Kyra's husband got attacked tonight. I need to know all about her." Dina's sharp intake of breath in his ear spelled doom. She wasn't going to betray her friend. "Dina?"

"Why are you asking? Kyra's not a suspect is she?"

"No, she's not. But everything I find leads back to a friend of hers. Someone's got a hard-on for her. How long have you known them?"

"I've known them for about five years. The divorce didn't surprise me."

"Why?"

"Kyra seemed restless. That's my opinion. She was withdrawn. When she spoke of Trevor, though, her love for him showed."

"What about her gambling?" Tricky subject. Knowing full well he might be sued by Kyra for invading her privacy without a warrant. What trouble was he causing by telling Dina about her addiction? But it had to be asked.

"Tom used it as an excuse. Listen Jake, she's my boss. I like her, but we're only work friends, if you get my drift."

"I do. Has anyone bothered her, harassed her that you know of?"

"No."

Dina had started to shut down the conversation in the way she answered him. In his gut, he knew he'd better ask the right question before she refused to answer any more.

"Dina, I'm doing this for her safety. Whoever beat him up tonight threw her name and mine into the mix. They said the beating came from us."

"Oh, Jake, I'm sorry."

"Not your fault. Has she talked about a guy named Phil Lucci?"

"I don't...wait. There was a Phil who's been calling her the past several weeks."

Now we're getting somewhere. "What's her reaction to his calls?"

"Reaction? I'm not privy to the calls, but the little I can tell you is that she's pleasant, businesslike, nothing more."

"One more question. How many times has he called her in the past several weeks?

"I'd say...five times or so."

"Thanks, I owe you dinner for waking you."

Jake hung up. Dina's answers swirled in his head. Five times wasn't a lot to call a person over several weeks. What did Phil want? Was he trying to convince her to go out with him again? Or was it business? What business? Something niggled at the base of his skull , trying to get out. Jake reached for the aspirins, popped a couple as he racked his brain.

Questions with no conclusive answers. Then answers that led to more questions. He went to check his computer to see if his search had produced anything concrete. It was still running. He decided to get some shuteye.

An hour later he was back up, pacing his living room. A grisly idea refused to die. Though he tried to push away the most disturbing idea, it was the only one that seemed the most plausible. If it was business—Kyra and Phil's relationship—it had to be about her job. He wrote down words on his pad, moved them around. What was Kyra's specialty? Cemetery? Crematory? His pen stopped in midair.

Oh, for Christ's sake! NO! Not that.

He'd slept with her, had started to care for her. Was she disposing of bodies for Phil Lucci? What department did he start with at the state level? Whose job was it to audit cemetery records? How was it possible to prove what he imagined she was doing for Phil? Was Dina involved? Is this why Stack was killed? No. That didn't fit. Kyra had told the truth when he asked her about Stack.

Kyra, an accomplished liar? A sociopath? The workings of his mind mulled information around until it clicked into place.

Around six a.m. his cell phone rang. "Hello?"

His back ached. He'd fallen asleep in the recliner. He stood and stretched out the kinks.

"Jake, Byron Gates here. You called?"

"Byron, thanks for getting back to me. Who audits the cemeteries around the state?"

"My department. The State Health Department. You didn't find a problem, did you? After that scandal last year, we're right on top of things now."

"No, don't worry, nothing like that. Can we meet for lunch today? I'll explain everything when we meet up."

"You got my attention."

After making lunch plans, Jake hung up. Soon he'd know if she had falsified records. Shit, if she had, his career was over and she had made him a patsy. His phone rang again before he jumped into the shower.

"What's up, Louie?"

"I caught one. Do you want me to pick you up?"

"No, you're lead on this one. I'll be tied up with IA this morning."

"Stack?"

Jake grimaced, "No, me."

"You? What the—"

Jake cut him off. "Kyra's ex got beat up last night. Miller's division caught the case. Supposedly, the attacker said it came from me."

"That's bullshit, Jake. Miller's an asshole."

"He is, but I have to go through the motions. I'll fill you in after lunch."

Chapter 34

Kyra didn't sleep well. Up early, she decided to head into the office. Two burials yesterday and one today created a lot of paperwork. She had to update the files and record the permits. Outside of a cremation tomorrow, she'd be done. She understood that at the close of the day her career ended. She'd never be able to find work in this field again without recommendations. Kyra had trained Dina to do cremations, but she didn't like it. Kyra hadn't pushed her, now she was sorry for that. She didn't like leaving them in the lurch, but Trevor came first.

Who was she kidding? She was doing this to protect herself.

"Hey, you're here early." She jumped at Dina's voice.

"Morning. I'm trying to catch up on the paperwork."

"I heard Tom got beat up last night. Are you okay?" Dina said as she took a seat in front of Kyra's desk.

"How'd you hear that? Did it hit the morning edition?" Kyra's voice squeaked.

"No, Jake called me last night."

"Jake?" This wasn't going to be good. Her pulse quickened, her mouth went dry. Why didn't he believe her?

"Yeah. He asked a lot of strange questions. Kyra, are you all right? Sit." Dina helped her into her chair.

"I'm fine. What kind of questions?"

While Dina relayed the conversation she'd had with Jake the night before, Kyra calculated Jake's reasons. She'd need to leave sooner than planned. She needed to pull Trevor out before school ended. Why didn't things ever go smoothly?

Later, with the *Bargain News* in her hand, Kyra contacted the number in the ad. She made the appointment to look at a car at lunchtime. It was a 2008 Audi A4. She hoped there was nothing wrong with the car because it was going cross-country after she picked up Trevor.

* * * *

Jake walked into the Internal Affairs division with his shoulders straight, his manner professional. His surroundings reminded him of corporate America. The secretary took his name before he sat in the far corner facing both the hallway and the door. Annoyed at this interruption in his investigation, he picked up a magazine to control his anger. He thumbed through it, not comprehending what was on the page, his mind elsewhere. After twenty minutes, the lieutenant who came out surprised him. He knew him. In fact, Frank Rinaldi had worked cases with him before Rinaldi transferred to IA.

"Jake, I'll be handling this interview. Good to see you again. Please follow me."

Once inside the lieutenant's office, Jake took the seat in front of the desk while the lieutenant sat beside Jake instead of in his office chair. Two equals having a discussion, not a lynching. His nerves settled down.

"Jake, Sergeant Miller filed this complaint. I'm here to tell you that your captain has already called to express his opinion in this matter. As you know, every complaint, no matter who files it, must be investigated."

"I understand," Jake said.

"Good. I interviewed the victim last night and although he doesn't like you, he didn't see you doing something like this. I also interviewed his soon-to-be ex-wife and she appears to be innocent of this. The only thing we have here are allegations with no proof. You do date Mrs. Russell, correct?" Lieutenant Rinaldi asked.

"Yes."

"You were also the one to file charges against Mr. Russell for the attempted rape of Mrs. Russell."

"No, Mrs. Russell filed charges. I was a witness to the attempted rape. I subdued Russell and relayed my account of events to the officer who responded to the call. I'm the one who called for the uniforms, convinced Mrs. Russell to file charges. Mr. Russell was turned over to the uniforms who arrived on the scene after I called for a wagon."

"How did you feel about Mr. Russell attempting to rape your girlfriend?"

"The man should be locked up. Any person who attempts to rape anyone belongs behind bars. Men like that are cowards."

"It angers you?" Jake knew he was being baited.

"Yes, that's why I subdued him and called for backup."

"What are your long-range plans with Mrs. Russell?" Lieutenant Rinaldi asked.

"What does that have to do with anything?" Jake tapped his fingers on his legs.

"Answer my question, Lieutenant," Rinaldi said.

"Our relationship has run its course."

"Why is that?"

"It's personal."

"Nothing is personal in an IA investigation, Lieutenant, you more than anyone should understand that." *Again, with my rank. Rinaldi's putting me in my place. He's not letting me take control. Impressive.*

"I broke it off to resume a previous relationship."

"What relationship was that?" Rinaldi asked.

Jake ran a hand through his hair. "I'm in love with another woman. We decided to give it a second chance."

"I see."

Jake didn't fill the silence. He waited Rinaldi out. Where the hell were these questions leading?

"Do you have anything else to add to your statement, Jake?"

"That's it?" *Tread carefully here. What's Rinaldi up to?*

"Yes. Sergeant Miller was out of line filing this claim before he completed his investigation. He filed on hearsay, not evidence. IA agrees with Captain McGuire. Now, McGuire said you had a delicate matter to discuss with Internal Affairs?"

"A Detective Carl Stack—is he or was he under investigation by this department?" Jake asked.

"I can't reveal that, Lieutenant."

"Stack's dead, and my investigation into his death is leading me to some strange places." *It's not the time to give too much away.*

"Such as?" Rinaldi asked.

"See, I don't want to put a black mark against a man's name until I'm sure. His death is being investigated by the state police. It happened in their territory," Jake said.

"And you're involved, because?"

"Because I'm running Missing Persons right now and one of his cases doesn't hold together." Jake watched Rinaldi process the information.

"Yes, we were investigating him," Rinaldi said after a time. "He lives, I mean lived, above his means and always refused to work with a partner for the last couple of years," Rinaldi said.

"And?" It was like pulling teeth, Jake thought.

"And it looks like he associated with known criminals."

"Can I get names?"

"No. You have to follow your investigation. When you're further along, we'll compare notes."

Jake stood, reached out his hand, took Rinaldi's in his.

"I'll let you know, if and when you find anything to aid in our investigation," Rinaldi said.

"One other thing. Did the name Phil Lucci come up in your investigation?"

Rinaldi had answered his question without answering his question. *Thank you, Frank.*

On the way back to his office, Jake checked his watch and contacted Louie. Not bad. IA had detained him for an hour. Rinaldi went easy on him. What this told him was that they didn't put credence in Miller's complaint, but were required to go through the motions. His respect for Internal Affairs had increased.

"Are you still at the scene?" Jake asked cutting off Louie's greeting.

"Yep."

"Address?"

Jake wrote it down then headed out. He wasn't needed at the scene, but he was too antsy to sit at his desk. And truth be told, he needed Louie's calm and logic. Stupid as that sounded, even to him, Louie had been his rock his whole life. Louie's mind worked out things others missed. Jake wanted to bounce some stuff off him.

He pulled up to the scene. Let his gaze roam the area. He noted the bystanders. He drew back his jacket to expose his shield as he ducked under the crime scene tape.

"Where's Sergeant Romanelli?" he inquired.

The uniform at the door said, "He's in the back bedroom with the body, Lieutenant." Jake nodded as he continued walking into the house.

In the doorway, he stopped. He fixed his eyes on the victim. He liked to study the scene before he touched anything or anyone gave him information pertaining to the crime. The body always told its own story. Sadness filled him. A Caucasian woman, in her twenties, brown hair with blond highlights, five-five, one hundred twenty pounds. Manner of dress, suggestive, not slutty. Dress hiked above her waist told him most likely a sexual assault. The panties lay over by the bed as if they'd been whipped off and thrown.

The victim appeared to have been entertaining someone or had plans to entertain. A wide gap in her neck gave him probable cause of death. A sharp knife. Doc McKay would give him shape and size. He'd guess she'd been dead since last night. The eyes, already filmed over, stared at the ceiling, almost as if in prayer. A pretty girl in life, judging from the pictures he saw around her apartment. Death still showed some of that beauty, but in a creepy sort of way. Louie walked over to him.

"Meet Miss Ellen Laurel," Louie said and gave Jake the run-down.

"Any suspects or witnesses?"

"Nary a one."

"Nary? Seriously?" Jake loved Louie's expressions. "Who found her?"

"Her best friend, Cindy Kalen. She said Ellen didn't go into work today or answer her phone. At first she figured the date lasted longer than expected. The thing is, this girl always answered her phone. It's why her friend got worried."

"Will you be done by one?"

"Yeah, you want to grab lunch?"

"I have a lunch date, but I want to bounce some stuff off you."

Louie gave him the eye. "I'll look you up when I get back. Want to give me a heads-up?"

"Not here."

Back at the station, the day promised to be a long one. It was only ten thirty. In his pocket, his cell phone rang. Good, his snitch.

"Yo, Lieutenant." Caller Id. Jake needed to remember to block his number.

"Yo, back at you, Dickieboy."

"I hate that nickname," Dick Kendal, Jake's snitch, said.

"What have you got for me?"

"Stack was a weasel, man. He'd come down here to score. If you wanted to get paid for your product he'd threaten to lock you up on trumped-up charges. You ask me, he got what he deserved," Dick said, as he sniffed into the phone. Back on the coke, Jake figured.

"I didn't ask you. Why didn't someone work him over? If he was stealing from you, he had to be hitting on others. Right?"

"Because he was protected."

"By whom?" Jake asked.

"Come on, Lieutenant, you wanna get me dead?"

"No, I don't, Dickie. Give me something."

"You know how I love that show about the mob on HBO?" Dick asked.

Interesting. "Yeah. How long was Stack watching that show?"

"Gotta be a few years now."

"How long was Stack using?"

"I don't know. At first, he said it was for his girlfriend," Dick said.

"How long?" Jake pushed.

"A year or so. You got my cash?"

"I'll be around to pay you, Dick. Oh, one more thing. Do you know the name Phil Lucci?"

Silence. Jake checked his phone to make sure they were still connected. "Dick?"

"When Stack threatened me, he made it sound like he and Phil were good friends."

Chapter 35

Jake hung up, added the conversation notes to his file. Next he wrote up the timeline on his investigation into Stack's death. After reviewing the facts, he called Trooper Sergeant Cal McDermott.

"Hi, Cal, Jake Carrington here," he said when Cal picked up.

"What can I do for you today?"

"It's a courtesy call. I'm requesting a warrant to search Stack's condo."

"We already searched and shared the information with you. What's up?"

"I know, thanks. I'm searching for information on the missing person he was investigating. I also requested a warrant for Stack's home and cell phones. Did you get that far?"

"I haven't requested them yet. Are you going to share?"

"Yes. I'm looking for one number in particular."

"We took some stuff into evidence. I have several half-filled-out forms on a missing person. A Saul Church."

"That's the case I'm investigating."

"That so? I'll fax you copies. Give me your number."

Jake hung up and processed his warrants for both the phone records and Stack's apartment. He added his financials to the mix. As soon as the warrants came through, he called Joe Green and Louie to his office.

"Louie, I'm taking Joe with me to search Stack's apartment. You I want on the phone with the phone company. I want those records yesterday. Also, start the bank requests. Check offshore accounts too."

"Got it," Louie replied.

Jake and Green tossed Stack's apartment. It was messy to begin with. Their search added a little more. The state troopers had done a thorough job. Stack liked his alcohol. His fridge was stocked with beer, vodka, and very little food. His sink was full of dirty dishes. His desk piled high with unopened bills. Green started pulling drawers from the desk while Jake worked the bedroom. If there was one thing constant about police work, it was the tediousness of it. You talked to people, you searched records, you banged your head against a wall. And if you were lucky, you'd find something that led you to more answers and an arrest. Frustrated, they found nothing.

"Joe, come here. Help me turn this dresser over."

"Sure, Lieutenant. What are you looking for?"

Shrugging, he said, "I'll know when I find it."

They turned over the last nightstand and there, taped to the bottom, was a flash drive. He'd found his luck. *How in hell had Cal's team missed this?* Jake tapped a few keys to see if Stack had left his computer on. He had. It called for a password. Jake tried the obvious. He typed in 'Password' and the screen came to light. Stupid of Carl to be so lax even at home. Jake loaded the flash drive. It contained two files. A Word document and an Excel spreadsheet.

"Holy Mother of God," Jake said, as he watched the data load.

Jake's eyes widened as he scanned down the Word file. All there, in black and white, were the dates, case names and numbers along with a list of evidence Phil Lucci had requested Stack make disappear. It was a treasure trove. Carl Stack had kept a road map covering his ass. As a cop, Stack should've known better than to keep records implicating himself. Christ, he even named other cops. Jake noticed that he had a side note of the different people who'd gone missing, but didn't follow through. *Well, we will*, Jake declared. It was only right.

What he did notice was there was no reference to Kyra Russell in any of the files. She wasn't on Stack's radar. Was she clean of this mess? But his gut still told him she wasn't.

"I'd never have pegged him as stupid, but he detailed every transaction, didn't he? I worked alongside him and Carrusso every freaking day. I didn't have a clue. What does that say about me?" Green questioned him.

"Carl was covering his ass. But you're right, it was stupid, because it confirms he was dirty. IA is going to love this."

Jake hunted up two more flash drives, made copies, then flexed his fingers before taking the flash drive out of the computer. He also emailed a copy to his office and home units. He wasn't taking any chances of the original going missing. He'd lock up the second copy at home, away from the station for the same reason. Phil had to own more than one or two cops in Wilkesbury. The third copy was for McDermott. Jake put the original one in an evidence bag. The copy for McDermott he put in another. Again he questioned the state troopers search—who performed the search—Cal or one of his team members? How had they missed it? Did Lucci's reach hit them too?

As he climbed into his car, he dialed Louie's cell phone number. "Did you find the money?" he asked, with no preamble.

"I have traces. I'm working with the Electronics division to get the whole thing."

"We'll be back in ten minutes. Grab a conference room and ask Shamus to join us in there in twenty."

He hung up as he outlined in his head how to proceed with the case. What charges should be levied against the dirty cops and Phil Lucci. The corrupt cops he'd toss to IA, but he wanted Phil Lucci to himself for corrupting his department, murder of a cop, and screwing with Kyra's life. And his own.

As Jake entered the conference room he nodded to his captain and Louie. It didn't surprise him the captain had invited Lieutenant Rinaldi of IA to join them. Jake walked right to the front of the room and took charge. As he started talking, the others stopped.

"Green, shut the door please. What I'm putting up on the screen is only being shared with the four of you at this time." Jake clicked the remote in his hand and the overhead lit up with Stack's information.

"We need to proceed with caution. I've found five cops in this department that are on Phil Lucci's payroll. In Missing Persons there was Stack and Carrusso, in Electronics there's Al Murphy, and two uniforms assigned to Illegals."

"Isn't that Miller's department?" Lieutenant Rinaldi asked.

"Yes."

"Is he on the list?"

"Not that I found. I haven't studied the entire contents of the drive. There wasn't enough time, but I'll have all that information for tomorrow." Jake handed Lieutenant Rinaldi his copy of the information.

"I'm going after Lucci first. I believe he killed Stack." Jake let that sit out there for a minute before he continued. "No one gets away with killing a cop—even a dirty one."

"What else do you have, Jake? We can't go after Lucci based solely on this evidence. It's hearsay," Captain McGuire said.

"Can we present it as a dying man's last confession? The only reason I haven't picked up Lucci is that I agree with you. I've been putting together other things that will add weight to this evidence. Louie, how did you do with Stack's financials?"

"He has six accounts with local banks, totaling three hundred thousand dollars. He has four more accounts in New York banks totaling another two hundred fifty thousand. I haven't heard back from the offshore accounts or the Caymans. I don't expect an answer there until tomorrow afternoon at the soonest."

"Lucci is generous. That's five hundred fifty thousand dollars. We need to trace the deposits to their source."

"I'm already on them, Jake," Louie said. "I should have some information on that by tomorrow ."

"Good. Green, I need you to pull all the cases that Stack referred to in his notes. I also need the outcome from those trials. If anyone asks, I'm running you ragged."

"On it." Green left the room.

"What about Saul Church?" Captain McGuire asked.

"There's the pisser. We haven't found anything on the guy. Stack made only one vague reference to him. The man's disappeared into thin air."

"No theories?" Rinaldi asked.

"I'm working on one, but it's far-fetched."

"Care to share?" McGuire asked.

"Not at this time."

"Lieutenant Rinaldi, I'm going to leave the cops to you. Can you share what you glean with us tomorrow?" Jake saw him hesitate then added, "I'm looking for the gist of it. How it pertains to my part of the operation. I don't want to duplicate our efforts. At some point, I'm going to need to interview those cops."

"I'll speak to my captain and get back to you. You understand any investigation into an officer has to be confidential until he's charged or cleared."

"I'm not looking to hurt anyone." Frustrated, Jake ran his fingers through his hair. "I want this mess to go away. The publicity's going to smear the department yet again."

"I understand. We'll spin that if we can, but there will be fallout over this both from within and out."

He got the warning. He'd pay dearly for uncovering this mess. A mucked-up system at best. "Let's meet tomorrow at ten o'clock if your schedules are open." Jake gathered up his notes and the drives.

"Jake, you have a minute?"

"Yes, Shamus."

"Tread lightly here. I've done some research on Phil Lucci. I've connected with some people in the organized crime section of the FBI. They say Phil Lucci's one mean son of a bitch, but they warned that his sidekick, Angelo Rainford, is far worse. He's Phil's enforcer."

"I'm not going in until I'm sure we can get a conviction. I'm going to give the state trooper I've been working with a copy of the drive. He seems straightforward. I like the way he shared everything with me."

"Your call, but the more people who know, the more chance it'll get back to Lucci."

On the way back to his office, he found Louie unusually quiet. Expecting him to continue on to the bullpen, he was surprised when Louie walked into his office behind him and shut the door.

"What weren't you telling the others?"

"Nothing."

"Jake, I've known you long enough to know when you're hiding something. Not sharing with your partner? There's something in your head you're struggling with. Nine out of ten times it's right on the money." Louie tilted his head. Jake rubbed his.

"I'm not sharing right now, Louie. You need to back off."

Louie glared, then stormed off.

Freak it, I don't want to get into it with him on top of everything else right now. With Louie, there is no forgiveness. No, he wasn't going to put Kyra in his sights yet.

Chapter 36

Kyra popped into Jake's mind as he reviewed Stack's evidence. Relieved that there was nothing connecting her to Stack, Jake ran her financials. He knew he was walking a thin line without a warrant. Over the line, in reality, but if he linked her to Lucci, he'd have probable cause. His ringing cell phone killed his next plan of action. He picked it up, answered without looking at the caller ID.

"Hi." He'd been expecting Kyra's call. Instead, it was Mia's voice on the line.

Hmmm! "Hello."

"Everything all right?"

"Yes, I have a couple of cases hitting their peak, putting in some crazy hours to wind them up." Cops made lousy life partners. It took a special person to put up with the hours.

"How are things on the personal front?" What did she need? They weren't supposed to contact each other until Monday.

"My week has been interrupted with a cop killing. And I'm fighting insinuations that I had Kyra's ex-husband's beaten up. It's cramped our socialization, if that's what you're asking."

Silence from Mia. *Interesting.*

"Was the cop anyone I knew?"

"No, he wasn't at Louie's party." *The one where we met.*

"I guess I'm a bit jealous. That's new for me. I'm counting the days until Monday." It had to be hard for her to admit that. But damn it, he needed to focus on his cases, not his love life.

"I hope I can clear these cases soon. How about we plan on a long weekend away next month?"

"I like that idea. I won't bother you again until Monday."

"You're not bothering me. I have a lot on my mind right now. I'll call you tonight if I can."

* * * *

Kyra bought the car at lunchtime. The silver Audi looked to be in good shape. Title in hand, she dashed off to the Motor Vehicles Department and got temporary plates. Before she took it home, she stopped at Staples and picked markers to play around with the numbers on the temporary plate. She drove the car home, garaged it, then called a cab to pick up her car. At the curb, while she waited for the taxi to arrive, she placed a call to Dina. Nobody needed to know about the new car.

"Dina," she said, the minute the phone was answered. "I won't be back this afternoon. My errands are taking longer than I expected. Mark it off as vacation hours."

The cab arrived as she hung up. When she got to her car, Kyra headed to her parents' house to visit her mother. She feigned a headache and asked to lie down for a while. Once upstairs, she opened her old closet. She moved around several of her mother's hat boxes. In the largest one, she hid half the money, in case she got caught.

This money took care of Trevor's future. With the money secured in the closet, Kyra left an envelope addressed it to her parents on her old bed. Her mother vacuumed all the rooms every day. She'd find it tomorrow. It was a dramatic gesture, but she needed to let them know how much she loved them and trusted them to take care of Trevor if anything happened to her. She'd given them ammunition against Tom and his parents to make sure they got custody.

Back downstairs in her mother's kitchen she sat at the table while her mother made tea. The kitchen needed updating. It hadn't changed since her teens. The maple table displayed a beautiful arrangement of fresh flowers her mother had picked from her garden. The wallpaper, yellowed with time, needed to be changed out. She'd go nuts looking at those big blue flowers on the wall all the time, but her mother didn't seem to mind.

"What's the matter, Kyra?"

"Everything and nothing."

"Well, that makes sense." Her mother's concerned look almost had her confessing.

"Mom, someone beat Tom up last night."

"No." Fear and suspicion spread over her mother's face.

"Yes, I was questioned, but I didn't have anything to do with it. It seems he's been out drinking every night. I hate that Tom's been leaving Trevor with his parents most nights. It's not good for Trevor."

"No, it isn't. His mother's a horrible woman."

"She is. Trevor doesn't like her. I have a favor to ask, Mom."

"What is it?"

"If I can't get custody of Trevor, will you and Dad petition the court for it?"

Her mother didn't answer right away. She walked back to the stove, lifted the teakettle and poured the water into a cup. After a few seconds she turned and locked eyes with her.

"Yes, we will."

Kyra got up from her chair and hugged her mother. Pleased that Trevor's future was settled, Kyra left her parents' house to head to the school to pick him up. Before she reached the school her cell phone rang.

"Mrs. Russell?"

"Yes?"

"This is Sister Mary Joseph at All Saints School. Can you come immediately?" *Oh God, had something happened to Trevor?*

"Yes, what's wrong?"

"It seems during recess Trevor went into the building to use the restrooms and hasn't been seen since."

"What do mean he hasn't been seen? Someone abducted him?" Kyra screamed into the phone.

"Our cameras don't show him leaving the building again. I'm sure he's in a classroom playing somewhere."

Her hands trembled on the steering wheel as she pressed the pedal to the floor. Was he okay? Did someone take him? Was Phil involved? He'd better stay away from her son or she'd kill him with her bare hands.

"I'm a block away. I'm going to hold you personally responsible for finding my son. And he better be safe." She didn't care she was screaming at a nun. How dare they lose Trevor.

Kyra sped down the street and had to swerve to avoid hitting a delivery truck. She frantically called Jake, informing him of the situation and begging him to meet her at the school. As she pulled up to the building, she slammed out of her car and raced up the school steps. The information officer tried to stop her. "Get the hell out of my way. Why weren't you doing your job when my son went missing?"

"Mrs. Russell, please come to my office," Principal Sister Mary Joseph said.

"I want to search along with your team. If Trevor hears my voice he'll come out if here's still here." *Dear God please let him be here.*

Kyra rushed into the first classroom, pulled open every door and the closet, then moved on to the next one. Twenty minutes later her cell phone rang.

"Right out from under their noses. See how easy it is, Kyra. Make sure you stay loyal."

"Where the hell is my son?" she shouted into the phone, but the line went dead.

Jake rushed down the hall. Kyra saw him as she turned. "Do you have news?" she asked him.

"No, who were you talking to?"

"Someone, and I didn't recognize their voice, is taunting me. He said it was easy to snatch him from under their noses. Oh, Jake, we have to find Trevor."

"We will, Kyra, let's keep looking."

In the basement by an unused furnace, they found him in the corner playing with some toys.

"Mommy, I was scared."

"Who took you here?"

"One of the teachers told me to wait here. It was a game, but she never came back."

Well, at least they knew they were looking for a woman. But who?

"I'm your mother's friend, Trevor. Do you remember me?"

"Yes, you're a policeman."

"That's right, can you tell me what the teacher looked like?"

"No, she's a new one."

Kyra and Jake both looked over at Sister Mary Joseph. "We have two subs filling in today. Let's go talk to them."

The first substitute Kyra questioned wasn't the one, Trevor insisted. The second one was nowhere to be found.

The principal checked the cameras while she, Trevor and Jake watched the screen.

"There she is," Trevor shouted as a woman with her face partially covered dashed from the building.

"Do you know her, Sister? Kyra?" Jake asked.

"No," they answered in unison.

"She's never substituted here before?"

"No," Sister Mary Joseph said.

Kyra hadn't let go of Trevor since she found him. Her heart rate hammered away in her chest.

"Kyra, I need your phone. I'll put a trace on the caller. You said it was a man?"

"It sounded like one," she said as she handed it over to Jake. "I want the bastard caught and locked away, Jake."

Jake escorted Kyra to her pediatrician's office to get Trevor checked out.

"Where to now?" Jake asked when the doctor had finished with Trevor.

"I have to take him to Tom's, but I don't want to let him out of my sight."

"I understand that. I'll follow you there. After you drop him off we'll need to talk. I'm going to trace the number before we get together. How about we meet at my house?" Jake asked.

"It might be awhile, I have to update Tom."

"Not a problem, call me when you're done."

* * * *

Kyra sat with Trevor and Tom for over an hour. Her fear still had its claws in her. She understood who the call had come from. Though Phil wasn't in the area, he had somehow arranged it. While she played with Trevor, she realized she'd have to tell Jake everything for Trevor's sake. What ripped her heart apart was the realization that if she took Trevor with her, he'd be in constant danger. Something she didn't want for her son. No, she had to disappear and break all contact with him. Hopefully someday he'd understand.

"Mommy, you're smothering me."

"Sorry, honey. I was scared today. Remember always how much I love you. Promise."

"I promise."

She kissed Trevor goodbye and hugged him to her chest. At the door, she turned back for one last look. How had she ruined their lives? Gambling, but it was more than that, it was all rooted in her stubbornness. If she'd only gotten help in the beginning...now she had to pay the ultimate price. Her son.

* * * *

Sitting at the curb for a good ten minutes before she was able to steady her hands, Kyra put the car in gear then drove across town to meet with Jake. He'd picked his house for privacy. Was she walking into a trap? Did he find out who the caller was? Her anxiety level rose as did the bile in her stomach. A tidal wave crashing onto the shore, its contents rushing up before heading out again. Halfway across town she pulled to the curb, threw open her door, leaned out, and threw up. The horrible taste stayed in her mouth, but she didn't have any water to rinse it out. *Better get driving, Kyra. Relax. Jake can't know anything unless he's clairvoyant. Hold it together, and in two hours you'll be gone. Sentenced to hell. A life without Trevor.*

As she drove into Jake's driveway, his front door opened. Great. *What's he in such a hurry to tell me?* Kyra got out of her old car. Glad she was smart enough she didn't use the new one. At least something had gone her way today. She walked to the door and was shocked when Jake leaned down and kissed her. *Well, that's another good sign.*

"Come in. Do you want something to drink?"

"I promised Tom I'd be back. Trevor's still upset."

"Is it safe to be at Tom's?"

"Yes, Trevor's safety is our only concern. What do you want to talk about? Mia?"

"No, it's not. First the caller's number was a burner cell. We can't trace it. I want to discuss several things. A cop was killed the other day. It's looking like Phil Lucci is involved."

"Are you sure?"

"Yes, I'm positive. This cop was on the take. He ties into the Missing Persons' case I'm working."

"Who was the cop?"

"Carl Stack. I asked you about him the other night."

"I remember, but I didn't understand why you did."

"Because of your connection to Phil Lucci."

Kyra stared at Jake, dumbfounded. "Jake, my connection—two dates doesn't make a connection. We've been over this time and time again. Why do you keep asking?"

"You've had more than two dates with him, which you told me yourself. You went to his house for dinner a couple of times and to a restaurant in Rhode Island. Why?"

"He asked me. I didn't see the harm in it then. I won't go again, now that I know he's tied into a murder. I took your reaction as jealousy." Lord, she hoped he brought it.

He seemed to ignore her answer. "I asked myself over and over what Phil Lucci wanted with you. In the beginning, I kept coming back to the fact that you're a beautiful woman. Then I found out who and what he was. I had to ask myself the question again. Each time the answer I come up with is that he wanted to use you. It only made sense if it had something to do with what you do for a living."

She stood paralyzed. Sweat gathered between her breasts as she tried to find the strength to form an intelligent answer. It had to be a good one to appease him.

"You've got nothing to say?"

"I—I'm speechless. What exactly do I do for him?" *Dear God, don't make me only a few hours too late to leave.* A fist squeezed her heart until she almost burst open and confessed. *Hold it together. You're almost gone.*

"You're not that naïve." Jake hadn't broken eye contact with her since she'd walked in the door. Was he trying to intimidate her?

"What you're suggesting is obscene." They'd been standing. She walked farther into the room, took a seat in one of his chairs.

"I'm going to find my answers, Kyra. I hope I'm wrong." He sat on the coffee table in front of her and took her hands in his. "If you are involved with him, tell me now. I want to help you. I'll go to the DA and get you a deal. It's Lucci they want, not you."

Cops are liars. Was this a trick to nail her? What should she do? Christ, all she'd wanted was money to get custody of her son. Now she had money and no Trevor.

"After today, I trust no one." She stood. "Don't bother coming over tonight or any night, for that matter. We're done."

She turned. Started walking toward the door. He grabbed her by the arm, spun her around.

"Don't you understand that I care about you? If you're in trouble, I'll help you. You have to trust me."

"Trust is a two-way street, Jake."

She disengaged her arm as tears ran down her face. "This isn't how I pictured our last night together."

Chapter 37

Jake stared at her back as walked down his front steps. He was helpless to stop her. She'd lied again to him. She had all the classic tells. The question was, what was she lying about? He had no evidence of any wrongdoing. Was she right? Was he trying to push her away for good? It was rare for him to question his instincts, but she'd planted doubt in his mind. He locked up his house and headed back to the station.

As he walked through the lobby, McGuire called out to him. Shamus didn't engage in small talk. "I've got the FBI and the state's joint task force in one of the conference rooms. I need you and Louie there now."

"What joint task force?"

"The Organized Crime Task Force."

Alrighty, this was going to pop sooner than he'd thought. "I'll grab Louie and be right in."

The minute Jake and Louie arrived, the senior agent started talking. Jake guessed he was FBI, not state.

"In front of each of you is a file on Phil Lucci. The second file is on Angelo Rainford. Inside each you'll see the case we've been building to take them down. We, meaning both the FBI and the State of Connecticut." He paused. "My name is Special Agent Timothy Newton. I head this task force."

Jake wondered if "Special Agent" was engraved on this guy's underwear. Newton had on the standard blue suit, white shirt, and blue tie and wore his hair in a crewcut. Right off the bat, Jake pegged Newton as a company man. *Focus, Jake.* "I have one question before we move forward, Special Agent Newton."

"And that is, Lieutenant?"

"Are you tying my hands on my investigation?"

Jake watched the agent process his question.

"I'd like to think that we'll be working together for the same purpose, but, and this is a big but, I won't have two years of hard work thrown down the drain to boost your arrest averages. Do you understand?"

Jake's face burned. "The killing of a cop is not a minor offense, Agent."

"Jake," McGuire said. "Agent Newton, we won't back down on a cop killing, but we have no plans to ruin your operation either. I'm going to say this once to everyone in this room, and heed my words. Work together or the Wilkesbury Police Department will pursue its investigation into Carl Stack's death and not share any information with you. Am I understood?"

"You can't—"

"I most certainly can, and will, Agent. We have jurisdiction here. Your investigation is coincidental to ours. And remember, you're an invited guest. The purpose of this meeting is to share information to make the apprehension of Phil Lucci as smooth as possible. Our main goal is to make sure that when we arrest him, our evidence is solid and he doesn't walk. Any other agenda is secondary."

Jake watched the agent back off. McGuire's military background came out when he was confronted. He handled his command and conflict well. Jake studied McGuire. He still wore his hair cut short in the classic military style. His straight posture was plumb with the wall. He ran his department with precision, each operation timed to the second. McGuire believed in the rank and file and supported his men. Jake loved working under him. He was glad it was Newton, not him, who was at the receiving end of McGuire's wrath.

Jake opened the file on Phil Lucci first. The agents had been thorough. Transcripts of tapes, along with pictures of anyone Phil met or had dinner with. Damn. There was Kyra's picture. It showed her going into Phil's house. Others showed her dining with Phil in some fancy restaurant and going into Phil's house with another man. Jake turned the picture over and read the names on the back. The other man was Joe Dillon, her casino host. As he stared at the picture, Jake made a decision. He needed to disclose his relationship with Kyra.

Tapping her picture with his finger, he said, "I know this woman."

"Is that a fact?" Special Agent Newton said, pinging Jake's antenna.

"Yes, it's a fact." Stupid, of course. He was in the FBI's file too. "I've dated Kyra Russell."

"For how long?"

"It started about three to four weeks ago. I met her at a friend's party."

"Did you know she was associated with Phil Lucci?" Newton asked.

Jake saw McGuire studying him. "I knew she had a date with him. She said she met him about the same time she met me."

"And you didn't find that convenient on her part or Phil Lucci's?"

"No, I didn't. I met her at a friend's party. No one, including me, knew I was attending that night. When I questioned Kyra, she said it was one date. There was no reason to question her further."

"Captain McGuire, you can't expect us to work with Lieutenant Carrington on this?" Agent Newton said.

"Jake Carrington has my complete faith and support, Agent. His record and reputation speak for themselves. We don't play games here. So, I'm going to ask, what reaction were you looking for by putting Mrs. Russell's picture in the file?"

"You have to understand, Captain, I needed to know his involvement before we proceeded."

"Asked and answered. Move on," McGuire said.

"I have a question." Jake held up his own picture. "You're putting me in this file as a known associate of Phil Lucci? You're compromising me and my career for your own advancement?"

"You're dating the same woman," Newton said.

"This file needs to be scrubbed of my officer. I'll speak with your supervisor on this issue," McGuire told Newton. "And Agent Newton, for the record, I don't like to be coldcocked. Now, let's move on to the reason we're here today."

Jake was impressed with the way McGuire took over the room after dressing down Newton. "For the record, Newton, I dated Mrs. Russell, not Phil Lucci." Jake looked at his captain, got the go ahead. McGuire passed the floor and the operation over to him.

It warmed his innards when Newton's anger washed across his face. *Bastard barges in here and wants to take over my investigation. In a pig's eye.*

"Mrs. Russell and I are no longer dating. I'm resuming a previous relationship. I've questioned Kyra—I mean Mrs. Russell—several times about her association with Lucci. I'm not satisfied with her answers. I don't have any concrete evidence to dispute them. It's my instincts nagging at me. In fact, Mrs. Russell was never mentioned in any of Stack's files or on the flash drives I recovered."

The state guy interrupted for the first time. "Lieutenant, what was it about her answers that you didn't like?"

"As I said, it's years of doing my job. I questioned her when she said she had the one date with him, but I learned she had dinner with him at his home on other occasions." Jake saw the confusion on their faces. "If she hadn't told me, I would never have known that fact."

"The question is, why did she tell you?" Newton said.

"I won't know until I ask her. Now, I want to outline the plan we've developed. Who'll be involved when we execute the warrant on Lucci's home? I got a warrant for his enforcer, Angelo Rainford's, home too."

"You've been a busy guy, Jake." He tried to control his frustration when Newton interrupted. "When were you going to inform us that you already had everything in place for this operation?" Newton asked, annoyed.

"I'm telling you now. Until a half hour ago, Newton, you weren't part of this investigation. Mark it down as asked and answered. Having to explain the details to you is setting me behind on my timeline. Can we move forward now?" Jake stared Newton down before turning back to the board in the conference room.

In one column, he listed all the physical evidence he had against Phil Lucci. In a second column, he made a list of crimes he knew might be related, but had no proof Phil Lucci had either ordered or committed.

"What I'm hoping for here"—Jake pointed to the second column—"is that you, Newton, or the state—by the way, what's your name?" Irked that he was never introduced, Jake looked over to the state guy.

"I'm State's Attorney John Rudderman."

"Okay, John. What I'm hoping for here is that either you or Newton can fill in the blanks with your evidence pertaining to these crimes."

Jake watched them study his board and work through their files before they answered him.

"I have a Darlene Jones in my file, who went missing when she agreed to testify against Lucci. But I have no evidence pointing to him except for what you see there." Rudderman handed Jake a copy of his report.

"She was last seen with Lucci," Jake asked, as he looked at Rudderman. "How reliable are your witnesses?"

"They were solid at the time of the report. I can't answer for now. It seems every time we have a witness come forward, they back down at the last minute or disappear. I know Lucci's threatened them, but they won't verify that," Rudderman said.

"We have cases here in Wilkesbury with the same signature. Detective Stack detailed what evidence went missing per Phil Lucci's orders. I'm hoping to give Kyra— Mrs. Russell— another chance tonight to clear the air."

"If she hasn't given you any information up to this point, why would she now?" Newton asked.

"I've pulled file photos of Lucci's victims. I'm hoping to shock her into talking."

"You have more than you're sharing," Newton said.

"I don't have solid evidence, as I said, but I have another line of questioning that I haven't pursued. Also today, someone snatched up Mrs. Russell's son at school and hid him for about a half hour. She received a call from a burner cell warning her. I plan on using her fear for her son's safety to dig deeper. And I want Lucci in a cage first to make sure she and her son are safe. I'm bringing in State Trooper Sergeant Cal McDermott to execute the warrant. That's his jurisdiction."

"Can you trust him?" Captain McGuire asked.

"So far he's been solid. He's been cooperative and he's also kept me in the loop evidence-wise. Any questions?"

Jake scanned the plans, made a mental note as he detailed the number of officers he'd need. Outside of him, Louie, and Joe Green, he'd need Dunn, no not Dunn, for some reason McGuire wanted Epstein from the electronic division instead of Dunn. He'd also use the WPD SWAT Team. Beside Newton, his team included two guys from his division. Rudderman said he'd be there to make sure no one stepped over the line and cause the evidence to be dismissed once it went to trial. John also knew Cal McDermott and gave him the thumbs-up.

* * * *

She found it hard to stay away. Kyra knocked on Tom's door. "I needed to see him again."

"I understand. Today's incident has affected us more than him. Come in."

"Why don't we take him to The Burger Joint if you're up to it."

"I am. Give me a couple of minutes. Trevor, your mom's here," Tom called.

"Kyra, is everything okay? You sound funny."

"Everything's fine, Tom. Today's events rattled me." She'd forgotten how Tom was in tune with her every mood.

"Are you over today's excitement," she asked as she hugged her son. The scare that phone call from the school had put into her was indescribable.

"I promise to never leave my class again."

"It's not your fault, Trevor. You got to go, you go, but next time let your teacher know."

"I will."

"Your father and I are going to take you to The Burger Joint?"

"Can I have a milkshake?"

"Yes."

Her body vibrated with grief as she realized this was the last time she'd be with him before she disappeared. She fought back the tears as she followed in her car as they drove away from Tom's house.

Trevor played in the ball pit at The Burger Joint while she watched and wished for a lifetime of these memories. Tom seemed subdued. Every few minutes Trevor stopped and waved to them. After an hour of playing, she signaled for Trevor to join them. As a family, they walked out of the restaurant to their cars. Kyra gave her son a big hug.

"Mom, you're crushing me," Trevor complained.

"I'm sorry, honey. I love you more than anything in the whole wide world. You understand that, don't you?"

"Yes." Kyra kissed the top of his head as he got into Tom's car. Tom climbed into the driver's seat. "Mom, why are you acting weird?"

"I'm not. I want you to always remember how much I love you and how proud I am of you," she said as she fastened his seat belt for the last time.

"See? Weird. I can do my own seat belt." He giggled.

Kyra gave Trevor another hug and kiss before letting go of him.

"Kyra, this was great. Can we do it again?" Tom asked.

"I can never get enough of seeing him. I love him."

"I know. Are you going to follow me home?"

"No. If he needs anything give me a call."

She drove a block from the restaurant before she broke down and cried. A sharp pain in her heart stole her breath away. Clutching her breast, she doubled over the steering wheel while trying to force air into her lungs. Realization hit her. Alive, she'd never be able to walk away from Trevor. She'd have to talk to Jake and see what kind of deal he had in mind for her. With her mind made up, Kyra drove home. She'd call Jake in a little while, after she had control of her emotions.

Once home she sat at her kitchen table and detailed her meetings with Phil and the dates that she'd burned bodies for him, including the names of the legitimate bodies that burned with Phil's drop-offs. She left out the exact amount Phil had paid her to dispose of them. Standing, she headed to the garage, pulled her suitcase from the trunk, and went to her bedroom. She removed half the money and put it in her purse, the other half she put into a brown envelope addressed to Jake for when they spoke. She hoped he believed that's all she was paid for her part in this.

Kyra wrote another letter to her mother. She addressed and stamped it— she'd place both letters in the mailbox at the post office on her way to Jake's.

After pouring a generous amount of rum and coke into a glass, she sat and reread the letter she had composed for him.

It pained Kyra the embarrassment she'd cause her parents and Trevor. She'd never meant to hurt anyone, but she had been desperate. Tom had left her no choice when he cut off her funds. Kyra understood without facing her sins and asking for redemption she'd receive no penance or forgiveness.

She sat there fingering the bottle she'd stacked away for just such a time. Would she be brave enough to drink it?

As she debated, her cell phone rang. *Shit!*

"Hi, Phil," she said through her teeth.

"Kyra, how are things?"

"Great, what can I do for you, Phil? I'm on my way out."

"It's imperative that I see you tonight."

"Phil, I can't. I promised my son I'd stay with him tonight. There was an incident at school today that scared him." *And you damn well know that.* It took all her control not to shout at him.

"This isn't a request, Kyra. I'll see you in an hour." Phil hung up on her.

Do I go or not go? Phil's voice was off. If I leave without showing up will I get far? No, I'll leave from Phil's house.

She took the note she had for Jake and stuck it in an envelope and addressed it to him at his home address, along with the money for Trevor. Would Jake give it to him? If not, the money she left at her mother's would care for Trevor. She mailed the letters to Jake and her mother before she headed to the highway on her way to Phil's house.

Chapter 38

Phil paced his office, then bent over and checked the security cameras loaded on his computer. "Well, it's about time she showed up."

Phil sent Maria to open the door. Kyra was ushered in moments later. He stared her down but didn't say a word. Kyra stood at attention. "Sit."

"Phil, someone took my son this afternoon. I got a strange call telling me to behave. Was it from you?"

"No. What's going on in Wilkesbury?"

"What do you mean?"

"Jake Carrington is sticking his nose in my business. Did you put him up to it?"

"No, Phil. I told you we don't speak about our jobs. Though I do know he's mad about a cop killing. He's canceled several dates with me to investigate it. But he did call and tell me he wanted to see me later."

"What are you going to do?"

"I don't want to see him. He's asking too many questions lately. I threw it back at him as a way of getting rid of me."

"Did it work?"

"Yes, but I don't want to hang around to find out."

"You think you can take off."

"I'm here to ask your permission," she said.

"No, you'll wait through the heat like the rest of us. Have you seen Angelo today?"

"No."

Where the hell was Angelo? He's the one who should be dealing with her now. It wasn't like Ang not to show up or call. Phil dialed Angelo's cell phone again, and again it went right into voicemail. Something was up, but what? Phil didn't like it. Everything was falling apart. His phone rang.

"Phil, it's Angelo. Sorry, my son cut himself bad this morning. We've been at the emergency room."

He took a deep breath. *Everything's fine.* "I was worried when you didn't call."

"I'm fine and my son will be too."

"Good. When will I see you?"

"I should be there in a couple of hours, after I settle him down. Carmela went nuts when she saw all that blood. They gave her a sedative to calm her down."

"I got Kyra here, who wants to get away from everything that's going down. I need your help."

Phil looked down at Kyra's shaking hands as he hung up. Something was off with Angelo. It was unlike Carmela to overreact. Perhaps when it was your own kid it was hard to stay calm. Still he found it odd. He should verify and call the hospital... His phone rang again and Angelo's wife was forgotten.

He didn't recognize the number.

"Phil, it's Kevin Carrusso."

"Where are you calling from?"

"A pay phone in Wilkesbury."

At least he was smarter than Stack. "What do you need, Kevin?"

"Carrington called in the Feds on Church."

"Why?"

"With no trace of Church, he's handling this as more than a Missing Persons case. From what I gathered, his frustration level is high."

"Why did he call the Feds? A homicide?"

"No, I checked. He doesn't have one that crosses into their territory."

"Thanks for the heads-up."

Interesting. Didn't a crime have to be over state lines or a federal offense for them to join an investigation? Did Carrington always call in the Feds this early in a case? He didn't think so.

Phil came around his desk and towered over her. He yanked her from the chair by her neck and squeezed. "Phil, you're hurting me," Kyra choked out.

"What did you tell Carrington?"

"Nothing." she gasped.

She told the truth, but it didn't appease him. "I'm going to have Maria set you up here for now to keep you safe."

Later, when he calmed down, he'd have his play time with her before he disposed of her.

* * * *

Jake called Cal McDermott, told him to meet him ten miles from Phil's house at a diner off the highway. When he got there he detailed the whole operation to Cal and watched him process the information.

"Don't trust me, Jake?"

"It was on a need-to-know basis, Cal."

"I need men and permission to execute the warrant. My captain's not going to be happy about this."

"My captain's speaking to your captain now."

"I see. You think we have a leak in the department?"

"I don't know, but my department and the FBI do."

"Good enough. Your car or mine?"

"We'll take both." Jake led the way.

Happy McDermott was aboard, Jake hoped he didn't call anyone on the way.

Jake contacted the other members of the team to inform them he was on his way with McDermott. The pounding in his ears grew louder as he drove down the road. Jake recognized it—adrenaline. With every raid, every arrest, he experienced it. Two teams would hit simultaneously. One at Lucci's, one at Rainford's. If luck was on his side, Rainford would be at Phil's. If not, he hoped Louie's team cornered Rainford at his home. And, call him crazy, he was looking forward to interrogating Phil Lucci. He was sure everything he needed and wanted to put the bastard away was at his house. Anything they found at Angelo's would be gravy.

Jake pulled beside the Fed's car and rolled down his window. "Ready, Newton?"

"Yes, let's get it done."

Jake pulled up to the detective from Electronics, Stew Epstein, and the members of the WPD SWAT team.

"The system is down, Lieutenant," said Stew.

"Excellent."

Jake motioned to the SWAT officer. "Cosgrove, you go over the fence and come up behind the man at the gate. I'll come in through the front gate and distract him. Send your team over the grounds. I understand that he has several men who patrol the area."

The SWAT officer nodded to Jake and took off. Three minutes later, Jake pulled up to the front gate.

"Lieutenant Carrington to see Phil Lucci." Jake flashed his badge.

The guard looked at his board. Jake focused over the guard's shoulder, watched Cosgrove come up behind the man. Cosgrove put the gun to the guard's head and told him to open the gate. Jake loved a guy who knew how to do his job. And he loved when no shots were fired. *Now for the next part of the operation.* He hoped their luck held out.

"Take him to the wagon," Jake said, after Cosgrove cuffed the guard.

Once he got the signal from the other members of the SWAT team informing him their targets were secured, Jake got on his phone, giving the go-ahead to the Feds and the other team members to follow him into the house. He sped up the driveway with the element of surprise. Jake parked next to an Audi with temporary plates he didn't recognize. He palmed his gun as he rang the bell. When Phil's maid answered, Jake pointed his gun at her heart and put his right index finger to his lips to silence her.

"What room is Phil in?"

"His office is the third door on your left."

"Is he alone?"

"No, there's a woman with him."

Jake's stomach curled. He hoped to God it wasn't Kyra. Passing the maid off to the waiting officer, Jake watched while she was handcuffed. Jake tilted his head in the direction of Phil's office. McDermott nodded. Together they proceeded down the hall, stopping on either side of the door, guns raised. McDermott knocked. When Phil called out, they entered the room. Jake went to the right. McDermott left.

"What the hell is this? Where are my men?" Phil dove for his desk drawer as Jake and Kyra locked eyes.

Light glinted off the gun Phil pulled from his desk drawer. Kyra jumped in front of Jake as Phil raised his gun and then fired it. Jake hit the floor, pulling Kyra down with him and returned fire. He crawled to the front of the desk. It had a solid front, and for that Jake thanked the heavens. With his back to the desk, Jake checked his gun, four bullets left. He looked across the room and saw blood. McDermott was hit. Jake stayed put, otherwise he'd be in the line of fire. He pushed Kyra from his mind as he concentrated on Phil. Jake ignored the rush of footsteps coming from outside the door. He crawled to the end of the desk and peered around it, hoping to catch Phil off guard. The area was clear. He proceeded to the short end of the desk. His gun leading, Jake looked around to the back of the desk and there was Phil—reloading his gun and cursing.

Jake leaped, body slamming Phil as he led with his right. He put every ounce of strength he had behind each blow and smashed them into Phil's face. He cursed when Phil got one in under his guard. For a little guy, he had quite the punch. His head rang out in pain, Jake landed one dead center on Phil's nose. A satisfying crunch echoed under his fist—he'd broken Phil's nose, though it didn't stop Phil. After a few minutes Jake was able to gain control as he rolled on top of Phil. This time he sent his fist into Phil's stomach. Phil tugged on his hair. It seemed like the fight went on for an eternity, though it lasted no more than a few minutes. When Newton tried to pull him off Phil, Jake continued to throw punches.

"Jake, stand down. See to the Russell woman, she's been hit," Newton ordered.

Blood dripped into his eyes. Still sitting on Lucci, Jake turned to signal he'd heard him. Though he bloodied up the bastard good, Phil had gotten a couple of punches in. Once his adrenaline ceased pumping the pain would take over. Jake moved his jaw from side-to-side to make sure it wasn't broken and shook out his bruised hands. Lucci hadn't fared as well. There was blood in Phil's eyes. Not red liquid, but the 'I'll kill you red.' If Phil was ever let loose, Jake understood he'd come after him first.

Then it hit him. "Where is she?"

"In front of the desk."

Jake crawled to her. She'd been hit in the stomach. Dark blood oozed out of her stomach and mouth, paralyzing him. She'd saved him. Helpless to save her he lifted her into his arms.

"Kyra, do you hear me?"

"Yes," she said, coughing up blood. "I had to save Trevor. I'm sorry, I had no choice."

"Don't talk."

"I wish…we met before he crushed me…I love…"

"Kyra…" Her eyes rolled back.

"Jake, she's gone," Newton said.

Jake gently laid her on the floor. "I need you to leave the room for a minute, Newton. Go see about McDermott. He's been hit and needs a meat wagon. I'll take care of the prisoner." Jake refused to acknowledge Phil by name.

"Jake, I can't leave you alone with him," Newton said as he handcuffed Lucci.

Jake stared Newton down. He turned back to Lucci and dragged him up to his feet, then pushed him into his desk chair. "Someday, somewhere, I'll get you for this," Jake whispered in Phil's ear.

Newton called over one of his agents to stand guard over Lucci then pulled Jake across the room.

"Are you able to continue?"

"Yes."

"Epstein has gotten through one layer. I'll show you."

A swarm of bees started buzzing in his head. He didn't have to read the file—they'd found something connecting Kyra to Lucci.

Jake walked into the small office and looked over Epstein's shoulder and read the screen. A sadness enveloped him.

"Is this the first time she's mentioned?"

"Yes, but I'll dig deeper."

"Thanks, Stew. Bring everything back to the station," Jake said.

"Will do, Lieutenant."

"I'm taking the evidence in," Newton said.

"No, you're not. I understand your concern, but I'll get more information out of him than you will."

Jake looked across the room as McGuire entered. "Captain, can I speak to you outside for a moment?"

He filled him in. McGuire agreed Wilkesbury should handle the case. "I need your word that you're going to be okay, Jake," Shamus said. "I understand you cared for her."

"I did, but it won't interfere in my investigation, Captain."

Jake walked into Phil's office where Phil was screaming like a banshee.

Hate filled every pore of his being as he stared Phil down. It pissed Jake off the way criminals lived. This house, heck, this room cost big bucks, more than everything in his entire house. Why had Phil's activities gone on without detection? Jake understood, but it still got his goat. It would bother him long after he closed the case. Phil Lucci kept crooked cops in his pocket.

"You're going to regret the day you were born, Carrington," Phil spat.

Jake ignored him and read him his rights. "Do you understand your rights, Mr. Lucci?"

"What am I, an idiot? Of course I understand. But you don't understand anything, and you're going down Carrington. And you don't even get the girl. What a shame."

Jake leaned down, placed himself in front of Phil then he tweaked Phil's broken nose. Phil let out a blood-curdling scream. Jake waved away Newtown when he rushed into the office to see what had happened.

"He's looking for sympathy, Newton, don't pay any attention to him." Turning back to Phil, Jake whispered in his ear, "She never told me a thing. You got sloppy with Stack."

If it wasn't for the loss of Kyra, Jake might've enjoyed Phil's expression as his words landed. The shocked look on Phil's face alone was priceless. Phil continued to rant. Jake refused to be baited. He pushed Phil out of the way and searched the desk.

Jake turned to a uniform and said, "Put him in my car. I don't want him in with his men. I want Electronics in here next. Make sure all the computers, phones, answering machines, and cell phones are confiscated." Jake's eye caught Newton, who stood off in the corner.

Jake called out to Epstein.

"Lieutenant?"

"Stew, I want you to search specifically for records of jobs that Lucci or Rainford ordered. I want names of known associates, to begin with. And I need that fast, before word of the raid gets out."

"Can do," Epstein said, walking over to Phil's computer.

"Thanks. I'll be here for another half hour, then I'm transporting the prisoner."

Jake's cell phone rang. Looking down at the number, he pressed ignore. He'd need to call Mia later.

"Jake, I already looked at this computer and it's clean. None of the files are password coded. It doesn't make any sense." Newton pulled on his ear.

"The one in the other office seems to be the operational one. All of those files are password coded. Epstein's good. He'll break the codes," Jake said, sure of his guy.

Chapter 39

Jake pulled his cell phone from his pocket and dialed Louie. "What have you got there?"

"I've got an empty house. It looks like it was picked clean. The electronics guy, Todd Sweeney, said there's a virus uploaded in the computers here."

"Rainford was smarter than Lucci."

"Looks that way. How'd he know, Jake?"

"I don't know. When did they leave?"

"Last night. The next-door neighbor said Rainford told him his mother was ill and they'd be gone for about a week."

"Bring everything in anyway. I'm sure Electronics can pull something off of those computers."

"Jake, I heard—"

He cut off Louie. "Later." He didn't want to deal with Kyra's death right now. Jake walked out to his car. "Give me a few minutes, Officer."

He stood in front of Lucci. It was his turn to bait Phil. "Looks like Angelo and his family have done a vanishing act. He left you to take the heat." Jake smirked.

"Back the hell off. I have nothing to say to you until I see my lawyer. I'm filing police brutality charges against you." Lucci turned his head away from Jake.

"If that's the way you want to play it, Phil. It's your word against mine. I can tweak that nose anytime I want until I put you in the car where the cameras will capture everything." Jake grinned at Phil and nodded to the officer to put Lucci into the car. Jake returned to the house to update Newton.

"I'll put out a BOLO for Rainford and his family and notify Homeland Security," Newton said.

"Great, but we're a day late. He's out of the country by now."

"I agree, but it has to be done."

Newton grabbed his cell. Issued his orders. Jake listened in on how Newton interacted with his agents. Direct, no-questions-asked orders.

Jake took a last walk through the house before heading to his car. He put a uniform in the front seat and one in back with Phil. He wasn't taking any chances with him even though he wanted to be alone. Later, he'd grieve Kyra. Someone knocked on his window as he put the car in gear.

"What?" Jake asked, all but screaming it.

"We're taking Lucci to my office, what with the leaks at your place," Newton said.

Jake noticed Captain McGuire behind Newton.

"You agree, Captain?"

"I do, Jake. Until we can round up the others listed in Phil's file." Jake looked in his rearview mirror. The panic he read on Lucci's face lifted his heart. "I'll follow you, Newton."

Once they placed Phil Lucci in federal custody, Jake met up with McGuire and Newton in one of the FBI's conference rooms in Wilkesbury. Lieutenant Rinaldi been invited to join them. He looked up at McGuire. McGuire nodded, but didn't say a word.

"Jake, I'm going to get right to this. What we've found in Lucci's files implicates the Russell woman. You know that from what you saw at the scene. It's best that you leave Special Agent Newton here to continue the investigation into Stack's death."

"She's dead, Rinaldi. She jumped in front of me when Lucci started firing his gun and saved my life." His slow reaction was something he'd have to live with the rest of his. "Captain—Shamus, you know I'm not involved. Right now all we have is her name in his file. We need more. I'm going to search her condo with Louie. This is still my case, Newton, back off."

"Get it done, Jake," McGuire said.

* * * *

Jake and Louie methodically searched Kyra's condo. Under her bed he found the loose flood board with nothing under it. She might've stored something there but what? Probably money. According to Phil's records, he'd paid a large amount that should've been enough for her to gain custody. Is that why had she worked for Phil? It broke his heart. He understood. Once in, she wasn't able to get out. Phil was transferred to Wilkesbury's

Police custody after they found corrupt FBI agents on the local level. Phil continued to be tightlipped and refused to cooperate. The only thing he did every time Jake and Louie interviewed him was taunt Jake about Kyra. If the cameras weren't on he'd have hurt him.

"You know, Carrington, she only dated you on my say so. Miss Goody Two Shoes left you then came to me. How does that make you feel?" Phil laughed.

Jake didn't engage him.

"Phil, your lawyer has a list of evidence we have against you. Do you want to make a statement in your defense?" Jake asked between gritted teeth.

Jake didn't want Phil to defend himself. The state's attorney was going to prosecute him. Rudderman was an honest man. Jake had to trust in his abilities to nail Phil to the wall. It was his only consolation.

* * * *

After things settled down, he was put on temporary suspension. Kyra's death had drilled a large hole in Jake's heart. He chided himself more than once. He should've seen it coming. At the bar, he threw back shot after shot. Trying for numb, he barely got to lightheaded. After a week he was cleared of any wrongdoing in the Kyra Russell case. His reinstatement didn't ease his pain. For the past week he'd been taking the jokes and the ridicule from the other guys and Miller. He looked like a fool for not noticing the signs earlier. For Christ's sake, he was a trained investigator. It took all his self-control to rein in his Irish temper. A few times he almost came to blows with Miller and his cronies. His immediate department knew better than to bust his chops, but hey, he was their boss.

He raised his glass and signaled Pat.

"What are you trying to do?" the bartender said.

"Get drunk."

"That isn't the way to handle this."

Pat knew everything, even though he was retired. Jake looked at him through bloodshot eyes. "What did you hear, Pat?"

"The usual bullshit."

"Yeah, well, I don't know how much longer I'm going to put up with all the comments and the fisheyes."

"You'll do it for as long as it takes."

"I don't want to talk about it."

"It wasn't your fault."

The vial they found in Kyra's purse was a slow-acting poison, derived from some kind of plant. The scientific name he used was *Zygadenus venenosus* otherwise referred to as death camas. If Phil hadn't killed her, it looked as if Kyra had intended to do it herself with that stuff. He should've seen it coming both from Phil and Kyra.

"Pat…put the bottle on the counter."

"No can do, Jake, you know the law."

"Well then keep it handy. I don't want an empty glass, got it?"

"Who's driving you home, Jake?" A good bartender knew when to walk away. Pat wasn't walking.

"That's none of your concern, Pat, just keep them coming."

Jake started to brood again as Kyra floated around in his head. A hand landed on his arm, tugging him from his pity party. *Jesus*, he'd never heard her approach.

"Jake?"

He stared, trying to focus on the figure before him.

"Can I sit down?"

"I'm not in the mood for company," he said, turning away.

"I understand. I'm sorry about Kyra."

He turned back. "Why are you here, Mia?"

"I figured you needed a friend and an ear to listen. Mine are free."

"Thanks, but no thanks."

"Then I'll sit here and drink with you."

"It's a big bar, suit yourself."

Would she walk away from him again? Pride kept him from asking her to stay. He turned back to the bar and downed his drink.

Damn her, she was going to wait him out. He should've called, but this last week he hadn't had it in him.

"What do you want?"

"I'm not going anywhere, Jake. You need a friend. I hope I'm still one."

"You're much more."

Mia nodded.

"Pat." Jake hailed the bartender.

"Yes, Jake?" He paused and turned. "Mia, right?"

"Yes. Hi, Pat."

"What'll y'ave," Jake slurred.

Mia motioned Pat away. "Why don't we get that drink somewhere else?" Mia suggested.

"Like where?"

"Your place or mine, it doesn't matter."

"Do you still love me, Mia?" Jake asked.

"Yes."

"Me too," Jake slurred.

"You love you too?"

"No, no, you know what I mean," he snapped.

"Relax, Jake, I understood what you meant. It was a joke."

"Do you want to leave?" Jake asked.

"Yes."

"Let's go."

* * * *

When they got settled in at Jake's house, Mia made coffee instead of drinks. Jake started telling her what and how thing went down. He didn't leave out any details. Instead of talking to his girlfriend, he used her as a shrink.

"Don't downplay her death or the effects it had on you. She was a good woman who got in over her head. Gambling's a disease. Hers happened to be terminal. I've been a little jealous of her since I first saw her with you that night. I'm not proud of that, but I felt betrayed that you were with her."

"Nobody can take your place. Do you understand?"

"Yes."

"Mia, I love you with everything I am…"

"Is this the Irish popping out?"

"What do you mean?"

She was making fun of him. And damn it, he'd had enough of that lately.

"Relax, the Irish love their misery. I understand, I love getting my Irish on."

"Let me finish, because I'm only ever going to talk about this once."

"Okay," she whispered.

He ran through their meet, the dates, his suspicions. How he'd ignored them. He stopped talking. Eyes focused in the distance, he picked up his coffee cup and sipped. "I'm sorry if this hurts you."

"It does, but I'm still here."

"She was insightful into everyone else but herself. Kyra had no self-respect left, toward the end. I saw it play out in her life and our relationship." He stopped to gather his thoughts and looked at Mia.

Silence.

"Well?"

"Well what, Jake?"

"Do you want me to continue?"

"Yes."

As he finished up, he took her hand. "I love you and I want to fix what's wrong."

"It was mostly me, but I do need my independence. I can't be suffocated."

"I suffocated you?" he asked, his anger peaking again.

"Shit. I'm screwing this up. No, you weren't, that's my point. I was."

"I'm confused."

"It's hard. I clung to you when things went wrong and hated myself for doing it. Then I pushed you away when things were going fine, and you... you walked away. You didn't even fight to keep me. That's what hurt the most. Why didn't you make me stay?"

"Make you stay?" Dumbfounded, he stared at her. "Because it's unlawful to restrain a person."

"You didn't try to stop me from leaving that night."

"I gave you what you asked for, what you wanted."

"No, you didn't."

"I'm a simple guy. You're going to have to explain."

"I see. This is hard."

"Well, if you can't, how am I supposed to understand?" *What the hell does she mean?*

"You were supposed to come after me, tell me we'd work it out," she said, tears clung to her long dark lashes. It broke his heart.

"Mia, were we even in the same room? You left me no opening, you made it final."

"No, you did. Your stubborn Irish pride said 'all or none.'"

At a loss for words Jake stared at her. If he lived to be a hundred, he'd never understand women, especially this one.

"So we weren't together because of me?"

"Yes...no...oh, Jake, we've both been such fools."

"You never said you loved me." He looked into her eyes as he pulled her into his arms.

"I love you, Jake Carrington."

He crushed her to his chest, kissed her with a month of buried pent-up passion. His anger dissipated as he deepened the kiss. Breaking away, he looked deep into her blue eyes.

"I need you in my life," Jake said. Soon he'd have to deal with the mental anguish of Eva's case and Spaulding, but for now he'd take comfort in Mia.

"I'm not going anywhere."

For now his world had balance. How long it lasted...

Acknowledgments

To my 'from the cradle to the grave friends', Dorothy, Maureen, and Kathy. My life is enriched from knowing and loving you.

A special thanks to Brenda Piel, Apieling Pictures LLC, for the great author picture.

Meet the Author

Photo by Brenda Piel, Apieling Pictures LLC

A self-described tough blonde from Brooklyn, **Marian Lanouette** grew up as one of ten children. As far back as she can remember, Marian loved to read. She was especially intrigued by the *Daily News* crime reports. Tragically, someone she knew was murdered. The killer was never found. Her Jake Carrington thrillers are inspired by her admiration for police work, her experience in running a crematorium, and her desire to write books where good prevails, even in the darkest times. Marian lives in New England with her husband. Visit her on Facebook or at www.marianl.com.

All the Pretty Brides

Don't miss the next Jake Carrington thriller by Marian Lanouette

Coming soon from Lyrical Underground,
an Imprint of Kensington Publishing Corp.

Keep reading to enjoy a sample excerpt . . .

Prologue

August 24th

Disappointment, yet again—why does she continue to deny me? Not once in all these years has she kept her promise? I've kept mine. All have refused my terms even with the wedding preparations completed. This one's like the rest of them—she cries all day and all night long. What more did she want? We have each other. That should be enough for her.

She lies, insists she's not my Ciara. And I'm saddened. I can see it in her eyes. My lovely Ciara's planning on running away again? Not this time, bitch. You made me a promise. A promise you will keep one way or another. Until death do us part. You will not humiliate me again. We're mated for life. That's what marriage means. If I can't have you no one else will.

The fake must die. The simple truth of it struck hard. *Though I've explained all this to her time after time, she doesn't listen. Not one of them have kept their promise. Don't they understand a promise is a commitment? Our wedding day has come and gone—five long years alone. And I haven't one clue to your whereabouts. Each time I wind up with a cheap copy. No marriage, no children. I'll give her one last chance though I understand deep in my heart it's useless. She's not Ciara—Ciara, never cries. Ciara, you're independent, wild, strong and beautiful.*

I will not...cannot live without Ciara. I must find you and end this charade with the imposter downstairs.

At the bottom of the stairs he stood, listened to the low whimper, then shut down his emotions. As he studied her he moved closer, and for the first time in weeks the differences popped out. *A charlatan—how did I miss it? Oh, how she made a fool of me. Not anymore—she'll join the other pretenders.*

Calmer, he walked over to her, unhooked the chains that bound her wrists and legs. With no fight left in her, he easily handled her. He dragged her up off the basement floor, spun her around, spooned her to his body and caressed the side of her face with his knife. He pressed the steel to her throat and drew a fine line until a trickle of blood appeared. He rested his head on hers and took a deep whiff, inhaling all the fragrances that bespoke of Ciara. Though her hair had been washed in Ciara's shampoo, her neck drenched in Ciara's perfume, this imposter was not his Ciara.

I've searched for you Ciara for five long years. How can anyone disappear off the face of the earth? Where are you? You bitch, you humiliated me in front of both our families and friends. You left me stranded at the altar on our wedding day. I waited hour after hour for you. You didn't show. You left with no explanation. Why? What an idiot I'd been...worrying something bad had happened to you. God, how I wished it had. Not one word from you, no explanation, no apology. Not a whisper or trace of you in all these years.

Your parents moved away—left me no forwarding address. Ah, but I know where they live. I've traced them through the internet. It seems Ciara, you don't live with them. My tracers on your social security number, your credit cards haven't turned up one clue. Though I almost had you once. Your mother's credit card was used in a different state and another one on the same day in the state where she lived. I jumped on a plane, searched the area where the purchases had been made, but I never sighted you. Aren't you working Ciara? Are you using a different social security number and name. Damn it, where are you?

"What is your real name?" he demanded.

* * * *

"It's…it's Nadia. I keep telling you. My name is Nadia," she screamed hoarsely. Broken, she almost was unable to remember her own name. Nadia knew deep in her heart she hated a woman named Ciara. A woman she had never met.

"It's not Ciara?"

"No." Nadia knew this was the end, and had even prayed for it.

She sent her prayers, her goodbyes and love to Donny, her parents, and her sister.

"Say goodbye, Nadia." He pressed the knife deep into her skin as he ran it across her throat, left to right, ending her life.

After weeks of torture, she barely registered the final insult.

Chapter 1

September 1st

"That's the best sex on or off planet a girl could've asked for first thing in the morning. But next time, put Brigh's bed in the living room." Mia pushed off Jake as his cell phone started to ring.

He grabbed it, looked down at the caller ID and cursed, before answering it. There went his day off. He reached for the pen and notebook he kept on his nightstand and started writing as he listened to the Dispatcher.

"Thanks. Notify Sergeant Romanelli and have him meet me at the scene." Jake disconnected the call and turned toward Mia. And wasn't it strange to have her back in his life. Life...wasn't it bizarre?

"I know. You're leaving me. Who's dead?"

"I don't know. Sorry, Mia. I'd hoped to spend the whole day with you." He got out of bed, pulled a pair of jeans from the bottom drawer, his socks and underwear from the top one.

"I understand. Call me later."

"Will do, go back to sleep." Jake stepped into the shower.

Fifteen minutes later, dressed, he walked back into the room and put on his shoulder holster along with his ankle holster, then reached into his closet safe for his guns.

"What?" he asked. Mia was sitting up in bed, staring intently at him.

"All that hardware—doesn't it bother you to carry it?"

"It'd bother me more if I had a situation and didn't have my weapons with me. Don't worry."

"I can't help it. Will I see you tonight?"

"I hope so. I'll let you know what's going on when I do." He leaned into her and glided his lips over hers, lingered there for a moment—something positive to take with him to the scene.

In the kitchen, he brewed a quick cup of coffee, toasted a bagel, and headed to his car. As he drove out of the garage Kyra's death weighed on him. He hadn't been able to get Kyra out of his head. It was Kyra who had helped him when Mia dumped him. He and Mia were still testing the ground of their newly resumed relationship. Trust had become an issue for him. He kept waiting for the other shoe to drop, for her to walk away again. Though Kyra dying had nothing to do with them getting back together it was still a touchy subject for him. A few times in the past couple of weeks Mia had tried to broach the subject. Hadn't he told her he'd only talk about that one time? When she brought it up, he'd cut her off. At least Mia had the sense not to throw Kyra's criminal history at him. Even with it, Kyra held a place in his heart. She'd saved his life when she jumped in front of Lucci's gun for him. Phil Lucci continued to refuse to offer insight in Angelo Rainford, or say where he had taken off to. All Lucci did was gloat about Kyra's death.

Oh, Kyra.

* * * *

Jake scanned the crowd as he drove into the Metro station parking lot. He counted six cruisers with their lights flashing. *Nothing like advertising a crime scene in the joined lot to the newspaper. Whatever happened to common sense? I bet the reporters got better pictures than we did.*

Disgusted, he gulped down the rest of his coffee and wiped his mouth before climbing out of the car. He wondered what the body count was for there to be that large of a police presence. The crowd consisted of not only the patrol car officers, there were a few who patrolled on foot, as well as CSIs, uniformed Metro employees, strangers he assumed were commuters who got more than a ride to work today. The crime scene tape was in place, installed to hold back the lookie-loos. He nodded to a couple of the uniforms as he walked by. Some turned away from him. He gritted his teeth. *Damn freaking 'Wall of Blue.'* Did they trust going through a door with a dirty cop? He'd refuse to go through a door with one. Jake continued to scan the line as he pushed down his anger. It didn't belong at a crime scene. He surveyed the crowd again for anyone who stood out. It was never that easy, though some killers did like to watch the police process the scene.

Dispatch had reported that two kids who had cut school this morning had gotten more than they'd bargained for. They had planned to walk along the tracks to get to a favorite party spot where there was no access by car, making it difficult for the cops to patrol it. Instead of enjoying the late summer day, they'd found a body. *It might act as a deterrent from cutting classes the next time,* he mused. A tough lesson for sure.

"This way, Lieutenant," Officer Martin Gregory said, approaching Jake.

"How contaminated is my scene, Marty?"

Jake followed him down the slight incline to the tracks while taking in the area. *Not an easy dump site,* he noted. Someone had lots of muscle if he'd carried the body this far. Jake pulled out his notebook, wrote down his first impressions before listing the questions that popped into his head. How much strength did it take to carry a body this far? It clearly had to be done early before people headed to work. But there's still be a possibility someone might've seen the perp. Where had he parked? Where had he entered the area? Did he drag or carry her?

"You got kids running around, the homeless, plus all the druggies use this spot," Marty said.

"Grab a couple of uniforms and walk the perimeter. See if he dragged her down here once he was off the road and out of sight. Look for tire marks in case he drove it."

Jake looked down the hill, still unable to locate the body. "And see if you find any bags large enough to transport a body."

"Yes, sir."

"Did Sergeant Romanelli get here yet?"

"He's with the victim, sir. My partner's with him."

It eased his mind knowing Louie had taken control of the scene. Someone called out to him.

"Lieutenant, is she the missing girl from July sixth?"

Anger burned a hole in his gut as he turned to face the speaker. Reporters in general annoyed him. Cretins in his opinion. They only cared about their next headline, not the victims or their survivors. But Matthew Hayes was the worst of the lot.

"Stay off my crime scenes. This is your last warning." Hayes was on the scene too early—again. Someone had tipped off the bastard. He turned to Marty. "Escort this person to the parking lot. If he asks you any questions, even one, arrest him." Turning, he headed toward the victim.

"You know, Lieutenant, a little cooperation might help you solve the Bride Murders," Hayes shouted out.

Jake knew better than to engage him, but he'd had enough of Hayes. He pulled up short and turned back to the reporter. The 'Bride Murders' the press had dubbed them for sensationalism. *Christ, if I find out who's letting Hayes onto my scenes, there'll be hell to pay. The victims deserved everyone's respect. They weren't headlines. They were people with families, lives and ambitions. Someone stole their lives, their futures.* If he let it, it'd fester until his sister Eva's case jammed into his head. *She didn't belong there right now.* It would cloud his judgement if he wasn't careful.

"The other women are still listed as missing, not murdered." Without another word he continued on to the body.

* * * *

"What have you got?" Jake asked, Sergeant Louie Romanelli, his partner for the last ten years and his life-long friend.

Louie's six-foot-two frame was crouched over the body as he examined some piece of evidence. His styled brown hair didn't budge in the wind.

"A Caucasian woman in her early twenties with dark brown hair, brown eyes, approximately one-twenty or less, she fits the description of the most recent missing woman," Louie replied, as he pushed up from his position.

"Same date?" Jake asked, looking into Louie's brown eyes.

"Yes."

"Don't give Hayes that information. It'll only give him more ammunition to tag the victim. I don't want these crimes referred to as the Bride Murders by any officer."

"You're a little touchy this morning," Louie said quietly for Jake's ears only.

"Hayes is on our scenes even before we are. We need to find out who's feeding him."

Louie nodded as he squatted down to pick something up with gloved hands. He placed it in an evidence bag and labeled it.

Jake looked around at the faces of the young and experienced cops as he pulled on his own gloves. In the car he had put on his booties. It was as good of a time as any to address the issue. "I understand you all heard what I said to the reporter. I want every victim treated with respect. It starts by referring to her by name. Not a nickname given by the press. Understood?" He looked to each person, not moving until he got a nod from each of them.

"Let's get to work."

Sympathy, pain, and memories flooded him as he crouched to examine the woman's face. It never failed to amaze him what human beings did to one another. Animals fought and killed to survive. Humans fought and killed for many reasons—sport, food, trophies. What kind of satisfaction did the unsub get from torturing a beautiful young woman? What switched on in a person's mind to cause this kind of brutality? After twelve years of being a cop, he understood self-defense, even instant rage. But murder and especially this kind of killing he hadn't a clue to the why of it. To abduct, torture and hold a person hostage took planning and organization. It said something about the killer.

"You ran her fingerprints through the computer? There's no mistake?" he asked Louie.

"Yes, it's Nadia Carren. According to her Missing Persons' file she was twenty-two at the time of her disappearance. She worked over at Feinberg & Feinberg as a paralegal. Besides her parents, she leaves a sister. Mr. and Mrs. Carren asked to be kept in the loop. The date's the same as the other missing women. Want to speculate?"

"Not at this time, Louie, we need more information. When we get back we'll bounce it around."

Jake knew questions like this would be directed at him from the brass. Last year he'd taken the FBI profiling courses at Quantico. He hoped it gave him an edge in this case, though it might not. This case fell to him even though it started out as a missing persons' case two and a half months ago. In that time, he'd been running only Homicide. Now he had the Missing Persons' department too. Now a homicide, a case this sensitive, that's been in the news, brought pressure from the candidates in an election year. The incumbent was running again, much to Jake's chagrin, and two others with no political experience. Jake'd take either of the new comers over Mayor Velky. Politics screwed with cases that drew large amounts of publicity. Velky'd have no problem using it as a stepping stone.

"I don't have a clue. We'll find out when we catch him. But it will never make sense to anyone but the killer," Jake said.

"None of the other victims have been found. He obviously wanted this one found quickly. Why is the question of the hour? And is it the same guy?" Louie asked.

"All good questions, Louie, but without the other bodies, we can't be sure."

"I'm only throwing it out there." Louie scratched his head.

Jake understood he partner's methodology. "I don't know. If someone came upon him dumping the body it changed his MO. Who knows if it's the same guy." Though deep down his gut told him it was. "He might've been tired of not getting the credit for his work." He heard the frustration drip from his voice.

Every July 6th for the past five years a young woman disappeared. Five beautiful young women ready to start their lives, all gone without a trace...until now. And Louie was right, it was a big question. Why now? What had changed?

"I hate that it ended this way, but at least now we have something to work with. I hope it'll lead us to the other women," Louie said.

Always the optimist. Jake wondered how Louie held on to it.

With a rhythm born from years of partnership, Jake and Louie worked side by side in silence, directing, gathering, and collecting evidence. Together they examined the train tracks near where Nadia's body was found. Jake stood beside the splayed body, eyeing the different ways the murderer might've brought her in without being noticed. If he'd done it himself, he'd have parked beneath the underpass.

This crime scene was covered in litter, empty crack vials, cigarette butts, fast food containers, cheap wine and liquor bottles along with used condoms and needles were scattered everywhere. It was a known party hangout. The area around the body had been cleared of debris. It pointed to an organized killer. Fingernails and hair looked recently washed. Bending closer to the body, Jake took a sniff. Yep, there went his trace, damn. *The perps learned how to spoil evidence from television. Why here, why now?* kept popping back into his head. The killer had a reason for dumping her where she'd be found fast. What was it? Jake's stomach churned. Whoever washed the body was familiar with police procedure. Was it a cop? God, he hoped not after the recent scandal of corrupt cops working for the mob. It didn't need more.

"Disease Haven" he'd dubbed this place years before when he was a uniform on patrol. Everyone hated to get stuck with duty down here. It was bad enough he had a contaminated scene, between the homeless and emergency response members. Jake wouldn't be able to get any decent footprints and the large amounts of garbage in the area hindered them further. He directed the CSIs to pick up every bit of litter they saw. Told them he'd supply uniforms if necessary. He wasn't taking any chances—he didn't want to miss one important piece of evidence due to laziness. One gum wrapper might nail the suspect. Louie had a couple of officers taking swabs from Neil McMichaels, the railroad safety inspector, who'd called in the report after his morning rounds, and any of the homeless still on scene to eliminate them from the mix. They had to wait for the parents before taking samples from the kids.

* * * *

After overseeing the collection of evidence, Jake walked back to the body and joined the assistant medical examiner. Louie had already bagged the hands and the feet. Doc McKay pronounced her dead on scene and made a notation of the time. It was a myth that medical examiners checked the body temperature at the scene. It served no purpose except to make the M.E. look efficient on television. Once he completed the other necessary tasks, McKay signaled to the morgue drivers. He turned from the corpse, took off his gloves, rolled them together, and placed them in an evidence bag as not to contaminate any of his other instruments. Next, he wiped his hands with an alcohol wipe, than swiped the wipe over his tweezers before putting them back into his bag.

"I heard what you said before to your team," McKay said. "You know, Jake, one of the reasons I like working with you over other detectives is your respect for the victims."

"Thanks, Tim." Embarrassed, Jake dropped the subject, and asked, "Do you have an approximate time of death?"

"No, I don't want to venture a guess. With the wild weather and the heat we've been having estimating time of death will take a while. I'll give you a heads-up when I finish my prelim."

Doc McKay was a respectful man who handled the dead with care. Next to him, Jake was a giant. McKay stood about five-ten, his thinning hair and a paunch showed his age. The Doc didn't seem to notice or didn't care about. On his scenes, Jake only wanted Lang or McKay.

"Good enough, Doc." He watched as the morgue assistants loaded up the body for transport.

* * * *

After he finished with the scene, he and Louie headed to the west end of town, to an affluent neighborhood, and a house lined with cheerful flowers along its border. After they delivered their news, it'd be a false façade. Out of all the tasks his job required, Jake hated notifications the most. Cop families knew when another cop knocked on their door the news was the worst. Civilians stalled hoping to delay the news and the outcome. Today he'd dash the hopes of the Carrens and change their lives forever.

Jake knocked harder than intended. A pretty, petite brunette in her late forties, who resembled the pictures of her missing daughter, answered the door. The smile dropped off her face when she spied their badges.

"You found Nadia? Is she okay? Where has she been?" Hope lived in her eyes.

"Mrs. Carren, is your husband home?" Jake asked.

"Yes, come in." She stepped back. Once they were inside, she turned and showed them into the living room. "I'll get him." She ran up the stairs outside the living room.

Mr. Carren walked into the room, followed by his wife and a young woman who resembled her sister. The man towered over his family. Shoulders squared, his face an emotionless mask, the man's body language told Jake he expected the worst.

"Officers, my wife said you have news of Nadia."

"Mr. and Mrs. Carren, I'm sorry to inform you that Nadia's body was discovered this morning in Wilkesbury."

Mrs. Carren let out a scream and collapsed into her husband's arms. Their daughter sank into the nearest chair, tears streaming down her face.

"Are you sure it's Nadia?" the daughter asked.

"Yes, I'm sorry for your loss."

Useless words, but he had no others. The family's grief coated him like motor oil coated an engine. It reminded him of his own family's grief when it had been his younger sister. The bastards of the world preyed on the young and innocent.

"Can I get you anything?" Louie asked.

"No, we need time to process this. We prayed—we hoped—we'd find her alive. I knew this was a possibility, but still…we need to process this," Mr. Carren said, never letting go of his wife.

"Mr. Carren, I know this is a difficult time, but we have a few questions we need to ask you to help us find her killer."

Weeping louder, Mrs. Carren curled into her husband. The daughter walked over to her and put an arm around her mother's shoulders and patted her father's back with the other. It hit him. A unit, united in grief.

"Ask, I'll answer what I can," the daughter said.

"I'm sorry, are you Nadia's sister?" Jake asked.

"Yes, I'm Rori."

The girl wiped tears from her face while she tried to gather her composure.

* * * *

They asked their questions, but got nothing new from the family. Everything they supplied was already in the Missing Persons' file. Rori offered to fax over a list of phone numbers and addresses of Nadia's friends. Jake and Louie left the family to their grief. Outside at the car, Jake looked around then climbed into the driver's seat. Louie in the passenger's.

"So how's Brigh?" Louie asked. *A change of subject won't clear my head today.*

"Good. She still shakes and loses it when strangers come to the door. I hope in time it stops."

"She and Mia are getting along?"

"Yep. Want to grab lunch before I drop you back at your car?"

"That sounds good. Where do you want to eat?"

"You pick it."

"Okay then, let's go to the chicken place on West Main Street."

"You have such childish tastes," Jake said, as he drove into the place.

"Sophia doesn't allow fried foods at home. I eat what I want at lunch and this way she's none the wiser."

"If Sophia was cooking for me every day, I'd brown bag it."

"You'd get tired of good food all the time. Hey, how are things going with Mia?"

"Good."

"No deets?" Louie looked over at him.

"There are none. We're going slow, kind of walking on eggshells right now until we sort everything out."

"What's to sort out? Didn't you guys talk and settle it while you were dating Kyra?"

"We did…it's freaking complicated. I don't want to talk about it."

"Okay. Sophia's gone from being sorry to being pissed at Mia now, because she hasn't returned any of her calls. Can you ask Mia to phone Sophia for my sake?" Louie looked hopefully at Jake.

"I can try, though I'm not promising anything."

"Great."

After lunch, Jake dropped Louie at his car. "I'll see you back at the station. I want to interview the fiancé next."

"I have one stop to make then I'll be back," Louie said, frowning as he looked down at his cell phone.

"Something wrong?"

Odd, Louie had walked away without responding.